Warwickshire County Council

MOBILE LIBRARY SERVICE

5|13		
2 3 JUL 2013	2 7 SEP 2016	
0 9 SEP 2013		
0 3 JAN 2014		
Wattons		
York Ave		
- 6 SEP 2016		
Hughes 18		

This item is to be returned or renewed before the latest date above. It may be borrowed for a further period if not in demand. **To renew your books:**
• **Phone the 24/7 Renewal Line 01926 499273 or**
• **Visit www.warwickshire.gov.uk/libraries**

Discover • Imagine • Learn • *with libraries*

Warwickshire County Council

Working for Warwickshire

Elizabeth Jeffrey lives in the small waterfront town near Colchester where she was born. She was educated at Colchester County High School for Girls. She began her writing career with short stories, more than a hundred of which were published or broadcast. In 1976 she won a short story competition which led on to writing full-length novels for adults and children. Elizabeth is married with three children and seven grandchildren.

GINNY APPLEYARD

When Ginny Appleyard's childhood sweetheart returns after his racing season aboard the yacht *Aurora*, her hopes that he is bringing her an engagement ring are shattered, as Nathan disembarks with Isobel Armitage, the daughter of *Aurora*'s owner. Nathan tells Ginny that he is following Isobel to London to pursue his dreams of becoming an artist. Already distraught at the tragic death of her father, Ginny is further devastated to hear that Nathan and Isobel are to be married. More heartache is in store for Ginny when she realises that she is expecting Nathan's child . . .

Books by Elizabeth Jeffrey
Published by The House of Ulverscroft:

STRANGERS' HALL
GIN AND GINGERBREAD
THE BUTTERCUP FIELDS
FIELDS OF BRIGHT CLOVER
IN FIELDS WHERE DAISIES GROW
FAR ABOVE RUBIES
DOWLANDS' MILL
HANNAH FOX
TO BE A FINE LADY

ELIZABETH JEFFREY

GINNY APPLEYARD

Complete and Unabridged

ULVERSCROFT
Leicester

First published in Great Britain in 2002 by
Judy Piatkus (Publishers) Limited
London

First Large Print Edition
published 2004
by arrangement with
Judy Piatkus (Publishers) Limited
London

British Library CIP Data

Jeffrey, Elizabeth
  Ginny Appleyard.—Large print ed.—
  Ulverscroft large print series: saga
  1. Love stories
  2. Large type books
  I. Title
  823.9′14 [F]

  ISBN 1–84395–347–1

Published by
F. A. Thorpe (Publishing)
Anstey, Leicestershire

Set by Words & Graphics Ltd.
Anstey, Leicestershire
Printed and bound in Great Britain by
T. J. International Ltd., Padstow, Cornwall

This book is printed on acid-free paper

To the memory of my mother,
With love

1

It was a bright, warm Saturday afternoon in late September; the tide was full and the sunlight danced a merry jig on the water. All along the river bank the crowd waited, pushing and shoving, tripping over cables and mooring ropes that stretched from the line of yachts already berthed there as they jostled for position, the lucky ones perched on bollards to get a better view. There was always a crowd to welcome home the big sailing yachts as they returned from their summer's racing, but today's crowd was bigger than usual. Because more than half the village had turned out to welcome back *Aurora*, the biggest and most successful of them all, returning triumphantly at the end of the season to spend the winter in her mud berth on the River Colne. A few of the people waiting were families of the crew, eager to welcome back fathers, sons and brothers after their summer away; but most had come simply to cheer the big yacht home.

Suddenly, the cry went up, 'Here she comes!' as the huge yacht hove into view, a magnificent sight as she sailed upriver, her sails spread like a giant butterfly, her prize flags fluttering in the afternoon breeze. For *Aurora*, owned by Sir Titus Armitage, the steel magnate, was a legend. She was coming back in a blaze of glory, having this year, the year of Our Lord 1934, won every race she had entered. There was not a yacht from the Clyde to Cowes to touch her, both for speed and the expert handling of her Colneside crew.

Ginny Appleyard was among the waiting crowd. She was a tall, slim girl of nineteen, with a pale, faintly freckled complexion, large brown eyes and thick hair the colour of ripe chestnuts that hung nearly to her waist. Ginny hated her long hair, which was caught back at the nape of her neck with a tortoiseshell slide. She wanted to have it shingled in the latest style but her mother forbade it and Ginny knew better than to disobey.

Shading her eyes with her hand and jigging excitedly from one foot to the other, Ginny watched as the yacht progressed majestically upriver, impatient for her to dock because her sweetheart, Nathan Bellamy, was one of the crew. She had managed to persuade Mr Stacey, of Stacey's Grocery Stores, where she worked behind the counter, to let her leave an hour early so that she could be there to

2

welcome *Aurora* home and she had put on her best pleated stockinette dress in the shade of green that suited her most and pulled the darker green tam o' shanter fetchingly over one eye in honour of the occasion. Nathan was the son of the yacht's captain. Often during races he would have to climb to the top of the mast, tightening or loosening the halyards, furling or unfurling the top sail according to the wind, working in all weathers and conditions. Ginny knew all this because her father was mate aboard the yacht, and he had told her so, remarking that he was never sure whether young Nathan was brave or just plain reckless.

Ginny always looked forward to *Aurora*'s homecoming but today's arrival was extra special. Because she was sure, well, almost sure, that Nathan would be coming back with an engagement ring in his pocket, bought with his share of the prize money that was traditionally divided among the crew and which promised to be quite considerable this season. He had hinted as much when he went off in April.

'If we do well, Ginny, and I get good prize money . . . Well, you never know, I might bring a surprise home for you . . . ' And he had winked as he set off jauntily along *Aurora*'s jetty, his sea bag over his shoulder, a tall, lean man of twenty-one, his cheese-cutter cap set at a rakish angle on his fair curls.

And now he was back — well, almost back and soon she would have a ring on her finger to proclaim that she was to be married to the bravest, most handsome man in Wyford. Her heart was full to bursting with happiness.

There was a huge commotion as the sails were furled, ropes were flung and expertly caught, the crowd backing away and surging forward again as men ran up and down the sea wall, taking the strain, guiding, shouting orders and securing ropes on bollards as the yacht was pulled neatly round into her berth, previously dug out from the mud in readiness and marked with a wand bearing her name, setting up bow waves that wetted the shoes of those not quick enough to get out of the way. Ginny had made sure to position herself well out of reach of the swell. She didn't want the salt water to spoil her new shoes.

A cheer went up as moorings were made fast bow and stern. Soon decks were cleared and eventually the crew began to appear, rolling down the jetty on sea legs, sea bags on shoulders. They were glad to be home after their successful season's racing, and were quickly swallowed up in the arms of their families. Impatiently, Ginny scanned the faces for Nathan, although she knew she would recognise him first by his height, but there was no sign of him.

Will Kesgrave, who, like Ginny, lived in Quay Yard stepped on to dry land.

'Waitin' for your daddy, Ginny?' he said, with a mocking grin, hefting his sea bag higher on to his shoulder.

Ginny turned her head briefly towards the dark-haired young man, tanned from long hours in the sun. 'I might be,' she said shortly. She didn't want to talk to Will Kesgrave, a reluctance ingrained in her by her mother from a very early age. The Kesgraves, Will, his mother and young sister, lived at the bottom end of Quay Yard. Annie Kesgrave, Will's mother, was 'no better than she should be,' according to Ginny's mother, which somewhat ambiguous phrase meant that Annie was free with her favours and hadn't the slightest idea which of her many lovers had fathered her children. This, in Ruth Appleyard's view, put the whole family entirely beyond the pale and she forbade Ginny to have anything to do with them, even though Annie had calmed down in recent years, since her looks and figure had gone, and begun to take her comfort from the gin bottle.

Quickly, Ginny turned away from Will to scan the last of the men as they came off the boat. But still she couldn't see Nathan.

There was a lull and the crowd began to disperse. Then her heart leapt as she caught sight of him. He was with a young woman of about twenty, who was wearing silky, wide-bottomed navy blue trousers and a white blouse with a sailor collar. To complete her pseudo-nautical outfit a round sailor hat was perched at a rakish angle on her dark, Marcel-waved hair. Ginny recognised her immediately as Sir Titus's daughter, Isobel. They reached the gangplank, where Isobel made a great play of nearly overbalancing into the water and she clutched Nathan's arm, laughing up at him as he helped her unsteady progress off the yacht.

He never even glanced in Ginny's direction as they went off together, still laughing.

A swift stab of jealousy shot through Ginny and lay like a lump in her breast. What could have happened during the season's racing that he should act in such a familiar way with the owner's daughter? Had she spent the whole summer on the yacht? Common sense told her that this was not very likely. Conditions on a racing yacht were not exactly luxurious, with everything below decks stripped down to the minimum to keep the weight down. She turned away from watching them and managed to smile and wave as she saw her father coming off the yacht, walking behind Captain Bellamy and the yacht's owner. Sir Titus Armitage was a short, rotund man, full of his own importance, dressed in immaculate yachting gear although in truth he hardly knew one end of a yacht from the other.

A wide grin spread across Bob Appleyard's face as he saw his daughter and he enveloped her in a bear hug. 'Thass my girl. Come to meet your owd dad. My word, you look as pretty as a picture.'

She leaned against his shoulder to hide her disappointment over Nathan and smelled the familiar tang of salty sweat. 'I'm glad you're home, Dad,' she said, her voice muffled against his guernsey. 'It's always better when you're home.'

He held her at arm's length, knowing exactly what she meant. 'Your mother only wants what's best, matie,' he said loyally.

'I know, Dad.' She made an effort and smiled up at him. 'She's made a steak and kidney pie for tea.'

'Well, thass worth comin' home for,' he said heartily. 'I'd travel half round the world for one o' your mother's steak and kidney pies.' He hitched his bag on to his shoulder and they turned for home. 'Did you see anything of Nathan?' he asked as they walked along the quay.

'Yes. But he didn't see me. He was too busy helping the owner's daughter off the boat.'

'Ah. Yes. Quite a fashion-plate, that one.'

Ginny waited for her father to say more but when he didn't she asked, 'Have they come all the way from Scotland on the yacht, Dad?'

He glanced at her. 'Who? Sir Titus and his daughter? No, they wouldn't do that. They came down from London by car and boarded at Brightlingsea so they could do the last little trip upriver on her before she's laid up for the winter. I 'spect the shuvver'll drive the car back here ready to take 'em back to London later on.' He grinned down at her. 'Thass all right for some, ain't it, matie!' 'Matie' was his pet term for his daughter.

Ginny digested this as they continued along the quay, past the Rose and Crown to Quay Yard. This was reached through a door set in the wall with a wonky latch and peeling black paint.

Quay Yard consisted of a row of four cottages in a cobbled yard. Two wash houses and two privies stood back to back halfway up the yard, each one serving two cottages. The Kesgraves lived at the bottom end, nearest the quay. Their cottage was squalid, with a rickety old table outside the back door

8

where heaps of rubbish, old boxes and bags of shrimp heads spilled off on to the cobbles. Outside the next cottage was a little but not much better. But numbers three and four, where Granny Crabtree and the Appleyards lived and shared the facilities, was always kept neat and tidy, the cobbles swept, the steps whitened and the curtains hanging crisply starched at the windows. In spite of the warm September day the door to number four was firmly closed. Ginny pushed it open.

'Mum, we're home,' she called, stepping into the kitchen. A table covered in checked oilcloth stood in the middle of the room, with four Essex chairs round it. A dresser displaying matching china on the shelves stood against one wall and an elderly couch draped with a patchwork blanket against the adjacent wall. Two Windsor chairs stood either side of the fire. Two peg rugs, one at the hearth and another just inside the door, were laid on the highly polished linoleum. There was not a speck of dust anywhere.

At Ginny's words Ruth Appleyard closed the oven door and straightened up. 'If I've told you once I've told you a thousand times not to use that bottom yard door,' she said irritably. 'There's no telling what you'll bring in on your feet coming up that yard. Why can't you come in that way?' She nodded out of the window to where two stone steps led out on to Anchor Hill. 'You know I don't like you carting through all that filth outside number one. That Annie Kesgrave's a slut.' She pursed her mouth in distaste. 'And Marjorie Oliphant's not much better. But at least she's got a husband,' she added grudgingly.

'It was nearer to come in from the quay,' Ginny said flatly, her happiness at being reunited with her beloved father slightly soured.

Bob went over to his wife. She presented a cool cheek for him to kiss.

'Ginny says you've made my favourite meat pie,' he said, obviously used to his wife's lack of warmth. 'I shall look forward to that.'

'It's not quite cooked,' Ruth said, flushing, though whether it was with pleasure or from the heat of the stove it was impossible to say. She was a woman of medium height, with hair that had once been the same chestnut colour as her daughter's but was now liberally streaked with grey. She wore it parted in the middle and looped into a bun just above her collar. Like Ginny, she had good bone structure, with high cheekbones and a small, straight nose, but there the likeness ended because Ruth's eyes were grey and hooded and her mouth was small and unused to smiling.

Bob sat down in the Windsor chair beside the kitchen range and began to unlace his sea bag.

'Don't do that in here. Take it out into the wash house. I don't want your dirty washing all over the floor in my kitchen,' Ruth said sharply, carefully placing knives and forks out on the table.

'I wasn't going to empty it, dear. I was only going to get these out.' Bob produced a box from the top of his bag. 'Presents I've brought for you both. Look, I've bought you a brooch in the shape of a thistle, Ruthy.' He held it out to her. 'I thought you'd like that. It's got a pretty mauve stone for the flower. You always used to like the colour mauve, didn't you. They told me in the shop it was amethyst.'

She took it. 'Yes. It's pretty.' She looked at him accusingly. 'I hope you didn't spend a lot of money on it, Robert.'

'That's for me to know and you to wonder, Ruthy,' he said ambiguously. He dived in the box again. 'And this is for you, Ginny. A little pendant on a silver chain. It's mother-of-pearl. And see, it opens out so you can put a photograph in it. Or a lock of hair. I saw it in a shop in Oban and I thought you'd like it.'

'Oh, Dad, it's beautiful.' Ginny flung her

arms round his neck and gave him a smacking kiss on his cheek. 'Thank you. Will you fasten it for me?' She held up her thick mane of hair so that he could fasten it round her neck.

'Well, at least you didn't want to know how much it cost,' he murmured under his breath with a glance at his wife, busily straining potatoes outside at the drain, the thistle brooch discarded on the table.

Ginny usually enjoyed her mother's meat pie but today, with the memory of Isobel Armitage hanging on to Nathan's arm still fresh in her mind, it tasted like nothing more than soggy paper. But watched by her mother's eagle eye she knew better than to leave any. She longed to question her father about Isobel Armitage. Had she joined her father in Scotland to be with him on the yacht? If so, how long had she spent there? A few weeks? Most of the summer? But she didn't want to appear too interested, so she forced down her meal and said nothing.

'You're quiet, matie. Still workin' at Stacey's?' Bob asked suddenly.

Ginny opened her mouth to reply but her mother forestalled her.

'Yes, she's doing very well there, too,' Ruth said. 'It's a good grocer's. The best in Wyford. Better than working in that canning factory.

She's too bright for that.'

'I only asked,' Bob said mildly. He turned back to Ginny. 'Do you like serving behind the counter, matie?'

Ginny made a face. 'It's all right. Anyway, it's only 'til . . . ' she stopped. Her parents didn't know quite how serious things were between her and Nathan. And she wasn't sure how they would react when they found out. It was all a bit difficult with Nathan's father being captain of *Aurora* because her father, as mate, was only his second in command. Captain Bellamy would be on what was called a retainer throughout the winter, which meant that all he would have to do was to keep an eye on the yacht and supervise anything that needed to be done on it; the rest of the time he could be a gentleman of leisure. But Bob Appleyard needed to earn his living in the winter months and this he did by fishing out in the North Sea, in the smack he had inherited from his own father. And Ginny's mother worked for Nathan's mother, which only added to the problem.

Bob was watching her carefully. 'Only till what?'

She smiled at him. 'Yes, I quite like working at Stacey's. I've been there five years now.'

'So you hev.' Satisfied, Bob held his plate

out for more pie. 'This is real good, Ruthy. We get good grub on board but there's nothin' to touch home cookin'. Specially your meat pies, girl.'

Ginny watched as her mother piled his plate again. Ruth showed no emotion, no pleasure when her husband complimented her on her cooking, no sign that she was even pleased to see him home after nearly five months away. But it was always like this. It seemed that the only thing that gave Ruth Appleyard any pleasure was the money in her post office savings account. Money she was saving towards a house at the 'better' end of the village so that she could take her family out of Quay Yard, which she considered to be squalid and beneath her.

Ginny knew that it was into this account that any prize money her father handed over would go. Not that there would be much of that. Most of his prize money was earmarked for keeping the *Emily May* in good order and this year he had promised himself a new main sail for the smack. But Ruth's bank balance was gradually growing with the money she earned from her work as cook for Captain Bellamy's wife and with that she had to be content.

Captain Bellamy and his wife lived in the 'better' part of the village, in Anglesea Road.

It was here that Ginny and Nathan, who was two years her senior, had first come together, longer ago than either of them could remember. As children they had often played together while Ruth worked. Not to do cleaning or rough work, someone else from the village did all that, Ruth was simply there to cook. Once or twice a week she would spend the day making pies and cakes and cooking delicious meals that could be left on the cold slab in the larder to be warmed up as required. What they ate for the rest of the week she didn't know, because that Mabel Bellamy never lifted a finger, Ruth had often been heard to remark. In fact she had got so far above herself, according to Ruth, putting on airs and graces since marrying Captain Hector Bellamy, that she must have forgotten they had all been at the village school together when they were children.

Ginny enjoyed her mother's 'cooking days' because while Ruth was busy in the kitchen she and Nathan would play together in the sail loft attached to the back of the house; sailing imaginary oceans, boarding pirate ships, surviving on desert islands, their fertile imagination knowing no bounds. Mrs Bellamy didn't really like them playing together, but she was torn between forbidding Nathan to have anything to do with a

15

child of a servant and being glad to get him from under her feet. Usually, she had been glad to get him from under her feet and so as Ginny and Nathan grew up they became good friends.

More than friends. Ginny didn't remember when she had first fallen in love with Nathan, probably when she was about fourteen, and although he had never actually told her so she was convinced he felt the same way about her. He even used to get her to sit for him sometimes, oh, not for a portrait, but as a figure in the distance when he was painting a landscape. He quite fancied himself as a painter and Ginny could see that he was quite good. Not to be outdone, Ginny would sit with her pencil and pad whilst he was painting and amuse herself sketching. She didn't have a paint box so she couldn't put any colour in her drawings but she managed to get the effect she wanted by careful shading and it was something she really enjoyed doing.

As they grew older and had begun to go about with some of the other young people from the village, somehow Ginny and Nathan usually managed to end up together when they paired off. He seemed more than happy about this and before he left on *Aurora* in April, he had kissed her, not for the first time, and his last words had been, 'If we do well, Ginny, and I win lots of prize money, I might bring you back a surprise!'

To Ginny, that could only mean one thing and each night she had gone to sleep picturing the kind of ring he would bring home for her. Sometimes it would have diamonds with a ruby in the middle, sometimes just a single diamond, sometimes sapphires.

But since she had seen the familiar way he was acting with Isobel Armitage a worm of doubt had begun to creep into her mind. Yet there *couldn't* be anything between them. Miss Armitage was the owner's daughter; she wouldn't want to get too friendly with the likes of Nathan Bellamy. Would she?

Once again the picture of the two of them together left Ginny wracked with jealous misery.

'I've got to go back to the boat to see to a few things. Do you want to come with me, matie?' Bob asked when the meal was finished and Ginny had helped her mother to clear it away.

'I don't know why you want to go back there. You've only just come off it,' Ruth said, sitting down and picking up her mending.

'I told you, dear, I've got a few things to see to,' Bob said patiently, getting to his feet. 'Comin', matie?'

17

'Yes, Dad. I'll come. I'll just go and change my dress.' Ginny hurried upstairs and took off the new green dress and put on her old work skirt and a jumper she had knitted herself. Then she pulled on a woollen cap and went downstairs to where her father was waiting.

'Better go out the top way,' he said, giving her a conspiratorial wink. 'Your mother'll be watching.'

Ginny laughed and led the way up the two steps on to Anchor Hill. 'Doesn't really make that much difference, does it?' she said, tucking her arm into his.

'It does to your mother, Ginny,' he replied. 'Makes a lot of difference to her.'

It was a warm September evening and the sun hung like a big red balloon low in the sky. The tide was leaving *Aurora* and with the odd creaking of timbers she was settling comfortably into her berth as if glad to be home after a busy summer. While Bob went below Ginny stayed on deck, leaning over the rail and watching the waves lapping lazily round the stern. Thinking about it now she realised she had probably been torturing herself unnecessarily over Nathan. The fact that he had helped that young woman off the boat didn't mean a thing. After all, she was the owner's daughter so she was hardly likely to look twice at the son of a humble yacht captain. No doubt when she saw Nathan tomorrow they would have a good laugh together at the antics of Isobel Armitage, stumbling off the boat all dressed up in her sailor outfit. She permitted herself a little smile at the thought.

She heard footsteps coming along the deck. 'Ready to go, Dad?' she asked as she turned.

But it wasn't Bob, it was Nathan coming towards her, an expensive-looking portfolio under his arm. He was smiling excitedly and her heart seemed to do a somersault at the sight of him. He held out his free hand to take hers.

'Ginny! I didn't expect to see you here tonight. But I'm glad because I've got something important to tell you.'

2

Ginny waited expectantly. Nathan was still holding her hand. 'Well,' she said, smiling eagerly, 'what is it you want to tell me?' Although she was sure she could guess, she wanted him to say it. Excitement bubbled inside her.

He looked round. 'We can't talk here. Anyway, what are you doing here on the yacht? Is your dad around?'

'Yes, he's gone below to tidy up or something.' She waved her hand impatiently. 'I stayed here on deck to watch the sunset on the water.'

'I see. Well, let's take a walk along the wall. It's more private.'

Ginny's heart turned over yet again. 'I'll just call down and tell Dad,' she said.

'It's all right, Mr Appleyard, Ginny's with me,' Nathan added when they heard Bob's muffled reply.

They left the boat and Ginny hoped Nathan noticed how confidently she stepped along the gangplank, with no need of a steadying arm. At the same time she hoped he hadn't noticed she was wearing her old navy serge skirt and a jumper that had seen better days. If she'd known she was going to see him tonight she wouldn't have changed out of her new smart green dress. She would have liked to look her best when he proposed. She pulled off her woollen hat and smoothed her hair; at least that was something she could do to improve matters, especially as Nathan was looking so smart. He had changed out of his sailing gear and was wearing grey flannel trousers and a check shirt, open at the neck to reveal a smattering of blond hairs on his chest. Her heart swelled with love for him.

They walked along the river wall in silence, stepping carefully over the mooring rings and ropes that littered the path. The only sounds to be heard in the soft evening air were the wheeling gulls and the plopping mud. Suddenly, she felt shy in the presence of this handsome, tanned man, his hair bleached almost white by the sun. He was so tall and broad walking beside her and it was so long since she had seen him that he seemed almost like a stranger.

When he showed no sign of breaking the silence she asked, 'Was it a good summer in Scotland?'

'It rained quite a bit. But the racing was good.'

21

They walked on again in silence. She was puzzled. This was not at all how she had imagined their meeting would be. He had released her hand before they left the boat and so far he had made no attempt to retrieve it, let alone to kiss her and tell her how much he had missed her. And there was as yet no sign of the ring he had bought her.

Maybe he was too shy and needed a bit of encouragement. She stole a glance at him. 'I've missed you, Nathan,' she said softly.

He didn't reply.

She tried again. 'You won a lot of races, didn't you? I'll bet that was exciting. Did you get a nice lot of prize money?'

'Yes, quite a bit.' He stopped and turned to her. 'Oh, yes, that reminds me. I brought you a little present, Ginny. I said I would, didn't I? I didn't forget, even though I spent nearly all my spare time with my painting.' He shifted the portfolio he was still carrying under his other arm and fished in his pocket. Looking pleased with himself he brought out a package and gave it to her.

She took and looked at it, frowning a little. It was quite the wrong shape for a ring box.

'Well, go on. Aren't you going to open it?' he said.

'Yes, yes, of course I am.' Puzzled, she pulled away the paper to reveal a tartan silk scarf. A very pretty tartan silk scarf but not quite what she had hoped for or expected. Perhaps he was teasing and the ring would come later.

He picked up a pebble and threw it into the mud, where it landed with a dull plop. 'I got it from Oban. I thought you'd like it,' he said, his voice casual.

'Yes, yes, I do. It's very pretty. Thank you, Nathan.' She waited, a half smile on her face, ready for him to produce the ring and tell her he was only teasing.

'I'm glad you like it. Well, go on. Put it round your neck,' he encouraged. 'That's it. It suits you.' He smiled at her in what was left of the fading light.

There was still no mention of a ring. Ginny shivered, but the cold came from inside her. 'I think I'd better be getting back,' she said. 'It's getting a bit chilly now the sun's gone down.'

He caught her arm. 'No. Don't go. Wait a bit. I've got something I want to tell you. Something exciting. I wanted you to be the first to know.' He was speaking in jerky sentences. 'Let's go down here and sit on *Vanessa's* jetty and I'll tell you.' Holding the portfolio carefully he held out his other hand to help her down the bank to one of several wooden jetties that stretched across the mud to the moored yachts.

His hand was warm in hers and this time he didn't let go as they sat side by side, their legs dangling.

'Well?' she asked, unsure now whether or not she was interested.

'I'm going away, Ginny,' he said, all in a rush. 'I'm going to London.'

'London!' Her jaw dropped. 'Whatever for?'

'To paint, of course.' There was a note of impatience in his tone. 'Sir Titus — you know, *Aurora*'s owner . . . '

'I know who Sir Titus Armitage is,' she interrupted, a trifle irritably.

'Well, Sir Titus saw my paintings when he came up to Scotland with his daughter — as I told you, I did quite a lot up there because the scenery is really grand, the lochs and mountains are really beautiful. I painted boats, landscapes, oh, all sorts of things. Look, I'll show you.' He undid his portfolio and Ginny saw some half dozen paintings, mostly sea and sky, it seemed to her as he flicked through them. 'Isobel reckons I've got real talent,' he confided enthusiastically, 'so she's persuaded her father to set me up in a studio in London.' He fastened the portfolio again and looked for Ginny's reaction to the momentous news, his eyebrows raised expectantly.

Ginny felt a sliver of ice move into her heart. 'Isobel?' she asked carefully.

'Sir Titus's daughter. She's twenty-three. That's a bit older than me but she says it's not important.' He warmed to his theme. 'She's beautiful, Ginny. The most beautiful girl you ever saw.'

'I know how beautiful she is. I've seen her,' Ginny said through dry lips.

'You have? Where?' He turned to her, surprised.

'I saw you come off the boat with her,' she said flatly.

'Ah, yes.' He chuckled. 'She hadn't quite got her sea legs, had she.'

Ginny made no answer to that. 'And she wants you to go to London so you can be with her?' she asked, giving the icicle that seemed to have lodged itself in her heart a masochistic twist.

'Yes. Well, no. Well, partly. Mostly because of my painting, of course.' He squeezed her hand. 'Don't you realise what this means, Ginny? I've got the chance to make a name for myself. I might even be famous one day!'

Carefully, Ginny pulled her hand away. 'Fat chance,' she said scathingly.

'Oh, come on, Ginny, don't be sour grapes. You don't know anything about art, how can you tell what's good and what isn't? But

Isobel can. Isobel says she can recognise talent when she sees it. She's been to art galleries all over the world so she knows what she's talking about.'

'Good for Isobel,' Ginny said in a tight voice.

He turned to her, frowning. 'What's the matter with you, Ginny? I thought you'd be pleased for me. I thought you'd be glad to know I've got a chance to make something of myself.'

Ginny said nothing. She stared out over the thin stream snaking its way between the mud banks, all that was left of the river at its lowest ebb. After a long time she said quietly, 'Oh, you'll make something of yourself, Nathan. A fool, if I'm any judge,' she said. 'You know very well you'll never be happy away from the sea.'

'Oh, I shall, Ginny. As long as I've got Isobel. And my painting . . . '

Ginny turned to look at him, her face serious. 'As long as you've got Isobel,' she mimicked. 'You mean as long as Isobel wants you. She's stringing you along, don't you realise that, Nathan? Your paintings aren't bad but you're not *that* good an artist. Good grief, I've seen drawings on the pavement that are better than anything you've ever done.' It was not true but she was past caring. Her voice rose. 'And have you thought what will happen when your beloved Isobel gets tired of you? Will you be prepared to starve in a garret for your art, or will you run home to mummy?' Her tone was biting.

He stared at her in amazement. 'Ginny! What on earth's come over you? I've never seen you like this before. I thought you'd be pleased for me. I thought you were my friend.' Then his face cleared and he grinned. 'I do believe you're jealous, Ginny Appleyard,' he said.

She gave him a withering look. 'Ha! Don't flatter yourself,' she said and gathering the remnants of her pride round her she got to her feet and stood looking down at him. 'I don't know why you bothered to drag me along here to tell me where you're going and what you're going to do because I'm simply not interested. I don't know why you ever thought I might be. You can go to Timbuktu for all I care.'

He stood up too and towered over her. 'We've been friends a long time, Ginny, so I thought you'd be pleased to know about my good fortune. But it seems I was mistaken,' he said. He shook his head, puzzled. 'I don't know what's happened to you over the summer but you've changed. You're not the same sweet-natured girl I left. When I talked to Isobel about you she said she thought you sounded a poppet . . . '

'Well, she was mistaken, too, wasn't she!' Ginny flashed. 'Maybe I've grown up. Maybe I've come to realise that there's as good a fish in the sea as ever came out of it.' She whipped the scarf from round her neck and threw it at him. 'Here, you can take this. Wrap it round Isobel's neck and pull it tight. Tell her the poppet sent it.' She went back along the jetty to the bank.

He followed her, laughing. 'You *are* jealous, aren't you, Ginny! That's what's wrong. But what are you jealous of? Is it because I'm going to London and you aren't? Well, you needn't be. When I get my own studio I'll hang some of your pencil drawings for you. How will that be? You never know, they might even sell.'

'Oh!' There was all the disgust she could muster in the sound. She turned away. 'You can hang yourself for all I care.' She shivered. 'I'm cold so I'm going home.' She climbed the bank and turned for home.

'Well, wait a sec. You don't need to be in such a hurry. I'll walk with you.' He scrambled up the bank behind her.

'Don't bother. If people see us together they might think we're walking out, and that would never do. Anyway, I'd rather go on my own. I don't want to talk to you any more.'

'Well, the least you can do is to wish me luck,' he called after her.

'Wish you luck? I reckon you're going to need a bit more than luck where you're going, Nathan Bellamy,' she called back over her shoulder.

'All I can say is, I hope when I come home again you'll be a bit better tempered,' he shouted.

'And I hope you'll have learned a bit of sense,' she shouted back.

She made her way home, tears blinding her eyes.

★   ★   ★

When she reached home her mother was sitting by the fire, mending. Her father was sitting opposite to her, staring into the bowl of his empty pipe. He looked up as Ginny walked in.

'Did you hev a nice walk with Nathan?' he asked.

'He's going to London,' she replied shortly.

'Ah, she's got round him then, and persuaded him to go,' Bob said with a nod. 'I fancied she might.'

Ruth looked up. 'Who?' she asked.

'The owner's daughter. Took quite a shine

to the boy, she did. Followed him around like a little dog, praised his paintings sky high, persuaded her father to buy two or three he painted in Scotland. Carried on about him being as good as some painter or other, Policeman, was it? No, Constable, that was the name.' He rammed tobacco into his pipe. 'Sprat to catch a mackerel, if you ask me.' He chuckled. 'Thass not his paintings she's interested in, thass other things.' The last few words, murmured into his beard, were lost in the scrape of his match as he lit his pipe and surrounded himself in a wreath of sweet-smelling tobacco. When he had got it drawing to his liking he got to his feet. 'I think I'll toddle round to the Rose and Crown for half a pint, Ruthy, seein' as it's the first night home.'

'Make sure it is only a half, then,' Ruth said sharply. 'I don't want you coming home as drunk as a lord.'

He spread his hands. 'Do I ever, Ruthy?'

She shrugged her thin shoulders. 'There's always a first time.'

Ginny went over and kissed him. 'Well, I shan't wait up for you, Dad, I'm going to bed. Goodnight.'

'Yes, you look as if you could do with your beauty sleep, matie. You look a bit peaky,' he said, concerned.

Ruth looked up briefly. 'She never carries much colour,' she said.

Ginny went to bed. But she didn't sleep. She lay staring at the ceiling, tears running down from the corners of her eyes on to the pillow, going over everything Nathan had said again and again. It was quite plain both from his words and what her father had said that he was completely bowled over by the beautiful Isobel Armitage. He had conveniently forgotten the words he had spoken to her, Ginny, before he went away — or, she tried to be fair — could it be that she had read more into them than he had intended?

Whatever the case, any fond notions she had cherished of a romance between herself and Nathan Bellamy could now be forgotten. He clearly had no regard for her and she no longer loved him. Or so her head argued. The trouble was, her heart was beating to a different drum. She turned her head into the damp pillow and sobbed.

She was still awake, her tears spent, when she heard her parents climb the narrow stair to bed. Through the thin wall she heard the creak as her father lowered his bulk into the bed beside his wife.

'Oh, come on, Ruthy, thass my first night home. I've missed you,' she heard him say.

There were further murmurings, then, 'Oh,

very well, but be quick about it,' from her mother.

After that, Ginny pulled the covers over her head. She didn't want to hear the sounds of her parents' lovemaking, if you could call it that.

Eventually, she fell asleep.

The next day was Sunday. Ginny got up early, pinched some colour into her cheeks and put on her best green dress, determined to show the world that she didn't care about Nathan Bellamy.

'I'm coming to church with you, Mum,' she announced over breakfast.

Ruth allowed herself a small smile of approval; usually Ginny made some excuse so as not to accompany her. 'That'll be nice,' was all she said.

'I'm not. I want to go and have a look at *Emily May*,' Bob said. 'She'll need a bit of a tidy-up before we start fishing and I want to see Billy Barr about the new mainsail. He should have it finished by now, ready for us to do it over with red ochre.'

Ginny looked up. 'I've often wondered, Dad, why do you paint the sails with that horrible red stuff? It stinks to high heaven.'

'Thass because of the fish oil mixed in with it. But we do it to preserve and strengthen the canvas, matie. Sails take a lot of strain when there's a good gale a-blowing.' He smiled at her. 'Thass a dirty owd job but Bert Grimshaw'll give me a hand. He's been keeping an eye on things for me over the summer.' Bert Grimshaw was several years older than Bob but they had been friends for years and they always fished the North Sea on *Emily May* together.

Ruth looked up from buttering a piece of toast. 'Bert Grimshaw's dead.' She spoke with about as much emotion as if she'd offered him another cup of tea. 'He had a stroke last July. Laid for a month, then had another that took him off. Didn't I tell you?'

Bob's jaw dropped and he looked stricken. 'No, you didn't. Oh, Ruthy, you might've written and said! Bert was a good mate of mine. You know that.'

She shrugged. 'I thought I'd told you.'

He scratched his wiry brown beard. 'I shall have to go and see his missus. Explain to her that I couldn't write because I didn't know. Oh, dear,' he shook his head from side to side, 'thass a bad job and no mistake. Poor owd Bert.' He sat staring at nothing in particular as the news sank in.

Ruth finished her toast and wiped her fingers on the napkin beside her plate — Bob never bothered with such niceties and Ginny sometimes forgot — then she pushed her chair back and got up from the table.

'Fetch the bowl, Ginny,' she said briskly. 'The breakfast things have to be washed up and the vegetables peeled ready for dinner before we go to church.'

Obediently, Ginny cleared the table and fetched the washing-up bowl from its shelf under the window sill. Then she poured water from the kettle on the hob and swished the mesh ball that held the last slivers of soap to make frothy suds. As she washed the china she put it on a tin tray beside the bowl to drain before drying it. When this was all done she emptied the water down the drain in the yard.

'When we get our house at the top end of the village we'll have a tap inside and a proper sink,' Ruth said, viciously stabbing the eyes out of a potato. 'But that won't be yet. Not while you throw all your prize money away on that old smack, Bob Appleyard.'

Bob got to his feet, still quite shaken at the news of the death of his old friend.

'*Emily May* is a good old fishing smack. She belonged to my father. She gives me — and you, Ruthy my girl — a decent living in the winter,' he said heavily. 'So it's up to me to make sure she's kept seaworthy. And that I shall do, for as long as I'm able.' He gave her a stern look. 'I don't think you'd

34

want me going to sea in a leaky owd tub like some do, making you a widder afore your time, would you?' He nodded as he saw the almost imperceptible shake of her head. 'No, I thought not.' He took his cheese-cutter cap from its hook by the door and screwed it on to his head. 'Now, I'm going to see Bert Grimshaw's missus. Then I shall take a look at the smack.' Without another word he left the house.

Ruth sniffed. 'Come on, girl, look sharp. Find your prayer book. The bells are ringing,' she said.

Ginny didn't really want to go to church. She had learned her catechism at her mother's knee and learned to say her prayers every night but she didn't have much faith in them being answered. But she was anxious to show Sir Titus Armitage and his daughter, should they grace the local church with their presence, that she didn't care a jot that Nathan was taking himself off to London.

Neither Sir Titus nor his daughter were there, as it happened. But Captain Bellamy and his wife were. They sat in the middle aisle, where the better-class people of the village sat — the shopkeepers, builders, yacht captains and the like. Ginny and her mother sat in the side aisle, near the front. Ruth Appleyard was not a person to skulk at the back when she went to worship her Maker.

After the service the congregation emerged into the warm September sunshine. The vicar stood at the church door, shaking hands with the more affluent of his flock, leaving space for those of lesser standing to slip out behind him.

Ginny and her mother were among those who left this way, unnoticed. Captain Bellamy and his wife were speaking to the vicar as they passed. The captain, wearing a blue serge suit, doffed his bowler hat to Ruth but Mrs Bellamy didn't even notice her. She was too busy telling the vicar of Nathan's good fortune.

'My son is to go to London, Vicar. To be an artist,' she said proudly.

'Indeed, Mrs Bellamy. How nice,' the vicar said.

'Oh, I shall miss him dreadfully,' she went on. 'But Sir Titus Armitage is so taken with his paintings that he's going to set him up in his own studio. You've heard of Sir Titus Armitage, haven't you, Vicar?' The daisies in her hat danced as she nodded at him encouragingly and she took a quick look round to make sure there was an audience for her words.

'I believe I may have, Mrs Bellamy.'

'Of course, one can't stand in the boy's

way, however much of a wrench it is . . . '

'No, of course not. Please wish him well from me, Mrs Bellamy. When will he be going?'

'Some time next week. Sir Titus has to have time to arrange things, of course.'

'Then maybe I'll see something of him before he goes.' The vicar shook her hand. 'Now, if you'll excuse me . . . Ah, good morning, Miss Brown. A lovely day . . . '

Mabel Bellamy swept up the churchyard like a ship in full sail, her husband in tow.

'I hope she'll have remembered to put the piece of beef in the oven,' Ruth remarked as she watched her progress. 'I left it all ready on the slab, vegetables done and everything. And an apple pie for afters.'

'Oh, I expect she can manage that, Mum,' Ginny said, without much interest.

Ruth glanced at her. 'You're upset about young Nathan going away, aren't you, girl?' she said.

Ginny tossed her head. 'I'll get over it. Like I told him last night, there's as good a fish in the sea as ever came out of it.'

She only hoped it might prove true. The trouble was, the way she felt at the moment it didn't seem very likely.

3

Throughout the next week Ginny see-sawed between hope and misery; hope that Nathan would have a change of heart and decide not to go to London and misery because common sense told her this was unlikely. In her more rational moments she didn't really blame him. She could well understand his excitement at the prospect of making a fortune with his painting if he went to London and she tried not to think about the fact that added to that he was head-over-heels in love with the beautiful Isobel Armitage, who would do all she could to help him fulfil his ambitions. But it didn't stop the heartache and her misery only increased when Mrs Bellamy came into the shop with her weekly order book on Wednesday, the day before Nathan was due to leave on his great adventure.

'I need a few extras for my son this week. He'll be going to London tomorrow,' she said to anybody who cared to listen as she sat herself down on the chair at the counter, thoughtfully provided for customers by Mr Stacey. 'It's because of his painting. He's a very good artist, you know. In fact, Sir Titus Armitage is so impressed with his work that he's offered to set him up in a studio of his own. Yes, two pounds of sugar and a quarter of tea, Ginny. No, not that one, Nathan likes Mazawattee. And a pound of custard creams, they're his favourites.'

The list went on and Ginny's unhappiness deepened although it might have helped to cheer her a little if she could have heard the conversation between Captain Bellamy and his wife in bed the previous night.

'Oh, Hector, isn't it wonderful? Such a marvellous chance for Nathan,' Mabel had said smugly as she reached out and switched off the bedside light.

'Hmph,' had come the enigmatic reply from the other pillow.

'Of course I shall miss him dreadfully,' she had gone on happily, 'but one must put one's own feelings to one side for the sake of his art, mustn't one.'

'Hmph.'

'What do you mean, *hmph*, Hector? Is that all you can say?' She had turned her head, spiky with curling pins and covered by a lurid pink hairnet, towards him in the darkness. 'Aren't you pleased that our son has this wonderful opportunity to better himself?' She had given him a nudge in the ribs. 'You never know, he could end up marrying Sir Titus's daughter,' she had said archly. 'That would be a feather in our caps, wouldn't it? Our son married to the daughter of a 'Sir'.'

'That's what I'm afraid of,' Hector had said, unimpressed. 'You don't know her, Mabel, but I can tell you she's a bit of a madam, that one. Twists daddy round her little finger. It was her idea, not his, you know, setting Nathan up in London.'

Mabel had been silent for some time. Then she had said huffily, 'Well, he must have agreed. And she must think he's good to have suggested it in the first place.'

'Oh, aye, she thinks he's good all right,' Hector had replied, remembering the afternoons in Scotland when Nathan had disappeared for hours at a time, appearing later with Isobel — Nathan looking a little sheepish, Isobel smiling like the cat who'd pinched the cream. It wasn't difficult to guess what had been going on . . . Hector had given another sigh. No good letting his thoughts wander in that direction, Mabel was no longer interested in that sort of thing. Not that she ever had been. Much.

She had warmed to her theme. 'I don't understand you, Hector. I don't understand you at all. I should have thought you'd be pleased at your son's golden opportunity. You never know, he could get hanged in the Royal Academy.'

Hector had smiled up into the darkness. 'I sincerely hope not, Mabel. I hope he'll never be hanged anywhere.'

'Well, hung, then. You know what I mean.' Irritated at his lack of enthusiasm, she had turned her back on him and settled down to sleep.

But Hector had stared up into the darkness for a long time. Unlike his wife he was not happy about what was happening to his son. In fact, he didn't like it at all. Oh, the boy could paint, there was no doubt about that, but could he compete with all those people in London who had been to special art schools? After all, Nathan had never had a proper lesson in his life. Another thing, would he be happy living among all those toffs in London? And perhaps even more to the point, would he be happy away from the sea? Hector had grave doubts on the matter. But who was he to argue when both Nathan and Mabel were so keen on the idea? He had turned over and tried to sleep.

But Ginny, of course, was unaware of all this. All she could see were Mrs Bellamy's excited preparations for her son's departure.

'Of course, we shall miss him terribly,' Mrs Bellamy continued, 'but it would be very

41

selfish of us to discourage him from going. After all, it's an opportunity in a lifetime. Yes, a half of short back rashers, Mr Stacey, please.'

Mr Stacey snapped his fingers. 'Roger! Half of short back rashers for Mrs Bellamy and look sharp about it.'

'Yes, Mr Stacey.'

Ginny gathered Mrs Bellamy's purchases and began putting them in a cardboard box while Roger Mayhew on the bacon counter cut the rashers. He was a pleasant enough young man of about twenty-three, with a rather pale face, black, sleeked-back hair and a neat moustache. He manipulated the bacon slicer — his pride and joy — with a certain flourish, making turning the handle and peeling off the slices into something of an art form. Ginny knew he did it only to impress her; he had asked her out several times but, faithful to Nathan, she had so far always refused. But she was fed up. Nathan was going away and there was a Fred Astaire and Ginger Rogers film on at the Regal in Colchester this week . . .

'What time bus shall we be catching tomorrow afternoon, Roger?' she asked as he walked over to put the neatly wrapped packet of bacon into Mrs Bellamy's box. 'Two o'clock? We want to get to the Regal in time for the start of the big picture.'

Roger flushed with surprise and pleasure. 'Oh, yes. The two o'clock'll give us plenty of time, Ginny.' He turned to Mrs Bellamy. 'Can I get you anything else, madam?' he asked politely.

'Yes, half a pound of butter, please.' Mrs Bellamy turned a frosty stare on Roger. She hadn't been aware that there was anything between him and Ginny and the knowledge rather spoiled her pleasure in boasting about Nathan, because part of the exercise had been to make Ginny Appleyard realise how futile her hopes of marrying her son had been. It was annoying, to say the least.

'How much is that?' she snapped, getting out her purse.

Ginny had been rapidly totting up the figures. 'That will be five and eleven three, please, Mrs Bellamy.' This was a kind of shorthand for five shillings and elevenpence three farthings.

'Have them sent up to the house.' Mrs Bellamy paid her bill and got up from the chair.

Mr Stacey hovered to escort her to the door. 'The delivery boy will bring them later on this afternoon, as soon as he gets home from school,' he said, holding it open for her.

'Thank you, Mr Stacey. I'd be obliged.' She

left the shop, her head held high.

'She must think she's somebody, just because her husband's a yacht captain,' Doris, Ginny's partner on the 'dry' counter remarked caustically, watching Mrs Bellamy walk past the shop window.

But Roger had his mind on other things. 'Did you mean it? Will you come to the pictures tomorrow afternoon, Ginny?'

'Well, it's our half day and I said I would, didn't I?' Ginny answered, busily packing the rest of the things into Mrs Bellamy's box.

'Yes. I just wanted to make sure you hadn't changed your mind, that's all.' He'd asked her so many times only to be refused that he could hardly believe his luck. Whistling under his breath, he went back to his own counter and began expertly and rather flamboyantly cutting off lumps of butter and patting them into shape.

When Ginny arrived home after work her mother was ironing. There was delicious smell of stew bubbling on the stove.

'Where's Dad?' she asked, taking off her hat and coat and hanging them on the hook behind the door.

'In the wash house, cleaning himself up. He's been doing whatever it is he had to do to that new sail,' Ruth said, her mouth pursed disapprovingly. 'Came home stinking of fish oil. I don't know why he needed to spend good money on a new one, the old one could have been patched again, I'm sure.'

As she spoke Bob came in, his hair and beard damp and springy from being washed and his face shiny with soap. He sat down heavily in his chair by the stove. 'Well, thass a good job done,' he said happily. 'I spread it out on the quay and got young Will Kesgrave to give me a hand to paint it with the stuff. Thass filthy owd muck to put on but he said he didn't mind. Poor owd Bert always used to help but now he's gone to the Better Land I had to find someone else.' He reached down his pipe from the mantelpiece. 'I shall miss owd Bert.'

Ruth slammed down the iron. 'Will Kesgrave? You asked Will Kesgrave? I should think you must want your head seeing to.'

'I don't see why. He's not a bad lad,' Bob said mildly.

'He's never sober. Like his mother, she's always drunk. And his sister will grow up just the same if I don't miss my mark.' Ruth vented her feelings on her husband's shirt. 'They're a filthy, Godless lot, that family. I'm surprised you have anything to do with them.'

Bob got his pipe drawing to his satisfaction, then he said, 'Will likes a drink, that I'll not deny. But if he can keep sober he's not a bad lad. And he's a hard worker, I'll say that for him. He was on *Aurora* with me and he shaped up pretty well. In fact, I was thinking I might ask him if he'd like to come fishing with me on the smack this season.'

'What!' Ruth nearly screamed the word.

He raised his eyebrows. 'Well, I can't see as how it'll make much difference to you, Ruthy, if I do. I'm not asking you to come along,' he said. 'Anyway, I only said I was thinking about it. I've got to find somebody to take Bert's place.'

'Well, I hope you'll think again about Will Kesgrave.' Ruth put the iron on the hearth and folded up the ironing blanket and put it in the cupboard under the stairs. 'I never heard such a thing.'

'I'll lay the table,' Ginny said. She was inclined to agree with her mother over Will Kesgrave but she thought it best not to join in the argument.

Almost as if on cue there was a knock at the door. Ginny opened it to find Will Kesgrave standing there, his cheese-cutter hat on the back of his head, his hands in his pockets.

'Hullo, Ginny. Is your dad in?' he asked.

'Speak of the devil and you'll hear the flap of his wings,' Ruth muttered under her breath.

Bob ignored her. 'Yes, I'm here. Come on in, bor,' he called from his armchair, also ignoring the vitriolic look she shot him.

Will stepped inside but didn't remove his cap. 'About that tar, Bob. I could fetch it from the gas works tomorrer and we could make a start on the hull. The weather looks set fair for the next few days so we oughta get on with it.'

Bob drew on his pipe, nodding. 'Yes. The sooner we get her ship-shape the sooner we'll be ready to fish. Right-o, bor. Thanks.'

Will made no attempt to leave. 'Your stew smells right good, Mrs Appleyard,' he said, grinning at her.

'There's only enough for three,' Ruth said without looking at him.

'Thass a shame. I'm partial to a good stew.'

'Well, you'd better get your mother to make one then,' Ruth said sourly.

'My mother!' He laughed. 'My mother make a stew! She can't even boil water without burnin' the pan.'

'Then it's time she learned. Shut the door as you go out.'

He took the hint and left.

'You were a bit hard on the boy, Ruthy,' Bob remarked.

'Hard on him! Why shouldn't I be hard on him? You know very well I don't have

47

anything to do with the Kesgrave family, dirty, slovenly lot that they are. I don't know what came over you, asking him into the house . . . Once they get a foot over the threshold you can never be rid of them, borrowing a cup of this and a spoonful of that. Granny Crabtree, next door, found that out.'

'Well, he never asked to borry anything tonight, did he?' Bob said drawing his chair up to the table.

'He as good as asked for some stew.'

'Well, it looks as if there's plenty,' Bob said, eyeing the saucepan.

'Not for the likes of him.' Ruth ladled it on to the plates and put the pan back on the stove. 'Tomorrow afternoon, Ginny, I want you to . . .'

'I'm going to the pictures, Mum,' Ginny said quickly. 'With Roger Mayhew.'

'And who might Roger Mayhew be, matie?' Bob asked, shovelling a potato into his mouth and rolling it around because it was hot.

'You know, Dad. He works on the bacon counter at Stacey's. Lives in Station Road with his mother and sister. They moved there a couple of years ago.'

'Oh, ah. I remember. He seem a decent enough chap from what I recall.' He glanced at her. 'Young Nathan's off to London tomorrer, ain't he?'

Ginny feigned surprise, trying to pretend the date wasn't burned into her brain. 'Oh, is it tomorrow he's going? I'd forgotten.'

'His mother was making great preparations, ironing his shirts and packing his case while I was up there this morning,' Ruth said. 'Got me to make some of his favourite rock cakes to take with him.'

'Is he very excited?' Ginny couldn't help it, she had to ask.

'Excited! If you ask me he can't wait to get on that train.' Ruth chewed a piece of meat thoughtfully. 'And I reckon once he gets settled in London that'll be the last we shall see of him.'

'Well, thass all right, ain't it, matie?' Bob said, smiling at his daughter. 'You've got other fish to fry now so it won't worry you whether he comes back or not, will it?' He was watching her intently as he spoke.

'No, it certainly won't,' Ginny said firmly, pushing her dinner round her plate without eating it.

'What's on at the pictures?' he asked.

'Fred Astaire and Ginger Rogers.'

'Oh, I ain't never heard of them.'

'They're dancers, Dad. And they act. And sing. Oh, they're wonderful to watch.'

'Thass good.' Bob nodded as he took a

doorstep of bread and began mopping up the last of the gravy on his plate.

* * *

Ginny took great care with her appearance for her outing on Thursday afternoon. She wore the new green dress and with it a darker green jacket that matched her tam o' shanter. With her black patent shoes and handbag she felt very smart, especially as she had coiled her hair up into a knot at the nape of her neck to make herself look older.

The look on Roger's face when he saw her proved that her efforts had been well worth while and the admiration in his eyes made her blush. He, too, looked smart. Having hardly seen him out of the white, high-necked, double-breasted jacket and long white apron that was his uniform when he was at work Ginny was amazed how different he looked in his best blue serge suit, which he wore with a pale blue shirt with a stiff white collar and a spotted tie. A grey trilby hat set at a slight, not too rakish angle, completed the picture.

And he was very kind and attentive, a real gentleman. He insisted on paying for her seat at the cinema as well as her bus fare and bought her a box of Milk Tray and an ice cream into the bargain. So she rewarded him by not pulling her hand away when he captured it, even though she got pins and needles in her arm and his hand was a bit sweaty. The film was good, too, although she couldn't help her mind wandering just a bit, wondering how far Nathan had got on his journey to London.

After the film they stumbled out into the daylight, slightly disoriented at moving from the unlikely rags to riches, lavishly costumed New York story on the screen to the slightly grubby Colchester pavements and the necessity of hurrying through the crowds to catch the bus home.

'Did you enjoy it, Ginny?' Roger asked, putting his hand under her elbow to guide her across the street.

'Yes, it was lovely. Ginger Rogers is beautiful, isn't she? And Fred Astaire! Oh, I think he's gorgeous.'

'I don't think Ginger Rogers is half as pretty as you, Ginny,' he whispered, blushing at his own temerity.

'Oh, go on. You don't mean that.' Ginny tossed her head, flattered.

'Yes, I do.' They walked on in silence. Then, 'Shall we go to the pictures again next week?'

'What's on?'

'Claudette Colbert. Don't you remember? We saw the trailer. I forget what it's called.'

'Oh, yes, Claudette Colbert. I like her. But I can't remember what it's called, either.' It must have been on when she was picturing Nathan's arrival in London, straight into Isobel Armitage's arms.

'Well?' he persisted.

'Well what?'

'Will you come with me again next week?'

'Yes. All right.'

They caught the bus and Roger walked her home from the bus stop.

'Thank you for coming with me, Ginny,' he said when they reached the steps leading down into the yard. 'I hope you had a nice afternoon.'

'I did. Thank you very much, Roger.' She didn't ask him in although she wondered if she should. But plenty of time for that later, she decided. No sense in rushing things.

'I'll see you at work tomorrow.' They both made a face at the thought of work.

'Let's hope old Stacey's in a good mood,' Ginny said with a laugh.

Roger took her hand and squeezed it. 'See you tomorrow, then.'

He went back across Anchor Hill and Ginny went down the two steps into the yard.

Ruth was laying the table. She looked up as Ginny opened the door.

'I've laid an extra place. I thought you

might bring your young man in to tea,' she said.

'Oh, Mum! He's not my young man. We've been to the pictures, that's all,' Ginny said, taking off her hat and shaking out her hair in front of the mirror over the mantel-piece.

'Well, he seems a nice enough young chap, from what I've seen of him. You could do worse,' Ruth remarked. 'You can't moon about for Nathan Bellamy for the rest of your life.'

Ginny gave an exasperated sigh. 'I'm not mooning over Nathan Bellamy, Mum. He's gone to London to be with his lady-love and there's an end of it. But just because I've been to the pictures with Roger Mayhew this afternoon and I'm going again next week, if you want to know, that doesn't mean he's my young man.'

'Oh, all right, Miss Hoity-Toity. No need to get your dander up. You can brew the tea. Your father will be in shortly, I expect.'

'Where is he?'

'Gone to the yacht with Captain Bellamy. They've gone to see about clearing things out ready to lay her up for the winter.' She pursed her lips. 'I daresay he's taken that Will Kesgrave with him, too.' Her expression changed and she returned to her former topic. 'If you're going out with Roger again next week you must invite him back for tea, Ginny. It's only polite.'

'I'll see.' Ginny was noncommittal. But thinking about it later she decided that Roger was really very nice and certainly knew how to treat a girl. There was a lot to be said for that. But there was no hurry.

4

Ginny went to the cinema with Roger the next week and the week after that. Before long the weekly cinema trip became a habit, followed by tea at Ginny's house one week and tea at Roger's house the next.

Ginny liked Roger's mother; she was a plump, homely woman who seemed very happy that her son had found himself a young lady. His sister was less easy. She was several years older than Roger and clearly felt that she should have been 'walking out' before her young brother. To Ginny's mind, if Elsie had been of a less miserable nature she might have stood a better chance of finding a husband. But she wisely kept this opinion to herself.

It worried Ginny a little how quickly everyone made the assumption that she and Roger were 'walking out'. She supposed they were, in a way, but only because she hadn't made any effort to put a stop to it. Being totally honest with herself, she didn't particularly want to put a stop to it. Roger was kind and attentive and treated her well and she quite enjoyed going out with him. It was nice to have a partner at the dances held once a month at the village hall, although she took care not to dance exclusively with Roger, and as well as the weekly jaunt to the pictures there were the Sunday afternoon walks that had begun a week or two later and become a habit before she realised what was happening. But he never tried to take liberties. She liked him for that.

But, a corner of her mind said, if she was in love with him wouldn't she *want* him to take liberties? Lying in bed thinking about it before she went to sleep she sometimes allowed her mind to wander to how she would feel if it was Nathan in Roger's place . . . When Roger bent to kiss her she always contrived to turn a cool cheek so that he missed her mouth, but even now she experienced a warm glow when she remembered how it had been on the few occasions Nathan had kissed her, full on the lips — she had gone all weak at the knees and wanted it to go on and on.

But it was no good dwelling on that. Nathan had gone and wouldn't be coming back. His mother made that quite plain each time she came into the shop. He was comfortably set up in his own studio, she was fond of telling anyone who cared to listen, and several people had shown an interest in his work. Next year, Sir Titus Armitage would probably hold an exhibition for him, she boasted. Ginny pretended she didn't care, smiling at Roger when he winked at her as he sliced the bacon and patted the butter and lard into shape.

In her spare time Ginny went down to the quay and helped her father mend his fishing nets. It was now November and *Emily May* was almost ready for her first trip to the Wallet or Swin where the sprat shoals were to be found. Will Kesgrave, warned by Bob that if he drank too much he wouldn't be included in the crew, had managed for the most part to keep away from the Rose and Crown. Saturday night was the only night he transgressed, and this he did regularly, reeling home loudly drunk at two in the morning, kicking everything in sight and singing at the top of his voice. Sunday mornings often saw Bob dunking his head under the tap in the yard and calling him everything he could lay his tongue to.

'I like a drink as well as the rest,' he would say, banging Will's head against the tap — not entirely by accident — and making him yelp, 'but I don't get stinking, filthy rotten drunk. You're a fool, Willy boy, piddling your prize money up against the wall the way you do. Why can't you take a couple of pints and leave it at that, same as I do.' Another rough jerk made Will yelp again.

'Hold hard, Bob,' he spluttered. 'I've got a head the size of a gasometer. You'll kill me if you carry on like this.'

'I shan't kill you, you great soft ha'porth. But I'll see you don't come aboard my smack. I ain't having men who can't hold their drink aboard *Emily May*. Thass too dangerous.'

'Don't worry, Bob, I shan't do it again,' Will promised every week as he surfaced, spluttering. 'And thass a promise. I feel too bloody rough.'

But he did. The next Saturday and the one after. And so it went on.

'I should think you've changed your mind about taking that Will Kesgrave on the smack with you,' Ruth said primly when Bob was making last-minute preparations for his first trip of the winter.

'He'll be all right, don't you worry. He won't get drunk at sea because there won't be any beer aboard *Emily May*.'

'Not unless he smuggles it on. And I wouldn't put that past him. You'll have to watch him, Robert.'

'I shall do that, Ruthy. Never fear.' He regarded her gravely but with a twinkle in his eye. 'I should think you'll be thankful to know I've got him with me. At least you won't hev to listen to the racket he kicks up every Saturday night when he's had a skinful.'

Ruth nodded. 'There's that much to be thankful for,' she admitted. She shuddered. 'Oh, he's a disgusting creature. I can't think why you have anything to do with him.'

'He's a bit of a rough diamond, I'll agree,' Bob said, drawing on his pipe. 'But there's good in him.'

'You see good in everybody,' Ruth snapped impatiently.

Bob smoked his pipe quietly for some time. Then he said, 'I ain't quite so sure about Ginny's young man. He seem a bit on the smarmy side to me.'

Ruth glared at him. 'I don't know what you mean. Roger's a very nice young man and I'm sure he thinks the world of Ginny.'

Bob nodded slowly. 'Yes. I reckon you're right. But I reckon I'd hoped she'd find somebody who'd got a bit more about him.' He sighed. 'But I 'spect somebody's got to cut up the bacon.'

'It's a respectable job. In fact I believe he's thinking of applying to the Co-op for a job. You mark my words, he'll end up as manager before he's finished.'

Bob pictured himself hauling in a full net in the teeth of a nor'easterly gale, wet through and frozen to the marrow, trying to keep his feet on a stinking, slippery deck. Somehow, he couldn't see Roger Mayhew surviving in such conditions. Neither could he see Ginny married to the manager of the Co-op, however well-paid and prestigious the post might be. He moved uneasily in his chair.

'I hope Ginny won't do anything in a hurry,' he said enigmatically.

'She's only nineteen. She can't do anything without our consent,' Ruth reminded him, adding, 'not that I'd have any objection to Roger as a son-in-law. He's a nice, steady man and he'll always have a good job if he moves to the Co-op.'

'Reckon you're right, Ruthy,' he said with a sigh.

Two days later, Bob and his crew, including Will Kesgrave, went off with the stow boaters, as the spratting fleet was called. It was hard, cold work in icy conditions in rough seas, but Will justified Bob's faith in him. He worked the long hours with a will and never a word of complaint, even when he was wet through and the water turned to ice on his oilskins.

Because Will was anxious not to let Bob down. He respected him and saw in him the father he had never known. While he was on board *Emily May* he signed the pledge, holding the pen with fingers that were like lumps of raw meat from handling the heavy nets and vowed never to touch another drop of alcohol as long as he lived.

But when they arrived back, with a full hold of the slimy silver sprats that would make a good price on the London market, he nipped into the Rose and Crown to let his mother know he was back and forgot his pledge. He was thrown out at closing time and crawled home on his hands and knees. He spent the next two days in bed, wishing he were dead.

On Christmas morning Ginny accompanied her mother to church, leaving Bob enjoying a quiet pipe beside the fire, with strict instructions to keep the fire well stoked up so the pudding didn't go off the boil. Ginny enjoyed church at Christmas. The atmosphere was festive, every window sill and ledge was decorated with holly and prize chrysanthemums from the rector's greenhouse and the crib scene was laid out on the font at the back of the church and lit with tiny candles. She loved singing carols, too, along with the choir and congregation. To Ginny this was an important part of Christmas, as important as going home to the large chicken her mother had left roasting in the oven, stuffed with chestnuts and sage and onion.

Wearing her best winter coat of warm,

rusty brown with the fur collar and the little fur hat and gloves that matched, Ginny walked across to the church with her mother. It was bitterly cold and everywhere was rimed with frost, which nearly made it a white Christmas. A glow of happiness spread through her as they crossed the square, the people they met all smiling and wishing them a merry Christmas. All it would need to make the day perfect was for Nathan to appear and say he'd had enough of London and was coming home. She shook herself mentally. Nathan was no longer a part of her life, she told herself sternly as she followed her mother up the side aisle to their usual pew near the front.

The church was full and the service took its usual Christmas Day form with plenty of carols for everybody to sing and the rector's usual Christmas Day sermon, which most people knew by heart. It was not until they left the church afterwards that Ginny realised that Nathan had been there, sitting with his parents. Although her heart began to thump uncomfortably she tried to pretend she hadn't seen him but he broke away and came over to her, grinning broadly.

'Merry Christmas, Ginny. How are you?' he asked, as if their parting three months ago hadn't been acrimonious.

'A Merry Christmas to you, too. I'm very well, thank you, Nathan,' she answered stiffly, trying not to look at him. 'And you?'

'Oh, things couldn't be better,' he said breezily. 'I've got my own studio and I've sold several paintings to Isobel's friends.'

'That's nice. I'm glad you like living in London.'

'Oh, I do. There's so much going on all the time.' He gave a little laugh. 'Isobel keeps taking me to so many places that I hardly have time to pick up a paintbrush.'

'You'll never make a living that way,' she couldn't resist saying.

'Oh, I do all right. Do you like my suit?' It was pale grey with dark blue braid round the lapels. Ginny thought it looked rather odd, especially with the dark blue trilby hat and — heavens above — *spats!* 'Isobel bought it for me. It's the latest fashion, you know.'

'Is it? I'm sure it's very nice.' She wasn't enthusiastic.

'But what about you, Ginny? Are you still working at Stacey's?'

She nodded.

'Why don't you leave and get out and see the world? You surely don't want to work in a grocer's shop all your life.' He grinned at her the way that always made her heart turn over. It didn't turn over today, in fact he seemed so full of himself that she found it slightly irritating.

'I don't suppose I'll be working there for much longer,' she said coolly. 'I daresay I shall be getting married before too long.'

His eyebrows shot up. 'Married! Who to?'

'Roger Mayhew. He works at Stacey's, too.'

'What, old Brylcreem!' he said in surprise, adding apologetically, 'We used to call him that at school because of the way his hair was so plastered down.' He paused, trying to find something positive to say. 'He was very good at mental arithmetic, as I remember.'

'He still is,' she replied coolly.

He was silent for a minute, studying her. Then he took a deep breath and smiled. 'Well, good luck, Ginny. I hope you'll be very happy.'

'Thank you. And the same to you.' She turned away and without looking back went up the churchyard with her mother.

'Nathan looks as if he's doing all right,' her mother remarked as they walked home. 'What did he have to say for himself?'

'Not a lot. He's enjoying living in London. Doesn't seem to be getting much work done, though.'

'He's managed to buy himself a new suit, I noticed.'

'Isobel bought it for him.'

'Ah. Like that, is it.' Ruth nodded sagely. 'I've have thought better of Nathan than that. But if she's got her claws into him to that extent we shan't be seeing him back in these parts many more times, unless I'm very much mistaken.'

'If he likes to turn himself into her lap dog that's his look-out,' Ginny said with a shrug. 'I hope Dad hasn't let the fire out,' she said, changing the subject.

Bob hadn't let the fire out. In fact, he'd gone one better and also lighted one in the front room, a room that held the best furniture, a green rexine three-piece suite, a spindly occasional table and a glass-fronted china cabinet, and was only used on very special occasions.

'It smoked a bit to begin with but I reckon that was because the chimley was damp, but thass all right now,' he said happily.

Ruth poked her nose in at the door. 'Still smells cold in there,' she said with a sniff.

'Well, then, time there was a fire to warm it up. You oughta put a fire in there more often. Ruthy.' He got to his feet. 'I think I'll get meself a little tot of whisky, seein' as it's Christmas. I'll take it there so I can keep an eye on the fire and give you more room out here to get the dinner.' He poured himself a generous tot from the bottle kept in the dresser cupboard for emergencies and went through to the front room while Ginny and her mother donned pinafores and bustled about putting the finishing touches to the dinner.

After they had eaten, they exchanged small gifts. Ruth had knitted Bob a pair of socks, Ginny bought him an ounce of his favourite tobacco. Ginny gave her mother a frilly apron to wear in the afternoon, Bob gave her a pair of slippers, which she needed. For Ginny there was a cream blouse and a box of handkerchiefs.

'Did you buy Roger a present?' Bob asked.

'Yes,' Ruth answered, before Ginny could open her mouth, 'She's bought him a paisley silk scarf. It's very nice. I'm sure he'll like it.'

'Yes, I dessay he will,' Bob nodded, his face impassive. 'Are you seein' him today, matie?'

'Yes. He's coming round this afternoon and he'll stay to tea.'

'Good thing I lit the fire in the front room, then,' he remarked, giving his wife a wink.

Roger arrived in time to listen with Ginny and her parents to the King's Christmas broadcast to the Empire. Bob had used some of his prize money to buy the new wireless and it stood on its own table in the corner of the room, with the two accumulators that powered it on the shelf beneath. These had to be taken to the garage at the top of the hill to be recharged when they ran down. Now, he twiddled the knobs importantly to get the best reception and then sat back in his chair to listen.

The others sat round the table, their eyes glued to the set, marvelling that the King, sitting in London, should be able to speak to them, here, in their own home.

When it was finished Bob turned the set off. 'He don't sound no different to anybody else,' he remarked, slightly disappointed.

'He speaks very nicely,' Ruth said, trying not to sound disappointed.

'Well, he's only a man, same as you or me,' Roger said with a shrug.

'Roger! You shouldn't say that. He's the King,' Ginny said, horrified. 'He's not like us at all.'

'Well, you know what I mean,' Roger said sheepishly, then quickly changed the subject. 'Shall we go for a walk, Ginny?'

'You don't want to do that. Thass cold outside,' Bob was quick to say. 'Why don't the two of you go in the front room. I've got a good fire going in there and thass a pity to waste it. I'm going to sit here and hev a smoke. Mother won't want me stinking her front room out with 'baccy smoke. Are you going to sit here with me, Ruthy?'

'No, I've got a bit more clearing up to do. Then I'll make a cup of tea and bring it in.' That was meant as a warning to the young couple not to get up to any 'hanky-panky'.

Roger followed Ginny into the front room and sat down beside her on the settee. Bob had made up a good fire but the room still struck chill after the warmth of the kitchen and Ginny shivered a little.

He immediately put his arm round her. 'I've brought you a Christmas present, Ginny,' he said. 'I hope you're going to like it.'

'And I've got something for you, too. Wait a minute. I'll go and fetch it.' Ginny ran up to her room and came down again with the scarf, carefully wrapped in tissue paper. She watched anxiously while he unwrapped it because it had cost her much agonising before she chose it, worried that it might be too expensive a present if he was just a friend — or not expensive enough if he was more than a friend. It was not made any easier because she wasn't sure in her heart which she wanted him to be. She was relieved by his smile of appreciation.

'Oh, it's very nice. Very posh. And just what I need to go with my new overcoat. Thank you, Ginny.' He leaned over and gave her a smacking kiss on her cheek. 'Now, I've got something for you.'

He reached into his pocket and brought out a small square package. 'Well, go on, open it,' he encouraged.

Carefully, almost fearfully, she undid the wrapping to reveal a blue velvet box. Inside, on a bed of satin, sat a gold ring set with a cluster of seven tiny diamonds. 'Oh, it's . . . it's beautiful, Roger,' she breathed. In truth she had never seen such a lovely ring before.

'It's an engagement ring, Ginny,' he said eagerly. He went on in a rush, 'I came round and had a word with your dad while you were at church this morning. I told him I'd got it and I asked him if he had any objections to us getting engaged. He said if you were happy about it then so was he but he hoped we wouldn't rush into getting married. I said no, I hadn't thought we'd get married for a couple of years or so and he said that he thought that was about right . . . ' His voice tailed off. 'What's the matter, Ginny? Don't you like it?'

She looked at him, her eyes shining with tears. 'I think it's the most beautiful ring I've ever seen, Roger,' she said softly.

'Well, put it on, then. See if it fits,' he urged.

'No, you put it on my finger,' she held out

the fourth finger of her left hand and he slipped the ring on to it.

'Whew! What about that! It fits,' he said, lifting her hand and kissing it. Then he gathered her into his arms. 'Will you marry me, Ginny?' he asked softly. 'Not yet, but in a couple of years?'

She wound her arms round his neck. 'Yes, Roger. I think I'd like that,' she said and this time she let him kiss her full on the lips and when his hand wandered to cup her breast she didn't pull away.

Half an hour later Ruth came in with the tea tray and Bob followed with the Christmas cake.

'We're engaged!' Ginny said excitedly. 'Look, Roger's given me the loveliest little ring.' She held her hand out for inspection.

Bob came over and kissed her. 'I hope you'll be very happy, matie,' he said. Then he turned to Roger and shook hands with him. 'You, too, bor. But you mind and take care of my little gal or you'll hev me to reckon with,' he said with a smile.

'I shall do that, never fear, Mr Appleyard,' Roger said.

He went over to Ruth, who presented a cool cheek for him to kiss. 'You won't be naming the day yet, will you,' she said, ever practical. 'I think you should wait until Ginny is twenty-one before you think of marrying.'

'Indeed, that's what we intend to do, Mrs Appleyard,' he assured her. 'We don't mind a long engagement, do we, dearest?'

Ginny blushed at the term of endearment. 'No. We don't mind at all,' she agreed, twisting the ring this way and that to make it sparkle in the firelight.

A little later they went to tell Roger's mother and sister the news. Mrs Mayhew was delighted at the prospect of Ginny as her daughter-in-law but Elsie was less cordial and gave a disparaging sniff when she was shown the ring.

'I suppose it will be left to me to help mother out with the household expenses now,' she remarked with a trace of bitterness. 'You'll be wanting to keep all your earnings to save up to get married.'

'I shall give Mum the same as I always do,' Roger said levelly. 'I don't expect to live here for nothing.'

'The boy is always generous in what he gives me,' his mother said loyally. 'I don't know why you need to carp, Elsie.'

'My sister's only jealous because she hasn't got a ring on her finger,' Roger said, squeezing Ginny to him as he walked her home in the dark.

'Maybe if she was a bit more cheerful she

would have,' Ginny ventured.

'That's exactly what I keep telling her.' He stopped and turned to kiss her under a street lamp. 'You see, Ginny. We already think alike. I love you, Ginny.'

'I love you, too, Roger.'

But lying in bed later that night, the little ring safely in its box on her bedside table, Ginny wondered if she really did love Roger or whether she was in love with the idea of being engaged and wearing the pretty little ring. And it worried her a little that the first thought that had come into her head as Roger put the ring on her finger was that this would prove to Nathan Bellamy that she didn't care about him.

5

It all seemed so ordinary, so mundane, that until she looked at the pretty little ring on her finger Ginny at times wondered if she had imagined the whole thing. In her dreams an engagement meant being swept off her feet on to cloud nine by a handsome young man (no, not a *bit* like Nathan Bellamy, she told herself sternly) who covered her with passionate kisses that she returned without reservation. And from then on every moment apart would be wasted, every moment together blissful.

In reality there was nothing very romantic in watching Roger slice the bacon and she tried to avoid meeting him in the stock room because he always tried to kiss and fondle her. She hated to admit it, but she didn't much like kissing Roger. His moustache was a bit bristly and she didn't care for the scent of his hair oil — she was sure it wasn't Brylcreem these days. And she didn't like him sticking his hand down her dress at every available opportunity; there was a time and a place for everything and eleven o'clock in the morning was not the time and Stacey's stock room was not the place.

But aside from these little irritations she was very happy to be engaged to Roger. If there wasn't a film they wanted to see on a Saturday afternoon it was nice just to walk round Colchester arm in arm, looking in furniture shop windows and choosing which bedroom suites and dining-room suites they would have in their house, when they got one. There was a slight hitch in that Roger preferred light oak or satin walnut whereas Ginny liked dark oak or mahogany and they couldn't quite agree on the kind of three-piece they might like for the front room — or lounge as Ginny liked to call it. Ginny thought uncut moquette was rather nice and very modern but Roger wasn't keen because he thought it would show the dirt too much. She shrugged off their differences, telling herself that there was plenty of time, no doubt things would sort themselves out as they went along. In the meantime, she enjoyed the occasional flowers that he bought her and the polite way he always walked on the outside of the pavement and held doors open for her.

Spring brought the big yachts to life again. After a winter spent fishing in the teeth of the North Sea gales, *Emily May* was laid up for the summer and Bob's attention was taken up in supervising, with Captain Bellamy, the fitting-out of *Aurora* for the coming summer's sailing and racing.

The sea wall was alive with activity as decks were scrubbed, hulls repainted, topsides varnished and brass polished on all the yachts moored there. While Captain Bellamy chose his crew, most of whom had sailed with him the previous season, Bob checked ropes and spars, and oversaw the loading of the sails, including the huge rolled mainsail, which was so big and heavy that it had to be carried on ten men's shoulders, progressing along the wall like a giant caterpillar, taken on board and carefully stowed.

At Stacey's, Ginny was given the task of making up the orders for victualling the yachts, stacking tea, sugar, coffee, tobacco, flour, butter, bacon and all manner of other supplies into large boxes clearly labelled with each yacht's name. She worked slowly and methodically because she knew that providing stores for the yachts made up the better part of the year's income for Mr Stacey so he was anxious that there should be no mistakes. As he reminded her frequently, Stacey's would suffer if they lost the franchise to any of the other, smaller, grocers in the village.

She was working on the last of the orders, for *Aurora*, just before closing time, when

Nathan walked into the shop. He was dressed in white duck trousers and a navy blue blazer with brass buttons and a new cheese-cutter cap. He looked very smart, much too smart for an ordinary crewman.

'Good evening, Nathan,' she said, walking past him, her list in her hand and giving him what she hoped was an impersonal, breezy smile, although in truth her heart had begun to do strange things at the sight of him even though she was nearly dropping with fatigue. 'I didn't realise you were home. Is there something you wanted?'

'Yes. I . . . ' he glanced round the shop. Then he noticed the label on the box on the counter. 'I've just come in to see how long it will be before *Aurora*'s stores are ready,' he said quickly.

She frowned. 'Are they needed in a hurry? I haven't quite finished packing. I suppose they could be collected tonight, but we can't deliver them because the boy's gone home. I thought it was all arranged that we should deliver them in the morning,' she said. 'I thought Mr Stacey had arranged it with the steward.'

'That's OK. I'm sure tomorrow morning will be fine. We don't sail till the three o'clock tide.'

'Oh,' she said with a lift of her eyebrows.

'Are you sailing, too? You look a bit smart for a crewman.'

He looked down at himself, slightly embarrassed. 'This is my shore rig. Isobel said I should . . . ' He stopped, shrugging his shoulders. 'My working gear is already stowed on board,' he finished lamely.

'I see.' She looked at the list in her hand. 'Well, I can't stop and talk now, Nathan, or I shan't get this done. It's nearly closing time already.'

'No, of course not.' For some reason he seemed reluctant to leave. He smiled at her. 'I'll see you later, perhaps.'

'Yes. Quite likely. It's Thursday tomorrow, my half day, so I shall probably come and watch the boat leave. Dad likes me to wave him off.' She went back to her list, congratulating herself on the cool way she had managed to talk to Nathan. He could have had no idea how her heart was thumping.

By the time she had finished making up the order the shop was closed and everyone, even Roger, who had pestered her with offers to help and been quite sharply refused, had gone. Only Mr Stacey, who lived over the shop anyway, remained.

'You're a good girl, Ginny,' he said as he unlocked the door so that he could let her out and lock it again after her. 'Thank you for staying late to get that done.'

'That's all right, Mr Stacey. We don't want to lose the orders from the yachts because we don't deliver on time, do we?'

She turned wearily for home, over the bridge and past the church. On the corner by the Grosvenor Hotel — a rather grand name for a rather shabby pub — men who, like thousands of others all over the country, were unemployed congregated to commiserate with each other and escape from under their wives' feet. Seeing them there she couldn't help wondering how they felt about the situation in the village at this time of year, when the wealthy owners of the large yachts laid up in the river arrived in their chauffeur-driven motor cars, having stayed at the best hotels in Colchester. These men knew next to nothing about sailing but they had money and they brought some employment and brief prosperity to the village. A village where industry, ironically mostly shipbuilding, was at a virtual standstill and tradesmen with a lifetime's skill at their fingertips were forced to stand every week in the dole queue for the bare necessities of life. They must have found it a bitter pill to swallow.

Then there were the yacht captains, the

elite of the village. They were answerable to the owner and paid by him throughout the year, but in total control of their yacht. They were responsible for choosing their crew from the local fishermen, who with their hard-won experience of the ways of the sea, fished — albeit for a pittance — all winter and fought, sometimes literally, for a berth on a yacht in the summer. Men came from miles around, on foot, sea bags on their shoulders, in the hope of a summer's yachting. Many went away disappointed.

Bob Appleyard, Ginny's father, was one of the lucky ones. He was a skilled seaman, he made a reasonable living fishing in the winter, and his position as mate on board *Aurora* was assured during the summer months when fishing was at a premium. This was so with most of *Aurora*'s crew. Captain Bellamy had gathered together a crew who worked well together and he saw no reason to change this.

Ginny was pondering all this as she walked home when suddenly Nathan appeared. He had obviously been waiting for her.

'I want to have a word with your dad so I thought I'd wait and walk home with you,' he said by way of explanation.

'That's very nice of you, Nathan. I'm afraid you've had rather a long wait though. I'm not usually this late.' She yawned as she spoke.

'That's all right. I didn't mind. I was talking to the chaps over there.' He nodded in the direction of the Grosvenor Corner, as it was known. They walked on a few steps, then he said, 'Congratulations on your engagement, Ginny. I saw the ring on your finger when I was in the shop. Is it still Roger Mayhew?'

She was surprised. It wasn't the kind of thing men usually noticed. 'Thank you, Nathan. Yes, Roger and I got engaged at Christmas.'

'I hope you'll be very happy together,' he said, glancing down at her without smiling.

'I'm sure we shall, he's a nice man,' she replied warmly. She looked up at him. 'But what about you? I didn't think you'd be going yachting this summer. I thought you were too busy with your painting in London.'

He shrugged briefly. 'I need to get a bit of sea air in my lungs. I miss the open spaces a bit,' he said. He gave a little laugh. 'I can't paint all the time, Ginny.'

'No, I suppose not. But what about Miss Armitage? Doesn't she mind you going off and leaving her?' There was a barb in the words but Ginny couldn't help herself.

Nathan didn't seem to notice. He kicked a stone into the road. 'As a matter of fact, it was partly her idea. She said it might give me inspiration.'

'Isn't the painting going well, then?' She had to ask, although perhaps it was a bit unkind.

'Oh, yes,' he said, a little too quickly. 'It's going really well.'

'Did Sir Titus hold an exhibition for you? Your mother said that was what he was going to do.'

'Not yet. I haven't got quite enough paintings finished to hold one at the moment. Next winter, perhaps.' Ginny couldn't detect much enthusiasm for the project in his voice. 'I'd send you an invitation, but I expect you'll be married by then.'

'No. Roger and I have agreed. We shan't marry until I'm at least twenty-one,' she said firmly.

'That's another eighteen months,' he calculated.

'Yes. Well, we've got to save up, haven't we.'

'I suppose so.'

They reached Quay Yard and she turned to face him. 'Perhaps you could see your way clear to giving us one of your paintings as a wedding present, Nathan,' she said on impulse. 'I should like that.'

'Would you really, Ginny?' He sounded surprised.

81

She shrugged, already regretting having asked. 'Only if you're not too busy selling them to the posh people.' She went down the steps into the yard, surprised when he didn't follow. 'Well, aren't you coming in? You said you wanted to see dad, I expect he's home by now.'

He shook his head. 'No, it doesn't matter. I'll see him tomorrow. It was nothing important.' With a brief smile he turned and walked away.

Thoughtfully, she went indoors. What was that all about? Nathan had come into the shop and bought nothing, then walked her home so that he could see her father and then wouldn't come in. It was all very odd.

To her dismay she found Will Kesgrave there. He had offered to take Bob's gear aboard and stow it for him and he had come to collect it. He was waiting while Bob made a last-minute check that he had everything he needed. Ruth was looking on, her expression making it plain that she didn't like Will Kesgrave in the house, even though under Bob's guidance he bathed regularly and combed his hair and only got drunk on Saturday nights. Bob knew this but still persisted in asking him in when he came to the door, which annoyed her even further.

'Evenin', Ginny,' Will said, looking up from

the bowl of soup Ruth had given him — reluctantly, and only because Bob had put her into a position where she could hardly refuse — from the pot simmering on the stove.

'Good evening, Will.' Ginny didn't like the man any more than Ruth did but she tried to keep her voice civil. In truth she felt a bit sorry for him, living with his slut of a mother, who had never cooked a proper meal in her life and wouldn't know where to begin to clean a house. And his sister was not much better.

'There we are, bor,' Bob said, pulling the string tight on his duffel bag. 'And don't forget the oilies. They're out in the wash 'us. We can't expect sunshine all the way, specially in Scotland.'

'There's another pair of socks on the airer,' Ginny pointed out.

'They're ready for tomorrer. Hev I got a clean shirt, Ruthy?'

'Of course you have. It's in the chest of drawers upstairs,' Ruth said.

'Thass that, then. Finished your soup, Will? Then off you go.'

Will hefted the sea bag on to his shoulder. 'I wish I'd got somebody to make sure my clothes was clean, Bob. My ma wouldn't notice if I wore the same things for a year.'

'I thought you did,' Ruth muttered unkindly under her breath.

Ginny's curiosity got the better of her. 'Who does your washing then?'

'I do it meself, mostly. And hang it up in the wash 'us to dry. Well, I'll be off. See you termorrer, Bob. Thanks for the soup, Missus.'

'Don't forget the oilskins,' Bob called after him.

'Dreadful man.' Ruth said with a shudder. 'I don't know why you have anything to do with him. Did you see the way he held his spoon? As if it was a shovel. No manners at all.'

'He's not all bad, Ruthy,' Bob said mildly. 'And he shaped up well in the smack. Did everything I told him and worked like a Trojan. You mark my words, he'll make a good fisherman when he's learned the ropes.'

Ruth shrugged her shoulders. She didn't want to antagonise Bob on his last night at home. She'd got used to him being there during the winter, when he wasn't out fishing and she knew that she would miss him when he was away for a full four months. He was a good man and she appreciated it although she was careful, for some reason she didn't fully understand herself, not to let him know this.

Meanwhile, Nathan was walking back to his mother's house in Anglesea Road. He didn't know why he had made a special effort to see Ginny Appleyard; she meant nothing to him and clearly she had no regard for him either because she had lost no time in getting herself engaged to somebody else. He didn't admire her choice. He remembered Roger Mayhew at school; he had always seemed a sight too fond of himself and a bit of a teacher's pet from what he could recall. He had never liked him much and he didn't think he was right for Ginny. But Ginny seemed happy enough with him and he supposed that was what mattered.

Not that he was interested in Ginny Appleyard's affairs, he thought sourly. Why should he be when he had Isobel? He still couldn't believe his luck that such a rich, beautiful, wonderful woman had fallen in love with him. Of course he hadn't told Ginny, but in truth his painting wasn't going too well. It wasn't that he wasn't able to paint, he was sure he could if he gave his mind to it, but there was rarely time these days. He was invariably late up in the morning because he and Isobel and her friends were often out on the town till all hours of the night, then Isobel came to his studio every afternoon and the minute she got there all either of them wanted was to go to bed. He had never known a woman like her — in truth his sexual experience of women until he met her had been practically non-existent. But she was insatiable and taught him things he would never have dreamed of. She laughingly called him her 'country boy' and delighted in shocking him with her abandoned behaviour. By the time she left to get ready for the evening round of theatres and night clubs he was usually so exhausted he had to have another sleep.

It was almost a relief when she agreed to his tentative suggestion that he should spend the summer on *Aurora*.

'Oh, yes,' she had agreed at once. 'And I'll book into a hotel at Cowes during Cowes Week and at Oban when you're racing in Scotland. It'll be fun, darling. A change of scenery will be good for the libido.'

He wasn't sure what libido meant, but if it meant what he thought it meant he wasn't sure she was right. Even at twenty-two, he feared his sexual drive wouldn't stand up to perpetual hard days' racing and hard nights' lovemaking and he worried a little in case one of these days he might let her down. That was what he feared most, that he might let her down and his goddess would tire of him. Fortunately it hadn't happened yet but it was no wonder his mother told him he looked tired.

As they left the shop at closing time on Thursday, Roger said, 'I'll meet you for the two o'clock bus, Ginny. You wanted to see that James Cagney film, didn't you?'

'No. I told you, Dad's sailing this afternoon. I want to go and watch the yacht leave.'

'All right, darling. I'll come with you. We can catch a later bus and go to the pictures tonight.' He gave her his usual swift peck on the cheek and left her.

She walked home. He was too compliant. It didn't matter what she suggested he always agreed. Sometimes — it was a small thought that she rarely allowed to surface — she found him quite boring. She stifled it almost before it had time to form, overlaying it with her mother's words.

'He's a good, steady man, with a good, steady job. You'll never see Roger standing on street corners or queuing up for dole money. He's too smart for that.'

But Ginny knew her mother wasn't altogether right. Being out of work had nothing to do with incompetence and everything to do with insufficient money to pay wages. She knew, too, that more and more men on the dole meant that more and more wives were forced to ask for credit, which Mr Stacey was too kind-hearted to refuse. Sometimes his actual takings in a week were hardly enough to pay his wage bill. If it wasn't for supplying the yachts Mr Stacey would have to get rid of most of his staff. And Roger wouldn't be exempt. It was a sobering thought.

6

Ruth had made a rabbit stew and a spotted dick for dinner. She always made sure that Bob went away with a good meal inside him; it was her farewell gesture, because she never went to see the yacht cast off any more than she ever came to see it dock. In a funny sort of way, which he quite understood, it was her way of telling him she was fond of him and would miss him, words that she could never actually bring herself to say.

But a good many people did line the sea wall and there was quite a festive air as *Aurora*, the last yacht home at the end of the season and the first to leave at the beginning of the next, slipped her moorings and was towed out into midstream just as the tide turned, to begin her passage out into the North Sea, her brightwork polished and shining, her topsides newly varnished, all set for a summer's sailing and racing.

Even Annie Kesgrave had come to wave her son goodbye, her daughter by her side, scratching absent-mindedly. Annie had once been an attractive girl, but too many men and too many back-street abortions, coupled with laziness and gin, had taken their toll and she was a wreck of a woman now, with a figure like a badly stuffed cushion, lank greying hair and a skin to match. What she had once been could vaguely be seen in the slightly vacant features of her fourteen-year-old daughter, Gladys, standing with her.

Annie turned to Ginny and grinned, showing several gaps where her teeth had given up the unequal struggle with decay and fallen out.

'My Will thinks a rare lot of your dad, Ginny,' she said. She gave a complacent shrug. 'Thass nice they get on so well together. I dunno what your dad 'ud hev done without him to give a hand on the smack this winter now old Bert Grimshaw's gone.' She nodded. 'Brought some nice fish home, too, he did. And cooked it for us. That was better'n fish and chips. Cheaper, an' all.'

Roger was tugging at Ginny's arm. 'Come on, darling, we shall miss the bus,' he urged in her ear. The yacht was already making her stately way down river so he couldn't see why Ginny wasn't ready to leave.

'Yes, all right, Roger.' Ginny shrugged him off and turned back to Annie. 'I'm sure my father would be even more pleased with Will if he didn't drink so much,' she said primly.

Annie threw back her head and laughed.

'Didn't drink so much! Your dad can sink a pint or two when he's let loose so he ain't got much room to talk. Anyway, a man ain't a man if he can't enjoy his drink, is he?' she said, and dug Ginny in the ribs. 'Mind you, the boy enjoyed it last night, all right. They had to carry him home. He's got a head the size of three this morning, I can tell you.'

'That won't please my father,' Ginny told her. 'I wonder he let him on board.' She felt Roger tugging at her sleeve again and said irritably, 'Yes, all right, Roger. I'm coming.' But still she stood, watching and waving, as the yacht rounded the bend in the river. There was a figure near the stern, waving back. It looked like Nathan, but it was probably only wishful thinking on her part. She gave a final wave, straining to see who it might be, remembering last September and the day *Aurora* had come back, covered in glory from her last summer's sailing. It seemed such a short time ago, yet so much had happened in those seven months. She sighed wistfully. She had been so full of excitement, so sure that Nathan would be coming back to her with a ring in his pocket. But she had been wrong. Horribly, miserably wrong, because any ring Nathan might have been bringing home was destined for Isobel Armitage's finger, not hers, while she was wearing the ring Roger had placed there. And before long, even next year perhaps, she would become Roger's wife. Life didn't always turn out the way you expected, she decided, turning to Roger and smiling brightly. Sometimes it was better.

She linked her arm with his and said, 'OK, Roger, let's go and see James Cagney.'

★ ★ ★

The summer passed slowly. Ginny missed her father's great bulk and booming voice around the house and she knew her mother did, too, although it was not in Ruth's nature to admit as much. But Ginny noticed how she looked for the postman every day and propped the cards up on the mantelpiece that Bob sent from the places he visited so that she could read them again and again. The messages were brief, as Bob was not a great scribe, usually something like '*I hope you are well as this leaves me. This is a pretty place*', or '*I hope you are well as this leaves me, lotta people here, racings good*'. Ginny looked for '*Owners here with his dorter,*' which seemed to be occurring rather more often than she wanted to hear.

Life with Roger had its own pattern. Apart from seeing him every day at work there were trips to the pictures on Thursday, dancing on Saturdays, a walk on Sunday afternoons, followed by tea at either his house or hers. (Ginny preferred it when tea was at her house because Roger's mother was not a very good cook and also her own mother made no coy attempt at 'leaving you two young lovebirds alone' in the chilly, mostly unused front room.) Roger was a very good dancer and knew it; Ginny thought privately that he rather fancied himself as a second Fred Astaire, with his complicated footwork and flamboyant way of twirling her about. But he was fun to dance with and she soon learned to follow him and even to add her own little twizzles and side-steps. Often people would stand aside and watch as they twinkled their way round the dance hall and they would applaud when the music stopped. Going home afterwards, with the rhythm of the music and the applause of the other couples still in her ears, she was happy to let him kiss and make love to her — as long as he didn't try to go too far. Her mother had warned her many times about what happened to girls who 'got themselves into trouble' — as if they did it all by themselves — and she was not prepared to take the risk.

But it worried her that Roger was becoming rather too possessive. If there was a film on that she wanted to see but that didn't interest him he refused to let her go with her friend Shirley, who worked at the draper's further up the road, saying Thursdays was their afternoon out and they didn't want anybody else spoiling it. So they would end up going to another cinema and watching a film that neither of them particularly wanted to see.

And the evening she went to a whist drive with Shirley instead of asking him to go with her he was furious.

'But I don't have to live in your pocket, Roger,' she said crossly. 'Anyway, you don't like playing cards. You've told me that enough times. And it isn't as if Tuesdays are one of our evenings together.'

'All the same, you should have told me what you were going to do,' he persisted.

'Why? We're not married yet, Roger,' she said with a frown. 'I don't have to answer to you for every move I make.'

'I like to know where you are and who you're with.'

'What about the nights you play billiards with your friends? I don't even know how many times a week you go.' And I don't care, she just stopped herself from saying.

'That's different. I'm a man.'

'Oh, for goodness' sake. I can't see what

difference that makes.' She turned away from him, then turned back as realisation dawned. 'Ah, I see what it is. You're jealous, aren't you? You don't believe I went out with Shirley at all. You think I went with another man, don't you?'

'Of course I don't,' he muttered. He shrugged uncomfortably. 'How do I know who you're with when you're not with me?'

'Because you ought to know by now that I'm not in the habit of telling lies, Roger. Don't you trust me?'

He tried to take her in his arms. 'Of course I do, darling. It's just that I love you so much I'm scared I'll lose you.' His voice took on a wheedling tone.

'Well, you're going the right way about it,' she said, pushing him away. 'Heaven's sake, I don't object when you go and watch a cricket match on a Saturday afternoon without me.'

'I always ask you to come,' he pointed out, huffy because she had rebuffed him.

'But I don't *like* cricket,' she said patiently. She heaved an exasperated sigh. 'Oh, let's go for a walk.'

After that there were several tiffs. Nothing particularly serious, but Ginny had the growing sensation that he was beginning to stifle her with his attentions.

At night, in bed, she would count up his

good points. He was kind and polite, generous to a fault, never letting her pay for anything when they went out together. And he was a wonderful dancer. Also, there was no doubt he was very fond of her. Perhaps that was the trouble, she thought with a sigh. Perhaps he was *too* fond of her. But she was sure it would be better after they were married because she would belong to him then and he would have no need to be so jealous. But supposing it didn't make any difference and he was still as possessive as ever? The thought of a lifetime of being constantly watched and questioned over every movement she made when she was out of his sight was not pleasant.

The summer wore on. Towards the end of August Ruth showed Ginny an advertisement in the local paper.

'Do you think Roger has seen this advertisement for an assistant on the bacon counter at the Co-op grocer's in Clacton?' she asked, pointing it out. 'And look, it says, 'with opportunities for advancement'.'

'What are the wages?' Ginny asked, immediately interested.

'It doesn't say, but it's bound to be more than he's getting at Stacey's, isn't it?'

'Yes. I reckon it must be. The Co-op at

Clacton is quite big.' Ginny nodded enthusiastically. 'I'll cut it out and show it to him. I'm seeing him tonight.'

Ruth raised her eyebrows. 'I didn't think you saw him on Tuesdays.'

She sighed. 'No, I don't, as a rule. I was going to the whist drive with Shirley but he's decided he'd like to come instead.'

'I didn't think he liked cards.'

'He thought he'd give them another try.'

Wisely, Ruth made no further comment.

Ginny was a good player and together with Shirley they often won prizes. In fact, she was gradually stocking up her bottom drawer with prizes she had won at whist drives. But not this particular night. Playing with Roger as her partner they lost practically every trick. And there wasn't even a chance of winning the raffle because he wouldn't let her buy any tickets, saying it was a waste of money when they were saving up to get married. By the time they left the hall Ginny was quite irritable.

'It's a lovely evening, let's walk home through the woods,' she said, hoping a walk in the cool evening air would improve her temper.

'Yes, all right. But we mustn't be late. Don't forget we've got to go to work in the morning.'

'Oh, that reminds me . . . ,' she began scrabbling in her handbag as they walked among the trees. 'Have you seen this advertisement in the local paper?'

The light was just beginning to fade so he had to stop to read it. He handed it back to her without comment.

'Well,' she said, with a trace of impatience. 'What do you think?'

'It's at Clacton. I'd have to catch the train every day.'

'So? A lot of people go to work on the train.'

'It's expensive. I don't have to pay train fares to get to Stacey's. I can walk there.'

'But if you got this job you'd be able to afford it because the wages are bound to be a good bit higher than you're getting at Stacey's. Look, it says, 'with opportunities for advancement'. That probably means you could end up as manager.'

'I don't know that I want to end up as manager. I'm quite happy at Stacey's where I can see you every day.'

It was like talking to a brick wall, she thought, exasperated.

She was silent for a few minutes, then she said firmly, 'Well, I think you should apply for it, Roger. After all, when we're married I probably won't be working at Stacey's. I probably won't be working at all so you'll need to find a job that pays more.' A sudden thought struck her. 'We could look for a house in Clacton. I think I should quite like to live in Clacton. By the seaside.' She smiled at him. 'We could do bed and breakfast. Probably make quite a lot of money.'

'I don't want to do bed and breakfast, Ginny. I don't want to live in Clacton and I don't want to work at the Co-op.' There was a petulant note in his voice.

'Then what *do* you want, for goodness' sake?'

'I want things to stay as they are, only I want to be married to you, darling.' He tried to take her in his arms but she pushed him away.

'Well, *I* don't want things to stay as they are. I want us to have a better life than we'll get if you stay on the bacon counter at Stacey's for the rest of your life, Roger. Haven't you got *any* ambitions?'

He shrugged. 'No. Not really.'

She stopped and faced him squarely. 'Well, I have. And either you go and apply for this job at Clacton or we're finished, Roger.'

The words hung between them. She was as surprised as he was that she had said them, but now they were out she felt somehow lighter. Liberated.

He was staring at her, his mouth open. 'You don't mean that, Ginny. You can't break off our engagement just because I don't want to go to Clacton to work. That would be silly when we love each other so much.' He stepped forward to take her in his arms.

She stepped back. It was just like doing the tango, she thought inconsequently. 'That's just it, Roger,' she said, listening to herself as if it was someone else talking. 'I don't think I do love you. In fact, I don't really think I've ever been in love with you. It's just the idea of loving you that I've been in love with. Do you understand what I'm saying?'

'No, I don't. You're talking rubbish,' he snapped. 'I've never heard so much nonsense in all my life. It's all the rubbish you've seen at the pictures, with your friend Shirley.' His tone was scathing.

'I don't go to the pictures with Shirley. You won't let me,' she said furiously.

'Well, you know what I mean.' Suddenly, he smiled at her. 'I know what's wrong with you, darling. This has got nothing to do with me working at Clacton, has it? You're just annoyed with me because I messed up your game of whist tonight. Look, I'm sorry. I shouldn't have insisted on coming. I won't come again and I won't mind if you go with Shirley another time. There, is that better?'

It felt like a metaphorical pat on the head and far from mollifying her, Ginny saw red. 'No, it isn't better!' she shouted. 'And don't patronise me, Roger Mayhew, because I don't like it.' She unscrewed the ring from her finger and held it out to him. 'I'm sorry, Roger, I can see now that our engagement has been a terrible mistake. What you need is some little mouse who'll be happy to do as she's told all her life while you slice bacon and pat butter for Mr Stacey. It just won't do for me.'

'Don't be silly, Ginny.' He tried to laugh it off. 'You're overwrought. Put the ring back on your finger — no, give it to me and I'll do it.' He took it from her and picked up her left hand. 'I'll take you home now. You'll feel better in the morning. Come on, darling, unclench your fist.' He tried to prise her fingers open.

'I shall not feel better in the morning.' Her teeth were clenched now as well as her fist. 'Didn't you hear what I said, Roger? We're finished. Washed up. It's all over. I don't love you and I don't want to marry you. I'm just glad I realised it before it was too late.' She turned her back on him and walked off through the wood, leaving him staring open-mouthed after her.

That night she slept like a baby. She felt as

if a great weight had been taken off her shoulders.

'You're late down, this morning,' her mother said when she appeared the next day. 'What did Roger say about the job at Clacton?'

Ginny grabbed a slice of toast and stuck it in her mouth while she combed her hair. 'Wasn't interested. The engagement's broken off,' she managed to mumble.

'Did you say broken off?' Ruth asked, amazed.

Ginny nodded, fixing her slide. She took the toast out of her mouth and gave her mother a wide smile.

Ruth looked at her uncertainly. 'You don't look very upset,' she said with a frown.

'Well, I wouldn't, would I? It was me that broke it off and I'm so relieved I could dance on air.' She glanced at the clock. 'And I shall have to do just that if I'm not going to be late for work. 'Bye, Mum.' She picked up her bag and ran out of the house.

Ruth watched her go running across Anchor Hill. She certainly seemed brighter and more carefree than she'd seen her for several months. And Roger was a bit stodgy, she had to admit, so maybe it was all for the best. She shook her head. Things might be difficult at work, though, with them both working at the same place.

Ruth was right.

At first Roger tried to pretend the broken engagement hadn't happened.

'Feeling better this morning, darling?' he asked cheerfully as she was putting on her overall.

'Yes, thank you, Roger. I'm feeling very well indeed.' Her tone was cool.

'Good. I realise you were overwrought last night, darling, so let's forgive and forget. Here, let me put this back on your finger.' He reached in his pocket and took out her ring.

'No, Roger,' she whispered fiercely, putting both hands behind her back. 'I meant what I said last night. I'm not going to marry you. And please don't call me darling.'

He looked amazed. 'But I love you, Ginny.'

'I'm sorry. I've already told you that I don't love you and I haven't got time to argue the whole thing out again. I'm already late and Mrs Peacock'll be in with her order shortly.' She did up the last button on her overall and checked her appearance in the mirror.

'I shall go away, Ginny,' he threatened. 'I shall write to my uncle in Australia. He owns a sheep farm, you know.' He came up behind her and put his arms round her, too far above her waist for comfort. His tone became wheedling. 'You say I'm not adventurous enough. Well, how about if I go sheep farming in Australia. Would that be adventurous enough for you? How would you like to live in the outback, Ginny?'

She pushed his arms away. 'Don't you understand? I don't want to live *anywhere* with you, Roger,' she said, exasperated. Now she had made the break with him suddenly she couldn't stand the sight of him. She was astonished how quickly and thoroughly her feelings towards him had changed.

'You'll regret it when I'm a rich sheep farmer, Ginny Appleyard,' he warned.

'I'd regret it a jolly sight more if I was to marry you,' she replied and escaped into the shop.

7

For weeks Roger persisted in pestering Ginny to take back her engagement ring. He followed her into the stock room when she went to make up orders, waited for her after work and generally acted as if it was only a lovers' tiff that had broken the engagement. It seemed there was nothing she could say that would convince him that their love affair was over.

In the end she went to see Mr Stacey.

'I'm afraid I shall have to hand in my notice and find work somewhere else, Mr Stacey,' she told him. 'It's no good, I can't stay here with Roger Mayhew any longer.' She blushed and gave him a brief, embarrassed glance. 'I take it you know all about Roger and me, don't you?'

He nodded. 'I had heard you'd had a bit of a difference of opinion, my dear,' he said with a fatherly smile. His bushy white eyebrows moved up questioningly. 'A lovers' tiff, shall we say?'

'It's a bit more than that, Mr Stacey,' she said, angry that he wasn't taking her seriously. 'I've broken off my engagement to him.'

'Ah, yes, Roger told me you got a bit cross. But he said . . . '

'Roger won't accept the fact that I've changed my mind. I no longer want to marry him, Mr Stacey,' she interrupted impatiently. She didn't want to hear the fairy tales he had been weaving to gain sympathy from the kind grocer. 'I've given him back his ring and told him everything is finished between us. I can't put it any plainer than that but he simply refuses to listen to what I say.' She gave a shrug. 'I suppose he thinks he'll wear me down in time but I can tell you he won't. In fact the more he keeps trying to make me change my mind the more I realise that I could never marry him. I don't know why I ever thought I might. I don't even like him any more,' she added gloomily.

'Oh my goodness, I didn't realise things were that bad, my dear,' Mr Stacey said, his voice suddenly full of concern.

'Well, I'm afraid they are, Mr Stacey.' Ginny gave a sigh. 'So you see I can't stay here with him pestering me to go back to him every five minutes. It's getting on my nerves. I'll just have to find a job somewhere else.'

A look of alarm crossed Mr Stacey's face. 'Oh, dear, you mustn't do that, Ginny. I can't afford to lose you, you're my best worker.' He stroked his moustache thoughtfully. 'Now that I know the full story perhaps I should have a quiet word with Roger. Tell him, man to man, to stop bothering you.' He looked up. 'I take it you're happy here apart from this little problem?'

She nodded and gave him a brief smile. 'Oh, yes, I'm very happy here.' The smile faded. 'But it isn't a 'little problem' to me, Mr Stacey, it's a great nuisance.'

He steepled his fingers. 'I understand. I'll talk to him.' He hesitated, tapping his fingers together. 'There is another thing, Ginny.' He hesitated again. 'I would advise you not to do anything in a hurry.' He fidgeted a little, stroking his moustache and then scratching his chin, then said in a rush, 'I'm afraid I may be breaking a confidence here, which under normal circumstances I would never dream of doing, but extreme circumstances call for extreme measures. Ginny, are you aware that Roger may not be here for much longer, anyway?'

'You mean he's leaving Stacey's?' She gave a little laugh. 'Oh, I don't think that's very likely, Mr Stacey. Not old stick-in-the-mud Roger. In fact, that's what we quarrelled about, in the first place.'

'Then he may surprise you.' He leaned forward. 'He tells me he's thinking of going to Australia. To live with his uncle who has a sheep farm. He's already written to him, I believe.' He stood up and came round and patted her arm. 'Why not wait a few weeks and see what happens. I don't want to lose you, Ginny. As I said before, you're my most reliable worker.' A frown crossed his face. 'Mind you, I suppose it would be a different matter if he were to ask you to go to Australia with him . . . '

She gave a little mirthless laugh. 'You needn't worry on that score, Mr Stacey,' she said firmly. 'I wouldn't cross the road for Roger Mayhew. Not any more. But thank you for telling me.' She smiled at him. 'And I'll do as you suggest and hang on for a week or two. But that's all. If he doesn't go soon, then I'll have to.'

'I'll talk to him,' Mr Stacey promised, adding with a wink, 'Oh, and Ginny, you'll find an extra half-crown in your wages this week. It's time you had a rise.'

She raised her eyebrows in surprise. 'Thank you very much, Mr Stacey.'

Ginny never discovered what Mr Stacey said to Roger but he stopped pursuing her into the stock room and hanging around waiting for her after work. In fact, he stopped speaking to her at all unless it was strictly necessary and then only in the curtest terms. And the looks he shot her from the bacon counter would have curdled milk. It all seemed very silly to Ginny. She couldn't see why a broken engagement meant they couldn't even be civil to each other but at least it was preferable to having to fight him off whenever they were alone.

She was relieved when Mr Stacey's prediction proved true and Roger sailed for Australia.

★　★　★

Aurora returned to her winter berth on an overcast, blustery day at the end of September. Once again she was covered in glory after the summer's racing, and in spite of the wind and threatening rain there was a good crowd on the sea wall to cheer her back to her mooring. This year, Sir Titus Armitage and his daughter found the weather too rough for them to board at Brightlingsea for the last leg of the homeward trip and they waited in the Daimler until she was safely berthed and all her mooring lines secured. Then the crowd parted deferentially to let them through, closely followed up the gangplank by photographers, who jostled for position as they made their precarious way on to the yacht, lugging their heavy tripods and cameras. One man fell in the water and had to be rescued, to the great amusement of the crowd.

Ginny noticed with amusement that Isobel was quite unsuitably dressed in a sleeveless dress of emerald green georgette with a fluted hem, with matching high-heeled shoes and cartwheel hat. There was a gasp of dismay when the wind caught the hat and tossed it into the water, but Ginny couldn't help a stab of malicious delight as she watched it float just out of reach of the men with boat hooks trying to retrieve it. Eventually it was rescued, soggy with mud and quite ruined.

Photographs were taken. Sir Titus at the wheel, Sir Titus with his daughter and the captain; Isobel at the wheel; the two of them with the captain and the crew; the two of them with the captain and the more important members of the crew (Ginny was gratified to see her father included in that one), the two of them with the captain and Nathan, and then several more of Isobel on her own in various nautical poses, looking quite out of place in her green georgette, the skirt of which kept blowing around in the stiff breeze in a most embarrassing manner.

At last it was over, the photographers left, followed soon after by Sir Titus and Captain Bellamy. Isobel came next, teetering down the gangplank possessively holding on to

Nathan's arm. As they drew level with Ginny Nathan paused.

'Hullo, Ginny. It's nice to see you again,' he said, smiling at her. He gazed round, surprised. 'But where's Roger? Didn't he come with you?'

'No.' She realised something more was needed but she didn't feel inclined to impart the knowledge that Roger had embarked for Australia less than a week ago. 'I've come to meet Dad,' she said. 'Like I always do when the boat docks.'

Isobel was determined not to be ignored. 'And who might 'Dad' be?' she asked, looking Ginny up and down as if she was something unpleasant picked up on her shoe.

'Ginny's dad is Bob Appleyard, Bella,' Nathan explained. 'Big, bearded chap; he's mate on board *Aurora*. I'm sure you know him.' He turned back to Ginny. 'Yes, you always come to meet him, don't you?'

Ginny said nothing. She was glad Nathan had no idea it was really him she had always come to meet in the past. Not any more, of course.

Isobel turned away, losing interest. 'Oh. Well, no doubt he'll be along when he's finished his jobs.' She gave Nathan's hand a shake. 'Come along, darling. Chop, chop. Daddy's organising drinks at the Falcon.'

111

Nathan allowed himself to be led away. 'I'll be seeing you, Ginny,' he called over his shoulder. 'I'm staying at home for a few days before I go back to London.'

'That's what *you* think, darling,' Ginny heard Isobel say, as she gazed up at him. 'I might have other ideas about that.'

Ginny stared after them. She couldn't imagine what Nathan could see in that woman; she looked as hard as nails even though she had a pretty face. No, her face wasn't pretty at all. Striking maybe, and beautifully made up, but not pretty. It must take her hours to put that face on every day, Ginny thought inconsequentially. But before she could dwell further on the matter she saw her father come striding down the gangplank and she went forward to be enveloped in his usual salt-laden bear hug.

Some time later, sitting in the warm kitchen, eating the steak and kidney pudding Ruth had made for Bob's home-coming and listening to the rising wind outside as the weather worsened, Ginny told her father about the broken engagement and Roger's harassment and eventual departure for Australia.

'Well, I'm not surprised he didn't wanta let you go, matie. Once he'd got the prettiest girl in Wyford promising to marry him he wouldn't wanta part with her, now, would he?' he chuckled, mopping up the last of the gravy on his plate with a lump of bread. 'But I ain't sorry. I never thought he was right for you. He hadn't got enough about him for my liking.'

'He was a good, steady man,' Ruth put in. She had liked Roger. 'She could have done worse.'

'She could do a damn sight better, too.' He got up from the table and moved over to his armchair and lit his pipe. 'There's plenty time, my girl. Plenty time.'

Ginny was relieved her father felt that way because her mother had always made her feel slightly guilty at the way she had treated Roger.

After the table was cleared and the washing-up done she fetched her embroidery basket and took out the tray cloth she was working on. It was always particularly nice the first night Dad was home, she thought contentedly, catching a fragrant whiff of his tobacco, because it meant that he was safe and the family was complete. Even her mother, sitting opposite to him with her knitting, looked happy tonight. The wind screaming round the chimney pots and the rain that had grown steadily heavier and was now furiously lashing at the windows only served to increase the sense of security and warmth. She looked at her parents and thought, I shall always remember this night, just the three of us here, warm and cosy and happy. Even Mum hasn't found anything to complain about. She chose another skein of silk and threaded her needle, humming one of the latest song tunes under her breath.

'Just hark at that wind. Seems like you got back about right, Robert,' Ruth remarked, leaning forward to put another coal on the fire.

'Aye. It's a bad night out there and no mistake.' He leaned back and closed his eyes. 'I said I'd meet one or two o' the boys in the Rose and Crown tonight, but I don't think I'll bother. I've had enough o' bein' out in all weathers.'

This pleased Ruth, although she tried not to show it. 'You could have a drop of whisky,' she said, keeping her voice casual. 'You know I always keep some by in case of illness.' She got to her feet and poured him a generous measure.

'Thanks, Ruthy.' He took a drink. 'Ah, thass a drop o' good stuff. Pity to waste it on illness,' he said with a grin.

'Well, you know I never touch it except in emergency,' she said primly. 'I don't think . . . ' Her words were cut off by someone hammering on the door.

They all looked at each other in surprise and then Ginny got up and opened it.

A man in dripping oilskins stood there. 'Is Bob there?'

'I'm here, bor. What's up?' He went to the door. After a few minutes' conversation he nodded. 'All right. I'll be along in a jiffy.' He closed the door and began to pull on his boots.

'Where are you going? Changed your mind? Going to the Rose and Crown with your cronies after all?' Ruth said with a frown.

'No. I've got to go and take a look at the boat. Young Gunn has just come to tell me one o' the sails has worked loose. Can't see how it could be, I thought they were all brailled up tight enough. But I wasn't the last one off today, so I didn't check everything before I left. Anyway, I'd better go and take a look. Make sure everything's safe.'

'You're not going on your own, are you?' Ruth asked, suddenly anxious.

'I'll give young Will Kesgrave a knock. He'll come with me if he's not in the Rose. If he's in the pub he'll be worse than useless.' He shrugged on his oilskins. 'I shan't be long, Ruthy.' He paused long enough to drink the rest of his whisky. 'I'll be ready for some cocoa when I get back.' He gave her an uncharacteristic kiss and went out.

Two hours later he hadn't returned.

Ruth sat, tight-lipped, her eyes straying to the clock on the mantelpiece every five minutes.

'I wonder why he's so long,' Ginny said anxiously.

Ruth gave a barking laugh. 'You may well ask. He's in the Rose and Crown, drinking his prize money away, if I don't miss my mark.'

'But he said he wasn't going there tonight,' Ginny protested.

'I know. But only because he was tucked up warm indoors. Once he'd got his oilskins on to go to the boat he'd think he might as well make a night of it and go to the Rose. Oh, I know your father of old.' Her knitting needles clicked faster and faster in disapproval.

Ginny got up and took her mackintosh off the hook on the back of the door.

Ruth looked up. 'Where are you going?' she asked sharply.

'I'm just going to make sure Dad's in the Rose and Crown. Oh, don't worry, I won't go in. But I just want to make sure he's safe.'

Ruth nodded. 'Well, don't be long.'

Ginny made her way along to the Rose and Crown, her head bent against the driving rain and peered in through the steamed-up window. The pub was crowded, mostly with men dressed in reefer jackets and cheese-cutter caps just like her father. With some difficulty she picked out Will Kesgrave, standing at the bar, but she couldn't see Bob.

Someone came out and she recognised him as old Zeke Bellamy, Nathan's disreputable old grandfather, the father-in-law Nathan's mother tried to disown because he lived in squalor on his old smack, tied up opposite the Rose and Crown.

'Mr Bellamy, is my dad in there?' Ginny asked, ignoring the fact that he was obviously preparing to relieve himself against the wall.

'Hey?' He looked over his shoulder, quickly adjusting his trousers. 'Who?'

'My father. Bob Appleyard. Is he in there?' She jerked her head towards the lighted window.

'No. I ain't seen him tonight.'

'Are you sure?'

'Course I'm sure. Why?'

'He went to look at the yacht a couple of hours ago and he hasn't come back. We thought he might have come for a drink.'

The old man scratched his beard. 'I'll goo and ask if anyone's seen 'im.'

He went inside and a minute later came out again with Will Kesgrave, none too steady on his feet.

'Wass the trouble, Ginny?' he asked blearily.

'Nothing you're in a fit state to do anything about, Will Kesgrave,' she said, her voice sharp with anxiety. 'Just you go back in there and fetch somebody who can still see out of their eyes to come and help me look for my dad.'

'I'll come.'

'You! I want help, not hindrance.' She eyed him up and down, then said impatiently, 'Well, come on then. I suppose he must still be on the yacht, but goodness knows what he can be doing.'

Will shook his head to clear it. 'Half a minute. I'll fetch a lantern. It'll be dark out there on the wall.' He dived back into the pub and came back with a lantern and two other men.

'You go home, Missy. We'll find your dad and bring him back,' a brawny man she recognised as Joey Green said.

'No. I'm coming with you. You never know, he might be hurt,' she answered, pulling up the hood of her mackintosh and tightening the belt.

Will was right. Once they were away from the lights on the quay the sea wall was in pitch darkness apart from the swinging lantern carried by Will as he stumbled along.

'For God's sake don't drop it, Will,' Joey shouted. 'Why don't you give it to me.'

'I'm all right, I tell you,' Will muttered, trying desperately to keep his balance against the wind and the rain and the effects of alcohol.

Ginny was glad of the company of the three men as they made their way along the wall to where *Aurora* lay because the wind screaming through the rigging of the yachts made an eerie, lonely sound in the blackness and there were ominous creaks and groans from the timbers as the yachts settled into the mud.

'Here we are.' Will led the way up *Aurora*'s gangplank and the others followed, with Ginny bringing up the rear.

Now they could hear, above the sound of the wind and rain, the heavy crack of a loose sail flapping up aloft.

'I reckon thass the tops'l come loose,' Joey said, trying to peer up into the darkness.

Will held up the lantern so that they could see the ghostly shape of the sail hurling itself about in the wind, fastened only by the mast hoops.

'She'll take off directly, the rate she's goin',' Joey said, craning his neck to see better.

'Never mind the sail. Where's my dad?' Ginny had to shout to make herself heard above the roar of the wind and rain.

'He's here.' The tone of the third man's voice made them all turn to where he was standing over a figure spread-eagled on the deck. 'Bring the glim, Willy boy.'

Will held the lantern so they could all see Bob. He was lying on his back in a pool of blood.

'Take the young lady home,' Joey said quickly. 'This is no place for her.'

Ginny pushed forward. 'But he's my dad. I want to know what's happened to him.' She went to kneel down by him but Joey pulled her away.

'Best you don't, dearie,' he said quietly. 'We'll find a plank and bring him back.' He turned to the third man. 'Alf, take the young lady home and fetch Doctor Dean. Tell him there's bin a accident. Not that there's much he can do,' he added under his breath.

Alf Mortlock took Ginny by the arm and led her back in the pitch darkness, walking at a pace she had difficulty in keeping up with.

'But what happened?' she kept saying. 'Did he fall? Is he hurt very badly?'

'We shan't know till the doctor's given him the once-over,' Alf said, although he had his suspicions.

They reached Quay Yard and Alf went in with Ginny.

'I'm afraid there's bin an accident, Missus. They'll be bringing Bob home shortly,' he told Ruth. 'I've gotta goo and fetch the doctor. Will you be all right till I get back or shall I ask my missus to come over and keep you company?'

Ruth frowned and said sharply, 'No, there's no need for that.' She turned to Ginny. 'Why? What's happened?'

Ginny told her.

After she had finished Ruth was quiet for several minutes. Then she said, 'Is he dead?'

Ginny's mouth dropped open. 'Dead! Of course he isn't dead. He's hurt, that's all,' she said furiously. 'What a dreadful thing to say, Mother.'

Ruth stared at her for a minute. Then she nodded. 'I'll make some cocoa,' she said.

8

The cocoa stood on the table, untouched and growing cold, when they heard the sound of footsteps in the yard. Ginny flung open the door and Will Kesgrave and Joey Green came in, water streaming from their oilskins, carrying Bob strapped to a plank. At Ruth's silent direction, still in their muddy seaman's boots, they carried him through to the rarely used front room and laid him carefully down on the carpet.

'Hev you got a sheet, Missus?' Joey said quietly. 'That'd be respeckful to cover him up.'

Every vestige of colour drained out of Ruth's face. She shot a look of alarm at Joey, who gave an almost imperceptible nod in return.

She stared down at her husband, the back of her hand pressed against her mouth, then knelt and touched her lips to his forehead. 'I'll fetch one,' she murmured, getting to her feet.

Ginny had followed them in, surprised that her mother had allowed these dripping men in their dirty boots to trample over her precious carpet instead of carrying her beloved dad up to his bed.

'Alf's gone to fetch the doctor,' she said eagerly. 'He won't be long.' She looked down at the figure on the floor. It was her father, her big, bluff, cheerful father lying there, yet somehow it was as if he wasn't there, as if she was looking down at an empty shell. She couldn't understand why he didn't open his eyes and speak to her and she frowned as she stared into his familiar, weather-beaten face, wanting to kneel and kiss him as her mother had done, yet for some reason not daring to in case he was asleep and she disturbed him.

Joey came and laid his arm round her shoulders. 'Thass good, Missy. But I'm afraid thass too late for him to do any good.'

'What do you mean?' Ginny turned agonised eyes on him. 'You don't mean . . . He can't be . . . '

He nodded. 'Yes, dearie, I'm afraid so. He musta died the minute he hit the deck.'

'Hit the deck?' Ginny heard someone say the words in a high, shrill voice, her brain too numb to realise she had spoken them herself.

'Thass right. As we see it, he musta climbed up the mast to try and make the tops'l fast and somehow missed his footing. The spreaders 'ud be greasy, the weather bein' what it is.' He spread his hands.

'Or it coulda bin a sudden gust o' wind caught him and blew him off the spar if he hadn't got a hand for hisself,' Will said. 'But what exactly happened we shan't never know for sure, I'm afeared, cause there worn't nobody there to see.'

'No. He's not dead. My dad can't be dead,' Ginny said, shaking her head to deny the truth. 'He's strong. He'll be all right. When the doctor comes he'll tell you. You'll see.' She folded her arms tightly across her chest, holding herself together.

Ruth had come back, a white sheet in her hands. She turned to Will Kesgrave. 'I thought he was going to take you with him to the boat,' she said accusingly.

'No, Missus. I was in the Rose. I never saw him,' Will said, shaking his head. The events of the evening had sobered him up completely.

'Ah. He said you'd be no use if you'd started drinking,' she said wearily. 'But he should never have gone alone.'

The two big men stood awkwardly waiting in the small room, mud and water dripping unheeded on to the carpet. There was nothing more they could do yet they were reluctant to leave the two women alone with the body of the man they had both respected and admired. When Alf arrived with the doctor, a young clean-shaven man not long out of medical school, they stood in a line, shoulder to shoulder, shielding the two women from the terrible sight of the back of Bob's skull, where it had smashed into the gunnel as he fell to the deck.

The doctor made his examination, then got to his feet, blood smearing his trousers. 'I'll arrange for the . . . him to be taken to the mortuary,' he said.

'No!' Ruth stepped forward. 'This is his home and this is where he'll stay.'

'But ma'am . . . ' Alf and Joey said together.

'There are things to be done, Mrs Appleyard,' the doctor said gently. 'There will have to be an inquest. Because nobody saw him fall.'

'But it was an accident.'

'Yes.'

'Then why?'

'Because it's the law, Mrs Appleyard.'

Bob Appleyard was wheeled up to the mortuary, a bleak little building hidden away in the far corner of the cemetery, on a covered trestle pushed by Alf and Joey, with Will following behind.

After they had gone Ruth closed the door on the chaos in the front room that was her pride and joy and poured two glasses of whisky. She handed one to Ginny.

'You won't like it, but drink it. It'll give you strength, girl,' she said, screwing up her face as she sipped her own. Ginny took a sip, shuddered and her face crumpled. 'It isn't true,' she sobbed. 'Oh, it can't be true. Dad can't be dead. Not my dad. Tell me it isn't true, Mum.'

Ruth pulled her to her feet and gathered her into her arms, stroking her hair. 'It's true, my girl,' she said unsteadily, staring blindly over Ginny's head. 'We're on our own now, you and me. So we've got to be strong.'

The inquest recorded a verdict of accidental death. As the men who had found him rightly testified, going to the yacht alone on that stormy night, Bob must have climbed up the mast in order to secure the tops'l that had broken free. This would not be an easy matter in heavy-weather gear and in such rough conditions and it was clear that he had either missed his footing or been knocked off the mast by the flailing sail and fallen to the deck below, smashing his head on the gunnel as he landed.

Ruth winced as this was said. Other than that her face betrayed no emotion and her expression didn't alter. The only sign of her feelings was that what little colour she had drained away, leaving her face completely ashen. Someone helped her out into the fresh air.

★ ★ ★

Exactly a fortnight after coming home after his summer's yachting, ironically on one of those beautiful sunny days that happen so often in the middle of October that they are known as St Luke's little summer, Bob Appleyard was laid to rest in the cemetery beside his parents.

The church was full for the funeral service because Bob was well liked by all who knew him and the deep voices of the local yachtsmen and fishermen echoed through the church in Bob's favourite hymn, 'Eternal Father, strong to save'. Of course, Captain Bellamy was there with Nathan and even Sir Titus Armitage had come down from London to pay his last respects to the mate of *Aurora*.

When it was all over, the last cup washed and the last crumb brushed away — Ruth had kept herself busy in the intervening days by doing what she did best, cooking pies, cakes and pastries to feed all those who she knew would come to offer comfort and support after the funeral — Ginny and her mother sank down in the chairs either side of the fireplace and looked at each other.

Ruth passed her hand across her face. 'In a few minutes I'm going to put my coat and hat on and walk up to the cemetery to look at the flowers,' she said quietly. 'I know there were so many wreaths that they were spread on the grass all round but I didn't really see . . . and I should like to take a proper look at them before they all fade. Do you want to come with me?'

Ginny shook her head. 'Not really, Mum. Not unless you really want me to. I don't think I . . . '

'That's all right, my girl,' Ruth said quickly. 'To tell you the truth I'd rather go on my own, but I didn't want you to think . . . ' Her voice trailed off. This was the way they had both spoken over the past days, sentences begun and not finished, sentiments unexpressed, taking refuge in everyday matters because there were no words for the enormity of what had happened to them.

After a few minutes Ruth got up and put on the new black coat and hat purchased specially for her husband's funeral and that she would wear for the next six months. 'Will you be all right here, on your own?' she asked, turning from the mirror to look at her daughter. 'Do you want . . . ?'

'I'll be OK, Mum,' Ginny said quickly. 'I'll

have the kettle boiled when you get back. Make a cup of . . . '

'Tea?' Ruth smiled faintly and Ginny managed to smile back. 'I reckon we've drunk enough tea these last few days to last us a month of Sundays, don't you?'

'All right. Cocoa, then.'

'We'll see.'

After Ruth had gone Ginny looked round the pristine kitchen. Every last cup and plate was back in its rightful place, the carpet in the front room had been brushed and the cushions plumped. The house was neat and tidy. And empty. So quiet and empty that Ginny wished now she had taken the mile walk up to the cemetery with her mother, just to get away from the emptiness. Yet she was used to her father not being here because ever since she could remember he had been away, either yachting or fishing, for most of the time. The difference was, this time he was not coming back. Ever. Someone, they didn't know who, had followed custom and taken her father's smack from her mooring at the quayside and anchored her in mid-stream, her bow pointing out to sea, symbolically ready for her skipper's last journey. Ginny had thought she had no tears left to shed, she had cried so much over the past fortnight, but remembering the sight of *Emily May* riding

129

the current her eyes welled again and she got up quickly and fetched her embroidery. Best to keep busy.

But before she could sit down again there was a knock at the door.

It was Nathan.

'Can I come in, Ginny?' he asked awkwardly, 'Or is it inconvenient?'

She brushed the tears aside. 'No, it's not inconvenient, Nathan. It'll be nice to have someone to talk to. Mum's gone up to look at the flowers in the . . . ' she swallowed.

'Yes. I just met her. She said you were at home.'

He stood awkwardly just inside the door, turning his cap in his hands until she gestured to him to take a seat. Then sat down on the old couch opposite the fireplace, where a small fire burned in the late afternoon chill.

'Would you like a cup of tea?' she asked, then managed a wry smile. 'I make a good cup of tea. I've made that much today I've had plenty of practice.'

'No thanks, I don't want tea.' He leaned forward and his voice softened. 'How are you, Ginny?'

She shrugged and sat down in the chair she had just vacated, clamping her lips together, not trusting herself to speak.

'Where's Roger? I noticed he was nowhere about today, just when you needed him most.' He looked round, as if expecting to find him lurking in a corner.

'Gone to Australia.'

'Australia!' He stared at her in disbelief. 'What's he gone there for?'

'His uncle's a sheep farmer there.' She looked down at her hands. 'I suppose it was my fault, really. I realised I could never marry him. When he wouldn't even apply for a job at Clacton I gave him his ring back and told him he was too much of a stick-in-the-mud for me. But he couldn't have been that much of a stick-in-the-mud, could he, because when I broke off the engagement he upped and went off to the other side of the world.' She glanced up at Nathan and gave a little giggle in spite of herself.

'Didn't he want you to go with him?' Nathan asked, watching her carefully.

'Oh, yes. He asked me to go, but . . . ' she shook her head.

'It was too late?' he prompted.

'No. Not too late, exactly,' she said thoughtfully. 'It was a mistake. The whole thing was a mistake. I should never have got tangled up with him in the first place.' She stared into the flickering fire. 'When it came

131

to it I realised that we'd got nothing in common. In fact, I didn't even like him much.'

Nathan spread his hands. 'Then why did you get engaged to him, Ginny?'

She was too tired, her emotions too raw after the events of the past days for any pretence. 'It was after you went away. I thought, well, I suppose I thought if you didn't want me Roger was as good as anybody else.' Her shoulders moved slightly. 'But of course it didn't work out like that. You can't turn love on and off like a tap.' She had shifted her gaze and was staring out of the window as she spoke.

'Oh, Ginny,' he breathed, as realisation dawned. 'I'd no idea . . . '

'No, well, you wouldn't have, would you,' she said, pulling herself together, her voice brittle with annoyance because she had allowed him to see how she felt. 'After all, my mother is only your mother's cook. It's only natural you wouldn't look in my direction. As Captain Bellamy's son you'd be sure to set your sights higher.' She turned to look at him. 'How is Isobel, by the way? Things going well? Selling a nice lot of paintings? I expect your feet are itching to get back . . . '

'Stop it! Stop it, Ginny!' He almost shouted the words.

She stared at him, wide-eyed with surprise.

'I'm sorry.' He passed his hand across his brow, then sat forward, his elbows on his knees, looking down at his hands, loosely clasped between them, a picture of dejection. 'It isn't working, Ginny,' he said, his voice barely above a whisper. 'That's what I came to tell you. I hate London. I can't paint there, the city stifles me. The thought of going back to that dreadful studio after the months I've spent on the yacht in the fresh air fills me with dread.'

Ginny digested this, then, careful to keep her voice level, said, 'Have you told Isobel how you feel?'

He shook his head impatiently. 'She wouldn't understand. All she understands is . . . Oh, God, how can I tell you . . . you of all people.' He put his head in his hands. 'I've been a bloody fool, Ginny, I can see that now. I was just bowled over to think that the owner's daughter was taking an interest in me. And I really thought she loved me. She . . . we . . . it was as if she couldn't get enough of me.' He looked up, then away again. 'Oh, God, Ginny, I shouldn't be talking to you like this. I shouldn't be telling you all these things, especially not on a day like this, when you're still so upset about your dad. I'm sorry. Look, I'd better go.' He made to stand up but Ginny got up from her seat and went over and sat beside him.

'No, don't go, Nathan. It's all right, really it is. I'm your friend, remember? We've always been friends, ever since we were little. If you can't tell me your troubles, then who can you talk to?' She was desperate for him to go on talking because in some strange way the hurt of his words was helping to make bearable the other, even more terrible hurt inside her.

'If you're sure?' He looked at her uncertainly. When she nodded he relaxed back into his seat. 'Isobel is totally spoiled,' he said flatly. 'Her father indulges her every whim. Whatever Bella wants, Bella must have.' He gave a small shrug and a quirky smile played round his mouth. 'I suppose you could say I didn't stand a chance against that.'

'But you love her. You told me yourself you'd fallen in love with her,' Ginny said, deliberately twisting the dagger of hurt inside her.

He nodded. 'Oh, yes. I fell for her all right. Well, what man in my position wouldn't, Ginny, if he was singled out for the attention of such a rich and beautiful woman?' He sighed. 'But she's like a bloody leech. Once she's got you in her clutches she won't let go.'

'But do you want her to?'

'What? Let go?' His voice rose and he turned to look at her. 'Yes, I do. I want to get away from London and come home to Wyford. I've had enough. That woman is wearing me out, Ginny. I don't go to bed till three most mornings and then she's round at the studio before eleven. It's no wonder I can't paint. I'm too bloody tired, apart from anything else.' He turned his head away.

Ginny took a deep breath and forced herself to say, 'Have you thought that perhaps she might like to come and live in Wyford with you, Nathan?'

'Oh, God forbid. I wouldn't want her spoiling my life here,' he said vehemently.

'But I thought . . . ' Ginny frowned. 'You said you were in love with her. Surely, if that's the case you want her with you.'

'I *was* in love with her. Or thought I was,' he said. 'But not any more.' He gave her a twisted smile. 'A bit like you and Roger, I suppose. I don't even like her much any more.' His voice dropped. 'In fact, to tell the truth, Ginny, I've only just begun to realise what love, real love, is.'

She closed her eyes. This was going too far. She didn't think she could bear it if Nathan was going to confess to yet another love affair. She felt him get up from beside her but she turned her head away, hoping he would just go away and leave her. She couldn't take any more, not today, of all days.

Then she felt him take her hands in his. 'Oh, Ginny, you're the one I love. I guess I've always loved you but been too close to you to realise it.'

She opened her eyes. He was kneeling in front of her, looking up into her face. 'It's probably because you've always been around, we've done things together ever since we were children, you've just always been a part of my life.'

He put her hands to his lips. 'It wasn't until I saw you wearing Roger's engagement ring that it hit me. I realised that some other man had dared to stake a claim to Ginny. My Ginny. I couldn't bear it, Ginny. I was so jealous I could have murdered Roger Mayhew. You can't imagine how I felt.'

Ginny smiled down at him although her eyes were brimming with tears. 'I think I can, Nathan,' she said. 'Don't you remember? It was about this time last year, the night the yacht was berthed after the summer's sailing, and you asked me to meet you on the wall because you'd got something special to tell me. I was so excited because I was quite sure you were going to give me an engagement ring, bought with your prize money. But instead of a ring you gave me a silk scarf and told me you were going to London to be with Isobel Armitage.' She shook her head. 'Don't talk to me about being jealous, Nathan,' she said bitterly. 'Don't talk to me about a broken heart. I don't have to imagine it. I know all about it.'

He got to his feet and pulled her up with him. 'Oh, Ginny. Darling Ginny. I'm so sorry. So dreadfully sorry. I've been such a fool. I was so dazzled by Isobel Armitage that I couldn't see what was right under my nose. Can you understand? More than that, can you forgive me, Ginny?'

She nodded, her eyes shining with tears.

He looked at her for a long moment, then slowly bent his head and kissed her, his tears mingling with hers.

For a moment she gave herself up to his kisses, her mouth opening under his as the dream she had cherished for so long became reality. Then she pulled back and looked up at him.

'What about Isobel?' she asked.

'Don't talk about Isobel.' He pulled her to him again. 'I'll tell her it's finished between us. I think she knows it is, anyway,' he said, his mouth finding hers again. 'I'll tell her I'm going to marry you.' He lifted his head enough to look into her eyes. 'You will marry me, won't you, Ginny?'

'Oh, Nathan. Of course I will.' She wound her arms round his neck and pulled his head down again. 'I just wish Dad had lived to see this day,' she whispered, her voice catching on a sob. 'He would have been so pleased, Nathan. Oh, God, why did he have to die like that?' She clung to him, her emotions in such a turmoil that she couldn't tell whether she was crying for her father or crying with happiness because at last she knew that Nathan loved her and wanted to marry her. As he kissed away the tears from her eyes and then his mouth slowly moved over her cheeks to her throat, a passion such as she had never known rose within her to match his.

'Oh, Ginny, I love you so much,' he whispered, lowering her back on to the sofa.

'And I love you, too, Nathan,' she murmured, tangling her fingers in his hair and pulling him down with her.

'I should go,' he whispered, his mouth against her, making no attempt to move. 'Your mother will be home before long.'

'Not yet,' she whispered back, her insides melting as he began to fumble with the buttons on her dress. 'Here, let me . . . ' She undid them herself, guiding his hand inside her bodice to caress the soft white flesh.

'We should go upstairs,' she murmured in his ear as he bent to kiss the pink nipple.

He caught his breath. 'No, it's too soon, Ginny,' he whispered, lifting his head. 'You've got to be sure it's what you really want. I love you far too much to want to hurt you. We shouldn't . . . not yet. We should wait . . . '

'Why?' She put her hand over his. 'Haven't we waited long enough? Why should we wait any longer?' Her eyes met his. 'Don't you want me, Nathan?'

'Oh, Ginny, if only you knew . . . ' he said in a muffled voice.

'Then show me, my dearest love,' she said softly.

9

Lying in bed that night, Ginny relived the events of the day. She was exhausted both mentally and physically, yet she couldn't sleep. Over and over again she recalled the details of her father's funeral, the deep voices of the men singing in church, the flowers, the words over the open grave, and the heavy thud of the handfuls of earth she and her mother had symbolically dropped on to the coffin as it lay in its final resting place. And afterwards, the people that crowded into the little house — the yachtsmen and fishermen she had known all her life suddenly all seemed so *big* — holding Ruth's best tea plates in their great ham fists and drinking tea from her best china tea cups instead of the thick enamel mugs they were used to. It had all seemed totally unreal and she had gone through the day as if in a dream from which she would wake at the sound of her father's voice calling her 'matie' and enveloping her in his great bear hug.

And the dream, the sense of unreality had gone on, the dreadful sense of emptiness, until at last the realisation broke through that this really was the end, that Bob Appleyard, the father she adored, the solid anchor of her life, had gone for ever.

And then Nathan had come.

Looking back, it was almost as if her father had sent him and she felt no shame or guilt about what had happened in the living room downstairs, only hours after he had been laid to rest. It had been as inevitable as the sun rising in the morning and setting in the evening. And equally right. She gave a great sigh of contentment. Nathan loved her, really loved her, he had told her so, over and over again as he held her, touched her, loved her. She felt a shiver of delight at the memory of the way his hands had caressed her, the caring gentleness of him as he tried not to hurt her, even in the tide of passion that had swept over them both. He had hurt her, but the hurt was nothing to the joy she had felt at their mutual expression of love. Afterwards, lying wrapped in each other's arms they had acknowledged that Isobel Armitage and Roger Mayhew had been nothing more than an irrelevance in their lives. They, Ginny and Nathan, were meant to be together and it had always been thus; there was a rightness about it all, an inevitability that couldn't be denied. Need no longer be denied.

She shifted her position and lay watching a

shaft of moonlight coming through the window, the same moon that was shining through Nathan's window, she thought in the manner of lovers the world over. Tomorrow he was going back to London. But only briefly, to collect his belongings and tell Isobel their affair was over, something he had been trying to find the courage to do all summer, he had confessed to Ginny, holding her close. Then he would come back to Wyford to stay and they would begin their proper courtship. Then, after six months or so, when the time of mourning was over — not that she would ever stop mourning the death of her dad, how could she? but it would be over in the eyes of the public — they would marry.

They had it all planned. All wonderfully planned. As she fell asleep there was a contented smile on her face.

★ ★ ★

Ginny and her mother went numbly through the days following Bob's funeral. Ginny returned to Stacey's and Ruth resumed her work for Mrs Bellamy. For some reason she didn't fully understand Ginny was reluctant to speak to her mother about the love she and Nathan had for each other; in a funny kind of way it was as if she was afraid that to speak of her own new-found happiness might be like rubbing salt into the terrible wound of Ruth's loss. So she kept quiet and spoke only of other things, waiting for the time to be right.

'Are you going to sell *Emily May*, Mum?' she asked one evening, knowing how much her mother had resented Bob's affection for the smack.

Ruth stared into the fire. 'I don't know. I hardly like to part with her, to tell the truth. Your dad set a lot of store by her.'

'If you sold her you could buy a house, like you've always wanted,' Ginny said slowly.

Ruth nodded doubtfully. 'I suppose I could. I've already got a bit put by.' She sniffed. 'But we've got to think carefully about how we'll manage, my girl, now we've no bread-winner. The only money we'll have coming in is what I get from Mrs Bellamy and your wages from Stacey's. Things are going to be tight.' She stroked her chin. 'Of course, there should be a bit of insurance money. Dad was always careful to keep up the payments. And I suppose the owner might pay a bit, but we can't bank on that.' She was quiet for several minutes, then she said, 'I might see about getting a new gas cooker. Perhaps I could sell some of the cakes I make . . . ' her voice trailed off.

'That's a good idea, Mum.' Ginny was enthusiastic. When she and Nathan were married Ruth would need to support herself with more than a few hours a week at Mrs Bellamy's. In any case, Nathan wouldn't want his mother-in-law working for his mother. That wouldn't do at all.

On the other hand . . . She voiced her fears. 'Who would buy cakes if you made them, Mum? With all the unemployment most people round here haven't got enough money to buy bread, let alone cakes.'

Ruth shrugged. 'There are always people like the Bellamys. And Mr Stacey might take a few and sell them in his shop . . . '

'You'd have Cracknell's the bakers after you for taking their trade if you did that.'

'Yes, you're right.' Ruth gave a sigh. 'I wonder if it might be better to get somebody to work the smack for me, instead of selling her. That would bring a bit in, wouldn't it?' She sighed again. 'It's difficult to know what's the best thing to do about that, isn't it? We can't leave her to rot, can we?' She looked up at Ginny, her eyes bleak.

'Well, there's plenty of time, you don't need to make up your mind for a bit,' Ginny said, wondering if now was the time to speak of her own love and deciding that perhaps it would be better to wait. Nathan would surely be back tomorrow or the next day, time enough to speak then.

The days passed slowly. Ginny tried hard not to be impatient; after all, Nathan had been in London over a year, he would have quite a lot of things to attend to before coming home for good.

More things than either he or Ginny had envisaged.

* ⋆ ⋆

Nathan had been back two days and was busily sorting through his canvasses in his London studio. He had put off letting Isobel know he was back because he was still rehearsing how he would break the news to her that he was leaving and going back to Wyford. He still hadn't perfected his speech when she walked in. She always walked straight in; it never occurred to her to knock; after all, why should she? Daddy was paying the rent for the place.

'Ah, so you're back at last,' she said, her voice petulant. She waited and when he didn't turn round, said, 'Well, aren't you going to say hullo to me, Big Boy? Don't you realise I've missed you while you've been staying in that dump of a village? Why did you stay away so long?'

'You know perfectly well why, Isobel,' he said over his shoulder. 'I stayed so that I could go to Bob Appleyard's funeral.'

She went over to his bench and picked up a palette knife. 'Oh, yes. I'd forgotten.' She put it down again and went over and wound her arms round his neck as he bent over his paintings. 'Well, you're back now so we can make up for lost time, can't we?'

He straightened up, at the same time loosening her hold. 'Can't you see I'm busy, Isobel?' he said, trying not to sound impatient. He didn't want to quarrel with her, what he had to say was far too important to be said in the heat of the moment. 'I'm trying to sort out my paintings.'

'Why? They're all right where they are, aren't they? The exhibition won't be yet. Daddy said . . . '

He turned to look at her. 'I don't think there will ever be an exhibition, Isobel. I don't think your father ever intended that there should be one,' he said, keeping his voice level. 'It's only because you've kept badgering him that he's agreed to even think about it. I'm not that good an artist.' A bitter smile twisted his lips. 'Do you think I haven't realised that the only paintings I've sold have been to your cronies? And only then because you've persuaded them.'

She smiled her little cat smile. 'Doesn't matter, darling, does it? At least it had the desired effect and they bought them.'

'Yes, it does matter, Isobel. It matters to me. I want to sell my paintings because they have some merit, not because your friends don't want to offend you. I have my pride, you know.'

'Pride comes before a fall, darling. Come and fall with me.' She tried to pull him over to the bed in the corner.

'No, Isobel. Not any more.' As he spoke he released himself from her grasp. 'I've done a lot of thinking while I've been away and I realise that although I've had a wonderful time here in London with you it isn't what I want to do for the rest of my life. I've had enough of sponging on your father. I've had enough of trailing round one London night spot after another . . . '

She gave him a slinky, sideways look. 'Had enough of making love to me?' she asked, sliding off her orange satin trousers she was wearing and undoing her blouse.

'Since you ask, yes, I have,' he said bluntly. He turned away from her. 'I've had enough of this whole scene and I'm going home. I'm just not cut out for a life of doing nothing but enjoy myself. Not that I do enjoy myself, I hate this life,' he added, a touch of viciousness in his voice.

She came and stood in front of him. She hadn't bothered to fasten her blouse or to put on her trousers again. 'There's someone else, isn't there,' she said, her lip curling.

He nodded. 'Since you ask, yes, there is.'

'I bet it's that little mousy creature who was waiting for dear daddy when the yacht came in.'

'Yes. It's Ginny. And she's not a little mousy creature, she's a wonderful girl. It was her father who died on *Aurora*, as you may or may not remember.'

'So you feel sorry for her,' Isobel remarked.

'Yes, I feel sorry for her. Good God, Isobel, she's just lost her father. Of course I feel sorry for her.'

'That's no reason to give up a good life here, with me. To throw up your career.'

'I haven't got a career and well you know it,' Nathan said savagely.

'Do you think you're going to marry her?'

'Yes, I do.'

Isobel went over and sat on the bed, looking at him out of the corner of her eye. 'I'm sorry to hear that, Nathan,' she said sadly. 'Of course, I won't stop you from going to her if you love her. But I must say the news couldn't have come at a worse time as far as I'm concerned.'

He spun round, frowning. 'What do you mean?'

She shrugged. 'Well, I had such a wonderful homecoming planned for you.'

'In what way?'

She picked at the eiderdown. 'I was going to take you out to dinner tonight and ask you how you felt about becoming a father,' she said, keeping her voice light.

'You mean . . . ' Nathan swallowed, staring at her.

'Yes, darling. I'm sorry to spring it on you like this, but the fact is, I'm pregnant.' There was a triumphant light in her eyes.

He swallowed again. 'But you said . . . You told me you could never have children. You said you'd had an operation when you were young and it had gone wrong . . . '

She smiled. 'It must have put itself right, darling, mustn't it? Or perhaps it was you. Perhaps you put it right. You're very — energetic when you're roused, darling, aren't you?'

He sat down on the nearest chair and mopped his brow. 'Can't you . . . ' he could hardly bring himself to say what was in his mind, ' . . . do something about it?'

She frowned. 'Nathan! What a thing to say. I'm sure you don't mean it.' She patted her still flat stomach lovingly. 'You surely can't

149

want me to get rid of the product of our mutual love?'

'But you're not cut out to be a mother! You're too damn fond of a good time,' he exploded.

'There are such things as nannies, Nathan.' She smiled and stretched out on the bed. 'Daddy will be thrilled, I'm sure. He never expected to be a grandpa.' She curled round and sat up in one swift movement. 'But of course, darling, you realise that it will put paid to your idea of going back to the sticks and marrying Little Bo-peep, because you couldn't allow your child to be born out of wedlock, could you.'

He licked his lips. 'No. I suppose not.'

'You suppose not! That's no way to treat incipient fatherhood, darling.' She laughed, showing little pearly white teeth. 'I know it's a bit of a shock, but you could at least show a little enthusiasm at the prospect of having a son and heir. Or a daughter, of course.'

He tried to smile and failed. 'When will . . . when do you expect it?' he asked with an effort.

'Let me see. This is the middle of October.' She began an elaborate count on her fingers. 'Round about next May, I should think.'

'What do you mean, 'round about'? Don't you know? Haven't you been to a doctor? I thought they could tell to within a few days.' His voice rose sharply with each question.

'Well, yes, they can. And of course I've been. He said about the twentieth of May. Or the fourteenth. I can't remember which.' She giggled. 'You remember that afternoon we had together roaming in the heather on Mull? If it's a girl we'll call her Heather in memory of that afternoon, shall we?'

He put his head in his hands. 'Oh, God. What am I going to do?'

She looked at him through eyes that had narrowed to slits. 'You're going to marry me, darling. That's what you're going to do. Just a quiet registry office wedding. I don't want a great society do at St Martin's in the Fields with all the trimmings, because white doesn't suit me.' She got up and came over to him and ruffled his hair. 'So you'd better write to Little Bo-peep and tell her that Little Boy Blue won't be coming back after all, hadn't you, darling.'

He didn't lift his head but said in a muffled voice, 'When do you intend . . . ?' His voice broke and he couldn't finish the sentence.

'The wedding? Oh, soon. With a special licence . . . shall we say next Tuesday?' She patted her stomach. 'Mustn't leave it too long or our heir will be too apparent.' She laughed delightedly at her own joke, then went over to him again and wound her arms round his neck. 'It's been a bit of a shock to you, hasn't it, darling? But once you get used to the idea of being a father you'll begin to enjoy it.' She looked up at him with huge blue eyes and smoothed his hair away from his forehead. 'We've had some wonderful times together, Nathan, and we will again. Don't spoil it all now. I understand that you feel sorry for Little Bo-peep. It's only natural. You've known her a long time and her father has just died. But you don't love her. Not the way you love me. We belong together, Nathan, you and me and our baby. Come on, darling, let's celebrate.' She led him over to the bed and this time he didn't resist. But their coupling was savage and entirely without love on his part.

10

Nathan had been gone eight long days — Ginny had been crossing them off on the calendar — when his mother came into Stacey's quite early one morning, beaming and bustling with news.

Ginny was busy bagging up sugar at the end of the counter so Mrs Bellamy handed her grocery list to Doris, the other girl who worked with Ginny on the 'dry' counter.

'I thought I'd better pop this in before I go to London,' she said in quite a loud voice. 'I'm in a bit of a hurry because me and the captain will be off very shortly.' (Her grammar sometimes let her down when she was excited.) She looked round to make sure she had an audience and was gratified to see that there were several customers in the shop as well as Mr Stacey himself. 'You won't have heard, of course, but my Nathan's getting married and we're just off to his wedding. He's marrying Sir Titus Armitage's daughter, you know.' She put up her hand and fluffed her hair under its wide-brimmed hat. 'Of course, me and the captain knew it was only a matter of time. They're *so* in love.' She gave a little tinkling laugh. 'But I must say we expected to be given a little more notice than this. He only phoned to tell us yesterday! I haven't even had time to buy new clothes.' She smoothed the skirt of her powder-blue dress with its matching three-quarter length coat. 'But he says it doesn't matter a bit because I always dress well.' She leaned forward confidentially. 'It's a registry office wedding, would you believe.' She simpered a little. 'Just like Isobel to be different. Says she doesn't want to be married in church because white doesn't suit her!' She peered short-sightedly at the tiny gold watch on her wrist. 'Oh, dear, I must fly or I'll miss the train. The captain's gone ahead to get the tickets.' She reached the door and called back, 'You'll make sure the groceries are delivered tomorrow, Mr Stacey, won't you. Mrs Appleyard will be there to take them in if me and the captain ain't — aren't back. Thank you so much.'

Before anyone else had time to say a word she was gone.

Ginny had continued weighing out sugar from the sugar sack into the dark blue two-pound bags, her hands working auto-matically, as she heard what Mrs Bellamy had to say. But as the words sank in the shop began to tilt and spin, faster and faster, then everything went black.

The next thing she knew, Doris was leaning over her, a glass of water in one hand, waving the smelling bottle under her nose with the other.

Ginny spluttered and waved the smelling bottle away. 'What's happened? What do you think you're doing?'

'Trying to bring you round, you daft thing. You fainted,' Doris said. 'One minute you was weighing out sugar, the next you was flat out on the floor. Here, sit up and drink this.'

Feeling decidedly groggy, Ginny struggled to sit up and took several sips of water.

'And have another whiff of my smelling salts. That'll clear your head. God, you look as white as a sheet. There. Better now?'

Ginny gave her a shaky smile. 'Yes, I'm OK now, I think. I feel a bit sick, that's all. I reckon it was the smell of that gorgonzola over on the cheese counter. It always turns me up.'

'Well, sit here for a few minutes till you get a bit of colour back in your cheeks.' Doris fetched a chair for her. 'Did you see Mrs Bellamy, all dressed up like a dog's dinner? Mind you, I didn't think that powder blue suited her. A woman her age ought to wear something a bit darker. Said she was going to Nathan's wedding. In London. Did you hear what she said? Or had you fainted by then?'

Ginny took another sip of water. 'Yes, I think I heard her say something about it.' That was an understatement if ever there was one because the words had exploded into her brain, sending her dizzy and faint. But it couldn't be true. There must be some mistake. Nathan couldn't possibly be marrying Isobel Armitage.

She gave her head a little shake. She hadn't dreamed it, Nathan had told her on the day of her father's funeral that he was going to London to finish with Isobel because it was her, Ginny, that he loved. He *couldn't* have been lying when he told her that he loved her. He would never have made love to her if he hadn't meant it; with all his faults, Ginny was sure she knew him well enough to know that he couldn't have been that cruel. Yet Mrs Bellamy was going to his wedding. It didn't make sense.

'You still look a bit peaky,' Doris said. 'I think you should go home. Have a lie down and come back this afternoon when you feel better. I'll cover for you. We're not that busy.'

Ginny staggered to her feet. 'Yes, I think perhaps I will. I don't know what came over me. I've never fainted before in my life. I'm sorry, Doris.'

'I expect it's the time of the month,' Doris

whispered in her ear.

'Yes, I expect it is,' Ginny agreed wanly.

She walked home slowly, the same thing kept going round and round her brain. Why should Mrs Bellamy say Nathan was getting married to Isobel if it wasn't true? Yet how could it be true when he had gone back to London on purpose to tell her their affair was over?

On the other hand he had been away over a week now, which was more than time enough to pack his things and come back to Wyford.

Yet Ginny still refused to believe that Nathan hadn't meant it when he said he loved her; she *knew* he'd been speaking the truth when he said the affair with Isobel was over. She'd known him nearly all their lives and even when they were children she could always tell when he was being evasive or not telling the truth, like the time when he denied burning a hole in his mother's armchair with a cigarette. That was when he was about ten; Ginny had never forgotten his guilt-ridden look when he denied all knowledge of it. It had made her giggle it was so obvious.

And another thing. He would never have made love to her . . . Her face flamed at the memory because she knew that hadn't been altogether his fault. She had been equally to blame, if blame there was. In fact, if she was totally honest she had been even more eager than Nathan to seal their love. And she didn't regret it, not for a single minute. But perhaps he did . . . ?

She let herself into the house, thankful that her mother wasn't yet back from the Bellamys' and sank down on the sofa, her aching head in her hands, trying to calm her queasy stomach and make some sense out of what she had heard in the shop.

After a long time she got up and went across to pull the kettle forward to make herself a cup of tea and take an aspirin. It was then that she noticed the letter propped up on the mantelpiece. It was addressed to her, it had a London postmark and she recognised Nathan's handwriting. She turned it over in her hand, half afraid to open it, then in one quick movement she slit the envelope and pulled out the single sheet of paper.

My darling Ginny (she read),
I don't know of any way to tell you this gently and I know you will be as devastated as I am. I can only tell you how desperately sorry I am to have to hurt you in this way.

When I got back here Isobel greeted me with the news that she is pregnant. She had always thought she could never have children after an operation that went wrong a few years ago so she is naturally quite delighted and so is her father. This means of course that I have no choice but to do the decent thing and marry her. They are both determined that our wedding should take place as soon as possible, in spite of the fact that Isobel knows I no longer have any feeling for her. It's damnable that this should have happened just now but what can I do? I can't walk out on her and more than that, I could never forgive myself if I allowed a child of mine to be born a bastard. I can't let his life be ruined even if mine is. I hope you can understand.

Please, Ginny, always remember that I meant what I said to you on the day of your father's funeral. I love you with all my heart. You are the love of my life, you always have been and always will be. If only I had realised it sooner I wouldn't have messed up my life like this. I was a fool and now I am having to pay for it. I'd give anything to know that you weren't having to suffer too, as I know you will.

Try and be happy, Ginny. Find someone else to love if you can.

Always yours,
Nathan.

She read the letter over and over, her tears falling on to the paper and blurring the words. Happiness had been so nearly in her grasp and now it had been snatched away. By Isobel Armitage. A surge of rage welled up inside her, swelling until it filled the whole of her body and she felt as if her head would burst. Then, as quickly as it came the rage left her. What was the use? Things were as they were and there was no going back. As Nathan said in the letter, he had been a fool and now he was paying for it. And so, God help her, was she. In her heart she knew that Nathan would be suffering as much on her account as his own. She drew a perverse kind of comfort from this and vowed that since she couldn't have the man she loved she wouldn't marry at all.

She washed her face and combed her hair and when her mother came home she had the table laid ready for dinner.

'You're home early,' Ruth said in surprise. She peered at her daughter's ashen face and the dark rings under her eyes. 'What's the matter, my girl? Aren't you well? You look washed out.'

'No, I don't feel all that good. I fainted at work. I think it was the gorgonzola on the cheese counter. I hate the smell of that cheese.'

Ruth frowned. 'It's never happened before, has it?'

Ginny shook her head.

'Maybe you'll feel better when you've had a bite to eat. I made Cornish pasties up at Mrs Bellamy's this morning so I've brought a couple home for us. I know you like them.'

'I might manage a half,' Ginny said without enthusiasm.

'The Bellamys have gone to London,' Ruth said as they sat down together. 'It seems Nathan's going to marry that Isobel Armitage. You could have knocked me down with a feather when I heard. I never thought it would come to that.'

'Mrs Bellamy was full of it when she came into the shop this morning. You can imagine, can't you.' She managed to bite into the pasty and was surprised to find she was quite hungry after all.

'Oh, I can. It's just what she's always wanted,' Ruth said with a nod. 'But it's a bit of a rush job, it seems to me. I reckon it's a case of having to, myself.'

'I shouldn't be surprised.' Ginny was amazed how calm her voice sounded.

'Ah, well. Marry in haste, repent at leisure, as the old saying goes. I can't see much good will come of it, myself. She's a flighty one, that Isobel, from what I've seen. Will you have the other half of this pasty?'

'Yes, please. It's good. I didn't realise how hungry I was.' She held out her plate.

161

Ruth gave her the pasty and regarded her thoughtfully. 'He'd have been a sight better off with you, my girl, to my way of thinking,' she remarked. 'Instead of that flibberty-gibbet.'

At that all Ginny's resolutions fled, she dropped her plate on the table and her face crumpled. 'Oh, Mum. If only you knew,' she said and pulled the tear-stained letter out of her pocket and gave it to her.

Ruth smoothed it carefully and read it several times before she looked up.

'Ah, so that's the way of it.' She studied her daughter for several minutes before saying, 'You'll get over it, my girl,' the stark words belying the compassion in her eyes.

Ginny shook her head. 'I don't think I shall, Mum. He's always been the one for me, ever since we were little.'

'I know that, Ginny. But you've got your whole life in front of you. You mustn't let Nathan Bellamy's stupidity ruin your life as well as his. He's not worth it.'

Ginny sniffed. 'Poor Nathan.'

'Poor Nathan, indeed!' Ruth said, her voice rising. 'It serves him right, to my way of thinking. He's made his bed and he'll just have to lie in it. I've no sympathy for him. No sympathy at all.' She reached over and took Ginny's hand. 'It's you I'm concerned with,

Ginny.' She stroked her daughter's fingers thoughtfully. 'In a way I suppose you could say we're both in the same boat, you and me. I've lost my man and you've lost yours, because as far as you're concerned now Nathan might as well be dead.' She took a deep breath. 'We've no choice, my girl. We've just got to get on with life, and make the best of it.'

Ginny managed to smile at her mother through her tears. 'I reckon you're right, Mum, but it's not going to be easy, is it?'

'No,' Ruth said quietly. 'It won't be easy, Ginny. Nobody's pretending it might be.'

★   ★   ★

Ginny dragged herself through the following weeks by the simple expedient of never looking more than a few hours ahead. When she got up in the morning she concentrated on putting on her clothes, washing her face and forcing down the piece of toast her mother insisted she eat. At work she gave all her attention to the customer she was serving, or the order she was making up, never letting her mind wander beyond the immediate task.

The evenings were worst. She and her mother sat either side of the fire, listening to

Henry Hall and his orchestra or Jack Payne and his band on the wireless, while their hands were busy with knitting or embroidery. Bob's reefer jacket still hung behind the door; neither of them had the heart to remove it.

'Why don't you and Shirley go to the whist drive?' Ruth asked one evening. 'You haven't been out for weeks. You always used to enjoy a game of whist.'

Ginny sighed. 'I don't feel like it, Mum. In any case I don't like to leave you here by yourself.'

'You don't need to worry about that, my girl.' She gave a wry smile. 'You never used to, when your father was away and you were out every evening, either with Roger or Shirley.'

'It was different then. We knew Dad was coming back.' She packed up her knitting. 'I think I'll go to bed. I'm very tired.'

'It's only half past eight.'

'I know. I'm always tired these days.' Ginny got to her feet, then sat down again quickly.

'What's wrong?' Ruth said sharply.

'Nothing. I went a bit dizzy, that's all.' She massaged her forehead.

'You need a good tonic, my girl. A lot's happened to you in the last few weeks, what with losing your dad and then the business with Nathan. These things take their toll, you know.'

Ginny nodded wearily. 'Mr Stacey's got some good stuff in the shop. You're right, Mum, what I need are some buck-me-up-pills.' She grinned. 'Doctor Pepper's Pink Pills for Pale People.' She got to her feet, more carefully this time. 'It's my half day tomorrow. I might take my sketch pad on to the quay and do a sketch of *Emily May*.'

'It's November, child. You'll get frozen sitting on the quay,' Ruth said in some alarm.

'I'll only go if it's a nice day like it's been today. Anyway, I want to sketch her before you put her up for sale. You are going to sell her, aren't you?'

'I still haven't quite decided,' Ruth said, looking at her thoughtfully. 'There's no hurry.'

The following afternoon was sunny, although there was a cold nip in the air. Ginny put on her thick winter coat and hat and wrapped a scarf round her neck. Then she picked up her sketch pad and pencils and a stool and walked down the yard to the door in the wall at the end. There was a little bit of trellis separating Granny Crabtree's cottage from the other two cottages in the row, the Oliphants' at number two and the Kesgraves' at number one, and this was a good thing Ginny thought, picking her way through the accumulated rubbish of the two cottages at the lower end of the yard, because the contrast between the squalor at that end and the immaculate neatness of the other was truly remarkable. As she went through the door in the wall and out on to the quay she scraped something she preferred not to name off the bottom of her shoe, wishing she had gone the long way round, along East Street and down Rose Lane.

She set her stool down just outside the yard door. In the lee of the wall and with a wintry sun shining it was not at all cold and she unwound her scarf as she looked around. Most of the fishing smacks were away at the fishing grounds but *Emily May* was riding at her mooring and several children were playing on the quayside nearby among the tangled ropes and discarded fishing nets. Only one child had any shoes, the rest were barefoot and their thin clothing was no protection against the chill air. But they didn't seem to notice — perhaps they had never known what it was to be warm — and they screamed in mock fear as the boy in the shoes chased them with a dead crab. Then they all crowded round to examine it.

Quickly, Ginny sketched the scene. *Emily May* in the background, one girl standing and looking on, her hair falling across her face, screwing the skirt of her tattered frock round in her fingers, two boys leaning down, one with a patch cobbled on to the seat of his trousers, the other wearing a pair that had obviously belonged to an older brother, because they were pulled up under his armpits and tied with string and still reached well below his knees. They both wore torn and grimy shirts, one had a pullover with a gaping hole in it and both wore caps that were so wide that they appeared to be held up by their ears. Another girl, slightly older, sat on a bollard swinging her legs. She had a large tear in the hem of her skirt and she was fast growing out of her blouse; what buttons there were left strained at their buttonholes. Her feet were bare and grimy.

After a while she wandered over to where Ginny was sitting and busily sketching the scene, trying to get the essence of it; the details could be filled in later.

'What you doin' then?' she asked in her sing-song northeast Essex voice.

Ginny smiled up at her, recognising her as Sally Oliphant. She was about thirteen and the oldest of seven in the Oliphant family. 'Can't you see? I'm drawing a picture of you children. Go back to where you were sitting and you'll be in it.'

'Dunno as I wanter be in it,' the girl said truculently.

'All right. Please yourself.' Ginny went back to her sketching.

The girl put a grubby finger on the pad. 'Thass my bruvver you're drawin' there,' she said. 'I can see thass him by his cap.'

'But the other boy's got a cap just like it,' Ginny said, looking up with a smile.

'I know. But he ain't my bruvver,' Sally said. She wandered off and carefully arranged herself back on the bollard.

Absorbed in her sketching, it was several minutes before Ginny realised that Will Kesgrave had come up beside her. She knew it was him by the smell. It was a distinctive smell of stale tobacco, shrimps, burnt fat and unwashed bodies that always seemed to emanate from the Kesgrave house and which permeated even the clothes they wore.

'Seen all you want to see, Will Kesgrave?' she asked, without looking up.

'I was jest thinkin' you ain't a bad artist,' he remarked, without taking the clay pipe from his mouth. 'You've got them children bang to rights.'

'Thank you for nothing,' she retorted. 'And for your information, I don't like people looking over my shoulder while I work.'

'Oh, work, is that what you call it?' He leaned on the wall. 'Well, thass a free country. If I wanta lean on the wall outside my house I don't know as there's any law to stop me. An' if you happen to be settin' there an' drawin', well you can't stop me takin' a look now an' then if I'm so minded.'

By this time the children had got tired of watching the crab and wandered off and Ginny had as much detail as she was going to get. She shivered and rubbed her hands together. She hadn't realised how cold it had grown now that the sun had gone.

'No. Lean on the wall for as long as you like.' She began to gather her things together. 'But you won't look over my shoulder because I'm going home now.'

'Now thass a pity. I always like talkin' to a pretty girl.'

'Hard luck. I don't like talking to you, Will Kesgrave.'

'All right, Miss Hoity-Toity.' He pulled himself upright. 'Do you want me to carry your gear for you?'

'No, thank you. I can manage quite well.' To her annoyance the tin that held her pencils slipped out of her hand and fell open. The pencils rolled in all directions.

With a grin he gathered them up and put them carefully back in the tin. 'Are you sure?' he asked cheekily.

She snatched it from him, pink with anger. 'Yes, thank you. I said I could manage.'

'I know. I heard you.' He went off, grinning, his hands in the pockets of his reefer jacket and Ginny walked home, up Rose Lane, along East Street and into the yard at the Anchor Hill end.

'Had a good afternoon?' her mother greeted her.

'Yes. Look, I've been sketching the Oliphant children and their friends.'

Ruth looked. 'You've caught them to a T,' she said admiringly. 'You've always been good at sketching, haven't you, ever since you and . . . ' she bit her tongue. Now, when Ginny seemed to be coming to terms with the fact that Nathan Bellamy was lost to her for ever, was not the time to remind her of happy days spent with him in their childhood. 'I'll make a cup of tea, you must be cold,' she said instead.

11

The last days of November crept out in a thick fog, which rolled up the river and enveloped the whole village in a depressing, sound-deadening grey blanket. Then overnight a bitter wind blew the fog away and December came in, celebrated by much rattling of shrouds and slapping of riggings on the yachts stationed in their winter berths alongside the river wall.

In the winter Ginny often walked that way on her half days just to look at the majestic sight of the big yachts lying snug in their mud berths, their decks protected by a winter coat of thick varnish, hatchways and skylights covered with canvas jackets, and those spars that hadn't been wrapped in sacking and carried off to be stored in the spar sheds coated with a sticky mixture of red or white lead and tallow to preserve them from the weather. But this winter she didn't go near the river wall at all. She couldn't bear to think about, let alone look at the sleek lines of *Aurora*, the yacht that had not only taken her beloved father's life but had been instrumental in taking Nathan away from her. She had come to hate the yacht as the cause of all her misery and more than once she had contemplated the possibility of sinking her by sneaking aboard one night at full tide and opening all the sea-cocks. But she knew she would never do it.

Thursday afternoons now were largely spent at home. If it was not too cold she would take her sketch pad out on the quay and make rough sketches of the men mending their nets, often helped by their wives, the children playing, the old men on the bench outside the Rose and Crown, their clay pipes clamped in toothless gums, or simply a fishing smack riding at its mooring. There was never any shortage of material for her pencil and her quick eye and a few judiciously placed lines would be enough to serve as a reminder of a scene so that she could sit by the fire and finish it, taking infinite pains, especially with her drawings of children, to capture movement and expression. Losing herself in her sketching was the only way in which she could forget the dull ache that she carried perpetually in her heart.

Her mother came in as she was sitting at the table, bathed in the light of the oil lamp, busy with her sketch pad and pencils late one Thursday afternoon. A steady rain had been falling all day so dusk had fallen early.

Ruth took off her wet coat and hat and hung them up, then she went over and lit the two gas mantles, one each side of the chimney breast, flooding the room with their soft yellow light. 'There,' she said. 'That's better, isn't it?'

Ginny looked up, blinking. 'Yes, I suppose it is. I lit the oil lamp because I could place it where I wanted it.' She began to gather her pictures together as Ruth began to unpack her basket.

'I got a couple of fresh herrings from Green's,' she said, unwrapping them. 'I thought you might like one for tea. You don't eat enough to keep a sparrow alive these days.' She sat down, her elbows on the table. 'You worry me, Ginny. I know how much you're grieving for your dad, and what happened with Nathan coming on top of it was a bitter blow, but don't forget I've lost my man, too,' she said quietly. 'However cruel it seems, my girl, life has to go on and we have to deal with it as best we can.'

'I know, Mum. And I am trying. I just don't feel like eating, that's all.' She didn't add that she felt permanently sick these days, a sickness that she was terrified had nothing to do with grieving for her father and everything to do with Nathan and the declaration of their love; a declaration that

173

had been far too premature in the event. She gave her mother a brief smile. 'I feel a bit sick, to tell you the truth. I expect I've been sitting hunched over my drawings for too long.'

Ruth chewed her lip, regarding her daughter thoughtfully. 'Your monthly's late, isn't it? I'd noticed you hadn't put any cloths out to be washed lately and I put it down to the shock of your dad . . . And then there was the trouble with Nathan, of course.' She paused. 'Things like that can upset nature. But of course, there could be another reason, couldn't there?' She was watching Ginny intently as she spoke.

Ginny flushed up to the roots of her hair. 'I don't know what you mean,' she said with a careless shrug, pencilling elaborate patterns on the corner of her sketch pad.

'Ah.' Ruth gave a great sigh. 'I think you do, Ginny.' And when Ginny didn't speak. 'Who was it? Roger?'

At that Ginny looked up, 'Roger!' Her tone was scathing. 'I wouldn't let him touch me with a barge pole.'

'So it must have been Nathan.' Ruth sighed again and her mouth twisted. 'I must say he didn't waste any time in bestowing his favours around.'

'You mustn't blame Nathan. It wasn't his

fault, Mum,' Ginny blurted out. Then realising what she'd admitted, mumbled, 'well, it wasn't altogether his fault. We love each other, it seemed right.'

'It's never right without a wedding ring on your finger,' Ruth snapped. 'You should know that.'

Ginny hung her head. 'We only . . . It was only once. After Dad's funeral. It was just as if Dad had sent him to me . . . And I didn't think . . . it was only the once . . . I didn't think I could get . . . People don't. Not the first time. And anyway, he was coming back to me so it wouldn't have mattered if I had . . . ' Her voice petered out.

Ruth digested this, massaging her forehead with her fingers. Finally, she looked up. 'Well, you were wrong on both counts, weren't you. You've found it *can* happen the first time,' she said. 'And he hasn't come back. What's more, he's *never* coming back.' Her voice sharpened. 'And don't you dare put the blame on your dad for what happened. My God, he'd turn in his grave if he knew what you'd done.' She stared at Ginny, her shoulders sagging. 'As if we hadn't got enough to contend with, now this.' She put her head on her hand. 'I don't know what we're going to do. We manage all right as it is, with your wages and what I earn.' She looked up. 'But what shall we do when you can't work and there's another mouth to feed, tell me that.'

Tears began to roll down Ginny's face. 'I'm sorry, Mum.'

'Sorry! Sorry's no good. Sorry won't put food on the table, will it.' She glared at Ginny. Then she shook her head. 'But it's no good sitting here talking like this. The damage is done now and we've got to think what's to be done. One thing's certain, the dirty little beggar can't marry you, since he's already got his fancy woman in the family way.'

'Oh, Mum. Don't talk about Nathan like that,' Ginny began to cry again. 'He'd have married me if . . . '

'Exactly. If he hadn't been forced to marry somebody else. Randy little sod. He ought to have his flies stitched up.' With this totally uncharacteristic statement Ruth got up from her chair and began viciously poking the fire. 'Now, do you want a fresh herring or don't you?'

Ginny stared at her mother. She had never, ever heard her use such language before.

'No, I don't think so, thank you, Mum. I think I'm going to be . . . ' Suddenly, the smell of them overpowered her and she made a rush for the door.

When she came back, looking very white, the herring were nowhere to be seen and a cup of tea stood on the table. Ruth pushed it across to her. 'Drink that. You'll feel better,' she said, her voice not unkind.

'Thanks, Mum.' Shamefaced, Ginny slipped back on to her chair.

'Now,' Ruth sat down opposite to her, elbows on the table, her cup poised ready to drink. 'We've got to find you a husband. And quick about it.'

Ginny opened her eyes in horror. 'But there's nobody I want to marry.'

'Maybe not. But the child needs a father.'

'No, he'll be all right. He'll have me. And you. We'll manage, Mum.' Ginny even managed a hopeful little smile as she spoke. But it was soon wiped off her face as Ruth's cup crashed down on its saucer.

'We shall *not* manage, my girl,' she said. 'I'll have no bastard child born in *this* house!'

'Dolly Mason had a little boy. You know, little Frankie Mason. She's not married,' Ginny persisted. 'Her mother looks after him while she works at the clothing factory.'

'Dolly Mason's no better than she should be,' Ruth said shortly. 'Everyone knows she's a trollop. She's the talk of the village. I'm not having you talked about the way she is. I'm not having my good name besmirched. No, either you'll find yourself a husband or I shall have you put away.'

'Put away?' Ginny said, puzzled. 'What do you mean?'

'I mean,' Ruth said, slowly and clearly, 'that I shall have you put away in Severalls Mental Hospital. That's what happens to girls from good families who get themselves into trouble.'

Ginny licked her lips. 'You wouldn't do that, Mum. You wouldn't do that to me. I'm your daughter.'

'Oh, wouldn't I! And I wouldn't be the first, either. Severalls is full of sluts who'd have brought disgrace on their families if they hadn't been put away.' Her face was wooden.

'That can't be right, Mum. Severalls is for idiots.'

'Exactly. And there's no bigger idiot than a girl who gets herself pregnant by a man who can't, or won't marry her.'

Ginny tried another tack. 'But how can I get married, Mum?' Her voice began to rise in panic. 'I don't know anybody . . . Nathan is married, Roger is in Australia . . . I don't know anybody else well enough . . . I can't go round saying to every man I meet 'will you marry me, I'm in the family way'.'

'You should have thought of that beforehand,' Ruth said, totally implacable.

'I couldn't . . . I told you . . . ' she looked round the room as if searching for help. Then she said eagerly, 'Look, Mum. I'll go away. I'll go right away where nobody knows me and when I come back with the baby I'll be wearing a wedding ring and I'll say my husband's dead. That wouldn't bring disgrace, would it?'

Ruth nodded. 'Oh, yes. And where would you go? What would you do for money?' she asked sceptically.

Ginny's shoulders crumpled and she shook her head. 'I hadn't thought of that.'

'No, my girl. It seems there are a good many things you haven't thought of,' her mother said. She leaned forward. 'But you'd better start thinking, and quickly, because I'm telling you this. There will be no bastard child born under my roof and that's my last word on the matter.'

But it wasn't.

Ginny spent a totally sleepless night worrying and wondering what she should do, appalled at the seeming callousness of her own mother. At five o'clock, her mind made up, she crept downstairs, a hastily packed suitcase in her hand. She had a little money so she would take the train to Ipswich, that should be far enough away. There she would find a room to live in and a job. There must be a grocer's shop that would take her on; Mr Stacey always said she was his best worker.

She would tell them her husband had been killed in an accident and she would work and save enough money to tide her over for the weeks after the baby came when she couldn't work. She knew she could do it, she had recently read a novel where a girl had done just that.

She had her hand on the latch when a voice came from the shadows.

'And where do you think you're going?'

'Mum!' She swung round. 'I thought you were still in bed.'

'Still in bed? I haven't even *been* to bed,' Ruth said, passing her hand wearily over her hair.

Ginny put the suitcase down. 'Well, I haven't slept much, either. But I've decided what I'm going to do,' she said in a flat voice. 'I shall go away, like I said last night. I'll go right out of your life where I shan't bring shame on you and I'll never come back.'

'No. I can't let you do that.' Ruth got up from her chair and went across and put her arms round her. 'I spoke harshly last night and I'm sorry,' she said, the words wrung from her unwillingly. 'I've sat here all night wondering the best thing to do and I think I've found a solution to the problem. In fact, it would solve two problems.'

Ginny looked up at her, her eyes

frightened. 'You won't have me locked away. I won't be locked away. I'll kill myself first.'

Ruth shook her head and gave a ghost of a smile. 'No. I realised last night that I could never do that to you. But you might not like my idea much better.'

Ginny frowned. 'Well?'

'You'll marry Will Kesgrave.'

Ginny stared at her mother, her jaw slack. There was total silence in the room except for the ticking of the pendulum clock on the wall, its brass weights gleaming in the light from the fire. She licked her lips and shook her head slowly from side to side.

'No. I can't do that. I don't even like him. And he doesn't like me. Anyway, he won't . . . He's not that daft.'

'I think he will,' Ruth said quietly, 'when he hears what I have to say.' She went to the door. 'I'll go and tell him I want a word with him. The sooner it's done, the better.'

'You can't do that. It's not six o'clock yet.'

'Ah, no, I hadn't realised. I suppose I'd better wait till eight.' She riddled the fire and pulled the kettle forward. 'I'll make some tea. Take your coat off and sit down. You're not going anywhere.'

Ginny did as she was told. Everything seemed unreal, even the chair she sat down on felt as if it wouldn't bear her weight.

'I mustn't be late for work,' she said automatically.

Ruth looked her daughter up and down and shook her head. 'You'd never manage a day's work, the state you're in. When I go down the yard I'll ask one of the Oliphant children to take a message to Mr Stacey to tell him you're not well. It's no word of a lie, by the look of you, you're as white as a sheet.'

Ginny watched dully while her mother made the tea and speared a slice of bread on the toasting fork and held it in front of the fire. When it was nicely brown she spread it with butter and pushed it across to Ginny.

'Eat that and don't argue,' she said.

Ginny did as she was told. She hadn't the strength to argue. She couldn't even be bothered to point out that news of her condition would be all over the village once Will Kesgrave had been told. She would be the laughing stock . . . she could just imagine the way he would jeer. Suddenly, startlingly, the cold waters of the river seemed to invite her. Just to walk across the mud until the water closed over her head, out of this mess, out of all her problems . . . She rested her head on her hand and let the comforting, almost cosy thought wash over her.

She was brought back to reality with the sound of her mother's voice saying, 'I'll go and fetch him. It's nearly eight now,' and realised that in her musings she had dropped off to sleep over her tea and toast.

She opened her mouth to protest but Ruth had gone and a few minutes later she heard her say briskly, her voice carrying easily from the other end of the yard in the clear morning air, 'Well, stick your head under the pump and then come along. You'll need a clear head for what I'm going to say.'

Seconds later she came back into the house.

'That Kesgrave place is a disgrace,' she said, pulling the kettle forward to make more tea. 'Goodness knows when the floor last saw a broom, let alone a scrubbing brush. And the windows . . . Ah, come in, Will,' in answer to the knock at the door.

Will Kesgrave entered, his face red and his hair wet from the dunking under the pump.

'Cup of tea?' Ruth asked.

He nodded. 'Thanks, Missus.' He cocked a questioning eyebrow at Ginny, who looked the other way. From across the table she caught a whiff of the stale smell of the Kesgrave house on his thick Guernsey.

'Well, sit down, boy,' Ruth said, cheerfully. 'We've got a proposition to put to you.'

Will frowned suspiciously. He wasn't even sure what the word 'proposition' meant.

Ruth poured three cups of tea, then she sat down between Ginny and Will.

'Now . . . ' she began.

Ginny stood up, her chair scraping on the lino, and tossed her head. She wasn't going to be haggled over like a prize cow, she would speak for herself. 'I need a husband, Will Kesgrave,' she said, with an air of truculence. 'And my mother seems to think you'll do.'

Will took a slurp of tea and choked. When he recovered his breath sufficiently he eyed her insolently up and down. 'Oh, yeh? In the pudden' club, are you? And want me to carry the can?'

'Something like that.' She sat down and turned to her mother. 'There you are,' she said, her voice a mixture of resignation and relief. 'I said it wouldn't work.'

'He hasn't heard what *I've* got to say on the matter yet,' Ruth said.

'And I hevn't said I wouldn't do it,' he said. 'Not that I'm sayin' I would,' he added hurriedly, 'but I've always had a soft spot for you, Ginny Appleyard.' He rubbed his chin and the three days' growth of beard made a rasping sound. 'Mind you, damaged goods . . . Been playin' around with Roger Mayhew and he upped and went to Australia where you couldn't get at him when he knew you

184

was in the fam'ly way, I s'pose.'

'That's right,' Ginny said quickly. She didn't want Will Kesgrave to know the truth.

'I daresay you've sown plenty of wild oats in your time, Will, so you've no call to shout,' Ruth remarked.

'Yes, but I don't carry the results of 'em round for all to see,' he said with a grin.

'No, you leave somebody else to do that,' Ruth said, quick as a flash.

He nodded. 'Reckon you may be right at that, Missus.'

'Well,' Ginny said, tired of the conversation. 'What's it to be? Will you marry me, Will Kesgrave?'

He looked at her thoughtfully. 'What's in it for me? Apart from a warm bed o' nights in the lee o' bum island?'

'Isn't that enough?' Ginny tried to keep the disgust out of her voice.

He sniffed. 'No. I'd want more'n that to saddle meself with another man's brat. I ain't that daft.'

'Then think about this, Will Kesgrave,' Ruth said. 'I need somebody to skipper *Emily May* and who better than my own son-in-law? You've been out fishing in her with my husband a good many times and from what he's said you've learned well. Do you reckon you could take the job on for a quarter share in the takings?'

Ginny's eyes filled with alarm. 'But you were going to sell the smack, Mum,' she cried.

'I've changed my mind. If my son-in-law is willing to work her it might be more profitable to keep her.' She turned to Will. 'You can have a quarter share, the crew can have a quarter share between them, and I'll have a half share, out of which I'll keep the smack well-founded. How does that strike you?'

His eyes lit up. 'I'll make us a fortune, Missus,' he said, full of confidence.

'I doubt it. Even Bob couldn't manage to do that and he knew the fishing grounds like the back of his hand,' Ruth said dryly.

'I'll get Ammy Bartlett and Jim Crow to crew,' Will said enthusiastically. 'They sometimes came out with Bob and me so they know the boat. Oh, yes, we'll do all right, Missus, don't you never fear.' He rubbed his hands together. 'I'll set to work on her today and get her ready to sail. She ain't had nothin' done to her since . . . ' he hesitated, 'not since . . . '

'Not since last winter,' Ruth said smoothly. 'But aren't you forgetting something?'

'What?' He looked blank.

'I think she means me,' Ginny said, with a lift of her head.

'Oh, you're the icin' on the cake, darlin'.' He leaned over and gave her a wet bristly kiss which turned her stomach over. 'Jest name the day an' I'll be there.'

12

After Will Kesgrave had gone — and he didn't stay long because he was eager to get *Emily May* ready for her first trip with him in charge — Ginny put both hands on the table and heaved herself wearily to her feet.

'Well, you've got your own way, Mother,' she said without looking at her. 'You've made sure I don't bring disgrace on you. I just hope you're satisfied.' She turned dull brown eyes on her mother. 'Of course, you realise, don't you, that we shall be the laughing stock of the village when word gets round. And it will. The Kesgraves will see to that. For my part I could have born the scandal better.'

'I think you're wrong, Ginny,' Ruth said, gathering up the cups and saucers and putting them on a tray ready to be washed. 'I think Will will keep very quiet about the reasons for marrying you. For a start he'll want people to think he's got charge of *Emily May* on his own merits. And for another thing he won't be anxious to let people know he's taking on another man's child. *He'd* be the laughing stock if that was made known.' Ruth nodded complacently. 'I think, by and large, we've done very well.'

'Except that you've condemned me to a life with a man I despise, who drinks himself stupid at every opportunity and stinks to high heaven,' Ginny said bitterly. 'Oh, yes, Mother, *you've* done very well. Not me. Don't include me. I think I'd be better dead.' With that she took her coat and hat off the hook behind the door.

'Where are you going?' Ruth asked, the complacency wiped off her face and replaced with alarm.

'I'm going to work.'

'But I sent a message to Mr Stacey by the Oliphant child to say you wouldn't be in because you were ill.'

'Well, I've recovered, haven't I.' Ginny didn't even look at her mother. After what Ruth had done to her she knew that relations between them would never be the same again.

★ ★ ★

Virginia Appleyard and William Kesgrave were married in St Mary's parish church on Christmas Eve 1935 at eight o'clock in the morning. Will had obligingly and at Ruth's suggestion bathed himself in the rusty tin bath that hung outside the wash house door

189

of number one and put on a pair of new moleskin trousers and a flannel shirt that had belonged to Bob. His guernsey had been washed and hung over the kitchen chair for three days to dry. Unfortunately, it had also absorbed the distinctive odours of the Kesgrave household. Ginny wore her best green dress under her black mourning coat and carried an ivory prayer book that her mother had given her. Ruth of course, was still in deepest black. By contrast, Annie Kesgrave had decked herself in lilac georgette, slightly old-fashioned in style and not quite up to the task of covering her ample figure. Will's sister Gladys acted as bridesmaid, wearing a sleeveless pale pink dress that her mother had chosen despite the wintry weather and which didn't suit her pasty colouring. The only other guest was Granny Crabtree, who had never been known to go outside her door wearing anything other than a navy blue serge costume with a skirt that reached down nearly to her ankles and almost obscured her long buttoned boots, a snowy white high-necked blouse and a shapeless felt hat. The verger, of course was in attendance and he was none too pleased at having to open the church at such an ungodly hour on the day before Christmas. The church was freezing, in spite of the tortoise stoves having already been lit in preparation for the Christmas services.

It took less than twenty minutes to tie two people who didn't even like each other very much irrevocably together. Afterwards, with the exception of the rector and the verger, they all went back to number four Quay Yard to drink sherry and eat fruit cake.

'I s'pose you ain't got a drop o' gin, dearie?' Annie Kesgrave asked Ruth hopefully, spreading herself comfortably on the couch.

'No. We only keep spirits for medicinal purposes,' Ruth answered, trying and only just failing to sound friendly. She had been watching and had seen that Annie Kesgrave had already downed four glasses of sherry.

'Thass what I want it for, dearie,' Annie said with a wink. 'Medissnal purpp . . . Never mind. I always keep a little with me in case I'm took bad.' She rummaged in the cracked black handbag she carried and fished out a small bottle. 'Ah, this'll keep me goin' for the time bein',' she took a swig from the bottle and wiped her mouth on the back of her hand. Then she leaned over to where Ginny was sitting. 'I've always liked you, Ginny gal, an' I'm glad to welcome you inta the Kesgrave fam'ly. Come here an' give your owd mum-in-law a kiss.' She held out her arms.

Reluctantly, Ginny went over and planted a brief kiss on Annie's flabby cheek.

'Thass right. Now, you listen ter me.' Annie wagged an unsteady finger at her. 'There'll ollwus be a welcome at number one for you an' don't you forget it. We ollwus hev shrimps for tea of a Sunday night.' She tapped the side of her nose. 'I manage to keep enough back for us when I pick 'em for the cannin' factory. That'd be nice if you an Will was to make a reg'lar thing of comin' to tea on Sundays.' She smiled encouragingly.

Ginny managed to stretch her lips in return. 'We'll have to see, Mrs Kes . . . '

'Mum. I'm Mum to you now,' Annie said with a complacent shrug of her shoulders.

'We'll have to see . . . Mum,' Ginny said, the word nearly choking her.

She was thankful when the sherry and cake were all gone and there was no reason for Annie and Gladys to stay any longer, but she felt a stab of pity for Gladys, a rather inadequate figure in her pathetic pink dress, helping her mother in her unsteady progress down the yard.

Granny Crabtree had sat in the corner watching and saying nothing, eating a few crumbs of cake and taking only a tiny sip of sherry. When Will had taken himself down on to the quay for a quiet smoke — he had already come up against the first of his mother-in-law's rules, no smoking in the house — and Ruth was gathering up the glasses and plates, Granny beckoned Ginny over to sit beside her.

'I can see as far through a brick wall as most people, child,' she said quietly, 'and I can see that this marriage is not altogether to your liking.'

Ginny pressed her lips together, on the verge of tears, shaking her head.

The old lady put her gnarled hand over Ginny's as it lay in her lap. 'I'm afraid we don't always get what we'd like in this life, Ginny,' she said. 'The secret is to be strong inside. You're your father's daughter. Life was not always kind to him but he made the best of it and never lost his cheerful smile. Remember that, child.' She looked across to where Ruth, her mouth in a thin line, was washing the plates in the bowl on the table as if her life depended on it. 'Your mother can be a hard woman at times. She likes her own way. Just remember I only live next door and I don't gossip.' She reached for her stick. 'Well, I must be going,' she said in a louder voice. 'I can't sit here all day doing nothing. Thank you, Ruth. It's been very nice. I hope you'll always consider you've done the right thing by your daughter,' was her parting shot as she went out of the door.

Ruth frowned at the old lady's back. 'What does she mean by that, nosy old besom,' she said. She gave a shrug. 'Well, never mind. Get these things dried up and put away, Ginny. I want to get the chicken stuffed ready for dinner tomorrow. Do you think Will will come to church with us as it's Christmas?'

'I don't know. You'll have to ask him.'

Will stayed on the quay until it was dinner time, then he went back and ate roast pork and apple sauce with Ginny and her mother.

'Cor, this is good. We never hev meals like this at 'ome,' he said rubbing his stomach appreciatively. 'Oh, 'course, this is 'ome now, ain't it. I keep forgettin'.' He turned to Ginny. 'I thought we might take a walk together, you an' me, this ar'ternoon, seein' as we shan't hev a lot o' time to ourselves.' He grinned at Ruth. 'Not that I object to livin' with me mother-in-law, Ruthy, don't think that. I don't object at all.'

'Well, I object to being called Ruthy,' Ruth said sharply.

'Do you? I'll try and remember that.' He turned to Ginny. 'Well, are you ready, wife?'

Ginny glanced at her mother. 'I'd better help with the washing-up . . . '

Ruth shook her head. 'It's all right. I'll do it.'

'Thass it. Ruthy'll do it.' He grinned and clapped his hand over his mouth. 'Oops, sorry. Shouldn't hev said that.'

Buttoned up in her thick black coat and with her hat pulled down over her ears, Ginny walked beside Will along East Street, through the passage known as Grant's Watch, along the Folly and out on to the sea wall, carefully averting her eyes as they passed *Aurora*.

As they walked Will talked. He talked about what he was going to do with *Emily May*, the improvements he intended to make, the fishing grounds he was going to explore, the bumper catches he would bring home and the fabulous prices he would get for them.

Ginny listened with half an ear, too busy with her own thoughts to pay much attention to what he was saying. She watched the seagulls padding about in the mud or wheeling and screaming in the air above it, wondering what Nathan would say when he found out the predicament their afternoon of love had landed her in. Would he be jealous when he discovered she was married to Will Kesgrave? She closed her eyes briefly. Heaven knew, he needn't be; there was no love lost between her and Will, even though he was now her husband. Then she realised. Nathan would never know because he wouldn't come back to Wyford, not now he was married to Isobel. A feeling of sheer desolation swept over her at the thought that she would probably never see or speak to him again.

' . . . an' you don't need to worry, I shan't treat Roger's child no different to me own, when they come along. Kids is all the same to me.' Ginny dragged her thoughts back to what Will was saying. Roger's child? What was he talking about? Suddenly, she remembered that he assumed the baby belonged to the man she had been engaged to and her hand automatically moved to protect Nathan's baby lying under her heart.

'That's very generous of you, Will,' she said quietly.

He took her free hand. 'I reckon you an' me can rub along together all right if we set our minds to it, Ginny,' he said.

'Not if you come home drunk every night,' she warned.

'No,' she could hear the doubt in his voice. 'But you wouldn't grudge a man a pint or two in the Rose an' Crown after a hard day's work, now would you?'

'A pint or two, no. A gallon or more, yes.' She looked up at him, because although she was above average height he was nearly a head taller, 'You thought a lot of my dad, didn't you, Will?'

'Aye. I did. I still feel bad about him dyin' the way he did. Thass why I was keen to look after his smack for him. I thought it was the least I could do.'

'Well, you could do something more. You could stop drinking altogether. Sign the pledge.'

He thought about it, kicking a stone along the icy ground as he walked along, then he shook his head. 'I ain't quite ready for that yet, Ginny. I like me beer too much. But I'll cut down, that I will.' He grinned at her. 'An' I shan't go to the pub tonight. They won't expect me. Not on me weddin' night. I gotta keep meself . . . well, you know . . . ' he gave her a knowing wink.

She knew all right and the knowledge gave her no pleasure, especially as she knew that her mother would be lying in the next room, separated from them only by a thin wall and able — indeed forced to — listen to every squeak of the bed springs.

But when it came to it, Will was no Clarke Gable or Charles Laughton, as she had seen them playing out tender love scenes at the pictures. He took what he wanted and the whole thing was over and he had rolled away before she had time to worry about whether or not her mother could hear what was going on.

On Boxing Day Will announced that he was going to make his first trip in *Emily May*. It was a bitterly cold day and there was a fresh north-easterly wind blowing.

'I think you'd be unwise to go today, Will,' Ruth said. 'There'll be snow before nightfall.'

'Nah. Thass not cold enough for snow, Ruthy,' Will argued.

Ruth winced at his deliberate use of her name and went over to tap Bob's barometer, hanging at the bottom of the stairs. 'The glass is dropping fast, I tell you the wind will get up and there'll be snow before nightfall,' she insisted.

'Well, I shall go jest the same. I'll stand to get a better catch if there ain't so many boats out there. Ammy Bartlett and Jim Crow said in the Rose the other night that they're ready whenever I say the word.'

Ruth put her hands on the table and leaned towards him. 'I say you shouldn't go. It's not safe,' she said. '*Emily May* belongs to me and I don't want her taken out today.'

''Course thass safe. An' I shan't do nothin' daft with the smack. I'll hev two experienced men with me. And I ain't a fool, meself.' He collected up his sea boots and oilskins. 'We shall be back afore the New Year.'

Ruth swung round to where Ginny sat by the fire, roasting chestnuts. 'Say something, girl. Persuade him not to go. He's your husband,' she said.

Ginny shrugged. 'He'll please himself whatever I say,' she said without much interest. In truth, she hoped he would go, then she would have her bed to herself again, without his brief, but none-the-less unwelcome attentions.

As Will made his way to the smack and made her ready to sail he realised that Ruth had been right. The wind was rising and snow clouds were gathering, black and ominous on the horizon.

'Think we should give it best, Will, boy?' Ammy asked, ramming his souwester back on to his head as he scanned the skyline. 'No sense askin' for trouble.'

But Will was not going to admit that his mother-in-law had been right and he'd been wrong. 'That'll pass over,' he said optimistically. 'We'll hev a good breeze to take us out to the Wallet.'

Three days later *Emily May* returned to her berth. It was a calm day and the sun glinted on the remaining snow, but *Emily May* was a little the worse for wear. One spar was broken and a sail had been ripped by the falling timber, the result of trying to fish in the teeth of a gale. Will came in soaked to the skin and frozen to the marrow.

'Well, I hope the catch was big enough to pay for the damage,' Ruth said grimly when she heard.

'We never caught nothin',' Will admitted. 'That was too bad out there.'

'I told you it would be. Perhaps in future you'll listen to what I say, Will Kesgrave.'

'I ain't bein' dictated to by no woman.' His voice was surly.

'While you work *my* smack and live under *my* roof you'll do as I say.' She slapped a plate of mutton stew down on the table. 'Now, get out of those wet things and eat this.'

When Ginny returned from work Will was eating the meal Ruth had cooked for him wearing his late father-in-law's best trousers and shirt. The atmosphere was icy. As soon as the Rose and Crown opened he went out and got drunk.

'You see what you've condemned me to?' Ginny said to her mother as she got ready for work the next morning while her husband snored his hangover off on the couch, having been too drunk to find his way up the stairs when he came in.

Ruth looked at him in disgust. 'Well, he won't do it again because he won't have the money.'

'Then he'll borrow from his mates. Or get it on the slate.' She slumped down on her chair. 'God, why did you make me marry him?'

'To give your child a name. Just remember you brought it on yourself. If you hadn't acted like a trollop there wouldn't have been the need.' Ruth pushed a cup of tea over to her. 'You'd better get a move on or you'll be late. We can't afford for you to lose your job, not now I've got the expense of getting the smack repaired.' She sat down in what used to be Bob's chair. 'I'll have to see Billy Barr about getting the sail patched and your dad always used to get Clarence Kidby to do the woodwork on the boat so he'll mend the spar. Goodness knows how much it'll cost.' She glanced over at Will, still sprawled on the sofa. 'That smack was supposed to make us money, not cost us,' she said viciously.

'Then you should have sold it, like you intended to in the first place,' Ginny said, entirely without sympathy. She took her coat from its hook on the back of the door, rammed her hat on and left for work without so much as a glance at her snoring husband.

13

Nathan Bellamy spent Christmas with his wife Isobel in the flat her father had bought for them as a wedding present. It would have been a pleasant flat, two floors of a tall Georgian house overlooking a quiet, tree-lined London square, if Isobel hadn't insisted on furnishing it in the latest Art Deco style, a style which clashed badly with the tall, elegant rooms and the ornate plasterwork on the ceilings. Nathan had quickly come to realise that although Isobel had expensive tastes she had no real 'taste'.

In the days before Christmas he spent most of his time at his studio, only five minutes' walk from the flat, putting the finishing touches to the painting of *Aurora* he intended to give Sir Titus, his father-in-law, for Christmas. His painting style had changed since his marriage; instead of his former meticulous execution of the smallest detail he was now using big, bold brushstrokes that showed a savage intensity, a disregard for detail in favour of a broader, impressionistic canvas. This was the way he painted now, the way he unconsciously vented his frustration and misery at the turn his life had taken.

Yet he told himself he was not altogether unhappy. The perpetual ache of love he carried around for Ginny, the terrible guilt at the way he had been forced to let her down, was a hair shirt he wore willingly. He deserved to suffer for the way he had treated her; he only hoped and prayed that she would find it in her heart to forgive him without bitterness and go on to find happiness with someone else. Someone else. The thought of that was like someone twisting a knife in his gut.

Two things made his life bearable. One was his painting. Once again he could paint all day, losing himself in dark, sombre storm scenes or bleak, empty landscapes, often with a lonely figure in the distance. And with his new, aggressive style his paintings were beginning to sell, for quite high prices too, which amazed him. And he wasn't selling simply to Isobel's friends, either. He was beginning to make quite a name for himself in the art world.

The other thing was the thought of the coming child. He looked forward to the birth of his son — it was always a son; to taking him by the hand as he grew old enough and walking with him in the park or taking him to the zoo; to buying him his first paint box

. . . teaching him to paint . . . And perhaps by the time he was old enough it wouldn't be too painful to take him to Wyford and show him his father's old childhood haunts.

These were the things that sustained him as he tried to meet the sometimes quite unreasonable demands of his spoilt and pampered wife. He found it increasingly hard to love her when he didn't even like her very much.

Her father came to spend Christmas Day with them and share the evening meal, turkey with all the trimmings followed by Christmas pudding, that Ethel, their maid, would have given up the best part of the day to prepare and cook for them. Ethel and her husband, who acted as chauffeur and general handyman, lived in the basement flat and therefore were expected to be on duty at any time of the day or night that Isobel decreed.

Nathan had suggested giving Ethel the day off as it was Christmas but Isobel wouldn't hear of it.

'Who's going to cook the turkey, if Ethel isn't here, darling?' she asked, raising one eyebrow in the quirky way he used to find attractive but didn't any more.

'Can't you do it? I'm sure we could manage between us. After all, it's Christmas, it's not fair to ask Ethel to work,' Nathan said.

'Don't be silly, darling. I wouldn't have the least idea how to cook a turkey. And anyway, Ethel doesn't mind. She expects to cook for us. She's quite happy to do it. That's what servants are for, darling. To serve.'

'In that case. If you think it's all right for Ethel to work on Christmas Day you won't mind if I spend a few hours at the studio, will you. The painting I'm on at the moment . . . '

'Oh, darling, you're not going to leave me. Not on Christmas Day,' she pouted.

'Only for an hour or two. You'll be going to church with your father this morning, anyway.'

'I thought you'd be coming too.'

'No.' He smiled at her. 'I have to go to the studio to get your Christmas present.'

'Oh, well, in that case . . . ' She wound her arms round his neck. 'You'll be back for lunch. Two o'clock sharp. It's cold collation because we're eating the turkey this evening.'

'I'll be back.' He planted a kiss on the tip of her nose. 'Be good.'

'Of course I'll be good, darling. I'm going to church.'

Nathan escaped to his studio and stood for

a long time staring out over the London roof-tops, thinking about Wyford, the ever-changing yet always constant river, the big yachts in their winter covers, the fishing smacks with their red sails, the wind rustling the tall grasses on the marshes, the wide skies where clouds scudded, chasing each other and merging together in ever-changing patterns. He had refused his mother's invitation to spend Christmas at home, afraid that if he went back to the village he would never tear himself away from it again.

And not only the village.

He left the window and went over to the corner where a heap of canvasses were stacked against the wall. From the very back, where it was carefully hidden from prying eyes, he took out a half-painted portrait of a woman and stood it on his easel.

It was Ginny. Painted entirely from memory, she was wearing her green dress and her hair was loose, tumbling over her shoulders in a thick, chestnut wave, with curly tendrils escaping across her cheek as if in a gentle breeze. Even now, only half finished, the likeness was striking, the tawny brown eyes, the straight nose, the clear complexion just lightly spattered with freckles, the mouth unsmiling, lips slightly parted. He had had trouble with the mouth, he had wanted to make her smile but somehow he couldn't get it right and so she looked out at him with a serious, slightly wistful expression that twisted his heart.

He had been secretly working on the portrait for several weeks, in fact, ever since his marriage to Isobel. Some days he couldn't face it, his sense of loss was too great; other days he couldn't wait to work on it. What he would do with it when it was finished he had no idea; maybe it would never be finished to his satisfaction. Two things were certain: it would never be sold and he would never let Isobel see it.

He worked on the portrait until nearly two o'clock, then with a whispered, 'Happy Christmas, Ginny,' he put it back in its hiding place and went back to the flat, carrying the picture for Sir Titus, Isobel's present safely in his pocket.

After the 'cold collation', a selection of cold meats, pork pies and various cheeses that Ethel had prepared, the three of them went into the blue and gold drawing room, with its huge white leather armchairs and settees, spindly light oak occasional tables and spiky lampshades and ornaments, to open presents in front of the huge fire Ethel's husband had lit earlier.

Sir Titus was delighted with the picture

Nathan had painted for him and in return gave Nathan a gold cigarette case. It said much for the old man that he had never noticed that his son-in-law rarely smoked.

Nathan then gave Isobel her present, a long, double strand amber necklace with matching earrings that hung almost to her shoulders, bought from the proceeds of the sale of one of his smaller pictures.

She made suitable noises although he could see she was disappointed. What on earth did the woman want? She'd got practically everything else money could buy. 'They're beautiful, darling. Just what I wanted,' she said, blowing him a cool kiss across the room.

'You'll have to wait a little while for my present to you, Bella,' Sir Titus said mysteriously.

She frowned. 'Why? Why can't I have it now?'

He smiled indulgently. 'Because it's a summer present. A cruise round the world to celebrate the birth of my grandson.'

'That'll be nice,' she said lightly. 'Only it won't be to celebrate the birth of your grandson because there isn't going to be one.'

Both men stared at her in disbelief for several seconds while she rummaged in her handbag for a cigarette, lit it and picked a speck of tobacco off her tongue.

Nathan found his voice first. 'What do you mean, there isn't going to be one? You're pregnant. You said . . . '

'No, I'm not, darling. I made a mistake.' She gave him a brittle smile.

Nathan frowned. 'How can you have made a mistake? You told me you'd been to see your doctor.' He was out of his depth. He didn't understand the workings of women's bodies, it was not something that was ever discussed in his own family and men's talk was only of the inconvenience to their needs at certain times of the month.

'I did go to see my doctor. But not about that.' She stubbed out her half-smoked cigarette and fished for another one. 'I just went for a routine check-up.'

Nathan stood up, towering over her. 'Are you telling me you knew perfectly well you were not pregnant when we married?' he asked, his voice dangerously low.

She looked up at him and gave a nervous little laugh. 'No. I really thought . . . well, I thought there was a chance that I might be.' She shrugged. 'I have terrible trouble keeping track of dates, you ought to know that.'

Silence hung between them for several minutes. Suddenly, in the distance the front door banged as Sir Titus left the house. Neither of them had even noticed that he had got up and left the room.

Nathan began to pace up and down, his face white with suppressed rage. After a minute he stopped and turned to face her. 'I married you because you told me you were to have our child, and I knew I had to do the decent thing,' he said furiously. 'It never occurred to me in a million years that you might be lying. Not over a thing like that.' He clenched his teeth. 'My God, Isobel, how could you do such a thing?'

She stood up now, lifting her chin, clenching and unclenching her fists as she spoke. 'I did it because you were going to leave me and go back to that — that village trollop. You should know by now, Nathan, I don't play second fiddle to *anybody*, and certainly not to some rustic village maiden.' She turned away, her eyes filling with tears. 'I also happen to be in love with you, you great stupid fool.'

'Well, I must say you've got a bloody funny way of showing it.' He watched her quite dispassionately. After what she had done to him he was reluctant to believe anything she said or did. 'And I'll thank you not to call Ginny a trollop.'

She turned to him and held out her arms, large tears rolling down her cheeks. 'We've had some good times together, Nathan. And we will again. I know we will. Maybe I *will* have a baby. One day. Who knows? We've plenty of time. The doctor did once say an operation might . . . '

'You lied to me,' he interrupted coldly. 'You trapped me into marrying you.'

She hung her head. 'I know. I'm sorry, darling. Really sorry. But we can make it work. I know we can.' She saw his wooden expression and her voice trailed off. 'You can't leave me . . . Not after what Daddy's done for you . . . '

He shook his head. 'No, Isobel, I won't leave you. I'll honour my debt,' he said quietly. He turned away. 'I'll go and tell Ethel she can have the rest of the day off. I don't think any of us are in the mood for festivities tonight.' He reached the door and turned, with his hand on the door knob. 'And I shall sleep in the spare room. Quite frankly, Isobel, I don't think I want to touch you ever again.' He went out and closed the door quietly behind him. It was far more ominous than if he had slammed it.

Isobel sank down on the sofa again and lit another cigarette from the stub of the last one. She blew a smoke ring and watched it change shape and dissipate into the air. She hadn't expected him to take it quite so badly and she realised it was going to take a great deal of strategy to get him back into her bed. But she was confident that she would manage it. In time.

* * *

With the dawn of the year 1936 Ginny made a resolution. There was no looking back. Things were as they were and it was up to her to make the best of them. Nathan had gone out of her life and would not be coming back, but she had the memory of his love and the precious gift of his child growing under her heart and this she treasured.

She tried to be optimistic. Will was not a bad man when he was sober. He kept himself clean and well-shaven, except when he was at sea when a beard was more practical. His table manners had improved, too. He soon learned, under Ruth's eagle eye, that it was not acceptable to shovel food into his mouth or lick his knife.

And he was hard-working, nobody could deny that. Over the course of the winter he made many fishing trips, out in all weathers, his hands chapped and chilblained, with deep, painful cracks that never healed in spite of the ointment that Ginny rubbed into them.

But somehow he never quite managed to get things right. If he made a good haul then he stayed at the fishing grounds too long, returning home behind all the other boats so that there was no market left for his sprats and they had to be fetched in tumbrels and spread on the land as fertiliser. Or he chose to fish in the wrong place and caught nothing. Another time a squall blew up unexpectedly and his nets snagged as he was trying to reel them in. There was always something that prevented him making the fortune he had predicted. Ruth blamed him for not listening to her advice and he told her to keep her nose out of something she knew nothing about. Tempers often ran high and Will would slam out of the house and seek refuge in the Rose and Crown, putting his drinks on the slate when he had no money, stumbling up the stairs late at night to subject Ginny to his rough attentions if he was not too drunk.

'He's as headstrong as an ox,' Ruth complained, counting out the money for yet another repair to the smack. 'He never listens to what I tell him. He'll be the ruin of us before he's finished. And he's always in the Rose and Crown when he's home. You need to speak to him, my girl.'

Ginny sat in the elbow chair by the fire, watching her mother. She had continued to work at Stacey's until February, when she could hide the fact that she was pregnant under her overall no longer, paying off Will's debts at the Rose and Crown out of her wages.

She got up from her chair. 'If you ask me, he's got enough trouble with one woman nagging at him all the time without me joining in, Mother. You never stop picking on him when he's at home.'

'Well, he's a lazy . . . '

Ginny rounded on her. 'Will is *not* lazy. You can level a good many complaints at him but not that. He works hard.' She sighed. 'It's just that he never gets things quite right.'

'Perhaps he'd do a bit better if his head wasn't addled with drink most of the time.' Ruth scooped the few coppers left and dropped them with a clatter into the tin where she kept them and replaced the tin on top of the dresser.

'He goes there to get out of the way of your tongue. You're always moaning at him about something. If it isn't one thing it's another.' Ginny glared at her mother. 'You might just remember that it was *you* who arranged this marriage, *you* who thought Will would be a suitable husband for me. Now, I'm having to make the best of it, and God knows, I'm trying, I'm trying very hard, whereas you do nothing but carp and complain about him. Well, if he isn't proving to be such a grateful lap dog as you'd hoped, jumping through all the hoops you prepared for him, that shows he's at least got a bit of spirit and a mind of his own. I admire him for that, if nothing else.'

Ruth sat down again with a bump, her jaw dropping. 'I never thought I'd hear you defend him. You always said you didn't even like him.'

'Liking doesn't come into it. He's my husband, thanks to you. And everybody's got their good points if you look hard enough to find them. He's not all bad.'

But when he stumbled home drunk yet again that night and woke her with his fumbling attentions she remembered those words and found herself counting the weeks to the yachting season when, with any luck, he would be away for months on end. She could hardly wait.

14

1936 began on a sombre note with the death of King George V at the end of January. Although he had been much loved and respected there were of course those who welcomed the prospect of a new, young King. Arguments raged among those Wyford men who, with no work and little prospect of finding any, congregated each day on the quay. Some were confident that with the advent of a new monarch the country's fortunes would somehow be lifted and the depression and consequent unemployment that held the country in thrall would miraculously end.

Others were less optimistic. 'Don't see what he can do. King he may be, but sittin' in Buckingham Palace bein' waited on hand an' foot, what do he know about people like us an' what we're goin' through? His kids ain't got empty bellies, nor ever likely to hev,' Harry Jones, a man of thirty, who looked sixty, said bitterly.

'He ain't got kids. He ain't married,' Percy Millet pointed out.

'Lucky bugger,' said Sid Oliphant, father of

the family who lived next to the Kesgraves in Quay Yard. 'He ain't got a wife at home goin' on at him all the time to get work when there ain't none to be had.' He held out his hands, soft and uncalloused through lack of handling the tools of his trade. 'Look at them, smooth as a baby's bum. I'm a damn good riveter, although I say it as shouldn't. That ain't right I should hev to waste my time standin' on street corners.'

The others nodded. 'Take away a man's right to work an' you take away his dignity,' they agreed, spitting over the edge of the quay in unison.

An older man, who had been silent up till now, rubbed his chin. 'There might be work sooner than you think,' he said darkly. 'I don't like the sound of what's goin' on in Germany. This Herr Hitler fella is gettin' too big for his boots, if you ask me. You mark my words, there'll be trouble there afore long. Power crazy, thass what he is, him an' his Nazi Party.' (He pronounced it Narzy.)

'Power crazy he may be, but there ain't no unemployment over there,' Sid said.

'P'raps we could do with him over here, then,' Harry said. 'Thass time suthin' happened to get us back to work. I'm fed up with Owd Brookie at the Labour Exchange wantin' to know the ins and outs of a duck's

217

arse afore he'll cough up a few pence dole money. 'Hevn't you gotta pianner you can sell?'' he mimicked Mr Brook's voice, adding gloomily, 'Where does he think I'd get a bloody pianner from?'

'He told Jack Marshall to go and sell rock on Clacton sea front,' Percy said. 'I wonder Jack didn't knock him down. He's a fiery bugger at the best o' times.'

'I still say this Hitler fella's trouble,' the older man said. 'I don't like him an' I don't like what he stands for.'

And so it went on, the same conversation, the same arguments, day after day, week after week among these men who had nothing better to do. Men who were skilled tradesmen, denied the opportunity to work because all the local ironworks and shipyards apart from a couple that dealt exclusively with the needs of the big timber-built yachts had all closed and only the lucky ones had found employment further afield.

Will Kesgrave was one of the lucky few in work. Fishing in the North Sea in the middle of winter was cold, dangerous and back-breaking, and with the fickleness of wind and tide profits were never guaranteed, but it was work.

At twelve o'clock one frosty morning in March he left *Emily May*, where he had been cleaning down the decks, and made for the bar of the Rose and Crown where he could slake his thirst and at the same time warm his bones by the fire.

'Thass all right for Will Kesgrave,' Harry Jones said, hunching his shoulders against the east wind and enviously watching him disappear through the door. 'He's always got money for a pint since he took over Bob Appleyard's smack. He's got a cushy little number there, if you ask me.'

Sid Oliphant shook his head sagely. 'Thass as maybe. But would you wanta be ruled by Mrs Appleyard? That woman's got a face as 'ud turn the milk sour and a tongue to match. I don't reckon he hev it all honey in that house, not by any means, even though he is married to Bob's pretty little gal. Bob's wife always did rule the roost in that house even when he was alive and thass a damn sight worse now she's a widder.'

'I reckon I could put up with it. I reckon I could put up with a lot to hev money for a pint to jingle in me pocket, like Will's got.' Harry turned his pockets inside out to show how empty they were.

'Come off it. You had plenty o' money. Thass all fell out through that hole in your pocket,' the others teased him.

Angrily, Harry stuffed his pockets back

where they belonged. He wasn't in the mood to joke.

'Anyway, you wouldn't jingle it for long if you had it. You'd tip it down your neck,' one of the others laughed.

'Too bloody true, I would,' he said with feeling, looking longingly towards the door of the bar.

As if he'd heard their words Will poked his head out of the door. 'Wanta pint, boys?' he asked, jerking his head towards the bar.

'Yeah, I'll hev a double whisky. Just wait a sec while I pawn me watch,' Percy said with more than a trace of sarcasm.

'No, I mean it. Come on in. Thass my round, chaps. Name your poison,' Will said beckoning them. 'We got a good haul this last trip so I'm in funds.'

The four men didn't need asking twice, the prospect of the warm bar almost as attractive as the promise of a drink.

But Will's funds didn't last long between five men plus a few more who had slipped in unnoticed and when the landlord refused to put any more on the slate they all left and reeled home, several of them wracked with guilt to think they had drink inside them while their children were still hungry.

Will was wracked with guilt, too. He paced the quay for a long time before he plucked up the courage to go home and tell his wife he'd drunk all his profit and more beside and to beg her for the means to pay off his debts at the Rose and Crown.

He waited until they were in bed that night.

Ginny knew there was something on his mind because he hadn't made any attempt to touch her. She waited, saying nothing. She didn't have to wait long.

'I stood some of the boys a few drinks in the Rose,' he whispered in the darkness. 'Poor buggers, they never get the taste o' beer, these days, livin' on the dole. Tell the truth, I felt a bit guilty, goin' for a drink when they couldn't.'

'You could have stayed away from the pub. Then you wouldn't have any cause to feel guilty,' Ginny replied unhelpfully.

'Oh, surely you don't grudge a man a pinta beer when he's bin at sea for days on end,' he said, exasperated.

'Keep your voice down. Remember Mum's only the other side of the wall.'

'I ain't likely to forget that, am I! The thing is . . . '

'The thing is the landlord at the Rose and Crown won't let you put any more on the slate till you've paid off what you owe so you've come to me like you always do. How much?'

'Only half a crown.'

'Only half a crown!' Ginny tried to smother her voice under the sheet. 'And where do you think I'm going to get half a crown from? I'm not earning any money. I had to finish working at Stacey's at the end of February, you might remember. I'd have worked longer but my overall was getting tight and Mr Stacey didn't think people would like it if they could see I was expecting. That means I don't get wages now.'

'Hevn't you got any saved up?' he asked hopefully.

'How do you think I could save anything? All my spare money goes to pay off your debts. If it isn't drink it's betting on horses that always come in last. You can't even get that right. I think you always choose horses with wooden legs.' She turned over and thumped her pillow.

'What am I gonna do, Ginny?' he asked on a plaintive note.

She sat up. 'You'll have to stay away from the Rose and Crown for a start. And you'll have to go out and fish some more. That's what you'll have to do.'

'Thass gettin' near the end of the season. There ain't a lot about.'

'Then get yourself a berth on one of the yachts. See if they'll take you back on *Aurora*.

They'll be fitting her out shortly. They'll need men for that.' She threw herself back on to her pillow. 'Now go to sleep.'

He was quiet for some time, then he said, 'That wouldn't be so bad if we was in our own place, Ginny. I'm sure we could make a go of things if we was on our own. But your mother's always moanin' at me, always watching what we do. Even here we hev to be quiet so we don't disturb her.' He sighed. 'I only go to the pub to get out of her way.'

'You only go to the pub because that's what you've always done,' Ginny said tartly. But there was truth in his words and she knew it. 'We will get our own place, Will. When we can afford it,' she said, her voice more gentle.

'God knows when that'll be,' he said gloomily.

'When you stop drinking and gambling and start to save a bit.'

'I told you. I only go to get out of *her* way.'

It was a vicious circle.

★   ★   ★

'Why don't you let me do that?' Ginny asked as she watched her mother making pastry one morning. She was fed up with only being allotted the menial tasks.

Ruth stopped, her rolling pin poised and

turned to look at her. 'But you've never made pastry,' she said in surprise.

'Only because you've never given me the chance. I've watched you enough times to know how it's done. And just because I'm not working at Stacey's now doesn't mean I want to sit and twiddle my thumbs all day.'

'That's true.' Ruth sat down, the rolling pin still in her hand, chewing her lip. After a few minutes she nodded thoughtfully. 'Mrs Bellamy has hinted once or twice in that smug way of hers that some of the other yacht captains' wives are jealous of the fact that I bake for her and not them. I've never taken her up on it because I've had more than enough to do working for her. But I reckon I'd only have to say the word and I could be cooking for several of them. And if I taught you . . . between us we might manage it. Goodness knows we could do with the money. That good-for-nothing man of yours . . . '

'Don't start that again, Mother. Remember it's your fault . . . '

'Well, he's slipped back into his old ways now he hasn't got your dad to answer to. He's so headstrong he won't listen to advice and we've had to have so many repairs to the smack that it's beginning to eat into the money I've got saved towards a house in The Avenue, or Belle Vue Road now. We'll never move out of this place at the rate we're going.'

'I don't know that I want to move out of this place,' Ginny said perversely. 'It's where I've always lived, where Dad lived, too.'

'We could do better. There are some nice houses at the top of the village. It's what I've always wanted.'

'Well, you'll have to want for a bit longer, won't you. We can't afford to move.' Ginny got to her feet. 'Now, what are we making?' she asked, changing the subject. 'It must be apple pies. I've peeled enough apples to feed an army this morning.'

Their little spat over, they spent a surprisingly companionable morning together and over the next few days Ruth was surprised — and, if she was totally honest, a little jealous — at the lightness of her daughter's pastry and the way her cakes rose in the oven.

'You're a born cook,' she remarked, as a tray of fairy cakes with peaks like tiny mountains emerged from the oven. 'I must have taught you well.'

Ginny smiled at her mother's determination to take most of the credit. 'I'm enjoying myself. It's better than working behind the counter at Stacey's. I ought to have started before. We could open a shop . . . '

'Just hold on. You have to walk before you

can run. It takes more than a few fairy cakes and the odd apple pie to run a shop, my girl.'

'Well, it's a start, anyway.' Ginny sat down, rubbing her side. 'Tiring, enough.'

'Yes. Don't get too ambitious. You'll have your hands full with the baby in a few months, remember.' As she spoke she was carefully placing cakes in the big, lined basket she used to transport the things she had baked to Mrs Bellamy's.

'Not till July. It's only March now. There's plenty of time,' Ginny said with a yawn.

Ruth covered the basket with a cloth. 'I'll just take these up to the house and they'll be out of Will's way. If he gets his hands on them there'll be none left for Mrs Bellamy.'

Ginny didn't reply. She was tired of her mother's continual carping about Will. It was her fault the marriage had taken place; the last thing Ginny had wanted was to marry Will Kesgrave. But now they were married she was trying hard to make the best of things and she had found that Will was not a bad man at heart, he was just weak. All he needed to mend his ways was a bit of encouragement. Instead of which he got nothing but nagging and complaints from Ruth. The poor man could do nothing right in her eyes. It was no wonder he spent all his free time at the pub.

Ruth reached for her hat and coat. 'It's a

bit blustery out there,' she said, jabbing in a hat pin. 'I shan't be gone long.'

She picked up the basket and left the house. A minute later Ginny heard a thump, for all the world as if a sack of flour had been dropped in the yard, followed by a cry of pain.

She hurried outside and found her mother half sitting, half lying in the yard, her foot twisted under her, cakes strewn over the yard. She went to help her up but Ruth waved her away.

'No, no, you'll do the baby a mischief. Just give me a minute and I'll manage.' She sat massaging her ankle. 'Pick those cakes up and see if they're all right. They shouldn't have taken any harm, I scrubbed the yard only this morning.'

'What did you do?' Ginny was at the tap, getting her a drink of water.

'I think I must have tripped over that lump of rope your husband left lying in the path.'

'I don't think it was that,' Ginny said, frowning. 'That rope is over near the wash house, nowhere near where you'd be walking. It looks to me as if you missed your step as you went up on to Anchor Hill.'

Ruth took a drink of water. 'Ah, that's better. Well, come on, get those cakes picked up.'

Sid Oliphant, in the wash house chopping up an old chair given to him for firewood by an old lady whose garden he looked after, had heard the noise of Ruth's fall and he came up the yard to see what was wrong. 'You'd better let me give you a hand, Missus,' he said. 'You'll never manage to get up on your own. Put your arm round my neck now. Thass right.' He put a brawny arm round her waist and helped her to her feet. 'Now, lean on me. I'll hev you indoors in no time.'

'I can't walk. I've twisted my ankle,' Ruth snapped, unhappy at being aided by the likes of Sid Oliphant.

'Well, lean on me an' hop,' he said. 'Thass it.' Half carrying her, he got her into the house and deposited her in the chair beside the fire.

'Thank you, Mr Oliphant,' Ginny said, because her mother seemed disinclined to show any gratitude. 'It was very kind of you to help.'

'I'm sure we'd have managed,' Ruth said ungraciously.

'Yes, I dessay you would,' Sid said cheerfully. 'Well, if thass all I'll bid you good day.'

'Perhaps you'd like these cakes to take home for the children,' Ginny said, putting three or four cakes on a plate. 'You can let us have the plate back any time.'

A warm smile spread across the man's face. 'Thass real good of you, Miss — I mean Missus. They'll be a real treat for the kids.'

After he had gone Ruth said, 'You shouldn't have done that. He'll always expect it.'

'Don't be silly, Mum, I was only showing a bit of gratitude for his help. You wouldn't have wanted to be left lying in the yard, would you? Anyway, the cakes had got a bit squashed when they rolled out of the basket so you couldn't have taken them to Mrs Bellamy.'

Ruth gave a shrug. 'We'd have managed.' She looked round. 'Where's the basket?'

'Here. I brought it in. It's all right. Nothing else got spoiled.'

'Let me look.' Ruth examined the contents of the basket. 'That's good. Well, you'll have to take them. Mrs Bellamy will be expecting them. I told her she'd have them by four this afternoon and it's a sure thing I can't take them.' She looked at her rapidly swelling ankle and wriggled her toes.

'I'll get a cold compress, that'll take the swelling down. You can wiggle your toes so I don't think anything's broken.' Ginny fetched a bowl of cold water and a cloth. 'There you are. Dip the cloth in. Keep it cold.'

Ruth waved her away. 'Never mind me. Get those pies up to Mrs Bellamy.' She leaned back in her chair and closed her eyes.

'I'll make you a cup of tea before I go,' Ginny said. 'There's not that much hurry and I could do with one, too.'

Half an hour later, she made her way to the Bellamy house in Anglesea Road.

15

Walking along the road to the Bellamy house, Ginny's thoughts turned, as they did far too often for her peace of mind, to Nathan. She hadn't replied to his letter and he had never written to her again. Not that she had expected him to, since he had told her it would be better if she forgot him altogether. As if she ever could! He should have known better than to even suggest such a thing. But perhaps it was this suggestion that had prompted the small niggling suspicion at the back of her mind that his letter had been nothing more than a sop to his conscience. A suspicion that had grown with the child inside her. For if he had loved her as she loved him there could be no question of forgetting. For either of them. Ever.

If he could speak of their relationship so lightly, if he intended to put her out of his mind, to forget her as easily as he seemed to think she could forget him, it could only mean one thing. He had never intended to marry her; never intended to leave Isobel. She kicked a stone savagely. To think that she had been such a fool as to believe him when he said he loved her. Worse than that, fool enough to give herself to him — throw herself at him if she was brutally honest. And it was no excuse to blame her behaviour on the fact that it happened on the day of her father's funeral, when she was in a highly charged emotional state and so desperately needing the comfort of a shoulder to cry on. The brutal truth was that she had made a terrible mistake. She had thought she knew Nathan Bellamy, thought she could trust him. But she had been dreadfully, horribly wrong and her mistake had cost her dear; in fact she would have to suffer for it for the rest of her life, shackled to Will Kesgrave.

She lifted her chin as she pushed open the gate of Captain Bellamy's house. Whatever happened, Mrs Bellamy must never know. She was the last person Ginny would admit her unhappiness to. She rapped on the knocker and waited. There was a porch with a seat on either side so if there was nobody at home the cakes could be left quite safely there in their covered basket. She was preparing to put it down when the door opened. She straightened up, ready with a bright smile, but to her consternation it was not Mrs Bellamy who stood there, it was Nathan.

For a split second Ginny thought she

would faint. Her heart was pounding, her mouth was dry and she could feel the colour leaving her face. But she was determined not to let him see the effect he had on her, so she held out the basket.

'My mother sent these cakes, Nathan,' she said, amazed at how cool and steady her voice sounded. 'She would have come herself . . . '

'Ginny!' His voice cut through her words. 'Oh, Ginny!'

She ignored it. 'She would have come herself but she fell and hurt her ankle. I think Mrs Bellamy will find everything there she asked for.' She turned to go.

'Wait. Ginny. Wait.' He looked at her and then at the basket in his hand. 'Don't you want to take your basket back?' he asked with a sudden flash of inspiration.

Reluctantly, she turned back. 'Oh, yes, please. I'll wait here while you empty it, if you don't mind.'

'I do mind, Ginny, what's come over you?' he said with a frown. 'Why don't you come in like you've always done?'

'Is Mrs Bellamy at home?' she asked, her voice still cool.

He ran his fingers distractedly through his hair in a gesture that was so familiar it tugged at her heart. 'No, as a matter of fact she isn't. I don't know where she is, to tell you the truth, because I've only just got home. I caught an earlier train than I was expecting to, that's probably why she's not back; I wasn't due till five.'

'Then it wouldn't be right for me to come in,' Ginny said primly.

'Oh, come on, Ginny, we're old friends!' he exploded.

'You're a married man,' she pointed out, then before he could answer, 'And I'm a married woman.'

He took a step back and his mouth dropped open. 'You? You're *married?*' he said incredulously.

'Why shouldn't I be?' she asked with a lift of her eyebrows.

He passed his hand across his brow. 'Oh, for goodness' sake, come in and sit down.' He caught her hand and almost dragged her into the house and through to the kitchen, the kitchen where in the past they had sat companionably drawing and painting for hours on end.

'Now tell me, Ginny, who is it?' he asked, sitting her down. 'Who are you married to? Has Roger Mayhew come back from Australia and swept you off your feet? Why didn't my mother tell me?'

'I don't suppose she thought it would be of any interest to you,' Ginny said, folding her hands in her lap. 'But if you really want to know, no, Roger Mayhew hasn't come back, as far as I know. I'm married to Will Kesgrave.'

'Kesgrave!' A look of pure disgust crossed his face. 'Oh, Ginny! What on earth possessed you to marry that . . . marry him?'

She stared down at her hands, lying in her lap. Suddenly, she felt unbearably hot and unthinkingly she unbuttoned her coat and let it fall open. 'He has his good points,' she said. 'He's hard-working.'

'When he's not drunk.' He suddenly caught sight of her thickened waistline. 'My God, he didn't waste any time in getting you pregnant, did he?'

'No, he didn't. Not any time at all,' she said quietly. 'But I hardly think you're in a position to make a judgement. I seem to remember your own wedding was arranged in rather a hurry.' She looked straight at him. 'When is Isobel's baby due?'

He ran his fingers through his hair again and then leaned his head on his elbow. 'Isobel isn't pregnant,' he muttered without looking at her.

'Ah. I see.' It gave her no pleasure to realise she had been right in her conjecture. She got to her feet.

His head shot up. 'What do you mean, 'Ah,

I see'? You don't bloody see at all.' His tone was belligerent.

'I see that you intended to marry Isobel all along. But of course it would sound better after all the things you'd said . . . ' she hesitated, ' . . . and done — to me if you told me she was pregnant. So you made out you had no choice.' Ginny stared out of the window as she spoke.

He stood up now and came round the table, towering over her. 'You really think that, Ginny?' he asked, his voice ominously quiet and she realised that for some reason she didn't understand he was having difficulty in keeping his temper in check.

She risked a glance up at him. 'What else do you expect me to think?'

He pushed her down into her chair again and slumped back in his own. 'Try this,' he said bitterly. 'After I left you I went back to London and began packing up my things. God, I was so happy! At last I'd plucked up the courage to escape from Isobel and come back to the girl I loved. When Isobel arrived I told her I was leaving, that I was coming back to Wyford to marry you.' He paused and chewed his top lip, trying to control himself. 'She was extremely nice about it, *too* nice I realise now. She said it was a pity I'd decided to leave, since she had intended to take me out to dinner that night and break the news that I was to be a father.' He shook his head. 'Oh, I can see now that she thought the pregnancy thing up on the spur of the moment; she would have done anything to stop me from leaving and coming back here. But I was too shocked and stupid to realise this at the time and I believed her, fool that I was.' He gave a great sigh. 'So I did what I considered the only decent thing and married her.'

'So what you told me in the letter was quite true,' Ginny said.

He looked surprised. 'Of course it was. I wouldn't lie to you, Ginny. Surely you know me better than that.' He paused for a minute, then his mouth twisted in a parody of a smile. 'I even tried to pretend I was happy, looking forward to the birth of my son, thinking of all the things I would do with him . . . trying not to think about how much I had hurt you . . . what might have been . . . ' His voice changed, became harsh. 'Then at Christmas the bitch announced that she wasn't and never had been pregnant.' He stared out of the window. 'I don't give a sod about her, but I would have liked a son,' he said sadly.

Ginny gave a ghost of a smile. 'Maybe you'll have one,' she said quietly.

He shook his head violently. 'No. Never. I

can't bear to go near her any more. Not after what she's done to me.' He got to his feet again and began pacing up and down the room. 'It's all such a bloody mess. There's me tied to that lying bitch and you . . . ' he spun round. 'Why in the name of all that's holy did you marry Will Kesgrave of all people, Ginny?' He sat down again with a thump. 'No, don't answer that, I've no right to ask you.' He put his head in his hands.

'I married Will Kesgrave because I needed a father for my child,' she said, her voice still quiet. She smiled at him, a real smile. Because she had been wrong. Nathan really did love her. At this moment nothing else mattered.

His head shot up and he looked from her face to her waistline and back, realisation dawning. 'You mean . . . ?'

She nodded, tears shining in her eyes. 'It's your baby, Nathan.'

He came round and pulled her gently to her feet, then held her close, stroking her hair tenderly. 'Oh, Ginny, my dearest love,' he whispered. 'We could have been so happy . . . '

She remained in the circle of his arms for a few precious minutes, then with a great effort took a step back. 'It's no use, Nathan. You have a wife and I have a husband. There's no future for us together,' she said sadly.

His hands slid down her arms to her hands when she pulled away from him and he was still holding them. 'I can't let you go, Ginny,' he said, his voice anguished. 'I love you and I know you love me. And there's the child. Our child . . . '

'Nobody knows it's your child except my mother and me,' she told him. 'Will thinks it belongs to Roger and I've let him go on thinking that. It's best that way.'

'Is he . . . ? He doesn't . . . ?' There were a hundred questions he wanted to ask.

'He's away a good part of the time,' she said with a shrug. 'We'd be all right together if it wasn't for my mother continually nagging him. Well, at least he probably wouldn't get drunk quite so often.'

'Oh, Ginny.' Nathan moved to take her in his arms again but she avoided him.

'Funny, really,' she went on as if he hadn't spoken. 'It was my mother that insisted I should be married. I didn't want to. I wouldn't have cared about the scandal. We'd have managed, the three of us. But she said she'd have me put away if I didn't agree to marry Will Kesgrave.'

He frowned. 'Put away?'

'Into Severalls, the lunatic asylum. That's apparently where loving parents put their daughters who 'get themselves into trouble'.'

'Good God. I didn't know that!'

'Neither did I. But it's true.' She gave a shrug. 'Well, it was either that or marry Will Kesgrave.'

'And he, of course, didn't need any persuading to marry the loveliest girl in the village,' Nathan said bitterly.

'No. Especially when my mother offered him Dad's smack to skipper as an incentive,' she replied, her mouth twisting.

He closed his eyes. 'Oh, God, it gets worse,' he groaned.

Ginny turned to pick up her basket. 'Being married to Will really isn't too bad,' she said, attempting to be cheerful. 'He isn't a bad man. He's weak, that's all.' She gave a little smile that tugged at Nathan's heart. 'I think he's quite fond of me, in his own way.'

Nathan took her arm. 'If he loves you one quarter as much as I do it would be enough,' he said, his voice rough. 'Ginny, I'm sorry, so sorry. I've messed up my life, well, that's my own fault, but to think I've made such a mess of yours, too . . . it's almost more than I can bear.' He picked up her hand and held it in both his.

She touched his cheek with her free hand. 'Knowing you love me is enough, Nathan.' She hesitated, her eyes filling with tears.

'Well, it isn't, of course it isn't, but it makes everything else bearable.'

He turned his face and planted a kiss in the palm of her hand just as a key turned in the lock of the front door. 'I love you, Ginny,' he whispered. 'Always remember that. And if there's ever anything . . . ' his voice changed, became louder as Mrs Bellamy could be heard coming down the hall. 'Thank your mother for the cakes, Ginny. I'm sure they'll be fine.'

'Oh, Nathan. Dear boy. I wasn't expecting you till five.' Ignoring Ginny, Mrs Bellamy went over and gave her son a delighted, perfumed kiss. 'It's wonderful to see you.'

'That's good, because you'll see plenty of me over the next few weeks. I'm here to help Dad oversee *Aurora*'s preparation for the sailing season,' he said with a grin, and Ginny knew he'd said it more for her benefit than his mother's. 'Now, if you'll excuse me, I'll just see Ginny to the door, Mother, then I'll go and unpack.'

'Oh, yes, of course. The cakes. Wait a minute, Ginny. I haven't paid for them,' Mrs Bellamy said, impatiently fishing for her purse. 'Oh, drat it, I haven't got any change.'

'Never mind, Mother. I'll take the money to Mrs Appleyard tomorrow. I'm sure she'll trust you till then,' Nathan said over his

241

shoulder as he followed Ginny along the hall. 'That gives me an excuse to see you tomorrow,' he whispered. When they reached the door he bent his head and gave her a lingering kiss, then looked down into her eyes. 'It's all my fault, Ginny. I've messed things up and I'm more sorry than I can say. But we both know we belong together,' he whispered. 'Just hang on to that. And one day I promise . . . '

She put a finger to his lips. 'No promises. Let's just say we'll always be friends,' she said softly.

★ ★ ★

Ginny walked home glowing inside with the knowledge that she had been wrong and that in spite of everything she was the one Nathan loved. But as she neared Quay Yard sanity prevailed as she realised that in spite of their love for each other there was no hope of them ever being together. Isobel would never let Nathan go, she was too jealous and possessive, and her own marriage to Will had been 'for better or for worse'. The words, 'till death us do part' rang ominously in her ears. Nevertheless, it would be a great comfort to have Nathan as a friend. Comfort? A voice inside her said. Or torture?

Will was at home, sprawling on the couch, when she arrived.

'He won't even lift a finger to make me a cup of tea, the lazy lout,' Ruth complained as soon as Ginny set foot inside the door.

'I've only jest this minute got in off the smack,' Will said, a picture of injured innocence. 'She might at least let me get me feet under the table afore she start naggin' at me.'

'I'll make you a cup of tea, Mother,' Ginny said with a sigh. 'But I made you one just before I left to take the cakes to Mrs Bellamy so you can't be needing another one already.'

'That was an hour and a half ago,' Ruth said petulantly. 'And did she pay you?'

'Was it? I hadn't realised. No, she hadn't got any change. Nathan said he'd bring it tomorrow.' Ginny busied herself at the stove to hide the blush which had spread over her face. She took a deep breath. Would it always be like that whenever Nathan's name was mentioned?

'Oh, he's home, is he?' Will said. 'Do you reckon he's got a berth on *Aurora*, too?'

'Sure to have,' Ruth said firmly. 'Sir Titus is his father-in-law. And what do you mean, *too*? Have you got yourself a berth on *Aurora*?'

'Aye. I hev an' all. We sail in a fortnight.'

243

'That's good, Will. You're lucky to be taken on. They only take the most skilled men on *Aurora*,' Ginny said, trying her best to sound encouraging.

'Yes, well, they knew Bob Appleyard thought a lot of me,' he said smugly.

'Then you'd better be sharp and lay the smack up for the summer,' Ruth said, shifting her foot on the stool Ginny had placed for it. 'We don't want it going to rack and ruin while you're away.'

'Can I jest drink me tea afore I go an' do it?' Will said, his voice heavy with sarcasm.

'Oh, don't take any notice of her, Will,' Ginny said with a sigh. 'You've got a fortnight. It doesn't have to be done tonight.'

'You encourage him in his idleness, my girl,' Ruth said. 'You'll regret it, you mark my words.'

'I regret a lot of things,' Ginny said under her breath as she gritted her teeth and got on with preparing the evening meal. When they had eaten it, with Ruth still carping at Will, about the way he held his knife, the way he slurped his tea, the way he gobbled his food, Will pushed back his chair and announced that he was off to the Rose and Crown.

'Well, don't you come home drunk. I'll need you to help me up to bed,' Ruth called as he went out of the door.

'He wouldn't go to the pub if you were to stop nagging him, Mother,' Ginny said, clearing the table. 'I don't know what's got into you.'

'I'll tell you what's got into me. I can see all the money I've saved towards a house in Belle Vue Road going into repairs on the smack, that's what's got into me. He won't listen to what I tell him. That's the trouble.'

Ginny put her hands flat on the table and leaned towards her mother. 'And why should he, Mother? *You're* not out in the North Sea, looking for the best fishing grounds. *You're* not there when the nets get fouled by an old wreck. *You're* not trying to haul nets in a gale with decks too slippery to keep your feet on. Have you seen Will's hands? Like lumps of raw beef. But he never complains, he just gets on with it. And then he has to put up with your nagging all the time he's home. It's no wonder he goes off to the Rose and Crown. For two pins I'd go with him!'

Ruth gripped the arms of her chair. 'I won't be spoken to like that, my girl,' she said fiercely. 'I'm going to bed.'

'You're not. You can't get up the stairs till Will gets back.'

'You'll have to help me.'

'And risk harming my baby? No. You'll just have to wait.'

'I'll sleep on the couch.'

'Please yourself. I'm going to bed.'

Ginny was asleep when Will came in but she woke when he got into bed.

'Did you carry Mum up to bed?' she asked.

'No, she was asleep so I left her there,' he said and she could hear the grin in his voice. 'It'll be a treat to know she ain't lyin' next door listenin' to what we're up to. Come here, girl, I got suthin' here you'll enjoy.'

To Ginny's surprise and in spite of everything, he was right.

16

As he had promised, Nathan arrived the next morning with the money for the cakes and also the basket, which Ginny had completely forgotten in the joy of rediscovering his love for her.

But if he had expected to be welcomed at number four Quay Yard he was sorely disappointed. It was Ruth who hobbled to the door in answer to his knock and she made no attempt to ask him in even though he craned his neck for a glimpse of Ginny. Instead, she thanked him coolly for bringing the money but said it could have waited until she came to work at Mrs Bellamy's again, which would be later in the week, when her ankle was better. When he told her, with what he hoped was a winning smile, that it was no trouble since he was on the way to *Aurora* anyway, she said that then she mustn't keep him and almost, but not quite, closed the door in his face.

'There was no need to be quite so rude, Mother,' Ginny said, disgusted at the smug, self-satisfied look on her mother's face. 'It wouldn't have hurt to ask him in for a minute.'

'What, so that he could make sheep's eyes at you? He must think I was born yesterday if he thinks I'm letting him anywhere near you again, my girl. I used to think he was a nice lad, but not since he got you . . . ' she pursed her lips and gave a disapproving nod towards Ginny's swelling stomach. 'And at the same time as his wife, too. I think it's disgusting.' She gave an expressive shudder.

'For your information his wife isn't pregnant. She only said she was to force him into marrying her,' Ginny said flatly. 'If it hadn't been for that he would have married me.'

Ruth was silent for several minutes, digesting this surprising piece of news. Then all she said was, 'Well, it's too late now, you've made your bed and you'll have to lie on it.'

'Correction, Mother. *You've* made my bed. It wasn't my choice to marry Will Kesgrave.'

'Well, you couldn't have married Nathan Bellamy anyway, because he's already married.' Ruth thumped the mixing bowl down on the table. 'Now, you'd better make a start on this pastry.'

'Make it yourself. I'm going out.' Ginny knew her mother didn't believe her over

248

Isobel and she felt she couldn't stand her presence a moment longer.

'What about my ankle? I don't know whether I can stand for long enough . . . '

'Then you'll just have to sit down.' Ginny snatched her coat from its hook behind the door, picked up her sketching pad and went out.

There was a lot of activity on the quay. Will and the two men who fished with him were busy on *Emily May*, and he gave her a wave when he saw her. They were making the smack ready for her long summer rest, taking down the old fishing basket that habitually hung from the top of the mast to show other boats that she was fishing, brailling the red sails to the mast and scrubbing her decks and hold clean of fish scales. Ginny had to admit that Will was taking quite a pride in looking after her father's smack; he was not a bad man when he kept off the drink and she knew he was quite fond of her in his own rough and ready way. The trouble was he was not the man she loved.

She surveyed the scene on the quay, choosing what she would sketch. Her eyes lit on old Zeke Bellamy, Nathan's grandfather, who was watching the men on *Emily May* from an ancient armchair on the deck of his leaky old smack, which was permanently tied up opposite the Rose and Crown since it was no longer fit to go to sea. He had a filthy old clay pipe clamped between the only two teeth left in his head and now and again he would remove it, spit in the river and jabbing the air with its stem, shout instructions to Will and his crew as to the best way to carry out whatever task it was they were engaged in.

They took no notice at all.

Neither did the constant stream of men carrying spars, sails, ropes and items of furniture to the yachts being made ready for the season's racing or holidaying. Some of the bigger yachts were furnished like country houses and one, it was rumoured, even boasted a grand piano, but *Aurora* was a racing yacht so her furnishings were necessarily kept to a bare minimum.

Ginny perched herself on a bollard and took out her sketch pad. With a few deft strokes she had the filthy old armchair, stuffing escaping from its arms, standing on the bow of the blackened hulk of old Zeke's boat among old bits of rope and chain, bottomless buckets and wicker fishing baskets. Then came the old man, with his straggly walrus moustache, his cheese-cutter cap pulled down over his wispy grey locks, his clay pipe jabbing the air as he leaned forward to make a point to some unseen audience.

Ginny smiled to herself as she sketched. It was no wonder Mabel Bellamy had disowned her disreputable old father-in-law, he was no asset to her social-climbing aspirations. But Ginny knew that Captain Bellamy kept an eye on his father. She remembered that when she worked at Stacey's there had been a box of groceries, ordered and paid for by the captain, delivered to the old boat most weeks, even when the captain was away, sailing. And she knew that Nathan visited too, taking his grandfather tobacco and peppermints and getting sworn at for his pains.

'That's excellent, Ginny. You've got the old devil to a T.' Suddenly, Nathan's admiring voice spoke from behind her. 'You're really very good, you know.'

She swung round. 'I thought you were . . . '

'I am. I'm overseeing things but I've come down on to the quay for a breather.' His voice dropped. 'I hoped I'd see you, Ginny. I came here hoping you'd be here. Did you hope to see me, too?'

'No, of course not,' she said, a bit too quickly.

'I think you did,' he said, and there was a smile in his voice. 'I don't think your mother likes me very much any more.'

Ginny sighed. 'I don't think my mother likes anything or anybody much these days.

She's very difficult to live with.' She lowered her head and sketched in a few lines. 'You should go. Will is on *Emily May* and he won't like it if he sees us talking.'

'Does he smell a rat?'

'No, of course he doesn't. And I'm anxious that he shouldn't.'

'Very well, sweetheart, I'll go.' He leaned down as if he was examining her picture. 'I love you, Ginny.'

Before she could answer he had straightened up and gone whistling along the quay.

She stared down at her sketch pad, her pencil still poised. Is this how it would always be? She closed her eyes. In some ways it had been almost easier when she had thought Nathan had betrayed her, at least she could try to put him out of her mind. But now, knowing that he was the one who had been betrayed . . . that he still loved her . . . She gave a great sigh. Why, oh, why was life so complicated?

★ ★ ★

It was Will who broke the news that Nathan had been elevated to the position of mate on *Aurora*, the post held by Bob Appleyard until his death. Ginny and Will were sitting and eating their evening meal with Ruth when he made the announcement.

Ruth let her knife and fork fall with a clatter on to her plate. 'Nathan Bellamy? Mate on board *Aurora*? He's not fit to take the place of my husband,' she said scathingly.

'Reckon he is, Missus.' Will had given up calling her Ruthy in an effort towards harmony. 'He's a good bloke. He'll do a good job.'

'Whether he'll do a good job or not has got nothing to do with it. His father is captain and his father-in-law owns the yacht and that's how he got the job, you mark my words. He didn't get it because he's a 'good bloke'. Good bloke, my foot! It's not what you know but who you know that gets you on in this world.' Ruth picked up her knife and fork and attacked her meal savagely.

'You're happy about it, Will?' Ginny asked quietly.

'Aye, Ginny, I am. And so is the rest of the crew. Whatever your mother says, Nathan's a man you can trust on a boat. I've learned a lot from him.' He stared at Ruth. 'And he got the job because he deserved it, not because of who he's related to. You don't win races by giving the best jobs on the yacht to your relations. And Sir Titus is a man who can't bear to lose.' His face broke into a smile. 'I'll hev another lump o' that pie, Missus. I see there's plenty left.'

Ginny said nothing as she digested the news of Nathan's promotion. Will seemed to have a high regard for him so it was imperative that he should never discover that Nathan and not Roger was the father of her child. It was also vital that he shouldn't discover they were still in love. She gave him another generous helping of pie as a kind of compensation. In some ways she couldn't wait for *Aurora* to set sail.

★ ★ ★

Nevertheless she couldn't resist standing on the quayside to wave goodbye to the yacht as she sailed away downriver for her season's sailing and racing. Halfway up the mast Will looked back and saw her waving her handkerchief and thought she was waving to him. This pleased him so he took off his cap and waved back to her. Nathan knew differently and raised his arm. Watching, Ginny wondered how the two men would manage to live at such close quarters for the whole summer. It was all right for Will, he had no idea of the real situation, but Nathan was a jealous man.

With a sigh, she put her handkerchief back in her handbag.

'Come an' hev a cuppa tea with yer owd mum-in-law,' a voice from behind her said. 'It'll cheer you up a bit, girl.'

Surprised, Ginny turned and saw Annie Kesgrave, all dressed up in an emerald green costume and matching hat. A pink feather boa completed the picture. 'Oh, I didn't realise you'd come to watch the boat sail, Annie,' she said.

'Oh, yes. I usually do. There's one or two on board I like to see off, for old time's sake,' she said enigmatically. 'Fellas I used to know well, as yer might say.' She grinned. 'I wouldn't like 'em to forget me altogether.' She linked her arm with Ginny and the girl had no choice but to accompany her back to number one.

The place was as squalid as ever and carried its usual stale, fishy aroma. Gladys, Will's sister, was sitting at the table, desultorily topping and tailing shrimps.

'Get the kettle on, Glad, we'm got a visitor. Well, you're not a visitor, are you, luvvie? You're fam'ly.' Smiling happily, Annie unpinned her hat, primped her peroxided hair and sat herself down, smiling smugly. Then her expression changed. 'Well, come on, Glad, like I said, get the kettle on!' she snapped.

Gladys pulled herself to her feet without

enthusiasm. She was wearing a stained blue dress that was several sizes too big. It was obvious both from Gladys's apparel and her own that Annie shopped at jumble sales. 'Why can't you do it,' she said grumpily. 'You're always orderin' me about. You left me to peel the rotten shrimps, now it's 'put the kettle on, Glad'. Well, I ain't your slave.' She pulled the kettle forward with a jerk that made water from the spout sizzle on to the hob and then sat down again.

'Don't be such a miserable little bitch,' Annie said sharply. 'Show a bit more of a welcome to yer sister-in-law.' Again her expression changed as she turned and smiled at Ginny. 'Don't take no notice of her, dear. She's olwuss bin a miserable little cow. An' a bit . . . you know,' she tapped her temple with her finger. 'I put it down to the fact that her father was a road sweeper an' I fell for her in the rain.'

Ginny's eyes widened. She had never heard such personal matters discussed so openly. To cover her embarrassment she looked round for a chair to sit on that wasn't already occupied, either with dirty washing or a cat.

'Shoo! Git orf that chair, Moggy.' Annie leaned over and gave the cat a cuff. It oozed lazily off the chair and began sniffing round the shrimp heads that had fallen on the floor.

Annie watched the cat for a moment, then gave a little self-satisfied wriggle of her shoulders. 'Will 'ud be ever so pleased to think you've called, Ginny. We don't see much of yer, even though you on'y live a spit away.' She paused. 'Don't see much of him, neither, come to think of it, but thass no great loss. Anyway, I 'spect he's otherwise occupied, as you might say.' She gave Ginny a knowing wink.

Ginny ignored the wink. 'I'm usually busy helping my mother,' she said, trying not to sound prim.

'Yes, I dessay yer mother's olwuss got a job for you,' Annie said, in a not entirely approving tone.

'Like you!' Gladys spat at her own mother.

Annie turned an unaffectionate gaze on her daughter. 'Kettle's boiled,' was all she said.

They stared at each other for several seconds but eventually Gladys backed down and made the tea and poured Ginny's into a cup that was almost clean. 'There y'are,' she said, then she picked up a penny magazine and retreated to the corner.

Annie watched her, shaking her head. 'No bloody manners, that girl,' she remarked. Then she brightened up. 'And how's me gran'child?' she said, nodding towards Ginny's stomach. 'Poddin' up nicely now, ain't you? Big baby, I reckon.' She frowned and pursed her lips knowingly. 'Don't look to me like you'll go till September.'

Ginny had already begun to wear a loose, shapeless overall under her coat to conceal her growing figure but the size of the bulge clearly hadn't escaped Annie's expert eye. 'I expect it's the way I'm sitting,' she said, pulling herself up straight in the chair. It didn't appear that Will had confided in his mother the full terms of the marriage.

'Hm. Either that or Will sampled the goods afore he bought 'em.' Seeing Ginny flush at her coarse words Annie burst out laughing. 'Ah, so thass the way of it. I thought it might be, the weddin' bein' in such a hurry, though Will never said. Well, all I can say, girl, is you were a damn sight luckier than I ever was. Both times I got caught the chaps buggered orf as soon as they knew I was in the fam'ly way and I've never seen hide nor hair of either of 'em since.' She sniffed. 'But I've managed well enough on me own, so I don't care.' She held her cup out to Gladys. 'Put a little drop o' gin in, girl.'

Gladys barely raised her head. 'Put it in yerself. You olwuss keep it handy.'

'So I do.' Annie scrabbled in the bag by her side till she found the bottle. 'Want some,

Ginny? Thass a drop o' good.' She held out the bottle.

'No, thank you, Annie.' Ginny shook her head. The tea was bad enough, with a marked fishy taste, without putting gin in it. Holding her breath she swallowed the last of it and got to her feet. 'I must be going. I told my mother I wouldn't be long.'

Annie grinned. 'You're a married woman now. You don't hev to be at your mother's beck and call all the time, you know.'

'No. I know. But I've got things to do. Will's things to clear up,' she added on inspiration.

Annie smiled approvingly. 'But you mustn't spoil him,' she said. 'He ain't used to bein' waited on hand and foot, you know.'

Thankfully Ginny managed to escape at last. As she walked up the yard she wondered what Gladys would have been like with a less slovenly mother, if she might have been less sullen and bad-tempered. Inadequate as she was, she had no incentive to take any pride in herself; she was too fat, her hair was lank and greasy and her complexion sallow. Ginny felt quite sorry for her.

She pushed open the door of her own home. The minute she got inside her mother sniffed.

'I know where you've been. You've been in

that Kesgrave house,' she said, making a face. 'I'm surprised at you.'

'I could hardly avoid it without being rude,' Ginny said, hanging up her coat. 'After all, like it or not, Annie Kesgrave is my mother-in-law, thanks to you.'

'There's no need to keep rubbing it in. At least I've preserved your respectability.'

'Oh, yes, you've done that all right, Mother.' Ginny made more tea to try and remove the taste of the cup she had been forced to drink in Annie's house. 'Do you want a cup?' she asked over her shoulder.

'No. I've only just come back from Mrs Bellamy's. I had a cup with her. She's always a bit low when the captain goes away. We had quite a chat.'

'Oh, yes.' Ginny waited, holding her breath, knowing she was about to hear all about it, and wondering what Mrs Bellamy's version of Isobel and the non-existent baby would be.

'Mrs Bellamy's very proud of the fact that Nathan's been made mate. Apparently, the captain says he's very competent.' Ruth paused. 'But she's worried about him, because he's not very happy living in London now,' she added carefully.

'Is she?' Ginny was carefully non-committal.

'Yes. And apparently her daughter-in-law is

not such a nice person as Mabel had thought.'

Ginny noticed she called Mrs Bellamy 'Mabel'. They must have had a real heart-to-heart to be on Christian name terms.

'It seems the wicked girl tricked Nathan into marrying her. She lied when she told him she was pregnant. She was never pregnant at all.'

'I told you that but you didn't believe me,' Ginny said.

Ruth gave a dismissive shrug. 'I thought you were making it up as an excuse,' she said, annoyed at having to admit that Ginny had been right yet unable to prevent herself from relating Mabel Bellamy's saga. 'Getting mixed up with Isobel Armitage was the worst day's work Nathan ever did, Mabel said.'

'I could agree with her there,' Ginny said.

'Of course, he doesn't live with her any more.' Ruth nodded several times in an effort to make Ginny understand. 'You know, *live* with her.'

'You mean he doesn't sleep with her,' Ginny said. 'He still lives in the flat, when he's not at sea, I suppose.'

'Yes, well, he'd have to, wouldn't he?' Ruth changed the subject. 'Have you heard of Sir Oswald Mosley?'

'Who?'

'Sir Oswald Mosley.'

Ginny frowned. 'Yes, I've read about him in the newspaper. What's he got to do with anything?'

Ruth dropped her voice. 'Well, it seems that Isobel has got herself mixed up with his followers, the blackshirts, I think they call themselves. She thinks this Sir Oswald is something wonderful, and she goes to his rallies, all dressed up in black, like the rest of them. I don't know what her father thinks about it all, I'm sure.'

'I'm quite sure Nathan wouldn't approve, if he knew,' Ginny couldn't help saying. 'Does he know?'

'Yes. He knows. In fact, Mabel says he's forbidden her to go. But she's headstrong. She doesn't take any notice of what he says.'

'And you learned all this today, from Mrs Bellamy?'

'Yes. She's really worried. After all, Isobel is her daughter-in-law, she's a Bellamy now so Mabel doesn't want her getting mixed up with that sort of thing. And neither does Hector. It's all to do with supporting this Hitler person, from what I can make out. He's got a great following in Germany, I believe, and there are some people over here who think he's a great man.'

'Sir Oswald Mosley for one,' Ginny said. She got to her feet. 'Well, there's nothing you or I can do about it, Mother.'

'No.' Ruth eyed her daughter up and down. 'But things might have been so very different, if . . .'

'If . . . If . . . If wishes were horses, beggars would ride,' Ginny said tersely. She crossed the room, pausing at the door to ask, 'I take it Isobel hasn't got any plans to join the yacht at Cowes, or in Scotland, like she usually does, if she's so taken up with her new cause?'

'Not that I know of. Mrs Bellamy didn't say.'

Ginny climbed the stairs unconvinced. Nathan may have thought he had escaped his possessive wife's clutches for a few months by going racing but knowing what she did of Isobel Armitage — correction, Isobel Bellamy — Ginny found it difficult to believe that even with this new interest in her life she would let an entire summer go by without checking on her husband.

17

Ginny's baby was born on the fifteenth of July in the year 1936. At the same time, her husband, together with the father — and grandfather, although he didn't know it — of her child, were battling it out in the Firth of Clyde on *Aurora* against some of the fastest yachts in the world. The child was born on the day they won the biggest race of the season.

The baby's birth was not without incident, although it was an easy birth.

Ruth had stipulated right from the very beginning that she would have nothing to do with the confinement. She made the excuse that she knew nothing about such things, she had been blessedly unconscious at the birth of her own daughter and had no wishes to witness the final mysteries of procreation. Her part in the proceedings would be to boil water, provide clean rags and linen and to send one of the Oliphant children for Nurse Canham.

Ginny said nothing, convinced that her mother would change her mind when the time came.

But she was wrong. Ruth stuck to her decision and when Ginny, white-faced and terrified, called her at six o'clock on the morning of the fifteenth, and said she kept getting a sharp pain in her side every ten minutes or so, Ruth abruptly sent her back to bed whilst she herself got up and dressed. Then she took Ginny a cup of tea and told her to stay where she was and went for Katie, the oldest Oliphant child still living at home, giving her a grudging penny in order to speed her on her way to Nurse Canham's house nearly a mile away. Then she stoked up the kitchen fire, poured out her own tea and sat down to wait for the nurse to arrive, drumming her fingers impatiently on the table and congratulating herself on the discreet way she had handled the situation.

But she hadn't taken Annie Kesgrave's eagle eye and ear into account.

Annie had heard the urgent whispered message under her bedroom window and immediately hauled herself out of bed. This was unheard of; Annie rarely surfaced before eleven, bleary-eyed and hung over, but she was determined not to be denied the privilege of being in at the birth of her first grandchild and she was at the door of number four, her hair hanging down in rats tails from its dowsing under the tap in the yard, before

Katie Oliphant was halfway up the High Street on her errand.

'What do you want?' Ruth asked rudely. 'Can't you see I'm busy?'

'Thass as much my gran'child as yourn,' Annie replied mildly, stepping past her into the spotless kitchen. She eyed the pan of water bubbling on the stove, the heap of snowy white linen piled on the table and the teapot on the hearth.

'If there's a cuppa tea in the pot I could do with it. I've got a mouth like a fisherman's boot,' she said, sitting herself down at the table. 'How often are the pains comin'?'

'Every ten minutes,' Ruth mumbled, busy with the teapot.

'Got a bit of a wait yet, then.' Annie folded her arms across her ample bosom.

Ruth poured Annie's tea. 'There's no need . . . ' she began.

'Like I said, thass my gran'child as well as yourn,' Annie said, pouring her tea into the saucer and drinking it noisily. 'When I've drunk this I'll go up and keep the gal company for a bit. I dessay she's a bit nervous, bein' the first.'

Ruth hadn't thought of that.

'Hev you got a waterproof on the bed?' Annie asked, finishing her tea. 'She might need it.'

Ruth hadn't thought of that either but she managed to find a waterproof sheet that she'd forgotten about.

Annie lumbered to her feet. 'I'll take it up. You don't need to come if you're squeamish,' she said.

'It's not that. But I need to stay downstairs to let the nurse in,' Ruth said haughtily.

'Jest as you like.'

Annie wheezed her way up the stairs and Ruth heard relief as well as surprise in the way Ginny greeted her mother-in-law. She poked the fire irritably, feeling guilty because she was not at her daughter's side and jealous that Annie Kesgrave was. But her fear was stronger and she remained downstairs.

It was an hour before Katie Oliphant returned.

'You've taken your time,' Ruth snapped, taking out her own inadequacies on the child.

'Well, thass a long way, an' all up hill,' Katie said, still breathless from running. 'I couldn't go no faster.'

'Where's the nurse?'

'She can't come yet,' the child panted. 'Mr Canham said I'm to tell you the nurse hev already been out on a baby case half the night and she sent a message to say she didn't know how long she'd be because they've had to call the doctor as well. He said he'll tell her to come to you as soon as she gets back.'

'Thank you.' Ruth shut the door on Katie and sat down on the edge of a chair wringing her hands. How was she expected to manage without a nurse? How was she expected to know what to do? She was a cook, not a nurse. And it wasn't only the actual birth, there was the cord to cut . . . she knew that if you didn't do it in the right place the mother could die . . . but where was the right place? And there were other things . . . all that blood . . . She shuddered and gulped.

After a few minutes she plucked up the courage to go upstairs. She hesitated at the bedroom door, then took a deep breath and went in. Ginny was walking up and down, supported by Annie, stopping every few minutes while Annie held her, saying, 'Thass it, dearie, take a deep breath. There, there. Thass it.'

Annie glanced over her shoulder at Ruth. 'She's doin' fine. Pains are comin' faster now. Is the nurse here?'

'No. She can't come. She's out on another case. They don't know when she'll be back.' Ruth looked round wildly. 'What shall we do?'

'Manage without her. The baby won't wait, thass for sure.' She supported Ginny as another pain washed over her. 'Come on, my girl, I think we'd better git you on to the bed,' she said, more confidently than she felt because she had never assisted at a birth before, let alone been in sole charge. 'Won't be long now, I don't reckon.' She glanced at Ginny, then turned to Ruth, saw the fear in her face and she realised she would be no help at all. 'Well,' she said, 'We shall jest hev to get on with it then, shan't we?' She frowned, remembering back to the birth of her own two children. Then her face cleared a little. 'Fetch me some rag so I can tie it on the foot of the bed for her to pull on, Ruth. Then you can bring us plenty of hot water and clean linen.' If Ruth wasn't going to be any help she was best out of the way.

Ruth scuttled away, relieved to be out of the room, ashamed at her own cowardice but glad to be of some assistance.

Granny Crabtree always rose early. She had heard Ruth run for the Oliphant child, and she had seen Annie lumber up the yard. She smiled to herself as she made her pot of tea; there was no hurry, these things took their time, you couldn't hurry nature. So she had eaten her breakfast, two slices of bread and marmalade and two cups of tea, her mind going back to the hundreds of children she had helped into the world in her time and then, quite naturally, to the hundreds more she had sat with while they left it. When she had eaten her breakfast, she washed her cup and saucer and plate and put them back on the dresser, took up her rag rugs and shook them, swept the floor and dusted the room. It was as she was folding the duster and putting it back in the drawer that she heard Katie Oliphant return and her breathless message. With a tiny smile of pleasure, Granny Crabtree put on a spotlessly clean and starched white apron, completely covering her 'morning' dress of grey serge, rubbed the duster over the buttoned boots that encased her stick-like legs, and tucked back a few strands of her wispy grey hair that had strayed from under the white mob cap she always wore to conceal the fact that she was practically bald. Then she went and knocked at the door of number four.

By the time Granny Crabtree rustled into the room Ginny was past caring about anything but the waves of agonising pain that were tearing her apart. She dimly heard voices and felt a blessedly cool cloth repeatedly wiping the sweat from her face and then, after what could have been hours or minutes, she had lost all concept of time; there was a final searing pain and then nothing. It was over. She lay with her eyes still closed, it was like floating in calm waters after a storm, blissfully peaceful. Then she heard a baby's cry. *Her* baby. Her eyes flew open as Granny Crabtree laid the tiny scrap of humanity in her arms.

'You've got a bonny little girl,' the old lady said, her wrinkled face beaming down at Ginny. 'She was in a hurry, too. I got here just in time to catch her! You were lucky, Ginny. First babies often take their time getting here. Mind, she's not that big. Six and a half pounds, I'd say.'

'Well, she's a month or two afore her time, ain't she?' Annie said, winking at Ruth, who had slipped into the room as soon as she realised the messy part was over.

'Yes. Yes, of course,' Ruth said hurriedly.

'She's a bonny little lass, all the same,' said Granny Crabtree, who was not deceived. 'And I think we could all do with a nice cuppa tea, especially Ginny, after all her hard work.'

'An' both her grannies could an' all,' Annie said heartily. 'Thass hard work birthin' a gran'daughter, ain't it, Ruth?'

Ruth nodded, sharing an unwilling bond with her slovenly neighbour who had turned out to be such an ally. 'Yes. Yes, indeed. I'll go and fetch the teapot.'

Ginny was immediately besotted with the little scrap that was her daughter. She gazed lovingly down at her and was amazed — and delighted — when the baby opened her eyes and stared back with eyes that were the same deep blue as Nathan's.

'What do you think you'll call her, Ginny?' It was her mother's voice, surprisingly gentle.

Ginny looked up, surprised. 'I don't know. I haven't thought. I didn't know . . . well, it might have been a boy.'

'It doesn't matter. There's plenty of time.'

'We'll hev to send a telegram to Will. Tell him he's got daughter,' Annie said excitedly. 'P'raps he'll wanta choose her name.' She slurped her tea noisily. 'I must go and tell Glad she's a auntie. Auntie Gladys. That'll please her.' She finished her tea and put her cup down and got to her feet. Then, after planting a noisy kiss on the baby's forehead she lumbered happily off down the stairs.

Ruth took the baby and laid her gently in the crib Ginny had prepared for her and a sudden, overwhelming relief enveloped her that the baby had no vestige of Kesgrave blood in her. It had been the biggest mistake of her life that she had forced Ginny to marry Will Kesgrave; she realised that now as never before, and she was both sorry and ashamed although it was not in her to admit as much. All she could do was to silently vow that she would do all she could to make life bearable for Ginny and this vulnerable little being she had just brought into the world.

⋆ ⋆ ⋆

The telegram was waiting for Will when the yacht arrived back at Oban after a hard race, in foul weather and heavy seas. The crew were wet, tired and hungry and not very good-tempered. They couldn't wait to get the sails furled and stowed, the sheets and halyards hanked, decks swabbed and the yacht made ready for the next race before they went below to clean themselves up ready for the hearty stew the cook had prepared for them.

The telegram was beside Will's plate.

He flushed when he read it. 'Seems I gotta little daughter,' he announced, grinning broadly.

Good humour was immediately restored all round. There were pats on the back, a good many unrepeatable, ribald comments and universal demands for Will to treat the crew to a drink 'to wet the baby's head' when they went ashore later.

Nathan, at the other end of the mess table, managed to smile but said little. Inside, he was consumed with a jealous rage because Will was receiving the congratulations that were rightly *his* due. It was *his* daughter, his and Ginny's; she didn't belong to this coarse rough-neck who was being patted on the back and called 'Daddy' by all and sundry. He was glad when they all went ashore in the dinghy.

It was an unwritten law that the captain and mate never drank at the same pub as the crew, and in fact on this night Nathan and his father didn't go ashore at all but had a quiet tot of rum in Captain Bellamy's cabin while they discussed the race; what they had done wrong, what they had learned from it, how they might have done better still if *Shamrock* hadn't nipped in and stolen their wind as they rounded the point. The atmosphere between the captain and his son was relaxed and intimate and Nathan was sorely tempted to ask his father to raise a glass to the baby that was rightfully his grandchild. But although he longed to share the wonderful knowledge, to acknowledge that he and not Will Kesgrave was the father of Ginny's baby, he held back, knowing that his father, a religious and God-fearing man who read a passage from his bible every night when he was at sea, would censure rather than congratulate him.

In fact, in this he was not altogether right. Indeed, Hector Bellamy was a God-fearing man, but that didn't alter the fact that he had been young himself once, and he sometimes wondered, with more than a twinge of guilt, if there could be a young man or woman in Tasmania bearing more than a passing likeness to Nathan, the result of a liaison that might well have come to more if he hadn't already been married to Mabel. The suspicion sometimes weighed heavily on him and he would have welcomed someone to confide in. But father and son were not sufficiently close for confidences of that kind and so they both remained silent regarding their indiscretions.

★   ★   ★

It was a beautiful moonlit night. The moon made a silver path across the calm, still water of the bay, so different from the angry waves *Aurora* had breasted through earlier. From time to time the peaceful calm was interrupted by raucous shouts and sounds of rude music hall songs floating across the water as dinghies loaded with drunken crews returned to other yachts anchored nearby.

It was very late before *Aurora*'s crew returned. As the dinghy approached the yacht's side a fight broke out, with the rest of the crew trying to separate the two sparring men and shouting to them that they would 'turn the bloody boat over' if they weren't careful.

Nathan was already on deck. His father had turned in over an hour ago and suggested that he should do the same, but he knew he wouldn't sleep, his thoughts were too full of Ginny and her baby. The baby that was his by rights.

He went and leaned over the side. 'Get aboard and shut that row,' he shouted, using the appropriate expletives that the men would expect to accompany his words. 'Do you want to wake the whole of Oban?'

The scuffling stopped and in the bright moonlight the men began to scramble up the rope ladder on to the deck and down into their hammocks. The two who had been fighting were the last to climb the ladder except for the hand responsible for making the dinghy fast.

'Git orf my bloody hand. You're treadin' on my bloody hand.' Nathan recognised Will Kesgrave's voice, slurred and belligerent with drink.

'Oh, shut yer face.' The man above kicked out viciously, hit Will in the face and knocked him off the ladder into the water.

There was a shout and those who hadn't already gone below went to the guardrail and stared owlishly down at the man floundering in the water below them. He couldn't swim, that was for sure, seamen hardly ever learned to swim, preferring to know that if they were shipwrecked death would come quickly. And he was weighted down with heavy sea boots and a thick woollen guernsey, quite unnecessary on such a warm summer night.

'Who is it?' one asked foolishly, staring down into the water.

'Will Kesgrave,' another answered. 'He'd had a good ole skinful tonight, I can tell yer.'

'Well, that'll sober 'im up.'

'Nah. He's a gonner, I reckon.'

'Yeh. Reckon so.'

While this exchange was going on, Fred Scales, the man in charge of the dinghy, who was not quite as drunk as the rest of them, was ineffectually waving the boat hook around in the water, trying to locate the drowning man.

Nathan, the only man there with a clear head, had already stripped down to his underclothes and dived in.

There was no time to lose. The tide was running fast and Will was being carried further and further away from the boat, flailing hopelessly. But Nathan, unusually for a seaman, was a strong swimmer and seconds later he reached him and grabbed him round the neck and managed to hold him up until

Fred could get the dinghy alongside so that between them, Nathan pushing and Fred pulling, they could haul him aboard. Once in the bottom of the boat, he spluttered and vomited as they sat on him and pummelled him to pump the sea water out of his lungs. When he was sufficiently recovered Fred rowed back to *Aurora* and Nathan slung Will over his shoulder and climbed back on board, where he dumped him down on the deck like a sack of potatoes.

'You saved my life,' Will muttered, maudlin and still half drunk as he heaved himself up to lean against the capstan. 'I can't never repay you for that, Mr Mate.'

Nathan nodded to those who were still standing and watching.

'All right. The show's over. Get below, the rest of you. I'll see to this one.' He turned back to Will.

Will was wagging his finger. 'No. Wait a minute. I gotta tell you suthin',' he insisted, his head rolling from side to side.

'It'll keep till morning. Come on, man, you're drunk and you've had a fright. You damn nearly drowned.' Nathan tried to haul him to his feet.

Again Will's head wagged, as he resisted Nathan's efforts. 'No. I gotta tell you,' he insisted.

'Well, come on then, man, what is it? I'm wet through, the same as you are. I don't want to be up here on deck all night.'

'The baby. Thass about the baby,' Will said, his voice still slurred.

Nathan looked over his shoulder to make sure nobody else was on deck. Suddenly, he felt cold inside as well as outside. 'Well?' he asked.

'They've all bin buyin' me drinks ternight, on account o' the baby, but she ain't mine, yer know. I on'y married Ginny ter get Bob's smack.'

Nathan licked his lips and said nothing.

Will leaned towards him and nearly fell forward. Nathan put out a hand and pushed him back. 'But I know who the father is,' Will continued, nodding his head up and down like a mandarin. 'Ah, yes. I know who he is, even though Ginny's never said.'

'Are you sure?' Nathan's blood ran cold. He was beginning to wish he had let the man drown. He had no wish to get into a fight, which was what Will must be spoiling for. Not that he was in any shape to put up much of a show, he was still half dead from his near-drowning.

'Yeh. Thass plain as a pikestaff. Roger Mayhew. Got her in the fam'ly way, then buggered orf to Australia rather'n marry her.'

Will frowned and looked up at Nathan. 'You won't tell nobody, will yer, Mr Mate. I don't wanna be the laughin' stock o' the ship.'

Relief flooded through Nathan. 'No, Will. I won't say anything.'

'I jest felt . . . I dunno, I jest felt funny about them buyin' me drinks for a baby that worn't mine.' His eyes filled with maudlin tears. 'Mind you, I shall care for the little maid as if she was mine. I shan't see her come to no harm an' I shall see she don't want for nuthin'.' He sniffed and wiped his nose on his sleeve. Then he looked up at Nathan. 'Mr Mate,' he said solemnly, 'I should be honoured if you'd consent to be godfather when the little maid's christened, 'cause you saved my life ternight.'

'I . . . ' Nathan began but Will held up his hand.

'I know Ginny'll agree when she find out what you've done for me,' he went on. He wagged his head. 'Oh, you don't wanta worry. I shall see to it that she's brought up God-fearin' like her mother and if you're her godfather I know you'll watch over her if anything happen to me so I can't.'

Nathan felt a prick of tears behind his eyes. Will Kesgrave, although he didn't know it, was asking him to stand godfather to his own baby. It was the highest compliment he could have paid him.

Unfortunately, he probably wouldn't remember in the morning.

18

It was nearly a week before Ginny heard from Will. He was no letter-writer, the most she got as a rule was a picture postcard saying, *We are here. Wether good (or bad, windy, wet, sunny,) I am well hope you are the same,* so Ginny was quite touched to receive a letter from him.

> *Dear Ginny,* she read,
>
> *I hope you are well as this leeves me. I went out and got drunk wen the telegram came about the little maid and I fell in the water and nearly drownded. Mr Mate saved me so I asked him to be Godfather I hope this is alrite with you. Your loving husband. Will Kesgrave.*
>
> *P.S. I hope she looks like me. Ha Ha.*

Ginny lay in bed, the baby by her side, staring out of the window. The words *Mr Mate saved me* seemed to burn into her brain. Supposing Nathan hadn't saved him? More, had he been tempted to leave him to drown? She shook herself impatiently at such an uncharitable thought. In any case, it would have made no difference because Nathan was still married to Isobel.

The baby began to cry so she picked her up and put her to the breast, stroking the soft downy hair on her head. She was Nathan's child, flesh of his flesh, blood of his blood. Nobody could take that away from her even though she might never know it. But Ginny knew it and for the time being that was enough.

Two days later there was a letter from Nathan. It was a letter the whole world could have read but Ginny knew what lay behind it.

Dear Ginny,

I am writing to congratulate you and your husband on the birth of your little daughter. I hope that everything went well and that you are making a good recovery. Nearly the whole crew went ashore the night the news came and raised a glass to Will. Not surprisingly, he came back a little the worse for wear.

What are you going to call her? Roberta, after your father? It's a nice name and I'm sure he would be pleased if you did. Will has already asked me to be her godfather when the time comes for her christening — with your approval, of course. As an old friend of the family I would be both

honoured and delighted to accept his
invitation if you are agreeable.
With regards,
Nathan Bellamy.

Ginny gave her mother both the letters to read.

Ruth sniffed when she read Nathan's. 'Roberta! That's a daft name if ever I heard one!' she said, throwing the letter back on the bed. 'In any case, what right does he think he's got to suggest that you should call her. Just because . . . ' she pursed her lips against saying any more, but couldn't resist, 'I think Elsie's a nice name. Why don't you call her Elsie?'

'Because I don't like that name.' Ginny picked the letter up and folded it carefully. 'And Nathan's got every right, Mother,' she said quietly. She smiled. 'It's strange. I'd already decided I would call the baby Robert, after Dad, if it was a boy, so why not do the same now she's a girl? Roberta's a nice name.'

'She'll get called Bobby,' Ruth said disparagingly. 'Or Robin. What kind of a name's that for a girl, I should like to know.'

Ginny smiled down at her little daughter. 'Bobby. I like that.' She bent and kissed her. 'You'll be proud to know you were named after your grandfather when you grow up, Bobby,' she said softly.

Ruth sniffed again. 'Hadn't you better wait and hear what your *husband* says?' she asked, laying great emphasis on the word. 'He might prefer her to be called Elsie.'

Ginny looked up, straight into her mother's eyes. 'What I call my baby has got nothing to do with Will Kesgrave,' she said quietly.

Ruth shrugged. 'He's your lawful wedded husband.'

'But he's not the father of my child.' She laid the baby back in her crib and leaned back on her pillows. 'I'm tired, Mother. I think I'll have a sleep,' she said, putting an end to the argument.

★　★　★

Roberta Kesgrave was nearly three months old when *Aurora* returned from her summer's sailing and racing. She met the yacht sleeping in her mother's arms, quite oblivious of all the excitement on the tow path.

Ginny stood with the waiting crowd, her feelings mixed. Last year when *Aurora* returned things had been very different. Then she had been waiting for her father, just as she had waited for him every year for as long as she could remember. She closed her eyes and pictured his burly, bearded figure striding down the gangplank and the warm salty smell of him as he enveloped her in a bear hug. A tear escaped and ran down her cheek at the memory. Maybe her mother had been right, after all and she shouldn't have come. Yet she couldn't stay away. This was what she had always done. And Nathan was on *Aurora* . . . She shifted the baby on to her other arm.

The yacht came upriver bedecked with all the winning flags and berthed amid the usual excited noise and cheering. After what seemed a long time the crew began to disembark, rolling down the gangplank, duffel bags on their shoulders, waving to friends and family as they came. They were happy to a man. It had been a good season for racing and they had money to jingle in their pockets.

Will was one of the last to leave the yacht. Nathan was right behind him and together they came over to Ginny, who was standing a little apart from the rest.

Will gave her a peck on the cheek and gave the baby a cursory glance. If he was honest he was not particularly interested in the child he thought Roger Mayhew had fathered although he had enjoyed the congratulations and the free beer in Scotland.

'When I saw you was waitin' on the shore I

told Mr Mate he oughta come and take a dekko at his god-daughter,' he said. He peered down at the bundle in Ginny's arms and she met Nathan's eyes over the top of his head. The expression of helpless longing there brought a lump to her throat but she managed to smile at him although her own eyes were moist.

'She's a bonny little maid, ain't she?' Will said in some surprise. He grinned broadly. 'Little Bobby.' He turned to Nathan. 'She's bin named after her grandad,' he said, as if Nathan didn't know. He touched the baby's hand and nodded. 'He was good to me, your grandad.'

'Yes, Bob was a good man,' Nathan said. Now it was his turn. He leaned over the baby and gazed down at her, hoping, yet fearful he would see his own likeness there. He pressed a coin into her little hand. 'I believe it's the custom to cross a new baby's palm with silver,' he said, smiling a little awkwardly up at Ginny. 'I don't want to be mean, but I thought a sixpence was about as much as she could grasp.' He straightened up. 'You're looking very well, Ginny,' he said softly. 'Motherhood suits you.' He held her gaze for a few seconds, then turned away, hitching his duffel bag on to his shoulder again. 'I must be going,' he said suddenly. 'I have to catch the train to London. Isobel's organised some kind of party for tonight and I promised I'd be there if I possibly could. But I shall be back sometime next week because there are things to be seen to on the yacht.' He raised his hand and went off.

'He went off in a bit of a hurry, didn't he?' Will said, frowning after Nathan's retreating figure.

'He said he'd got a train to catch,' Ginny reminded him. 'Well, come on, are you coming home? Mum's made your favourite stew.'

'Thass nice,' he said, without much enthusiasm. They walked along together in silence, taking the route along East Street and out on to Anchor Hill because they knew Ruth would complain if they came the other way. After a bit he said gloomily, 'I wish we was goin' to our own house, Ginny. I wish we didn't hev to live with your mother.'

'Mum doesn't mind,' Ginny said, although she was inclined to agree with him.

'No, but *I* do.' He stopped and turned to her eagerly. 'I got a nice bit o' prize money, Ginny. I reckon I've got nearly enough for us to rent a place for ourselves. And furnish it, if we go to Hatfield's second-hand place in Colchester. What do you say?'

She nodded thoughtfully. 'It would be nice,

Will.' She sighed. 'I must say I'd like to have a place of my own.'

He put his arm round her shoulders and squeezed. 'We'll go and see about it. Termorrer. An' thass a promise. There's some nice little places for rent in Alma Street. We can see if there's one o' them empty. That'll be nice for the little maid, too.'

It was the best she could hope for, Ginny told herself. Life, after all, was what you made it. Nathan had gone to his wife, he'd made no secret of that. Indeed, where else should he go but home to his wife? And Will was her husband, so it was up to her to make the best she could of life with him. He was rough and uncouth but that could change. And he wasn't all bad. He had been prepared to marry her and accept her child as his own. He wasn't afraid of hard work either. It was just the drink . . . But when they were in their own house maybe he wouldn't feel the need to spend every night in the Rose and Crown.

She tucked her free arm into his and smiled up at him. 'I'd like that, Will,' she said.

Predictably, it was Ruth's fault that things didn't work out the way they had planned.

It could have been envy at the way Ginny and Will came into the house smiling and talking to each other that triggered it off, but Ruth, never the easiest of people to please, could find nothing right in what Will did. She made him leave his duffel bag in the outhouse, saying it made the place untidy, she nagged at the way he held his knife, the way he slurped his tea; she made him take his boots off because he was putting mud on the floor, then made him put them back on because she said his feet stank. She complained that he didn't appreciate her cooking when he took longer than she thought necessary to eat his meal but when he asked if there was any more she accused him of greed. After the meal was over she refused to let him sit in Bob's chair by the fire and when he picked up a spill to light his pipe she refused to allow him to smoke in the house.

This was the last straw. He had borne her criticism and complaints without a word but now he stood up, ramming his pipe into his pocket. 'All right, Missus, you've made your point,' he said, reaching for his cap. 'Thass plain I ain't welcome here at the minute so I'll take meself orf somewhere else where the company's a bit more pleasant.' He turned to Ginny. 'You needn't wait up, gel,' he said, 'I dunno what time I'll be back.' He went out, slamming the door behind him.

Ginny rounded on her mother. 'Why did you treat him like that? The poor man couldn't do a thing right for you. And on his first night home, too.'

'Well, he's got to learn he can't do just as he likes in my house,' Ruth said, with an irritable shrug.

'It's your fault he came here in the first place, remember.' Ginny leaned over the table. 'But for your information, we shan't be living in your house for much longer,' she said triumphantly. She straightened up. 'Will's got enough prize money for us to rent a house in Alma Street. *And* furnish it. We're going to see about it tomorrow.'

Ruth's face fell. 'There's no need to be in such a hurry, Ginny,' she said. 'This place is big enough for the three of us, well, four with the baby. We can manage. Anyway, you'd be lonely on your own, with Will at sea most of the time. Don't forget he'll be off to the fishing grounds on the smack in a few weeks. You wouldn't want to be on your own when he's away, would you?'

'I shan't be on my own. I'll have Bobby,' Ginny said.

'But what about the cakes and pies? We're working up quite a nice little business now we cook for the other captains' wives as well as Mrs Bellamy. We don't want to let that slide, do we?' Ruth's tone was bordering on wheedling.

'There'll be no need. I can come here and work with you as well as look after my own house. It'll work very well.' Ginny picked the baby out of her pram, which stood under the window. 'And it'll give you more room. You often complain about the amount of room the baby's things take up.'

'It's only because you won't leave the pram in the wash house,' Ruth said.

'It's damp out there. I'm not putting my baby in a damp pram.'

'It's not damp. Well, only when we hang the washing there to dry . . . '

'I'm not arguing with you, Mother.' Ginny went to the stairs. 'I'm going to bed now and tomorrow Will and I are going to see about a house. If there isn't one in Alma Street there might be one in the Folly.'

'You wouldn't want to live *there*,' Ruth said, aghast. 'There's rats!'

Ginny began to mount the stairs. 'At the moment I'd be happy to live in a barn to get away from you,' she said under her breath.

She laid Roberta in her crib, then undressed and climbed into bed. Tomorrow, with any luck, she and Will would start a new life in a home of their own. He was not a bad man at heart; it was not his fault that his mother was a slut. Once they were on their own she would make a real home for him

. . . There would be more children . . . Life was what you made it and her life was with Will. Not Nathan. Nathan had gone home to Isobel, his wife. She turned her head on the pillow and found it was wet with tears.

But Ginny's dream of a house of her own was shattered when she got up the next morning and found Will a dishevelled heap snoring on the sofa. When he had arrived home, at heaven knew what time, he had obviously been too drunk to climb the stairs.

She laid Bobby in her pram and then went over and gave him a poke. He opened his eyes painfully and squinted up at her. 'Wasser matter?'

She held her hand out, tight-lipped. 'Where's the money?'

'Wha' money?' He hauled himself painfully up into a sitting position and put his head in his hands.

'Your prize money. How much of it have you got left?'

'Oh, stop naggin', woman.' He tried to roll back on to the sofa but she caught him by the shoulder and kept him more or less upright.

'I want to know how much of your prize money you've got left,' she said between gritted teeth. 'We're supposed to be seeing about a house in Alma Street today, remember? You had a lot of money in your pocket last night. Enough to rent a house of our own, and to buy enough furniture to put in it, you said. Over thirty pounds, you said. Where is it?'

He screwed his eyes up. 'Can't remember.'

She took him by the shoulders and, her temper giving her strength, hauled him to his feet and out of the back door. There she shoved his head under the tap in the yard. 'Perhaps this'll help to remind you,' she said, banging his head against it as the water gushed out.

'All right. All right.' He ducked away, shaking himself like a dog. He wiped his face with the towel she gave him as they went back into the house, then slumped back on to the sofa. 'You might go easy,' he said petulantly. 'I've got a head the size of a gasometer.'

'Serves you right. I've no sympathy.' She stood over him, arms akimbo. 'Now, about this money! How much have you got left and where is it?'

He rummaged in his pocket and threw a crumpled five-pound note on to the table.

'Is that all?' she asked, aghast.

He rummaged again and threw more crumpled notes down.

Carefully, Ginny smoothed the notes and counted them. 'Three pounds ten shillings. That's eight pounds ten altogether. What happened to the rest?'

'I got into a card school,' he said, hanging his head. 'And I had to stand my round . . . '

'Oh, spare me the details.' She waved an impatient hand at him, then turned her back and stared out of the window. 'I really thought you meant it when you talked about a house of our own,' she said bitterly. 'I really thought we could make a go of things. I went to sleep planning . . . '

'It was your bloody mother's fault. Nag, nag, nag. That was all she did, from the minute I set foot in the door. 'Do this. Don't do that. Take yer boots off. Put 'em back on again,'' he mimicked. 'Bloody woman didn't give me a minute's peace. I had to get away from her. So I went to the pub.' He looked up at her, willing her to understand. 'It was her. She drove me to it.'

Ginny sighed, folding her arms across her chest. 'I know. I don't know what got into her last night, really I don't. She isn't usually as bad as that.' She turned and looked at him and her voice sharpened. 'But you'll just have to put up with it because we've nowhere else to go now you've been and spent most of our money.'

He dragged himself to his feet. 'We could still see about a place of our own, Ginny,' he said hopefully, going to her and putting his arm round her.

'And what do you propose to furnish it with, orange boxes?' she asked, shrugging him off. 'Here comes mother,' she warned, as Ruth passed the window. 'We can't talk about it any more now.'

'Where's she been?' he said.

'I don't know. Shopping, I expect.'

Ruth came in, a satisfied expression on her face. She glanced at Will. 'Sobered up, have you?' she asked and for once her tone was not sarcastic. 'I hope so, because I've got something important to say. Sit down, both of you, you make the place look untidy.' She smiled at them.

Too surprised to do anything else, they obeyed and watched as Ruth took off her coat and hat, then pulled the kettle forward and picked up the teapot. 'You can get the cups, Ginny,' she said, her voice still amiable.

It was not until the tea was brewed and poured and they were all sitting at the table drinking it that Ruth dropped her bombshell. 'I expect you're wondering where I've been this morning,' she said, rubbing her hands together and looking from one to the other. Neither of them answered, so she went on, 'I've been to see about a house in Denton Terrace, off Park Road.' She paused, waiting for some reaction but when none was forthcoming she took a sip of tea and went on, 'It's not a bad little place at all. It's got its own flush lavatory and an inside tap, which is more than we've got here. There'll be plenty of room for all of us and there's even a garden for Roberta to play in when she gets old enough. It's not quite where I'd hoped to go but it'll be better than this place and the rent's not too high.'

Ginny glanced at Will. He was staring at Ruth with an expression that was not quite hatred on his face. Of all the times her mother might have chosen to speak about moving house this was just about the worst. The trouble was, she thought she was helping.

She smiled now and nodded towards Ginny. 'Well, aren't you going to say something?'

Ginny opened her mouth to speak but nothing came out. She didn't know what to say.

19

Ruth looked from Ginny to Will and back again. 'What's the matter? Cat got your tongue?' she asked, beaming at them both and oblivious of the tension round the table. 'Well,' she went on happily, 'I knew, when it came to it, *he'd* never do anything about finding a place to live, especially when I saw the state of him when I came downstairs this morning, so I took the bull by the horns and sorted it out myself. We can move in at the end of the month.' With a satisfied smile she finished her tea and poured herself another cup.

Will pushed back his chair, his face like thunder, and snatched up the notes that were still lying on the table. 'I'm goin' out,' he said, 'afore I say suthin' I shouldn't.'

Ruth raised her eyebrows in amazement, her cup in mid air. 'What's the matter with you? Aren't you pleased?' she said.

'No, I bloody well ain't,' Will said, rounding on her. 'And if you think . . . '

'Sit down, Will.' Ginny's voice cut across his words like a whiplash. He was so surprised he sank back on to his chair and stared at her open-mouthed.

Now it was Ginny's turn to stand. 'Now you can listen to me, both of you,' she said, without raising her voice, although it was obvious she was having difficulty in controlling her temper. She turned to Ruth. 'I'm glad you've found a house you like, Mother,' she said. She paused for a fraction of a second. Then, 'I suggest you go and live in it.'

Ruth gaped, her smug satisfaction disappearing like the air out of a pricked balloon. 'But you don't understand! I've got it for all of us. What about you? Don't you want to move to a better house?'

'No.' She hesitated. 'Well, yes. But my place is with my husband, Mother, and it's quite plain that you and he can't live under the same roof without sparks flying. So you can move to Denton Terrace and we'll stay here, in Quay Yard.'

'But what about our little business? The cakes and pies . . . ?' It was plain Ginny had completely taken the wind out of Ruth's sails.

'We can still cook together, either here or at your house. The fact that we no longer live under the same roof needn't make any difference to that.' Ginny looked round the room, then carried on in a businesslike tone, 'All this furniture and the household goods belong to you, of course, and you must take whatever you want. We'll make do with what's left till we can afford to get some things of our own.' She turned to Will. 'How does that sound to you, Will?'

He nodded easily, the tension gone out of him. He was full of admiration for the way Ginny was handling things. 'Thass fair enough, far as I can see.'

'Good. That's settled, then.' Ginny held out her hand to him. 'And I'll have those notes back, if you don't mind, Will. We shall need all the money we can scrape together for the rent and a few bits and pieces of furniture. I reckon you won't mind if we keep the bed, will you, Mother? I guess you won't need two.'

Ruth shook her head, flabbergasted at how Ginny had worked everything out in such a short time.

Will stood up and took the notes out of his pocket and gave them to Ginny. 'There y'are, girl. You'll look after 'em better'n what I shall. I'm off to the yacht now. There's a lot o' clearin' up to do there afore I start work on the smack.' He turned to Ruth. 'I take it you'll still want me to work the smack, Missus?'

Ruth nodded weakly. Events seemed to be moving too fast for her. She felt she was losing control.

'Thass all right, then.' He screwed his cap on to his head. 'I'll be back for me dinner, Ginny.'

'And stay away from the Rose and Crown,' Ruth warned, finding her voice.

'You mind your own business, Mother,' Ginny said, giving her a scathing look. She took a shilling out of her purse. 'One drink, Will, and no more,' she said, giving it to him.

He planted a kiss on her cheek. 'Thass a promise, girl,' he said, giving her a quick hug.

'Hm. His promises are like piecrusts, made to be broken,' Ruth muttered as he went whistling down the yard.

Ginny picked up the baby, who had begun to cry, and unbuttoned her blouse. 'What's the matter with you, Mother! Why must you keep nagging at Will!' She paused and settled the baby at her breast, then went on, 'Don't forget it's your fault he's living here. You insisted on me marrying him. I didn't want to, as you very well know. I didn't even like the man. But you gave me no choice. Well, I did as you wanted; now he's my husband and I'm trying to make the best of things. In truth Will isn't a bad man, he's got a good heart and if only he can leave the drink alone we'd manage together. I'm not saying we'd ever be really happy, but we'd manage. If it wasn't for you, that is. But you haven't got a good word for him. You nag him from the minute he gets in till he goes out again, he can't do a thing right for you. It's no wonder he spends all his time and money in the pub. He does it to get away from you!'

Ginny paused and made the baby more comfortable. When Ruth said nothing she went on, 'As I see it, you finding this house in Denton Terrace is the best thing that could have happened and the sooner you move there the happier we'll all be, because it wears me out trying to keep the peace between you and Will.' She gazed down at the little dark head, busy with her breakfast and oblivious to the drama going on round her, then looked up and said, her voice businesslike, 'And you'd better let me have the rent book, Mother, so I can get it transferred into my name. I'll take over the rent from this week.'

Ruth's head jerked up. 'Oh, so that's your little game. You want to turn me out of the house I've lived in for the past twenty years and more,' she said, pursing her lips.

'I'm not turning you out, Mother. You've just said yourself you've found somewhere better to live,' Ginny said, refusing to weaken. 'God knows you've complained about Quay Yard enough times. In fact, you've been talking about getting away from it ever since I can remember. Well, now you've got your chance. For heaven's sake take it and leave Will and me in peace.'

Ruth stared at her. 'Well! I never expected to be spoken to like that by my own daughter,' she said, affronted. She gave a shrug. 'But if that's your attitude I shall leave this minute.' She got to her feet.

'Oh, don't be so stupid, Mother, you've nowhere to go. You said yourself you can't move in till the end of the month,' Ginny said impatiently. She finished feeding the baby and put her back into her pram.

'Then I shall stay in my room.'

'Very well. I'll bring your meals up to you.'

★ ★ ★

The next two weeks were awkward, to say the least, with Ruth spending most of her time in her bedroom and refusing to speak when she was forced to leave it. But at last the time came for her to move to Denton Terrace.

Will borrowed a handcart and made four journeys with her furniture, which Ginny had cleaned and polished, and all her china, which Ginny had washed until it sparkled and wrapped carefully in newspaper. When Ruth was safely ensconced in her new home — without a word of thanks to her daughter and son-in-law — Ginny and Will returned to their own home, which contained nothing but their bed and the baby's cot. Ruth had vindictively taken everything else that was not actually nailed down.

'I'll go along to Green's and get some fish and chips,' Ginny said, trying to put on a cheerful face. 'I can't cook anything, she's taken all the saucepans. And we shall have to eat it out of the paper with our fingers because she taken every last bit of china and cutlery.' She bit her lip against threatening tears. 'I know it all belonged to her but I never thought my mother would be so unkind as to leave us with nothing at all. It wasn't as if she needed every single cup and plate.'

'Never mind, girl, we'll soon get some bits and pieces together,' Will said, more cheerful than she'd seen him for a long time. 'I'll go and borry a kettle and a coupla mugs off me mum so we can make a cuppa tea. And there's that old table in the wash 'us. We can make do with that till we can get suthin' better.' He grinned. 'She was so anxious to make sure she didn't forget the mangle she forgot the table. An' I didn't remind her.' He burst out laughing and Ginny couldn't help laughing with him. 'Thass better, girl. Now, you go off to the fish shop an' get us some grub, my belly think my throat's bin cut I'm that hungry. I'll hev the place right comfy, time you get back.'

Will was as good as his word. When Ginny arrived back with the fish and chips there was a bright fire burning in the grate and a somewhat battered kettle singing on it, the table was in place, laid with a clean newspaper and two odd mugs. There was a chair either side of the table and a brightly coloured rag rug on the floor.

'Where did you get all this from?' Ginny asked, amazed.

'The kettle and the mugs came from me mum.' He laughed and shook his head. 'Owd Granny Crabtree don't miss a trick. I'll bet she could tell you every pot and pan that went on that handcart to Denton Terrace. Anyway, she saw me on me way to Mum's for the kettle and called me. She said we'd need suthin' to sit on so would we like these two chairs. I said thank ye very much and she said we could hev the rug as well to make the place a bit more homely.'

Ginny's eyes brimmed with tears and Will went over to her and put his arm round her. 'We shall be all right, you an' me, Ginny, now we're on our own,' he said warmly. 'I'll keep away from the pub an' I'll work hard. An' we can go into Colchester termorrer an' see if we can get a few bits from Hatfields, the second-hand furniture place. The carrier'll fetch 'em home for us. You'll see. We'll make out all right.'

She smiled up at him through her tears. 'Yes. We'll make out, Will,' she said. 'Now, we'd better eat our fish and chips before they get cold.'

'Ah, yes. Well, they allus taste better outa the paper, don't they?' he grinned.

'And eaten with your fingers,' she grinned back.

★ ★ ★

Over the next few days they saw and heard nothing of Ruth. Ginny went to see Granny Crabtree, to thank her for the chairs and the rug.

'That's all right, dearie,' the old lady said, smiling her toothless smile. 'I didn't really need them cluttering up the place. I nearly always sit in my armchair by the fire.' She bustled to the chiffonier and pulled out a drawer. 'I've looked out a few knives and forks and spoons. You're welcome to them if they're any use to you,' she said. 'And I've got a couple of saucepans that are too big for my wants now.' She patted Ginny's arm. 'I know your mother didn't leave you much, child.'

'She didn't leave us *anything*,' Ginny said sadly. 'I never thought she could be so

306

unkind.' Her face brightened. 'But Will and me went into Colchester on the bus yesterday and ordered several bits from Hatfields. The carrier is going to bring them later on today. We bought a bigger table and a dresser and a dressing table and a chest of drawers for upstairs. And there was a whole bath full of china that Mr Hatfield said we could have for half a crown — goodness knows what's in it but I could see several dinner plates and some cups and saucers and a lot more besides. And we got everything for five pounds! What do you think of that!'

'I think you did very well, dearie,' Granny Crabtree said, smiling at her. 'I reckon Mr Hatfield must have liked the look of you.'

'Mind you,' Ginny said honestly, 'some of the furniture is a bit shabby and worn, but Will says he can mend it and with a good clean it'll be as good as new.' She looked at the clock on the mantelpiece. 'I'd better go. The carrier will be here soon and I want to be there when he comes. I'll call you in to see it when we've got it in place.'

Ginny was as good as her word. As soon as the carrier had delivered everything and Ginny had helped Will to put it in place, struggling up the stairs with the dressing table and the chest of drawers and replacing the old wash house table with the new one they had bought, she gave Will a shilling to slake his thirst at the Rose and Crown, made a pot of tea in the teapot she had discovered in the bath of china and invited Granny Crabtree in to see their purchases.

'These are *my* things, not my mother's, so it makes the place feel like a real home of our own,' Ginny said, running her hands over the dusty pine dresser. She smiled. 'Do you know, I'm almost glad she took everything with her when she left, although I thought it was mean of her, at the time.'

'You know why she did it, don't you, child,' Granny Crabtree said, pouring her tea into the saucer, blowing it and slurping it noisily.

'No, I don't. I thought she would at least have left me a kettle and a saucepan and a few knives and forks. I didn't think she'd take every single thing.' Ginny sipped her tea, then said thoughtfully, 'I can't think why she turned on Will the way she did, either. After all, it was her fault he was here, since she practically forced me to marry him. It wasn't what I wanted, at all. I'd have been quite happy to face the scandal and bring my baby up without a father.' She glanced at the old lady. 'But you knew all about that, didn't you, Granny?'

'Aye. I knew, child.' She leaned forward and put her cup and saucer carefully on the table. 'I thought at the time it was a mistake and she was being too high-handed, but it was not my place to interfere.' She looked up at Ginny, chewing her gums thoughtfully. Then she said, 'It's my belief that Ruth turned nasty with Will because you were beginning to make something of your marriage.'

'I don't love him,' Ginny blurted out.

'Maybe not, but love isn't everything. The thing is, you're both pulling in the same direction, and that's worth a lot.' She shook her head where a little lacy cap covered what was left of her hair. 'Your mother was as jealous as fire is hot, that was her trouble. She couldn't stand it when you sided with Will instead of with her. That's why she went off in a huff and took everything she could carry with her.'

'Will carried most of it for her,' Ginny pointed out.

'That only made matters worse, the fact that you were both so helpful,' the old lady said sadly. 'I reckon she thought you couldn't wait to be rid of her, even though she'd brought it on herself.' She patted Ginny's hand. 'Give her time. She'll come round. You'll see.' She got to her feet, encased, as always in their little buttoned boots. 'The baby's crying. You'll need to see to her so I'll be going.'

Ginny picked the baby up and walked with Granny Crabtree to the door. 'Thank you, Granny,' she said, 'You're very wise, aren't you.'

Granny Crabtree chuckled. 'I don't know about that. I keep my eyes open, that's all.' She went to the door. 'Now remember, like I told you once before, I'm always here if you need me,' she said. 'Everybody likes to be needed. Even your mother. And I reckon that's especially true right now.'

Ginny thought over Granny Crabtree's words a great deal in the following days but she still couldn't bring herself to visit her mother. She told herself she had no reason to go and she couldn't go without a reason. In any case, she was kept very busy at home. She was surprised how much more there was to do now that she was the only one there to cook and clean and care for the baby.

She was busy ironing one afternoon when Will came past the window, followed by another man. Ginny immediately recognised the figure as Nathan and her heart seemed to give a little jump, she wasn't sure whether with joy or trepidation.

'Come in, boy,' Will said. Then to Ginny, 'We've jest finished clearin' up on board the yacht and battened her down for the winter so I've brought Mr Mate back to see his god-daughter.'

'She's asleep in the pram,' Ginny said, nodding towards it.

Nathan went over and stood gazing down at his daughter, a look of adoration on his face. 'She's beautiful, isn't she?' he breathed.

Fortunately Will was standing behind him so didn't see his expression. 'Not in the middle o' the night when she's yellin' her head off, she ain't,' he said with a grin. 'She's got a voice like a fog horn.'

'She's not that bad, Will,' Ginny said, feeling strangely embarrassed at having Nathan in her rather shabby and bare living room, although she had tried to brighten it a little by pinning up a few of her pencil drawings on the wall. She took a deep breath. 'Would you like to sit down, Nathan?' she asked, hoping to keep him there for a bit longer.

'Thank you.' He gave her a fleeting smile and sat down at the table. He turned to Will, who had taken the other chair. 'And I think it's time you dropped the 'Mr Mate', Will, now we've finished the yachting season.'

'Right y'are, Nathan,' Will said easily. 'That suits me fine.'

The two men sat talking comfortably as

Ginny continued ironing on the other side of the table.

'What will you do with yerself over the winter, boy?' Will asked.

Nathan shrugged. 'I expect I shall spend a good deal of time in my studio, painting,' he said. 'That's what I do when I'm in London.'

'Do you like living in London?' Ginny heard herself asking, although she already knew the answer.

'No. I hate it,' he said vehemently. He turned to Will. 'I suppose you'll be spending the winter fishing?'

'Aye,' Will said seriously. 'An' I'm determined I'll hev a good season, too. I've got a bit o' work to do on *Emily May*, but soon as she's shipshape I shall be out lookin' for cod. Now th'owd woman has slung her hook I shan't hev to answer to her for every move I make.'

'You'll still have to pay Mother her share of the profits,' Ginny reminded him.

'Do you miss your mother, Ginny?' Nathan asked, looking at her thoughtfully, and Ginny was acutely aware of the faint golden shadow of beard on his jawline as he spoke, the deep blue of his eyes, bordered as they were by surprisingly dark lashes. She had a sudden urge to lean over and touch his cheek.

'I — yes, I suppose I do. A bit.' She spoke

312

vaguely, hardly realising what she was saying, afraid that he might have read her thoughts, that she had given away too much of her feelings under his gaze.

She pulled herself together. 'But it's nice to have the house to ourselves, isn't it, Will?' she said brightly, smiling at her husband.

'Oh, aye. Thass nice to know there ain't somebody in the next bedroom listenin' to every move you make.' He winked at Nathan. 'That can put you off your stroke, if you know what I mean,' he said with a grin.

Nathan didn't smile back and Ginny saw the look of pain that fleeted across his face. He drained his tea and got to his feet. 'I must be going. I've got a train to catch,' he said briefly. 'Thank you for the tea, Ginny.' He paused. 'If you're likely to be short-handed on the smack at any time just let me know, Will. I'll be glad to be out in a good old nor' easter to blow the London cobwebs away now and again.'

'I'll remember that, boy,' Will said. He didn't get up from his chair so Ginny went to the door with Nathan.

'Thank you for coming, Nathan,' she said quietly.

He put out his hand as if to take hers, then thought better of it and put it in his pocket. 'Goodbye, Ginny,' he said and strode away up the yard.

20

Ruth had been gone from Quay Yard for nearly three weeks before Ginny went to see her. And then it was only because Captain Hurley's wife had come to ask for some baking to be done.

Ginny could have baked the cakes and pies the captain's wife had ordered on her old kitchen range and she did consider this. But she and her mother had always worked together and the order provided an excuse to hold out an olive branch. If her mother refused to grasp it, Ginny decided, then that would be an end of it.

It was a crisp November day, the early frost still hanging in the trees, when Ginny tucked Bobby warmly in her pram and wheeled her along to Denton Terrace.

'Oh, it's you,' Ruth said rudely when she opened the door to Ginny's knock. 'What do you want?'

'I don't want anything, thank you, Mother,' Ginny said, keeping her voice level. 'At least, not for myself.' She waited, but Ruth, tight-lipped, made no reply. This was even harder than Ginny had anticipated. 'Aren't you going to ask me in?' she said, after a minute, 'Or would you prefer me to discuss our business on the doorstep for everyone to hear?'

'What business?' Ruth said warily. 'Oh, I suppose you'd better come in.'

'Thank you.' Ginny picked the baby out of the pram and followed her mother into the house.

It gave Ginny quite a shock when she entered the living room because it was just like walking into her old home. Everything was set out exactly as it had been at Quay Yard, even to the calendar hanging on a hook beside the mantel-piece. The only difference was the brass tap over the brown earthenware sink and the wooden draining board, where at Quay Yard the washing-up bowl was kept on a shelf.

'You've made yourself very comfortable here, haven't you,' Ginny said, looking round.

'And why shouldn't I?' Ruth snapped, sitting down at the table again and picking up the stocking she had been darning.

Ginny took a deep breath, determined not to lose her temper. 'I'm very glad you have, Mother,' she said gently.

There was an awkward pause, then Ginny tried again. 'Aren't you going to offer me a cup of tea?' she asked. 'Or would you like to nurse your granddaughter while I make one?'

Ruth gave an impatient sigh and threw down her mending. She got up and filled the kettle from the tap and put it on the gas stove and lit the gas. Then she sat down again. 'The teapot is in the usual place,' she said, holding out her arms for the baby.

Ginny busied herself with the tea things, keeping an eye on her mother, who was finding it difficult to maintain her stony expression in the face of her gurgling granddaughter.

'A proper sink and draining board. That's better than a bowl and a tray on the kitchen table,' Ginny said, warming the teapot and tipping the water down the sink.

'You could have had the same if you hadn't been so stubborn,' Ruth said shortly, without looking up from the baby.

'I know that. But it's better the way things are.' She poured the tea and pushed a cup across to Ruth. 'Will's finished on *Aurora* for the season and he's started to get *Emily May* ready for fishing. He asked me to tell you he's had to get Billy Barr to patch the corner of the jib and put in a new cringle, just so you know what the bill is for when it comes.'

'Hmph. Is that all you've come to tell me? That I've got to fork out money for his carelessness?'

Ginny closed her eyes and breathed a prayer for patience. 'It wasn't carelessness, it was a force ten gale that tore the cringle out of the sail last winter,' she said, keeping her voice level. 'And no, that wasn't all I came to tell you.' She picked up her cup and cradled it in her hands. 'Captain Hurley's wife came to see me this morning. She wants a birthday cake for her son and some pork pies baked.'

'Well?' Ruth looked up, her eyes cold.

Ginny banged her cup down on its saucer. 'For goodness' sake, Mother! How much longer are you going to keep this up? We were building up a little business between us, remember? Well, now you've moved house and that's good. For all of us, including yourself, because you must be glad of a bit of peace and quiet.' She took a deep breath. 'The point is are we going to continue to work together or not?' She glared at Ruth, then her expression softened. 'I'll be very upset if you say you don't want to work with me any more, Mum. I've always enjoyed our cooking sessions,' she said quietly.

Ruth jigged the baby on her knee for several minutes. Then she said briefly, 'I'll make the cake. You can come here and make the pies. Your pastry is lighter than mine and it comes out better cooked in the gas oven. Mrs Bellamy wants jam tarts made, too.

When can you come?'

'Tomorrow morning?'

Ruth nodded. 'I'll make the shopping list and get it sent up from Stacey's.'

'I'll drop it in on my way home, if you like.'

'All right. Fetch the order book and a pencil and we'll write it out.'

Ginny went to the bottom shelf of the dresser where the order book had always been kept and took a pencil from the jug beside it and sat down again. Together they listed the ingredients they would need for the next day's baking.

Ruth's tone was still cool but Ginny understood her mother well enough to know that she was beginning to thaw. But it was only a beginning. It would be a long time before the thaw was complete.

★ ★ ★

Will had a good season's fishing. He had learned where the best fishing grounds were from his earlier mistakes and he made his own decisions over weather conditions, instead of going out in all weathers in defiance of Ruth's nagging tongue.

Occasionally, Nathan accompanied him, usually when he felt the need to blow the London smoke and fog out of his lungs rather than because Will was short-handed.

He would arrive unannounced, often coming straight from the train without even paying his mother a visit and would wander along the quay to see if *Emily May* was tied up there.

If she was in her berth he would wander up the gang-plank and shout, 'Are you looking for a spare hand?'

'Aye, boy, you're allus welcome aboard,' Will would reply.

He didn't always get his timing right. Sometimes he would arrive as the smack returned with the catch, in which case he was equally happy to help with the unloading, the checking of the gear and the cleaning out of the holds before the next trip.

Occasionally, *Emily May*'s berth was empty and Will would be away at the fishing grounds. Then Nathan would call briefly on Ginny on his way to his mother's house, ostensibly to leave a message for Will that he was in Wyford for a few days. Ginny both welcomed and dreaded these visits, not that Nathan ever stayed long, but she felt unsettled for days afterwards, remembering his every look, every gesture. It was as if there was an invisible cord binding them heart to heart; she could feel it pulling them together however much she resisted it. She knew

Nathan felt the same and that for him, as for her, it was only loyalty to Will that kept them apart.

'I've brought Roberta a little Christmas present,' he said when he arrived one day near Christmas. He fished in his pocket and pulled out a little square box. 'Open it. See if you like it,' he insisted.

She opened it and found a little silver bracelet.

'It's beautiful, Nathan, but you mustn't ... ' she looked up at him, alarmed.

He closed her hand over the box and held it there. 'Please, Ginny. You must allow me to give my dau ... my god-daughter a present now and again,' he said quietly. 'It's all I can do, dearly though I would love to do more.'

She looked down at his hand, still closed over hers. 'I know.'

He squeezed her hand and then let it go. 'As it's Christmas?'

She looked up at him and nodded. 'Yes. All right. As it's Christmas. Thank you, Nathan.'

'Thank you, Ginny.' He stood for a moment, with no reason to stay except that he couldn't bear to leave.

'Will you be staying at Wyford over Christmas?' she asked.

He shook his head. 'No, I'll have to stay in London. We have to put up some kind of united front for the benefit of Sir Titus and my parents. Not that Isobel cares whether I'm there or not, she's too busy entertaining her cronies, or going on marches and shouting slogans. She's very committed to this Nazi movement and I can't make her see what a terribly dangerous thing it is.' He shrugged. 'Not that she ever listens to me, anyway.'

'Oh, Nathan, I'm sorry,' Ginny said sadly.

His mouth twisted wryly. 'You're sorry, Ginny! You're not the one who should be sorry. It's me. I've not only buggered up my own life, I've messed yours up as well.' He put his hand out and touched her hair. 'It's me who should be sorry, Ginny,' he said softly. 'And God knows, I am. I'd give twenty years of my life to turn the clock back so that I could ask you to marry me, instead of giving you a stupid silk scarf and going off to London with that bitch.'

'It's too late, Nathan,' she whispered, shaking her head. 'Clocks don't go backwards. But we can still be friends.'

'I want more than that, Ginny,' he said wretchedly.

'We can't have more than that, Nathan. You know that as well as I do. Will's turned over a new leaf. He works hard and never comes home drunk. He's not a bad man and you know how much he values your friendship.

And he trusts me. We can't betray that.'

He nodded. 'No, you're quite right. We mustn't betray his trust. I was wrong to speak the way I did. I'm sorry.' He gave a wry smile. 'I've done a lot of apologising this afternoon, haven't I?' He went over and dropped a kiss on the sleeping baby's head. 'Goodbye, little daughter,' he whispered, so softly that Ginny wasn't sure she'd heard aright. Then he straightened up. 'When do you expect Will back?'

'Probably tomorrow. But I'm not sure you'll get a trip in before Christmas, if that's what you're hoping, because I don't think he'll be going out again till the New Year. How long are you staying in Wyford?'

'If there's no fishing only a couple of days or so. Just long enough to get rid of the stink of London and get some fresh East Anglian air into my lungs.'

'You do hate London, don't you, Nathan?' she said sadly.

His face darkened. 'I loathe it,' he said.

★ ★ ★

Emily May arrived home the next day, the first of the fleet to arrive back, with a hold crammed full of silver sprats. By the time Will walked into the little house in Quay Yard he

322

had sold the lot to the London market for a good price.

'There y'are, girl,' he said, his weather-beaten face beaming as he threw a wad of notes on to the table. 'I learned my lesson. I wasn't goin' to be last back an' hev to sell the catch for farm manure. I raced the lot of 'em to be first back. An' I won!' He gave her a smacking kiss, his cold, unshaven face, smelling strongly of fish, reminding her of her father's greeting, when he used to return from the fishing grounds.

To hide the lump that rose in her throat, Ginny counted the notes into four equal piles. 'You've done well, Will,' she said, putting one of the piles in the biscuit tin on the dresser, two more in an envelope, her mother's share of the profits and a share, which Ruth still controlled, for the upkeep of the boat. The last one she pushed over to Will. 'That's to pay the crew,' she told him.

'I said I'd pay 'em in the Rose an' Crown tonight,' he said, stuffing the notes into his pocket. He looked at her anxiously. 'That'll be all right, won't it, girl? You wouldn't grudge me a drink on me first night home?'

'No, Will, I wouldn't grudge you a drink. But don't go drinking the pub dry, that's all,' she said with a smile.

He grinned back at her. 'You're a hard

woman, Ginny Kesgrave,' he said. He got up from his chair. 'I'll go out to the wash 'us an' hev a wash down and change me clothes. I can't say hullo to the little maid stinkin' o' fish.' He nodded towards the pram, where Roberta lay gurgling to herself.

'That's it. I'll have your meal ready when you come in,' Ginny said approvingly. He had come a long way. A few months ago it wouldn't have occurred to him to change out of his fishy clothes, let alone to wash himself, if she hadn't suggested it.

When they were sitting down to the steak and kidney pudding she had made she said tentatively, 'It'll soon be Christmas, Will.'

'Aye, I know that. But I shan't be idle. I've got a few jobs to do on the boat.' He didn't take his eyes off his plate.

'I wasn't thinking about you going fishing. I was wondering . . . Well, do you think your mother and Gladys might like to come in with us for Christmas dinner? And we could ask Granny Crabtree, too.'

He nodded, chewing thoughtfully. 'Thass all right by me, if thass what you want, girl.'

'And my mother?' She held her breath.

His head shot up. 'Her?' he scowled.

'Well, we can't really leave her on her own, can we, Will? And it is Christmas, after all.'

He mopped up the last of the gravy on his

plate. 'I s'pose you're right,' he said grudgingly. He moved over to the Windsor chair, bright with the cushions Ginny had sewn for it, beside the fire. 'This is new,' he said as he went to sit in it. 'Ain't seen this afore.'

'I went to Colchester and bought it with some of my cooking money,' she said proudly, delighted to have something to show for the work she did with her mother. 'The carrier brought it home for me. I made the cushions myself.'

He lit his pipe. 'Thass right comfy,' he conceded as she put the bowl and tray on the table ready to begin the washing up.

'Nathan called the other day,' she said, busy with the suds. 'But I told him you wouldn't be going out any more before Christmas.'

'No, thass right.' Will stretched his legs out in front of the fire.

'I think he's gone back to London now.' She dried her hands. 'Oh, I've got something to show you. He brought Bobby a Christmas present.' She gave the little box that held the silver bracelet to him.

'Thass nice,' he said admiringly. 'Musta cost him a pretty penny, too.' He smiled up at her as he gave it back. 'He think a rare lot of his little god-daughter, don't he?' he chuck-led. 'Pity her real father don't send her a present from Australia now and again.'

'Don't you think of yourself as her father now, Will?' Ginny asked carefully.

He got to his feet. ''Course I do.' He went over to the pram and tickled her under the chin. 'You're my little Lavender Water, ain't ye, bless yer heart.' He turned to Ginny. 'Where's that money? I'm off to the Rose and Crown to pay the boys.'

'You put it in your pocket.'

'Ah, so I did.' He held his hand out. 'But what about my share? Don't I get a drink outa all my hard work?' he asked with a grin.

She gave him two shillings.

'Shan't git drunk on that, shall I?' he said, looking at it disparagingly.

'I hope not,' she said. 'And don't go sponging on the other men,' she warned. 'Just remember, when they stand drinks all round you're tipping their children's shoe leather down your necks.'

He shook his head at her. 'You know how to ruin a good man's drinkin', don't you, girl,' he said. But he smiled as he spoke and Ginny knew she could trust him to come home reasonably sober.

Ginny had difficulty in persuading her mother to join them for Christmas but when she realised that Granny Crabtree would be there as well as Annie Kesgrave and Gladys she relented.

'I'll bring the Christmas pudding,' she said. 'I've got it in the pantry. I made an extra one when we made all the ones that had been ordered. Just in case it was needed.' She didn't say what she thought it might have been needed for and Ginny suppressed a smile. In spite of her reluctance to accept the invitation, her mother had obviously expected to be asked to join them for Christmas.

The day passed cheerfully enough. Annie came with bags of nuts and sweets and Granny Crabtree brought a bottle of her home-made blackberry wine.

Gladys came late. She had recently started work and was in service as kitchen maid at the Sheldrake's house in Belle Vue Road. She enjoyed her work there. The tasks were menial but suited her slow-witted temperament and she found the insistence on cleanliness there a pleasant change from the squalid atmosphere in which she had been brought up. In fact, cleanliness became something of a fetish with her, to her mother's consternation since this was something that had never loomed large on Annie's horizon. But to Gladys's credit she had already managed to persuade her mother to take a weekly bath and to smarten her appearance, although the distinctive, stale, smell of the Kesgrave house still managed to cling despite her efforts.

Gladys was late arriving because she had to stay and do the washing-up after the Sheldrakes' Christmas dinner. Nevertheless, she came in looking very cheerful, her face scrubbed and shiny, ready to enjoy the dinner that Ginny had kept hot for her over a saucepan. Then they all spent the afternoon roasting chestnuts in front of the fire, and drinking Granny Crabtree's blackberry wine.

Inevitably, they discussed King Edward's abdication, which had happened not much more than three weeks previously. Annie, an incurable romantic, thought it was wonderful that a king would give up his throne for the woman he loved; Ginny announced that she was glad because she had never liked that Mrs Simpson, anyway, and Granny Crabtree said she felt sorry for Bertie, or the new King George the Sixth as he was to be known, being plunged into a position he didn't want just because his elder brother had no sense of responsibility. Ruth agreed, adding that a man who was prepared to put his personal feelings before his duty to his country had no business to be King, anyway. Gladys frowned and said she couldn't tell which one was King Edward and which one was King George, at which they all smiled and Ginny carefully explained the situation to her. Whilst all this was going on Will sat smoking his pipe and dozing and Ruth and Granny Crabtree took it in turns to cuddle Bobby. It was all very warm and friendly.

The only blot on the day was when Annie nearly fell in the fire because she had liberally laced her wine, which was already quite potent, with gin. After that, Gladys took her home and put her to bed.

'You'll stay the night, mum?' Ginny asked, when the others had gone home. 'I've made a bed up in your old room.' She went to the window and pulled back the curtain. 'I believe it's beginning to snow.'

'Thass right. You stay here the night, Missus,' Will said, giving the fire a poke. 'You don't wanta turn out in the cold.'

Ginny held her breath as Ruth hesitated. Even Will had felt well enough disposed to his mother-in-law to invite her to stay the night in this the season of goodwill. She hoped her mother wouldn't spoil it by refusing the offer.

Suddenly, Ruth nodded, pulling her shawl round her. 'It's nice and warm in here. I must say you've made the place very comfortable. Yes, thank you. I will stay. Going out in the cold night air makes my joints ache, these days.'

'Good,' Ginny leapt to her feet. 'I'll put a bottle in your bed.'

21

The fishing went well over the early months of 1937. Catches were good and prices high. Nathan came down from London more and more frequently to join in the fishing trips, saying he was finding London claustrophobic. He usually managed a brief visit to Ginny, mostly with Will but occasionally on his own. Ginny found these visits increasingly difficult. Will had changed completely from the drunken slob she had married and was now a sober hard-working family man, so she felt disloyal to him in looking forward to Nathan's visits, although she was careful that there was never a word or gesture between her and Nathan that the whole world couldn't have witnessed. The trouble was, although she respected and admired Will for what he had become, she didn't love him, not in the way she loved Nathan. The way she had loved Nathan ever since she could remember and the way she guessed she would always love him, whatever he did. Over and over again she told herself that he was not worth her love, he had betrayed her by marrying Isobel and if his marriage wasn't happy he only had himself to blame. But it was no use. She couldn't get him out of her heart. Not even when she found she was pregnant again.

Will was delighted. Although he suspected there were one or two children running about the village that he had more than likely fathered, since his marriage to Ginny he had been faithful to her and the prospect of a legitimate son and heir pleased him inordinately. When spring came and fishing gave way to yachting he went off with Nathan and Captain Bellamy for the season's racing on *Aurora* a happy man.

The time passed very quickly for Ginny too, busy as she was with Roberta, the twice-weekly baking sessions with her mother and the preparations for the coming baby.

Ruth eyed her up and down one morning as she stood at the table making pastry one hot June day, her pregnancy advancing, a streak of flour down her face.

'I hope you're not going to be one of those women who produce a baby every year, my girl,' she said anxiously.

Ginny rubbed her aching back. 'No, I'll make sure of that, Mum. But Will deserves a son of his own, don't you think?'

'It might be a girl.'

'All right. A daughter.' She sat down and

wiped her hands on a tea towel. 'We didn't get off to a very good start, I know,' she said thoughtfully. 'But Will's changed a lot. I felt it was the least I could do for him, to give him a child of his own.'

'Doesn't he feel that way about Roberta?' Ruth asked with a frown. 'I've seen him dandle her on his knee plenty enough times. He seems very fond of her.'

'You know what I mean, Mother,' Ginny said, a trifle irritably. 'And you're quite right, he is fond of her. But I also know that at the back of his mind is always the thought that she's Roger Mayhew's child.' She gave her mother a warning glance. 'Yes, that's what he thinks and you're never to breathe a word that you know different. Nathan saved his life in Scotland and he's never forgotten it. They get on well together. If Will knew the truth it would finish everything.'

Ruth pursed her lips. 'You're skating on thin ice, my girl. To my mind the child grows more like her father, her real father, every day.'

'That's only because you know who her real father is,' Ginny said complacently. 'Nobody else would ever think that.'

'She's fair, like Nathan.'

'Yes, but her hair is gradually getting

darker. She'll have my colouring when she gets a bit older.'

'Her eyes . . . '

'Ah, yes. She's got Nathan's eyes,' Ginny said softly. 'I wouldn't want to change that.'

Ruth frowned. 'You're not still in love with that man?' she asked incredulously. 'Not after all he's done to you?'

Ginny made no reply but got up and went over to the oven. 'I can smell these cheese and onion pies are done,' she said briskly, putting an end to the conversation. 'Captain Harvey's wife won't want them if they're burnt to a cinder.'

★   ★   ★

Will didn't know he had a son until *Aurora* returned to her winter berth after the season's racing a week after he was born. However, he hadn't been surprised when Ginny hadn't met the yacht as she usually did because he knew she must be near her time.

'It's a pity she's not here,' Nathan said, looking round for her and trying not to show his disappointment, 'because I've got a little present for Bobby. I was hoping to see her here so I could give it to her before I catch the train. I'm off to London tonight.' He swung his kit bag off his shoulder and began

333

to unlace it. 'Never mind, you'll just have to give it to her, Will,' he said.

'You think a rare lot o' your little god-daughter, don't you, boy,' Will said, grinning. 'You better come home 'long o' me and give it to her yourself. That won't take you a minute. Thass not far outa your way. You'll still ketch your train.'

They walked along to Quay Yard together, talking amiably about the races they had won and the few they had lost and the tactical reasons for both.

Engrossed in their conversation they were quite surprised when Ruth greeted them at the door with the news of the baby's birth.

Will's face broke into a grin. He threw down his kit bag and took the stairs two at a time, shouting to Nathan to follow him.

Nathan looked uncertainly at Ruth, who gave a shrug and said nothing, so he followed more slowly.

When he arrived in the bedroom Ginny was lying propped up in bed, her wonderful chestnut hair spread round her like a halo, the baby nestled in the crook of her arm. Will had picked Bobby up and was sitting on the side of the bed cuddling her and smiling delightedly at his new son. A shaft of pure jealousy shot through Nathan, like a physical pain, making the gall rise in his throat. The scene would make a wonderful painting, but he could never do it.

'Come in, boy,' Will called proudly over his shoulder. 'Come an' see this little lad. He's a real chip off the old block. Look at him! Look at his thatch o' black hair! Look at his fists! They're like great hams.' He leaned over and took the baby's tiny fist in his own huge hand.

Somehow, Nathan managed to make the right noises. He gave Ginny a brief kiss on the cheek and said she was looking well, he admired the baby and gave Bobby a big hug and the box of bricks he had brought for her. Then he slapped Will on the back and escaped to catch the train to London.

And Isobel.

He hadn't seen her since he left in April, she was far too busy with her meetings and rallies to spare the time for holidays on the yacht these days. Not that this worried Nathan. He was more than glad that the season's racing hadn't been interrupted by her irritating presence.

But as the train bore him towards London and his beautiful, loveless home the memory of the scene he had just left haunted him. He had never seen Ginny looking so beautiful and the way she had been smiling at Will in his excitement over his new son had twisted his gut into a tight knot of jealousy that had left a dull ache of misery in the pit of his stomach.

He made a sound in his throat, something between a sob and a growl, making the other people in the railway carriage turn and stare at him.

He pulled himself together. Ginny was making a success of her marriage to Will. Maybe if he tried a bit harder he could do the same with Isobel, recapture some of the happiness of their first few months. Happiness? That was hardly the word; it had been more of an obsession. An infatuation based solely on sex. Nevertheless, they had been drawn together by something, even if it had been purely physical. If they both tried hard enough perhaps they could salvage something out of it all — if he could forgive her lies and deceits, if he could make her see that these friends of hers were a bad influence. Why she had ever allowed herself to be influenced by Sir Oswald Mosley and his cronies he simply couldn't imagine. He went over in his mind the conversation he would have with her to make her see sense. He was sure he could win her over. He yawned. He would make it come right between them. It was time he stopped yearning for a life he could never have and tried to make the best of what he had got. His mind made up, he dozed for the rest of the journey and woke up more tired than ever.

The minute he walked into the flat he heard the noise of music and partying going on in the drawing room upstairs. He threw his bag down in the hall and closed his eyes briefly. This was not a good beginning to the life he had planned. What he needed more than anything was a good hot bath and a large whisky. Like some kind of fugitive he crept up one flight of stairs, past the drawing-room door, and had his foot on the flight that led up to the bedroom and bathroom when Isobel caught sight of him.

'Darling! You're back!' she called gaily. 'Come and meet the gang. They're all dying to be introduced to my sailor boy.' She came out, a glass in one hand, and hooked her arm through his. She gave him an alcoholic kiss. 'Welcome home, lover boy,' she said and he noticed her voice was already slurred.

Carefully, he disengaged her arm from his. 'I need a bath and a shave, Isobel,' he whispered. 'I'll join you later.'

'No. We shall be going on to Jeronimo's soon. This is only the warm-up party, darling. You must come and meet my friends now. Then you can go upstairs and smarten yourself up. Dolores is dying to meet you, and so is Angela. Oh, and hundreds of others.

Come on, darling, don't be a spoil sport.' She caught his hand and dragged him with her into the room. 'Here's my Flying Dutchman, straight off his yacht, everyone,' she called. 'I told you he'd be back tonight.'

Nathan blinked. The room was full of noise and smoke and heavy with the mingled scent of perfume and alcohol. Bright young things with shingled hair, cigarettes in long holders dangling from their fingers, had turned to look at him, interrupting their urgent discussions with pale young men in evening dress, with sleeked-back hair and shiny shoes who looked like a lot of penguins to Nathan's tired mind. A gramophone was playing the latest songs and a few couples swayed in time to the music in the middle of the room.

It was like walking into another world, a world that Nathan, still in his navy serge trousers and woollen guernsey, the taste of salt still on his lips, didn't belong to and didn't like.

He nodded and smiled politely to those nearest and elbowed his way through to pour himself a drink. At the drinks cabinet he found himself next to a young man with an earnest face and a pencil moustache. 'Have you met Sir Oswald?' the young man asked excitedly, without waiting to be introduced.

Nathan frowned. Walking into this smart,

sophisticated gathering after weeks of battling against the elements in a yacht furnished with only basic necessities was almost more than his weary brain could take at the moment. 'Sir Oswald?' he said vaguely.

'Sir Oswald Mosley. He's meeting us at Jeronimo's later. Isobel's arranged it. Isn't it spiffing?'

'Ah. Yes. Spiffing indeed.' He slopped whisky into his glass and swallowed it, neat.

'You don't sound very impressed,' the young man said, clearly offended.

'I'm not. I wouldn't cross the road for him. In fact, I'd walk the other way. I think his opinions are misguided, to say the very least.' Nathan poured himself another shot of whisky although he knew it was unwise on an empty stomach. 'In fact, I think he's a dangerous man.'

The young man leaned forward confidentially and Nathan received the full blast of his hair oil. 'I wouldn't say that too loudly, if I was you, old chap,' he said, a trifle uncomfortably. 'We're all great admirers of Sir Oswald. That's what this party's all about.'

'Then I'm obviously in the wrong place.' Nathan swallowed his drink and banged his glass down and shouldered his way out of the room, furious with Isobel for organising this party when she knew he would be coming home exhausted.

He went upstairs and ran himself a bath, wishing he had brought another whisky with him. He closed his eyes as he sank into the steaming water and felt the warmth begin to loosen his aching muscles. He hadn't realised just how tired he was.

'Oh, good, darling. You're cleaning yourself up ready to come to Jeronimo's.' His eyes flew open as Isobel came into the bathroom. 'I wondered where you'd got to.' She leaned over and dropped a kiss on his forehead. 'Tired, are you, Baby? Never mind, a bath will refresh you. I've already put out your starched shirt and dinner jacket. Don't be long, will you, we're going in half an hour.' She turned to leave.

He yawned. 'I'm not coming, Isobel,' he said.

'Oh, darling. You must. I've told Sir Oswald . . . '

He sat up and reached for the soap. 'I don't want to meet Sir Oswald, Isobel. Not now, not ever. I don't like his politics. I don't like the way he supports that Hitler man. Can't he see what the monster's doing? I think he's at the best misguided and at the worst downright evil.'

Isobel ran a manicured hand over the curly

hairs on his chest. 'I love you when you're cross,' she purred. 'Hurry up and dry yourself. We don't want to keep the others waiting . . . But on the other hand . . . I'm sure they'll understand.' She slipped her hand into the water. 'It won't take me a moment to slip out of my dress. After all, you've been away for four whole months.'

He caught her hand and deliberately gave it back to her. 'Don't bother, Isobel. If I'd been away for four years I still wouldn't have any desire to make love to you.'

She straightened up. 'Well, let me tell you there are plenty of men who would,' she said, her face flushed with anger.

'And I daresay they do, knowing you,' he replied. 'Although whether you've managed to lure Sir Oswald into your bed yet . . . '

'I don't have to listen to this,' she said, going to the door. 'I don't know what's come over you, Nathan. I suspect you've spent too long on that yacht in the company of rough village men. You need to mend your manners. My friends downstairs were quite upset at the way you left the room without saying anything.'

'You can tell your friends downstairs to go to hell,' he said, 'or to Sir Oswald Mosley, which amounts to the same thing.'

'Oh!' She flounced out of the bathroom

and a little while later Nathan heard the sounds of the party leaving the house, chattering excitedly. Afterwards there was blessed silence.

Some time later, he got out of the bath and put on his bathrobe and went down to the basement, where Ethel made him scrambled eggs. Then he went back upstairs, looked in at the drawing room, a mess of overturned glasses, over-flowing ashtrays and canapés ground into the carpet. He leaned on the doorpost, surveying the scene. In spite of his determination to make the marriage work he knew, with blinding clarity, that however hard he tried, it could never be. This was not his life, the life he wanted to lead. These people were artificial, full of mannerisms and gestures, following causes because it was fashionable, not because they believed in them. Didn't they read the newspapers or listen to the wireless? Didn't they know what was going on?

Or did they? Did they approve of what Herr Hitler was doing to the Jews? Were they in favour of his idea of a superior Aryan Race? If they were, did they realise they would never be part of it?

He turned away, totally disgusted, and carried on up the stairs. There he wrote a brief note to Isobel, telling her he was leaving and wouldn't be back, then he dressed, packed a bag, collected his best paintings from his studio, and left, never to return.

To his surprise, Nathan didn't receive the welcome he had expected when he arrived back at his parents' house. His mother had become used to a life of ease, of pleasing herself what she did and when she did it. She found it bad enough when her husband came home and disrupted the smooth flow of things with his untidy ways and demands for regular meals — not that Captain Bellamy was untidy, but the newspaper left unfolded constituted a muddle in Mabel's eyes. But now Nathan had walked in with a suitcase full of his belongings and a huge portfolio of drawings, which he was expecting to put in his old room, the room Mabel had turned into a sewing room. It was too much. And she said so.

Captain Bellamy wasn't quite so unwelcoming but he pointed out, not unreasonably, that it would be rather embarrassing for him if Nathan were to come back home to live. After all, Hector was still captain of Sir Titus Armitage's yacht and being paid quite a handsome retainer by him for the winter, so he could hardly appear to condone the fact that Nathan had walked out on his wife, who was Sir Titus's daughter, by allowing him to return to the family home. Didn't Nathan appreciate that his father had his position to think of? Added to that, had Nathan considered *his* position? It was quite a ticklish situation since he was technically still mate on *Aurora*, and Sir Titus was still his father-in-law.

Nathan had. He wanted nothing more to do with Sir Titus, Sir Titus's daughter, nor Sir Titus's yacht. In fact, he had already written and resigned his position on *Aurora*. In answer to his father's further question he said that he had sufficient money to live on for several months, both from the season's prize money and from the paintings he had sold so if his parents were not willing to give him house room he would go and live with his grandfather on board his old smack until he could find himself a studio somewhere. But perhaps he could leave his paintings?

Mabel was torn between reluctance to upset her comfortable life and horror at the idea of her son living with his disgusting old reprobate of a grandfather. The comfortable life won and she let him go. Hector was content. If anybody could bring the boy down to earth, his grandfather would. However, the portfolio could stay. There wouldn't be space for that on the old smack.

Zeke Bellamy had made himself a snug little billet in his old smack, called appropriately the *Live and Let Live* and he was happy for his grandson to share it with him, the more so since he knew that Mabel wouldn't approve.

'Yis, boy, you c'n shake down in here with me for as long as yew like,' he said, through the blue fug of his old pipe. 'I shall be glad of a bit o' comp'ny. Yew c'n stow yer gear through there,' he pointed with the stem of his pipe to the foc'sle.

Nathan pushed his bag through the bulkhead and sat down opposite to his grandfather. It was just like old times. Ever since he could remember he had visited the old man, and listened to his tales of life aboard the various ships he had sailed in and the places he had seen; the fact that he was disobeying his mother giving an added spice to his visits.

'Wanta drop o' stew, boy?' the old man asked. 'There's a drop left in the pan.'

Nathan lifted the lid of the blackened saucepan on the stove. The stew was thick and greasy and full of meat and vegetables. It smelled good, if a trifle burnt.

'Git yerself a basin orf the shelf, boy, and help yerself.' The old man put his feet back on the bunk and puffed his pipe contentedly while Nathan ate the stew with obvious relish.

'I ollus make meself a stew or a suet duff. Every day,' Zeke said. 'I don't reckon that do any good to starve the inner man. Wanta drop o' beer?'

'No, thanks, grandad. I'm all right with the stew. It's good.' Nathan polished off the last of the stew in the basin, smiling to himself as he contrasted this meal, eaten on his lap out of a pudding basin of doubtful cleanliness with a bent spoon, with the elegant meals he had eaten with Isobel in their smart dining room, the table neatly laid with silver and expensive china, Isobel seated at one end and himself at the other, making polite conversation as they ate quails eggs and the like. He had never, ever enjoyed a meal in those surroundings like he was enjoying this one. When he had finished he wiped his mouth on the back of his hand.

'I think I'll turn in now, Grandad, if you don't mind,' he said. 'I've had a bit of a rough day, one way and another.'

His grandfather nodded. 'Home for good, are ye, boy?' was all he asked.

'Yes, Grandad. I'm home for good. I shan't be going back to London again.' There was almost palpable relief in Nathan's voice as he said the words.

22

It was nearly Christmas before Ginny discovered that Nathan had come back to live in Wyford. Since the birth of the baby in the middle of September her time had been fully occupied with the two children — Bobby had only been fifteen months old, little more than a baby herself, when he was born — plus the extra cooking she and her mother had been asked to do as Christmas approached.

They called the baby George, after the new King. Ginny had great admiration and respect for King George and after the Coronation, in May 1937, she bought a picture — they were on sale everywhere — of the King and Queen Elizabeth, his wife, with their two young daughters the Princesses Elizabeth and Margaret Rose, to hang above the mantelpiece in the front room. They looked a happy little family, even in Coronation robes, the princesses in ermine robes with little crowns on their head to match their parents'.

To mark the occasion all the village schoolchildren had been given a Coronation mug by the local council with a picture of the

King and Queen on it, so Ginny bought one for Bobby and the new baby so that they shouldn't be left out. George's was just a bit different in design from Roberta's but not enough to notice. She kept them both on the mantelpiece under the royal picture.

She was in the front room, having taken the opportunity to decorate the Christmas tree while the children were asleep, when Will came home. He had been doing some repairs on the boat after being caught out at sea in rough weather. The tree stood on a small table in the corner of the front room, which was fully furnished now with a square of flowered linoleum, a half moon woollen rug at the hearth and a green rexine three-piece suite. Ginny was very proud of her front room and the children were only allowed in on special occasions.

'Ah, you're in here,' he said, coming to find her.

She turned round from the tree. 'Don't you come in here with those filthy boots, Will Kesgrave,' she said sharply, her smile belying her words. 'I don't want this room smelling of fish and worse.'

He stepped back into the doorway. 'You'd better come and fetch these, then,' he said good-humouredly, holding out two parcels. 'Nathan gave 'em to me today to put under the tree for the children.'

'Nathan gave them to you? Is he back from London?' Ginny said in surprise, taking the two parcels from him and placing them carefully under the tree. She felt a sharp pang of annoyance, slighted because he hadn't brought them himself. Yet she had been telling herself for weeks that she was glad Nathan hadn't been back to Wyford. Seeing him always upset her for days afterwards, leaving her feeling restless and with a dull ache in her heart when she thought of how things might have been, so it was much better if he didn't come at all. But she had missed him. Oh, how she had missed him.

She followed Will through to the living room. 'We haven't seen him for ages, have we,' she said, keeping her voice light.

He sat down in the chair by the fire. 'I hev. Plenty times,' he said.

Ginny's eyebrows shot up. 'You have?'

'Oh, yes. He never stayed in London when he went back in September,' he said, pulling off his boots. 'In fact, he was back here the next day.' He nodded sagely at Ginny. 'He's never said, girl, but I shouldn't be surprised if he had a row with Isobel and walked out on her. Thass what I reckon. Anyhow, he's back here now, livin' with his old grandad on the *Live and Let Live*.'

Ginny sat down on the nearest chair. 'Living on his grandad's old smack!' she said incredulously. 'What's he living there for? Why isn't he living at his mother's house?' She frowned at Will.

Will shrugged. 'As far as I can make out his mother didn't want the bother of him and his father thought it'd be a bit tricky if he lived at home, seein' as he's still captain of Sir Titus Armitage's yacht.'

Ginny got up and went over to the stove. 'I can't see that would make any difference. Nathan's mate on the yacht, too,' she said, picking up the soup ladle to fill his plate with thick vegetable soup.

'Not any more, he ain't.' Will leaned back in his chair and filled his pipe. 'He's resigned.'

'How do you know all this?'

''Cause he told me so. He's been fishin' with me nearly every time I've bin out.'

Ginny felt another pang, this time of pure jealousy. 'Why didn't you tell me all this before?'

'You never asked.'

'Well, why hasn't he been to see us, then? He often used to pop in to see Bobby.' She corrected herself quickly. 'Well, not that often, but he sometimes used to come home with you to see her. He hasn't seen George since he was first born.'

He shrugged. 'Dunno. I've asked him several times but he's allus got some excuse why he won't come.' He smiled at Ginny through a haze of smoke. 'You ain't fell out with him, hev ye?'

'I haven't seen him to fall out with him,' Ginny said, more sharply than she intended.

'No, well, when he ain't bin fishin' with me he's bin busy with his paintin'. He's found hisself a studio up at the Cross, near the Horse an' Groom and he spends a lot of his time there, I believe. He's a bit worried about his grandad, too. That old smack ain't all that comfortable and Nathan's bin tryin' to do it up a bit an' make it a bit better for him. The old chap ain't up to much by all accounts. Some days he can't hardly move, his joints are that stiff an' his chest is bad. An' that old boat is as rotten as a pear; Nathan says he can't keep the wet out, try as he might. He's tried to persuade ole Zeke to go an' see the quack but he's as cussed as they come and on't hev nothin' to do with doctors.'

'Oh, dear,' Ginny said, 'that's a worry for him.' But she still felt slighted that all this had gone on and she hadn't known. 'Do you think Nathan might like to have his Christmas dinner with us?' she asked hopefully.

'No, he's gotta go to his mother's.' Will

finished his soup and held his bowl out for more. 'He wanted the old chap to go with him as well, but the stubborn old bugger on't leave his smack.' He chuckled. 'I reckon thass as well. I don't reckon Mabel Bellamy 'ud be any too happy if her father-in-law turned up on her doorstep on Christmas Day in his old moleskins.'

Ginny smiled briefly at the picture Will's words had conjured up as she refilled his bowl and poured some soup for herself. 'Dearie me,' she said as she sat down again. 'Fancy, Nathan's been living on that old smack with his grandad all this time and I never knew. He must find it a bit of a comedown from the posh house in London,' she said, unable to keep a trace of waspishness out of her voice.

'All I can say is, he seem a damn sight happier,' Will said.

His words gave Ginny little comfort.

On Christmas morning Ginny went to church. She took Bobby with her in the pushchair but left the baby at home with his father, saying when Will protested that there was plenty of help at hand if George cried. Granny Crabtree was only next door and Annie was just down the yard. Anyway, he was well fed and would probably sleep till she got back.

As she slid into the pew beside her mother Ginny saw that Nathan was there with his parents. They were sitting to the right and a little ahead.

All through the service she watched him, feasting her eyes on the back of his head, the way his hair grew — he had recently had it cut — the set of his shoulders, the line of his jaw as he turned his head slightly. She was sure he was thinner; his cheeks looked hollow under his weathered tan. It was fortunate that she knew all the hymns and carols off by heart because she couldn't even bear to take her eyes off him to look at the book in her hand and during the prayers she still watched him through a chink in her clasped fingers.

She knew she was being ridiculous but she couldn't help herself and when Bobby fidgeted and she had to take her eyes off him to quieten her she was unreasonably irritated.

After the service the congregation spilled out into the frosty Christmas sunshine.

'I must hurry home to baste the chicken and get the vegetables on to cook,' Ruth said, after they had received the rector's perfunctory greeting. 'You can fetch Will and the baby and come along when you're ready.' They were spending Christmas Day with Ruth this year.

Ginny turned Bobby's pushchair towards

the little kissing gate at the back of the churchyard behind the church, which was the quickest way to Quay Yard. She hurried in order to avoid bumping into Nathan, who she was sure hadn't even noticed she had been in church.

But she was wrong.

'Ginny.' She froze in her tracks at the sound of his voice behind her.

'Merry Christmas, Ginny,' he said quietly as he caught up with her.

'Oh,' she pretended to be surprised. 'Merry Christmas, Nathan.'

'Why were you hurrying away, Ginny? It's the season of goodwill, you know.'

She flushed. 'I didn't think you'd noticed I was here.'

'Of course I knew you were there,' he said with a trace of impatience. 'You were sitting in the pew behind me, a little to my left.'

She flushed again, wondering if he had seen her watching him. 'Thank you for Bobby's dolly,' she said, to cover her embarrassment.

He squatted on his haunches in front of the little girl. 'I see you've brought her to church, Bobby,' he said, leaning forward and kissing her cheek. 'Do you like her?'

Bobby laughed and nodded vigorously as

she hugged the doll tightly. 'My dolly,' she said delightedly.

Nathan straightened up. 'Yes, she's your dolly, Bobby,' he said, patting her head. 'Given with my very special love.' He turned to Ginny. 'I wanted to buy you a present . . .' He broke off as Ginny shook her head vehemently.

'No, Nathan. That would never do.'

'I know. But I wished I could.'

They were both silent for a moment, then she said, 'I didn't even know you'd come back to Wyford. Nearly three months you've been back and I didn't even know.' She spoke quietly but she couldn't keep the accusation out of her voice. 'Bobby's missed you,' she added.

'And I've missed Bobby.' But it wasn't Bobby that either of them were speaking about and they both knew it. He went on, 'I couldn't come to see you, Ginny. The last time I came . . . just after your son was born . . . you seemed such a happy family . . . so complete . . .'

'Will's a good man,' she said on a sigh. 'He's turned over a new leaf. He works hard and doesn't drink. At least not much. I owe him a lot.'

'Do you love him?' His voice was low.

She looked at him for the first time and he

saw the pain in her eyes. 'Oh, Nathan. How can you ask me that?'

He put his hand over hers on the handle of the pushchair. 'I'm sorry, Ginny.' He put slight pressure on her hand and then lifted his own. 'But that's why I don't come to see you now, Ginny. It's too painful. I'm jealous. I can't bear . . . ' He shook his head. 'And it's not fair to you, either.'

'No. It's best you don't come. We can't live our lives on what might have been. We have to accept things as they are.' There was only the merest trace of bitterness in her tone. 'But what about Isobel? She's still your wife.'

'Isobel?' His lip curled. 'I've left her. I'm never going back. I can't live her kind of life. It was killing me,' he said savagely. His mouth twisted. 'In any case, she's moved on. All she's interested in these days are her rallies and meetings with her Fascist friends. Sir Oswald Mosley is her hero.' He gave a shrug. 'I don't know whether she's actually been to bed with him but I wouldn't like to bet on it that she hasn't. Not that I care. She's got herself mixed up with a dangerous crew, to my way of thinking. If she's not very careful she'll end up in prison and then 'Daddy' will have to bail her out. Which of course he will.'

'Oh, Nathan, I'm sorry.' In an almost

involuntary gesture she put her hand on his arm.

He covered it with his own. 'Don't be, Ginny. I can assure you I'm not. Isobel means nothing to me. Nothing at all. In fact, leaving her was like lifting a great weight off my shoulders.' He grinned now. 'I'm far happier here, living on the smack with Grandad and his stinking old pipe. He's a cantankerous old devil and the smack isn't exactly the Ritz but we get on famously together. Mind you, I'm not there all that much. I do a lot of painting when I'm not out fishing with Will.' Suddenly, an idea struck him. 'You must come up to my studio, Ginny. It's at the Cross, opposite the Horse and Groom. I'd like to show you my paintings. There's one in particular I'd like you to see. Will you come?'

She gave him a rather sad smile. 'Do you really think that would be wise, Nathan?'

He smiled wryly in return. 'No, but I'd still like you to come, Ginny. Bring some of your pencil sketches and I'll hang them with my pictures. I'm still in contact with a few London art dealers who buy my pictures. I'm sure when they see yours they'll want them. You're very good, you know. And your sketches are quite unusual in the subjects you've chosen. Will you come?'

She nodded uncertainly. 'Perhaps. I'll see.'

She looked round at the churchyard, practically empty now. 'I must go. Will will wonder where I am.'

'Yes.' He hesitated. Then he said, 'As it's Christmas I'm going to allow myself a treat.'

She looked at him, puzzled.

He smiled into her eyes and said softly, 'I'm going to tell you that I love you, Ginny. I've always loved you, although I didn't realise it. And I know I always . . . '

'Stop it,' she said in a fierce whisper, her eyes filling with tears. 'For God's sake don't make things more difficult for me than they are already.'

With that she hurried away, back to her husband.

23

In the event Nathan spent very little time at his studio during the first weeks of the New Year. Old Zeke's arthritis got worse; then he contracted bronchitis. Nathan nursed him as well as the old man would allow but in the end, totally against his grandfather's wishes, Nathan called the doctor, who looked round with horror at the squalid surroundings and immediately ordered him into hospital.

'I ain't goin' to no horspiddle,' the old man croaked in Nathan's ear.

'You'll be more comfortable there, Grandad. It's only for a few days,' Nathan encouraged, trying to find a few decent clothes for him to take with him. 'You'll be back here before you know it.'

'I ain't bloody well goin',' Zeke insisted. 'I on't go. Not for Father Peter.' (Nobody quite knew who Father Peter was but he'd been called upon by his grandfather in times of stress for as long as Nathan could remember.) 'You can't make me.'

Nathan nodded. 'Well, we'll see about that.' Whilst the old man ranted and raged insofar as his weakened state would allow, Nathan washed him and combed and cut his sparse grey hair and trimmed his beard and moustache in readiness for his stay in hospital. 'There, you look a bit more presentable now, Grandad,' he said with a smile. 'Do you want to see how smart you look?'

'No. Leave me alone and go an' tell them doctor people I ain't leavin' my boat. They can give me a bottle o' jalop an' I'll be as right as ninepence. Thass all I need.' The old man was clearly frightened, his gnarled old hands were clinging to the wooden sides of his bunk for protection.

'There's really no need for you to worry, Grandad. I'll come in the ambulance with you,' Nathan said soothingly.

'You on't, 'cause I ain't goin' nowhere,' Zeke said, his voice growing weaker with arguing. He gave a long sigh. 'Fill me a pipe, will ye, boy?'

Nathan frowned. 'You shouldn't smoke, Grandad, not with your chest. They won't let you smoke that filthy old weed in hospital, you know.'

'All the more reason to hev it now.'

Nathan looked at him for a moment, then gave in. He could see the old man relax as he tamped the tobacco down and lit the pipe for him. Then he struggled up on to one elbow, took a few appreciative puffs and began to cough.

'I don't think it's doing you a lot of good,' Nathan said anxiously as the coughing went on.

'Can't do me a lotta harm. Not now.' He took another long pull. 'Ah, thass wunnerful stuff,' he said happily between bouts of coughing that shook his frame. He handed the pipe back to Nathan and lay back on the pillow. 'Shan't want no more,' he said, closing his eyes. 'I'm ready,' he said. 'They, can come an' git me now.'

Nathan smiled down at him. 'I'm glad you've changed your mind, Grandad. You won't be away many days, I'm sure. While you're gone I'll give the boat a good clean. It looks as if it could do with it.' He gazed round the smoke-blackened cabin. 'A lick of paint wouldn't come amiss, either.'

'You leave my boat alone,' the old man muttered. 'Thass bin all right for me all these years that'll last me out jest as it is, 'ithout your interference.' His voice weakened, then he sighed and whispered, 'I like it jest as it is. An' I ain't goin' to no horspiddle.'

'All right, Grandad, just as you say.' Nathan took his hand and held it.

The old man's eyes opened briefly. 'You're

a good boy, Nathan,' he said. 'We git along all right together.' Then, with a contented sigh he closed them again.

Nathan was watching as his grandfather drew his last breath. He waited a few minutes, then leaned over and kissed the weather-beaten old cheek.

Zeke had got his wish. He wouldn't be taken to hospital.

★ ★ ★

According to the old man's wishes, his body was towed out to the deeps beyond the estuary in the smack that had been his home for the past thirty years. There the boat was to be scuttled, sending the old man to a watery grave.

The operation didn't go altogether smoothly. At first the rector was not willing to conduct the funeral, in truth he was a bit afraid the sea might be rough and he would disgrace himself by being seasick.

Then there was the problem of getting the half-rotted *Live and Let Live* off the mud, where she had been settled for more years than most people could remember.

This was finally achieved, then a tow rope was attached to the *Emily May* and Will Kesgrave towed her out to sea, while Nathan and his father baled frantically in the bilges of the rotten old hulk in order to keep her afloat long enough to reach her destination. Then all they had to do was to scramble over on to the other boat and watch her sink below the waves while the rector stood on the bow of *Emily May* and read the funeral service. Then Hector Bellamy threw a wreath on to the spot where she had disappeared.

'What's Nathan going to do now? Where's he going to live?' Ginny asked when Will returned home and told her all that had happened. 'Will he go back to live with his mum and dad?'

'No, I don't think so,' Will said. 'He's found hisself a couple o' rooms near his studio and I think he's goin' to stay there for the time bein'. But he's speakin' of goin' back to London.'

'Oh, going back to his wife, is he?' Ginny asked, making a great effort to keep her voice level.

Will shrugged. 'I dunno. He didn't say. Jest said he'd gotta go back. He'd hev gone before if it hadn't bin for his old grandad.'

'I see.'

For days afterwards Ginny mulled over this news. She felt cheated. Betrayed. Furious with herself that she had believed Nathan's glib words in the churchyard on Christmas

Day. How could she have been taken in by his lies yet again, she asked herself. It was clear that he enjoyed keeping two women dangling after his affections; in all probability he had only come back to live in Wyford to make Isobel realise she couldn't live without him. She had probably written to him nearly every day begging him to go back and he would have gone to her before if it hadn't been for his grandfather. All those words about hating her and all she stood for had been so much eyewash. There was a saying that sailors had a girl in every port; well, it seemed as if the same could be said for fishermen and yachtsmen, too, when they were like Nathan Bellamy.

Furious with herself she banged saucepans and kettles about when she went to do the three-times weekly bake with her mother; she slammed the pastry down on to the pastry board and rolled it as if her life depended on it.

In the end her mother said, exasperated, 'What on earth's got into you, my girl? Has Will started drinking again?' She gave a disapproving sniff. 'Mind you, I thought it was only a matter of time before he would.'

'No, Will hasn't started drinking again, Mother,' Ginny replied wearily. 'He's all right. He's a good man, so don't keep looking for trouble.' She threw the rolling pin down and sat down at the table. 'I'm very fond of Will,' she said firmly. 'In spite of the way we got wed we've got a good marriage. He might be a bit of a rough diamond but he's good to me and he's good to the children. He works hard and keeps the smack in good order. As you know from your share of the takings he's done well at the fishing grounds this year. So don't keep picking on him.' She stood up and picked up the rolling pin again and attacked the pastry. 'I know you only do it because you're jealous.'

Ruth's mouth dropped open. 'Whatever put that idea into your head? Why should I be jealous?'

'Because you hoped I'd come running to you every five minutes complaining about him. Well, I don't, because I haven't got anything to complain about.'

'And who are you trying to convince, my girl?' Ruth said quietly. 'Me? Or yourself?'

'I don't know what you're talking about,' Ginny snapped. 'And pick the baby up, will you, I think he's got wind. My hands are all floury.' She looked down at Bobby, who was tugging at her skirts. 'All right, I'll give you a bit of pastry to roll in a minute,' she said impatiently.

Ruth sat rubbing George's back and

watching Ginny. Something was eating into the girl, of that she was certain. But if it wasn't trouble with Will — and Ginny had been so vehement in her defence of him that Ruth was not entirely convinced on that score — then what was it? She frowned. Surely, she couldn't still be hankering after Nathan Bellamy!

She planted a kiss on George's dark curls and laid him back in his pram.

'Mabel Bellamy told me the other day that Nathan's gone back to London,' she said casually, covertly watching for Ginny's reaction.

'Yes, I'd heard. I thought it wouldn't be long before he went back to his wife,' Ginny said, her back turned as she busily filled tarts with jam.

Ruth heard the bitterness that Ginny had been unable to keep out of her voice and nodded to herself, satisfied she had found the cause of her daughter's bad temper. She felt a trace of irritation. It was time the girl got over her infatuation for that man. Goodness knows he'd treated her badly enough over the years. 'Yes, well, it was only to be expected, I suppose,' she remarked. 'He was on to a good thing, wasn't he, marrying the boss's daughter. He'll never be short of a copper. No shortage of money there.'

Ginny put the jam tarts in the oven and slammed the door. 'Can't you think of anything good to say about *anybody*, Mother?' she asked, exasperated.

Ruth looked injured. 'What have I said now?'

'You're implying that Nathan has only gone back to his wife because she's got a lot of money. But I don't think that's the reason, at all. Nathan isn't at all short of cash, Mother. His pictures sell for quite a lot of money these days. He's a very good artist.'

'Then why has he gone racing back to London?'

'*I* don't know. Perhaps he's desperate to see Isobel.' Ginny turned quickly and knocked a basin of eggs on to the floor. 'Oh, damn. Now look what you've made me do.'

Ruth put her head on one side. 'Are you pregnant again, Ginny?' she asked.

'No, I'm *not* pregnant again. I'm just fed up with you making damn silly remarks,' Ginny shouted, then got down on her knees to clear up the mess of eggs, biting back the tears that threatened to spill over.

'I'll put the kettle on,' Ruth said quietly. 'I think we could both do with a cup of tea.'

After Ginny had gone home Ruth sat looking into her fire, thinking about her. It was quite obvious that the girl was still head over heels in love with Nathan Bellamy and from what Mabel Bellamy had let drop and in spite of what Ginny surmised Nathan wasn't happy with Isobel either. But there was nothing to be done; they were both married to other people and there was an end to it. Better if he stayed in London and never came back again. That way Ginny would forget him. In time.

And Will Kesgrave had turned out a better husband than could ever have been expected. Ruth had often agonised over that, fearing she had made a terrible mistake in shackling her only daughter to such a rough character. She'd known at the time it was a wrong thing to do, but she had been driven by fury. And shame. Shame that Ginny had turned out no better than her mother.

Irritably, Ruth got up and poked the fire.

★   ★   ★

March came in like a lion, with gales that lashed the east coast and brought the tides up higher than anyone could remember.

Will was restless. He worked on *Emily May* until there was nothing more he could do, then he sat at home, getting in Ginny's way, or went out on to the quay to pace up and down, watching the weather and waiting for it to improve so that he could go out and fish.

'I ain't earnin' any money standin' about like this,' he complained to Ginny. 'I can't afford to carry on like this much longer.'

'You're not standing about at the moment, you're sitting by a nice warm fire,' Ginny said with a smile.

'Well, you know what I mean.' He thrust his hands into his pockets.

'We'll manage,' she said cheerfully. 'I always put a bit by for a rainy day when you bring home a good catch and you've done well this winter. It won't be too long before you'll be yachting, so you'll be earning good money again.'

'All the same . . . '

'Have you ever gone without a shilling for beer?'

'No.'

'Well, stop moaning, then. This weather can't last much longer. March came in like a lion so it should go out like a lamb, so the old saying goes.' She looked at him, sitting hunched in his chair. 'But if you're so anxious to do something you can wash up the breakfast things. Or go up to Stacey's and get half a pound of butter. I forgot to put it on my list.'

He got to his feet and shrugged into his

reefer jacket. 'Thass women's work,' he said disparagingly. 'I'm orf out. See what the weather's doin'.'

'Dinner's at one o'clock,' she called after him.

He was back in an hour, looking more cheerful than she had seen him for several weeks.

'Wind's dropped,' he said cheerfully. 'We're goin' down on the tide.'

'Who's 'we'?' she asked suspiciously.

'Me and Albert Salmons and Sid Grimes. And Nathan. He's back. Got back last night.'

'Nathan's back?' she said in surprise. 'How long for?'

'Dunno. I never asked. But he's keen to come out with us so he must be here for a day or two.' He looked out of the window at the bright sunshine and rubbed his hands together. 'Ah, this is what we've bin waitin' for. This'll blow the cobwebs away.'

'Well, you mind and be careful,' Ginny said with a frown, watching as he gathered his gear together. 'Don't stay out there if it gets too rough.'

He gave her a smacking kiss on the cheek. 'Don't worry, girl. I've bin at sea long enough to know what I'm doin'.'

'Yes, I know. Have a good trip.' She waved him off with a smile.

After he had gone she sat down in the chair by the fire, heedless of the fact that the baby hadn't yet been bathed or that Bobby was amusing herself playing in the coal bucket. So Nathan had come back to Wyford again. That's what Will had said. But why? If he'd gone back to his wife why would he leave her again after only a few weeks? She stared into the fire. Of course, he could have returned simply to collect up his paintings. That was the most likely explanation. But in that case, he would hardly have had time to go out fishing with Will. Unless it was his final fling before he settled down to life in the Big City.

She got up and picked Bobby out of the coal bucket. 'You're a filthy little minx,' she said, planting an absent-minded kiss on the child's coal-streaked hair. 'You'll have to go in the tub as soon as George is bathed.'

Bobby had expected a smack. She looked up at her mother uncertainly and Ginny, seeing a sudden likeness to Nathan, gathered her up and buried her face in the child's golden hair. 'Oh, Bobby,' she murmured with a sigh, 'you get more like your father every day. What's to become of us?'

Usually, when Will was away Ginny relished having the bed to herself without him snoring beside her and she slept very well but that night she tossed and turned uneasily. She was anxious but she didn't know why. The wind seemed to have dropped to a stiff breeze so there was no reason for concern over the fact that Will had gone fishing. Her mother had been suffering from a heavy cold but that was much improved so there was no worry there. The children were both healthy and strong, for which she thanked providence.

She lay staring up into the darkness, knowing only too well that she had been skirting round the real reason for her anxiety. It was Nathan . . . Will said he had come back to Wyford. But why? If he had gone back to London to patch things up with Isobel why return to Wyford so soon? And how long did he intend to stay? Would she see him? It wasn't likely he would come to visit her but she might bump into him in the street, or on the quay. How could she be so desperate to see him yet dread meeting him at the same time?

She turned over and thumped her pillow. What was wrong with her? Why couldn't she put him out of her mind once and for all?

24

Emily May was away for five days. This was not unusual; sometimes they had to go further afield to find fish so Ginny wasn't worried on that score, but she began to get a little anxious when the weather began to deteriorate, with torrential rain and the return of the gales.

In the evenings, when the children were in bed and she only had the wireless for company, she would hear the wind howling above the music and she would send up a little prayer for *Emily May's* safety. But during the day she had little time to worry. Whether Will was at home or at sea much of her time was taken up with baking, mostly at Ruth's house. Appleyard's cakes and pies were becoming very popular with the more affluent families in the village and even beyond, although it worried Ginny that at the other end of the scale there were still a good many children who didn't have enough bread, let alone cake, because their fathers couldn't find work.

'It's a pity we can't open a little shop,' she remarked thoughtfully, surveying Ruth's kitchen table, laden with custard tarts, iced buns and fancy cakes. 'I'm sure we'd do well. I hear there's talk of reopening the shipyard, too. That would mean there's more money about.'

Ruth shook her head. 'I'm not sure that would be a good idea. Not the way things are at the minute,' she said doubtfully.

'I reckon we could afford to rent a place, Mum,' Ginny said, warming to her idea.

'I know that, Ginny, but I don't think it's a very good time. Don't you listen to the news on the wireless? It doesn't sound very good. This Hitler man seems to think he can walk into any country he likes and take it over. Sooner or later he'll have to be stopped. If there should be a war . . . '

'Oh, Mum, don't talk like that. There won't be a war,' Ginny said, more confidently than she felt.

'I sincerely hope you're right,' Ruth said fervently. 'The last one only finished twenty years ago. We've hardly got over that. But I wouldn't bank on it. The signs are all there. After all, there must be some reason for them considering opening up the shipyard again. And I heard on the wireless that everybody's going to be fitted with gas masks.'

'What for?'

'In case there's a gas attack, like there was

in the trenches in the last war.'

'But how can they?' Ginny said, alarmed. 'I mean, how would you fit a gas mask on babies like George?'

'I don't know. Perhaps it's just scaremongering.'

Ginny gave a little shudder. 'Let's not talk about it. It might not come to anything.'

'I hope to goodness it won't.'

Ginny pinched her lip. 'Mum, if they're going to reopen the shipyard, whatever the reason, there'll be more money about, won't there. It might be a good time to open a shop. I wouldn't mind living over the shop.'

'No, but Will might.' Ruth pressed her lips together. 'I think we should wait. We're doing all right as we are. We don't need a shop.'

As she spoke there was a knock at the door.

'See? That'll be the maid from Gurney Vale, come to fetch the pasties Mrs Bright ordered,' she said over her shoulder as she went to answer the door. 'Six. Put them in a bag, will you, Ginny? Oh,' her voice changed. 'You're not from Gurney Vale, are you.'

'No, madam, I'm afraid I'm not.' The man at the door tipped his hat. 'I'm looking for a Mrs Kesgrave. I've been to her house but there was nobody there. The next-door neighbour said I'd be likely to find her here.'

'Yes, I'm here,' Ginny said, coming to the

door and looking over her mother's shoulder. 'What do you want?'

He cleared his throat. 'I'd rather . . . not on the doorstep, if you don't mind.' He removed his hat, revealing thinning iron-grey hair. 'Might I just step inside . . . ?'

Puzzled, they both stood aside, Ginny wiping her hands on her pinafore and then smoothing back her hair. 'Well?' she asked. 'What is it you want with me?'

He cleared his throat again. 'I'm very sorry, Mrs Kesgrave, but I've come to tell you you're needed at the Colchester hospital.'

Ginny frowned. 'Who by? I don't know anybody . . . ' she began.

'It's your husband, I'm afraid.'

She sat down with a bump. 'Ah. Tell me.' There was no surprise in her voice. At the back of her mind she knew she had been waiting for it.

'Your husband's smack . . . *Emily May* . . . It was caught in a bad squall out by the Wallet . . . I'm afraid it went down . . . Fortunately, the men are all safe. Another smack managed to get alongside and rescue them.'

Ginny closed her eyes. 'Thank God for that,' she breathed. 'They're all safe, you say?'

'Yes. The smack that rescued them put in to Brightlingsea,' the man explained. 'There were a few cuts and bruises and of course they're all badly shaken, but fortunately nothing worse . . . '

'Oh, thank heaven,' Ginny said before he could continue, her shoulders sagging with relief.

'As I was saying, nobody is badly hurt,' the man went on uncomfortably, 'that is, except for your husband, Mrs Kesgrave. I'm told they think he may have broken his leg. Possibly, both his legs. The ambulance was called as soon as he was brought ashore and took him off to hospital.'

Ruth's hand flew to her mouth. 'Oh, my God.'

All the colour drained out of Ginny's face but she got to her feet quite calmly and took off her pinafore. 'Thank you for coming to tell me, Mr . . . ?'

'Goodwin. Charles Goodwin.'

'Thank you for coming, Mr Goodwin, it was very kind of you. Will's broken his leg, you say? Or legs? No matter, I'll find out when I get there. What time is there a bus?'

'If you'll allow me, Mrs Kesgrave,' he said, clearing his throat. 'I've got my motor car outside. I'd be more than happy to drive you there.'

'Would you really?' Ginny said, surprised. 'I'd be very grateful, Mr Goodwin. It would be so much quicker.'

He twisted his hat in his hands. 'It was because I've got a car that I was asked to bring you the news. It was the quickest way, you see.'

'Yes. Thank you, Mr Goodwin. I'll just get my coat and hat.'

'I'll get mine as well,' Ruth said.

'No, it's all right, Mother.' Ginny began to pin on her hat. 'I can manage on my own. I'd rather you stayed here to look after the children. I can't take them with me because I don't think they'd be allowed into the hospital but they'll be all right here with you.'

'Yes, of course. They'll be no trouble.'

Charles Goodwin said very little on the journey to the hospital, sensing that Ginny needed time to gather her thoughts and adjust herself to the news he had brought her. She seemed to him a very self-possessed young woman but you could never tell what was going on beneath the surface.

In fact, so many thoughts and fears were jostling for position in Ginny's mind that she couldn't think straight about any one of them. Will had a broken leg, well, thank goodness it was nothing worse. Would the insurance from the boat be enough to buy another one? Probably not. But a down payment and the rest in instalments, they could manage that, especially now Apple-yard's cakes were so popular. And there was always yachting in the summer months. She wondered what the price of a new or second-hand fishing smack might be. She had absolutely no idea. Perhaps Will would know. At any rate it would give him something to think about while he was convalescing.

Suddenly, the car drew to a halt.

'Would you like me to come in with you?' Mr Goodwin asked.

Ginny looked round her in surprise. She had rarely travelled in a car and she was amazed at how quickly they had arrived at the hospital. She smiled at him.

'No. I shall be all right. But thank you very much for your help. You've been very kind.' She made to open her purse to pay him but he put up his hand in horror.

'No. Please. I wouldn't dream of it. I was glad to be able to offer assistance. Would you like me to wait for you?'

'Indeed, no. I've taken up quite enough of your time. In any case I've no idea how long I shall be. But thank you all the same.'

He doffed his hat. 'I hope your husband will soon recover, Mrs Kesgrave.' With that he got back in his car and drove off.

Ginny watched him go, afraid she might have offended him by offering him money.

Then she made her way into the hospital and along the labyrinth of green-painted corridors to the ward she had been directed to. Everywhere was clean and quiet, with a definite aroma of carbolic hanging in the air, and her footsteps echoed on the polished linoleum.

There was a row of chairs outside the ward and to her surprise Nathan was sitting there. He had a bandage round his head and another round his hand and halfway up his arm. He looked very white and shaken.

He stood up when he saw her and it seemed the most natural thing in the world that she should walk into his arms. 'He's in the operating theatre, Ginny,' he said, stroking her hair with his good hand. 'He's been gone nearly two hours. I don't know how much longer he'll be but I thought you might appreciate a bit of company when you got here.'

'Oh, Nathan. Thank you,' she said, clinging to him, grateful for his presence. She looked up at him and touched the bandage round his head. 'But what about you? You got hurt, too.'

He released her gently. 'I got a bit of a knock when I slipped on the deck.'

'And your hand? Your arm?'

'Gashed it a bit and sprained the wrist. It'll be all right in a day or two.'

'You look pretty groggy, Nathan.'

'Yes, I must say I've felt more lively in my life. But I'll be OK.'

'You should sit down.' She sat down on one of the hard chairs and he sat on one beside her. After a minute she turned to him, frowning. 'Did you say Will's been in the operating theatre for nearly two hours?' she asked. 'I didn't think it took that long to set bones.'

'I think it's a bit more than simple bone-setting, Ginny,' he answered, taking her hand. 'They couldn't say exactly what the damage was but I think the bones are pretty badly shattered in both legs. But they're hoping they can save them.'

'You mean save his legs? You mean they might have to amputate . . . ? Both of them?' Her voice rose in alarm. 'Oh, God, Nathan! I'd no idea it was that bad . . . '

'Sssh, Ginny. They're hoping it won't come to that,' he said, but he didn't sound very convinced.

'But how . . . ? What happened?' she whispered. 'Mr Goodwin who brought me here said there was a storm . . . '

He gave a little mirthless laugh. 'There was a storm, all right. We all said we'd never known anything like it. Seemed to blow up from nowhere. The light was just beginning to fade. It had been a good day and the sea was as calm as a mill pond, then suddenly this wind blew up seemingly from nowhere and it was like being in the middle of a maelstrom, with forty-foot waves and a force eleven gale. Never known anything like it. None of us had. We were just heading back, too. Good catch. Been a good trip.' He heaved a great sigh. Ginny said nothing, sensing Nathan's need to talk the horror of it all out of his system. He went on, 'The boat was swamped before we knew it. Albert and Sid climbed into the ratlines but the way things were going that wasn't going to save them. Then the mast came down and brought them with it. Will was on deck, clinging to a stanchion and the mast knocked him down and trapped him by the legs. In a way he was lucky. If he hadn't been trapped he'd have been knocked overboard and we'd never have got to him. Anyway, eventually we managed to get him out although the boat was bucking about like nobody's business. We lashed his legs to a spar so they wouldn't get any more damaged, then we saw *Redoubt* steaming towards us. She was just about the most beautiful sight in the world and got to us just in time. It was a bit tricky, but if we timed it right, when the waves washed her close enough we could all manage to scramble or jump over on to her but we had to rig up a breeches buoy to get Will across. We'd only just got him off *Emily May* when she went down. It was a pretty close call.' All this had been related in a flat unemotional monotone. Now he turned and looked at Ginny. 'Sorry about *Emily May*, Ginny. She was your dad's smack.'

Ginny shrugged. 'She'd belonged to my grandad in the first place so she was getting a bit old, I suppose.'

'She was insured?'

'Oh, yes.' She nodded. 'Mum always made sure of that.'

Suddenly, there was the sound of wheels squeaking along the polished brown linoleum and a trolley pushed by a white-clad figure and with a crisply starched nurse hurrying along beside came into view. Behind it and walking more slowly was another white-clad figure, obviously the surgeon, just removing his face mask.

Ginny strained to see Will, but the trolley had passed on into the ward before she could catch more than a glimpse of his black hair.

The surgeon stopped. 'Mrs Kesgrave?'

Ginny nodded. 'And this is Nathan Bellamy.' She hesitated. 'He was with my husband when the accident happened.'

He regarded Nathan gravely. 'You didn't escape unscathed either, I see.' He turned to

Ginny and gave a brief smile. 'Well, the news is good, Mrs Kesgrave, insofar as we didn't have to amputate,' he said cheerfully.

'Oh. That's good news.' It was inadequate but she felt incapable of saying anything more.

He went on. 'We've done what we can to patch your husband up. His legs were in a bit of a mess, the right one was worse than the left.'

'Will he walk again?' Ginny heard Nathan ask the question and she darted a shocked glance at him. In her confused state it had never occurred to her that Will might be a cripple for the rest of his life.

The surgeon rubbed his chin. 'Too soon to say with any certainty, but I should think the answer to that is yes. Eventually. But probably not without some kind of support.'

'Crutches?' A little croak that Ginny recognised dimly as her own voice asked.

'Crutches, sticks, leg irons, something of that kind,' the surgeon said. 'That's what we're hoping. The operation — operations, I should say — went very well, considering the damage he sustained.'

'You mean he'll never walk properly again?' Ginny repeated, horrified.

The surgeon laid his hand on her arm. 'He could have ended up with no use in his lower legs at all, Mrs Kesgrave, with both shin bones smashed as they were. That would have been infinitely worse, I'm sure you'll agree. As it is, I don't *think* it will come to that, although of course it's too soon to be sure. Everything depends now on the healing process. Now, would you like to see him before you go? I warn you, he probably won't be properly round yet from the anaesthetic but I expect he'd like to know you're around.'

'Thank you,' Ginny said. Nervously, she took hold of Nathan's hand. 'You'll come with me, Nathan?'

'Of course. If you want me to, Ginny.'

They walked together down the ward to the screened area where Will lay. His face was chalk white in contrast to his black hair and several days growth of black stubble. As if he sensed their presence his eyes flickered open and rested briefly on Nathan. 'Thanks mate, you saved my life,' he murmured.

'What did he say?' Ginny whispered.

Nathan shook his head. 'Didn't catch it,' he lied.

Ginny bent over and took Will's hand. 'I'll come and see you tomorrow when you're properly awake,' she said softly. Then she smoothed his hair away from his forehead and dropped a kiss on it.

'Bring a bottle o' beer when you come, girl.

I got a thirst like . . . ' his voice slurred and his eyes flickered and then closed.

'You'd better go now,' the nurse said briskly, appearing round the curtain. 'And *don't* bring beer in for him, whatever he says. It's not allowed.'

'That's put us in our place,' Nathan whispered wickedly, as they left the ward. 'I don't know how Will will cope with her, she seems a real old battleaxe.' He smiled down at Ginny, but she was too shocked, too weary to respond. He put his hand under her elbow. 'Come on, let's go and find a café. What we both need is a cup of tea. Then I'll call a taxi and take you home.'

A little later, sitting in a dim little café with steaming cups of tea, Ginny looked across the table at Nathan, her eyes swimming with tears. 'Thank you, Nathan. Thank you for being with me. I don't think I could have managed today if you hadn't been there. And as for the future . . . '

'Take the future one day at a time, Ginny. Don't try to look too far ahead,' he said gently. His tone changed and became hard. 'Will will be all right,' he said, staring down into his cup. 'With you by his side to care for him he'll recover. He's a lucky man.'

She gave a wry smile. 'What, with two broken legs?'

He looked up. 'Even with broken legs I'd gladly swap places with him, Ginny. Any day,' he said fervently, then he looked away. 'But you know that, don't you.'

'You mustn't say that, Nathan,' she said fiercely. She stared out of the window, then said, her voice barely above a whisper, 'Especially when you know it isn't true.'

'Ginny! How can you say that when you know . . . '

'Oh, leave it, Nathan. I'm not in the mood for playing games,' she said, wearily pushing aside a strand of hair. 'Why don't you just stay in London with Isobel and leave me in peace?'

For a few seconds he stared at her, completely stricken. Then he opened his mouth to speak, changed his mind and got to his feet, saying briskly, 'Finished your tea? Come on, it's time to go.'

'Yes, let's go.' Emotionally drained, she stumbled out into the early evening behind him.

25

Will was in hospital for six weeks.

Ginny visited him as often as she could and when she couldn't go there were always his fishing friends ready to go and cheer him up. Even Ruth paid him a visit one Sunday afternoon when Ginny had to stay at home because George wasn't well.

'Quite concerned about me, she was,' Will said with a grin the next time Ginny visited. 'Brought me a nice fruit cake, too. Mind you, she had a dig at me because they make sure I shave every day.'

'Well, I must agree with her. You look a great deal smarter than you often do at home when you haven't shaved for three or four days,' Ginny said, smiling. He was sitting up in bed, washed and shaved, his hair more neatly combed than it ever was when he was at home.

He leaned over to her. 'Why hasn't my mate Nathan bin to see me?' he demanded, wagging his finger at her. 'The rest of me mates hev bin but I ain't seen hair nor hide of him. Where is he?'

Ginny shrugged, staring at the cage that

had been put over the lower part of the bed to keep the weight of the bedclothes off his legs. 'I don't know. He's gone back to London, I suppose. I haven't seen him since the day of the accident.' She didn't want to talk about Nathan, the hurt was too deep.

Will frowned. 'Is he all right?'

'How should I know,' she said impatiently. 'I suppose he is. Why shouldn't he be?'

'Because he got a nasty crack on the head when I smashed my legs. I wonder he didn't break his skull.'

She raised her eyebrows. 'Oh, he didn't tell me that. He just said he got a bit of a knock when he slipped on the deck.'

'Yes, when he slipped on the deck trying to get me out from under that bloody mast.' He frowned at her. 'Don't you understand, Ginny, if it hadn't bin for Nathan, I'd hev bin a dead man and you'd hev bin a widder? That man saved my life.'

'What, single-handed?' she asked sceptically. 'What about the rest of the men on the boat? Didn't they lend a hand?'

'No, they didn't. The buggers'd gone; they jumped on to the other smack as soon as they had the chance. They said afterwards they thought we'd done the same, they said they didn't know I was trapped. Well, thass fair enough, the way the boat was pitchin' and what with the wind and rain you couldn't see your hand in front of your face so they very likely didn't know I'd got caught when the mast came down.' He closed his eyes. 'But lucky for me Nathan saw what happened and he stayed with me. How he got me out from under that mast the Good Lord only knows; that was a miracle he didn't get hisself washed overboard, the way the boat was corkin' about, but somehow he managed it. Then he got 'em to rig up a kinda breeches buoy from the other boat and dragged me into it. He even waited till they'd pulled me across before he jumped hisself.' He opened his eyes and looked at Ginny. 'He's a brave man, Ginny. Thass twice he's saved my life. I owe him everything.' His voice rose and he thumped the sheet with his clenched fist. 'An' thass why I wanta see 'im. I wanta thank 'im. I wanta know he's all right. He's my mate. So you jest find out where he is and tell 'im I wanta see 'im, there's a good gal.'

The nurse came hurrying down the ward. 'Now, now, Mr Kesgrave, I've told you before, you mustn't get yourself all excited,' she said, straightening the already pristine coverlet.

'I ain't gettin' excited. I'm jest tellin' my wife what she's gotta do,' he said, glaring at her. He watched as she whisked away to straighten more beds. 'You can't fart in this bloody place 'ithout they come arter you,' he remarked morosely. 'I shall be glad and thankful to git home.' He sighed, then his expression cleared and he smiled. 'How are the kids? I miss seein' their little antics, you know.'

'I reckon it'll be a week or two yet before you come home, Will,' she warned. 'You'll just have to be patient. Your mum and Gladys are coming to see you next Sunday.'

'That'll be a real treat,' he said without enthusiasm. 'All Mum does is sit there and cry and tell me I shall never walk again while Gladys scoffs me grapes.'

'Well, your mother's wrong. The doctor told me they hope to have you on your feet in a fortnight.' The bell went and she got up and kissed his cheek. 'You can tell her that. And don't let Gladys eat all the grapes I've brought you today, they were expensive. Hide them in your locker.'

He caught her hand and kissed the back of it. 'You're a good gal, Ginny,' he said, squeezing it. He winked and gave her a wicked grin. 'When I git home I'll show you jest what I think of you. Thass only me legs thass out of action, remember. The rest of me's still intact.'

She smiled back at him. 'Now I know

you're feeling better,' she said.

'Remember what I said. I wanta see Nathan,' he called after her as she left the ward.

When she got home Ruth had fed the children and got them ready for bed and there were crumpets waiting for Ginny on the hearth.

As she ate them she told her mother what Will had said about Nathan.

'I'll have to write to him, I suppose,' she said, chewing thoughtfully. 'No doubt Mrs Bellamy has got his address in London.'

'Oh, he isn't in London,' Ruth said, surprised. 'I thought you knew. He's taken rooms at the Cross, near his studio.'

'I know he did that after his grandad died,' Ginny said, 'but I'd assumed he gave them up when he went back to London.'

Ruth frowned. 'No, I don't think he gave them up. He stayed with his mother for a fortnight or so after the accident, but only till he could manage on his own.' She cut Ginny a piece of fruit cake and handed it to her. 'To tell you the truth they don't get on all that well so I think she was quite glad when he left. He had a nasty gash on his arm, she said, and he'll always have a bit of a scar on his forehead but it's up near the hairline so it won't notice. Seven stitches they put in his head and ten in his arm. Lost a lot of blood, by all accounts.'

'Yes, so I believe. But where is he now?'

'I told you. He's got rooms at the Cross. That's where he'll be, I suppose.' Ruth poured Ginny another cup of tea. 'You say he saved Will's life?'

'That's what Will says. That's why he's upset Nathan's never been to see him. He wants to thank him.' Ginny sipped her tea. 'Oh, you make a lovely cup of tea, Mum,' she said, drinking it gratefully. 'I suppose I shall have to go and see Nathan,' she said when she had finished it and replaced the cup on its saucer. 'And I'll have to do it before the next visiting day too or I shall be in trouble with Will.'

'You don't sound very keen to go,' Ruth said, watching her.

'No. I'm not.'

★　★　★

The following morning Ginny set off to find Nathan. The walk to the Cross, about a mile, was too far for Bobby's little legs to manage, so she left her with Ruth and took George in the pram.

Ruth hadn't known Nathan's exact address so Ginny went first to his studio, which she recognised from the paintings in the large window at the front.

She tapped on the door and when there was no answer she turned to walk away.

'Ginny!' The door was suddenly flung open and Nathan stood there in a paint-streaked shirt and trousers. 'What are you doing here? Is Will . . . ?' He looked at her anxiously.

'Will's doing well,' she said.

'Ah, that's good.' He smiled and rubbed his hands together. 'The number of times I've asked you to come and see my studio and you've refused and now you're here without me having to ask. Come in. Please come in.' He stood aside and held the door for her to enter.

She peered into the pram. 'George is asleep. He'll be all right if I leave him outside.' She followed Nathan into the studio and looked round. It was light and airy although not very big. There were canvasses stacked against the walls, bits of material draped from the ceiling, and a bench covered with tubes of paint, palette knives, old bits of rag and several jars holding brushes of every size. A half-finished painting of a barge stood on an easel by the window.

He pulled up an old kitchen chair for her and perched himself on a stool.

'It's good to see you, Ginny,' he said, his

eyes searching her face. 'When we last parted I rather got the feeling that you didn't want to see me ever again.' There was sadness in his voice. Then he brightened. 'But clearly I must have been wrong, because here you are.' He got up from his stool and went to a bench in the corner. 'Can I offer you coffee? I can make coffee, I have a small primus and a kettle here. I can even offer you a biscuit if I haven't eaten them all.' While he was talking he was busily lighting the primus and putting the kettle on to boil so she had no option but to accept.

'Nathan, I've come . . . '

'Just a minute. The kettle's just boiled,' he said over his shoulder. 'I'll make the coffee and then I can give you my full attention. I'm afraid the mugs are a bit elderly but my mother wouldn't part with her decent ones,' he said apologetically as he handed her a mug with a border of faded flowers.

'I thought you'd gone back to London,' she said, scalding her mouth as she sipped her coffee.

'No. Why should you think that?'

'I thought that's where you lived.' She didn't wait for him to reply but went on, 'I've come with a message from Will. He wants to see you. He's most insistent. He can't understand why you haven't been to visit him.'

'How is he?'

'I think his legs pain him quite a bit although he doesn't complain. The doctors are hoping to get him up on to crutches next week or the week after.'

'Oh, that's good.'

'And you? How are you?'

He flexed his hand. 'Getting better. Fortunately it was my left hand so I can still paint.'

'You've got quite a scar on your arm. And on your forehead.'

He touched his head. 'They'll fade. In time. I was lucky things weren't worse.'

'Yes, so I believe. Will told me all about it. He told me you saved his life.'

He looked down into his mug. 'I nearly didn't, Ginny,' he said quietly, without looking up. 'God help me, I nearly left him to drown. I could have done. I could have jumped with the others. They hadn't seen what had happened to Will. Nobody would have known that I had . . . ' He drained his coffee and put his mug down on the bench with a crash. 'I thought — and this all went through my head in a flash — if I let him drown the coast will be clear, Ginny will be free and we can be married. It was so tempting that I was at the rail, waiting to jump as soon as the other boat came close enough. Then I recalled following Will up the stairs to see you after George was born. The picture of you with your new baby, smiling up at Will, with Bobby cuddled beside you, has never left me. You looked such a happy, complete little family I knew you'd be broken-hearted if Will died. So I went back to do what I could for him.'

Ginny swirled what was left of her coffee round in the mug. 'But even if Will had died, how could I have married you, Nathan?' she said. 'Have you forgotten you've already got a wife? In fact, I didn't know you were still in Wyford. I thought you'd gone back to Isobel again.'

He frowned. 'Gone back to her again? What do you mean, again?'

'Well, isn't that where you've been since Christmas? Back with Isobel?'

He let his breath out on something between a sigh and a snort. 'Not exactly, Ginny. In fact I didn't see Isobel at all.' He paused. 'Oh, I went back to London, all right, but not back to my wife.' He turned and stared out of the window. 'As a matter of fact, Ginny, I've been through a rather sordid divorce,' he said quietly. Now he looked at her. 'I'll spare you most of the details, but it involved going to a seedy hotel in Brighton and paying a woman I'd never met before and hope to God I never meet again to allow a photographer to burst in and photograph us in bed together. The fact that I was still wearing my trousers didn't actually matter as it didn't show up on the photographs.' He ran his fingers through his hair, revealing the angry red scar. 'God, it was ghastly, but worth both the embarrassment and the money it cost to get Isobel from round my neck.' He picked up his empty mug. 'I could do with more coffee. Want some more, Ginny?'

Wordlessly, she held out her mug. When he had refilled it she said, 'I'm sorry, Nathan, I misjudged you.'

He shrugged. 'You couldn't know. I don't suppose the newspapers that carried the pictures have much of a readership in this neck of the woods.' He cupped his hands round his mug. 'Ironic, isn't it? In a few months I shall be free. Free to marry the girl I love if it wasn't for the fact that she is already blissfully happily married to someone else.'

'I wouldn't say blissfully happily married, Nathan,' she corrected.

'No? Then what would you say? You certainly looked blissfully happy that day when I saw you . . . ' He got up and began pacing up and down the studio.

'Sit down, Nathan, and listen,' she said sharply. 'I married Will Kesgrave because I was pregnant with your child and you'd married somebody else.'

'You mean I was tricked into marrying that bitch,' he said viciously.

She waved her hand dismissively and went on, 'Will knew I was pregnant but he was willing to marry me because he liked the idea of taking over my father's smack. There was no secret about any of this; the only thing I deceived him over was the identity of Roberta's father. He assumed it was Roger Mayhew and I let him go on believing that.' She leaned forward. 'It was not my wish to marry Will, nor anybody else, for that matter, but it was either that or be turned out with nowhere to go except the lunatic asylum. So, to save my child from being labelled a bastard I had little option but to marry a man who was a wastrel and a drunkard.'

'Don't, Ginny. Stop it.' He came forward and tried to take her in his arms.

'No. Hear me out.' She fended him off. 'As it happened marriage was the best thing that could have happened to Will. He's become a changed man. He works hard and rarely gets drunk these days. He never even looks at another woman. So I gave him a son. I felt I owed him that. But I shall see to it that there are no more children and to say that I'm blissfully happy with him would be very far from the truth. He's a good man but I don't love him. Not in the way a wife should love her husband. I keep the house clean, I wash and cook for him, and I share his bed, but I don't count the hours and minutes while he's away, my heart doesn't beat faster when he appears, in fact, if he went out of the door and never came back I should be sad but not broken-hearted. Because my heart has already been broken by you. It was not only your life you messed up, Nathan, it was mine as well.' Her voice dropped to a whisper. 'God knows, I should hate you, Nathan Bellamy. But I don't. I hate myself because I can't stop loving you.'

'Oh, Ginny. My dear love.' Again he tried to take her in his arms and again she brushed him aside.

'No, Nathan.' Her voice strengthened. 'I'm telling you this so that you'll understand you're not the only one who's suffered. We both have. But that's no reason to inflict suffering on Will as well. He's happy. I'm a good wife to him and he's good to me. More than that I neither ask nor expect.' She stood up to go. 'Will regards you as a very good friend, Nathan. He trusts you, just as he trusts me. We can't betray his trust, whatever our own feelings might be.'

Nathan gave a deep sigh. 'You're right, of course, Ginny.'

She nodded. 'You'll visit him?'

'Yes, of course.'

'And when he gets home? You'll come and see him?'

He nodded. 'And Bobby. I haven't seen her lately.' He smiled wryly. 'My little *god-daughter*.'

'She's growing more like you, but fortunately Will doesn't see it. He's looking for a likeness to Roger Mayhew.'

He put his head in his hands. 'Oh, God, Ginny, what a mess.'

'It's even more of a mess than you realise, Nathan,' she said wearily. 'The doctors have told me that Will's lower legs will never mend properly. He'll walk again, but never without crutches.' Her eyes filled with tears. 'He'll always have to drag himself around on crutches, Nathan. That's the life Will's got to face so he'll need all the support we can give him.'

'Does he know?'

She shook her head. 'I haven't yet found the courage to tell him.'

26

Will came home from hospital at the beginning of May, looking pale and gaunt and with a pair of crutches that were supposed to help him to get about, after a fashion.

At first he was contented, simply pleased to be home. He liked nothing better than sitting in the open doorway with George on his knee, soaking up the sunshine and talking to Granny Crabtree. Sometimes his mother would come up the yard and sit with him, but he soon got irritated with her maudlin tears and sent her away.

'She keep all on about 'my poor boy' all the time,' he told Ginny. 'I can't put up with that. I keep tellin' her my legs are gettin' stronger every day but she don't seem to listen.' He bounced George up and down. 'We're doin' all right, ain't we, son,' he said, grinning as George chuckled with delight. 'We'll soon be out fishin' again, when we get the money from the insurance people for a new smack. An' when you're a big boy you can come with your old dad. You'll like that, won't ye, boy?'

But after a month or so the inactivity began

to pall. He had refused to use the crutches to begin with, saying he had only to wait till his legs strengthened and he would be able to walk without any aid, but Ginny began to insist that he should try to walk a little with them every day.

'They're no good,' he said. 'They don't go where I want 'em to.'

'And they never will if you don't make a bit more of an effort with them,' she replied, handing them to him.

'I keep makin' an effort, can't you see? But me legs don't seem to hev any more strength in 'em than they did when I first came home. I manage a damn sight better crawlin' around on my hands and knees or shuffin' about on me backside.' He took a few awkward steps, then, 'Oh, bugger it!' as the crutches went one way and he went the other and would have collapsed on to the floor if Ginny hadn't caught him and helped him back on to a chair.

'You'll have to persevere, if you don't want to crawl about the streets on your hands and knees,' Ginny said unsympathetically, although inside her heart was bleeding at his helplessness.

He pursed his lips grimly. 'Then I'll jest sit here till I can do 'ithout 'em,' he said.

'In that case, you'll never learn.' With an

effort she smiled. 'Come on, Will, you need to get out in the sunshine,' she insisted, far more cheerfully than she felt.

'It's a beautiful day today. You were doing much better with the crutches yesterday, once you got the hang of swinging your body as you walked. If you could manage to get down the yard and out on to the quay you could sit and watch the boats for an hour. The tide is full and there's sure to be somebody to talk to. You can call and see your mother on the way, to give yourself a bit of a rest and if you ask her she'll put a chair out on the quay for you to sit on.'

'I ain't callin' on her. All she'll do is weep all over me, specially if she's bin at the gin bottle.'

'Very well. I'll bring a chair for you. Here, take your crutches.'

With Ginny's help he propped the crutches under his arms and struggled to his feet, swearing under his breath all the while.

'That's it,' she said, 'Now, swing your body as you walk . . . Good. You're doing fine.'

He made his way slowly and painfully down the yard and she followed with the chair, watching his every move. His right leg was practically useless from the knee down and his left foot was twisted inwards so that he walked — if walk it could be called — on the edge of his toes. But by dint of dragging himself along on the crutches he got to the yard door without mishap and she put the chair by the wall just outside it. As he lowered himself on to it she saw the beads of perspiration running down his face.

'That's good. That's the furthest you've managed to walk,' she said with a smile. 'Now you sit here and sun yourself and I'll bring you a cup of tea later on.'

She hurried back up the yard because she never liked to leave the two children unattended, even for a few moments.

Inside the house she found Bobby, with the poker under one arm and the toasting fork under the other, hopping round the table, her tongue sticking out in concentration, trying to emulate Will's walk.

She snatched them away. 'Don't you ever let me see you do that again, you naughty girl,' she said, relieving her anxiety over Will by giving her a sharp smack.

'Like Daddy. Me walk like Daddy,' the child said, her face crumpling into tears.

Ginny swallowed and took a grip on herself. 'No, sweetheart,' she said, more gently, taking the little girl on to her lap and giving her a cuddle. 'You must never try to walk like Daddy. He doesn't like having to walk with those crutches and he would be very upset if he saw you trying to copy him. Promise me you'll never do it again.'

'All right.' Bobby stuck her thumb in her mouth and slid off Ginny's lap to go over to her box of bricks. There, she became completely absorbed in building a tower and forgot all about her father and his crutches.

★ ★ ★

Ginny sat down at the table. Will had been at home for well over a month now. Soon decisions would have to be made about the future. He still spoke optimistically about buying another fishing smack with the insurance money from *Emily May* and so far, afraid of what his reaction might be, Ginny hadn't plucked up the courage to tell him that his injuries had made that impossible. She simply couldn't face shattering his conviction that he would recover.

But with Will no longer able to support the family she knew that something would have to be done to keep the children fed and clothed and a roof over their heads. Up to now she had managed with the money she had put by from Will's fishing trips plus the money she made from the baking she did with her mother. But the fishing money was fast running out and up to now she wasn't making enough from baking for them to live on.

She had talked this over with her mother and although Ruth didn't really like the idea she had finally agreed that a proper cake shop would reach a wider market and so this might be the answer, if and when they could find suitable premises.

Ginny had the feeling that Ruth had only agreed because she was confident that it would be a long time before suitable premises became available.

In fact, Ginny had already found a shop. It was in a good position in the High Street and it had the added convenience of living accommodation behind it. It was absolutely ideal for their purposes, but it was for sale, not rent and even with the insurance money from the smack there would be nowhere near enough to buy it.

She traced a pattern on the tablecloth with her finger and went over the possibilities in her mind for the hundredth time. If they put all the insurance money down and took up a mortgage on the rest would the shop make enough money to support the family and Ruth and pay the mortgage? Would it even be worth making enquiries? More than that, would her mother agree or would she say it was only putting a further millstone round their necks? Ginny rubbed the back of her neck, weary with trying to see the right way forward for them all without worrying Will.

Suddenly, she heard a commotion in the yard and rushed to the door. Will was struggling up the yard, shouting obscenities at the top of his voice. Nathan was beside him, his arm round him, supporting him as best he could whilst avoiding the flailing crutches.

He managed to get him into the house and sit him down in the Windsor chair by the window. 'Now, calm down, old chap,' he said, 'It's not the end of the world.'

'It might not be the end of your bloody world. It's the end of mine!' Will shouted. 'An' some fine friend you are. Why didn't you leave me to drown under that bloody mast instead of condemnin' me to a livin' bloody death like this.'

'Will, what's wrong? What's the matter with him, Nathan?' Ginny asked, looking from one to the other and back again.

'Whass the matter? You may well ask!' Will shouted and then sank into morose silence.

Ginny frowned. 'What's got into him?' she said to Nathan.

Nathan straightened up and ran his hands through his hair. 'I don't know. All I can tell you is that I was at the other end of the quay, painting. Bill Herbert came along, stopped to speak and then saw Will sitting there. He said he hadn't seen him since the accident so he'd go and have a word. I said to tell him I'd be along later when I'd got my perspectives worked out. The next thing I heard was Will bellowing and trying to get up off his chair. I only just got there in time to stop him falling. Bill Herbert was nowhere to be seen. Goodness knows what went wrong.'

'I'll tell you what went bloody wrong,' Will said savagely. He gave Ginny a scathing look. 'I've jest found out suthin' you shoulda told me weeks ago on'y you didn't hev the guts, woman. 'Oh, you're doin' well, Will. You're much better today. Your legs is gettin' stronger every day,'' he mimicked her voice. 'Thass what you've bin sayin'. Now I've found out thass a lotta balls you've bin feedin' me. My legs ain't gettin' better. They'll never be better'n they are now. I'm always goin' to be a bloody cripple.' He banged his fist on the arm of the chair. 'An' I was the last to know! I wouldn't hev known now if Bill Herbert hadn't come up an' said how sorry he was to hear I'd lost the use o' me legs an' sympathisin' because I shan't never walk again. And there'd bin me, thinkin' it was on'y a matter o' time afore I'd be on me feet again. Why didn't you tell me the truth in the first place, woman?'

'Because I hadn't got the courage, Will,' Ginny said, shaking her head sadly. 'I've been trying to find a way to break it to you gently because I knew how you'd feel . . . '

'You didn't know how I'd feel! Nobody knows how I feel. I wish I was bloody dead.'

Nathan shook his arm roughly. 'Well, you're not dead, Will, and things could be a damn sight worse,' he said sternly. 'Do you realise, if that mast had fallen a foot or so in the other direction you could have been spending the rest of your life flat on your back.'

Will gave him a scathing look. 'Thank you for bloody nuthin',' he said.

'Where did Bill Herbert hear about you?' Ginny asked. As far as she knew the extent of the damage to Will's legs had been kept strictly within the family.

'In the Rose and Crown, apparently,' Nathan answered for him. 'You know how rumours circulate in there.'

'This was no rumour. Bill got it from me own mother, so he knew it was right,' Will said with a scowl.

Ginny nodded. She could just imagine Annie Kesgrave, maudlin with gin, telling anyone who would listen the terrible plight of her only son. Sometimes, she felt that throttling was too good for that woman.

Wearily, she pushed her hair back and repinned it.

'I'll make some tea,' she said. 'When you've calmed down, Will, perhaps we can discuss the future, now you know how things stand.'

'I ain't got no future,' Will said morosely.

She swung round from pulling the kettle forward on the stove. 'Yes, you have. And so have I. We might not like it but we're stuck with it, so we'll have to make the best of it,' she said brutally.

Nathan got to his feet; his face was full of pain. 'Perhaps I should go, Ginny,' he said. 'I don't want my presence here . . . '

'No, you stay,' Will interrupted. 'You stay an' hear about this marvellous future my wife has got planned for us.'

Ginny made the tea and poured three cups with a hand that was not very steady. Then she sat down at the table.

'Well,' she said, holding her cup in both hands as if for support, 'Now you've found out that you're never going to go to sea again, Will, you must realise that we've got to find some other way of earning enough to live on. The insurance money from the smack, when it comes through, isn't going to keep us for the rest of our lives . . . '

'Thass your mother's money,' Will said flatly. 'She's always made it plain enough thass nuthin' to do with us.'

Ginny ignored him and went on quietly, 'I've thought for quite a long time that I would like to have a little cake shop.' She turned to him. 'You know that, Will, I've talked to you about it, so don't pretend you know nothing about it.' She went on, her eyes fixed on the table in front of her, 'We do quite well, with the cakes and pies we make at my mother's house for the wives of the yacht captains and the people they recommend, but if we had a shop I'm sure we'd sell a lot more, especially as there's more money about in the village now that the shipyard has reopened.' She sighed. 'The problem is, of course, premises. There's quite a nice little shop in the High Street, with living quarters behind it but that's for sale, not rent, and it could be gone before we get the insurance money through. In any case, the insurance money probably wouldn't be enough. But if we could find somewhere that we could rent . . . what do you think, Will?'

He shrugged and stared out of the window. 'I don't care what you do. I'm useless. Do what you like.'

'Don't talk like that, Will,' Nathan said sharply. 'Ginny's trying to make the best of things, and God knows I admire her pluck, so you might at least show a bit of interest. And

'I'm sure there'll be plenty of things that you can do to help.'

'If you suggest I can serve in the shop I'll hit you with this bloody crutch,' Will said, glowering at him.

Ginny sipped her tea, grateful for its comforting warmth. She knew now she had been right in keeping from Will the extent of the damage to his legs. He was not yet in a fit state to cope with such shattering news. Her hand tightened on her cup. At that moment she would like nothing better than to break Annie Kesgrave's gin bottle over her head.

After a few more minutes Nathan said, 'I really think I should be going.' He went to the door. 'I'll come and see you tomorrow,' he said to nobody in particular but Ginny knew it was directed at her.

'Aye, come an' see us termorrer,' Will said bitterly. 'I shall be stuck here, you can be sure o' that, even if *she's* out lookin' for her bloody shop.' He nodded towards Ginny, a sneer on his face.

Ginny got up and went to the door with Nathan.

'Will you be all right?' he murmured anxiously. 'Can you manage him?'

'Yes, he'll be fine,' she said, loud enough for Will to hear. 'He's very brave, you know. But he's had an awful shock today. He needs time to get used to it. Thanks for your help, Nathan. You're a good friend to Will. He appreciates it.' She watched Nathan go up the steps to Anchor Hill, then turn and give her a quick wave, his face anguished. She managed to smile at him, then took a deep breath, pulled back her shoulders and went back into the house.

'Now,' she said, planting a kiss firmly on Will's forehead, 'from now on there'll be no more swearing in front of the children, Will. Bobby's like a little parrot now, she copies whatever she hears. You wouldn't like to hear her using some of the language you've come out with this afternoon, would you, now.'

'Well, it's enough to make a saint swear, what I've found out today,' he growled.

She sat down beside him and took his hand.

'Just remember, it's not easy for me, either, Will,' she said quietly. 'How do you think I feel, having to watch you struggle and knowing there's nothing I can do to help you? All I can do is to encourage you to make the best of things. And at the moment you can't see that there is any good anywhere. But think about this. You've got me. And you've got the children. Surely, that's something to be thankful for.'

He turned and looked at her and there

were tears in his eyes.

'Aye, Ginny, I thank the Good Lord for you every day of my life. I dunno what I'd do without you. Or the kiddies, there.' He turned away. 'But it galls me to think I can't ever provide for you again the way a man oughta provide for his fam'ly. I'm useless. B . . . ' Smiling, she put her hand over his mouth before he could say the word. He planted a kiss in the palm of her hand instead and gave her a sad smile. 'Useless,' he repeated.

She rested her head on his shoulder. She wished from the bottom of her heart that she could tell him that she loved him, that as long as he was by her side she could face anything. But she couldn't, because it would be a lie. In truth, he was a burden that she would have to carry for the rest of her days. But that was something he must never know.

She got up from her chair. 'I must get the children's tea,' she said briskly.

27

The following day was what Ginny called a baking day so she got the children ready and took them off to her mother's house, leaving Will with a heap of sandwiches for his lunch and plenty of books and newspapers to read. He had hardly spoken a word since the previous evening but there was nothing more she could do at present to help him to come to terms with his life. He knew as well as she did that they needed what money she could earn to supplement what was left of his fishing money so she had no choice but to leave him, whether he liked it or not.

'How is he?' Ruth asked, going to and fro from the table to the larder as she prepared for the morning's cooking.

'You may well ask,' Ginny replied and told her of the events of the previous afternoon.

'Annie Kesgrave always did have a big mouth,' Ruth said tersely when Ginny finished. 'It's time she learned to keep it shut.'

'Well, it's too late now, the damage is done. Will knows he'll never walk properly again and he knows I'm looking for premises so that we can open a shop.' She heaved a sigh. 'It was quite a lot for him to find out in one afternoon.'

'How is he this morning?'

'Hasn't spoken much. I've left him plenty to read, if he feels like it. I did think of getting all my bits of brass out and suggesting he might like to clean them for me but I thought better of it. He'd only say it was 'woman's work' and start off again about how useless he is.'

'He needs something to do to take his mind off himself.'

'Yes. But I don't think cleaning brass would be the answer.' Ginny sighed. 'I'll think of something.'

Halfway through the morning there was a knock at the door. Ruth went to open it, pushing stray ends of hair up under the cap she wore when she was baking.

She frowned when she saw Nathan standing there. 'If you've come for your mother's pies, they aren't out of the oven yet,' she said shortly. 'I told her we'd deliver them some time after twelve o'clock.'

'I haven't come for my mother's pies, Mrs Appleyard, I've come to see you and Ginny,' he replied, looking a little apprehensive. 'But I can see I've come at a bad time. You're busy.'

'It's all right, Nathan, we were just going to stop for a cup of coffee,' Ginny said over her mother's shoulder.

'Very well, you'd better come in, I suppose,' Ruth said with some reluctance. 'What do you want to see us for?'

'Thank you.' He took off his cap as he crossed the threshold and looked anxiously at Ginny. 'How is Will today, Ginny?'

She shrugged. 'He's hardly spoken.'

He nodded. 'I'll go and see him later on.' He looked at the table, laden with freshly baked cakes. 'My goodness, those cakes look and smell delicious,' he said with a smile.

'Would you like one?' Ginny asked.

He shook his head. 'No, they're your livelihood. But I wouldn't say no to your offer of a cup of coffee, if you're making one.' He turned to Ruth. 'I thought it best to come here rather than to Quay Yard, Mrs Appleyard,' he explained, 'because what I've come to say concerns you as much as Ginny.' He turned back to Ginny. 'And if you agree to what I propose to do it might be best if you're the one who breaks it to Will, Ginny.'

Ginny frowned. 'What are you talking about, Nathan?'

'I'm talking about the shop in the High Street that you seem to have set your heart on, Ginny,' he said.

She cleared a space on the corner of the table and put his coffee cup on it.

She shook her head. 'I'm afraid . . . ' she began.

'No. It's out of the question,' Ruth said firmly. 'We couldn't possibly afford to buy those premises.'

'No, Mrs Appleyard. I quite understand that. But *I* could,' he said, watching over the rim of his cup for their reaction. 'In fact, I have already made an offer and it has been accepted.' He put his cup down carefully. 'Quite simply, what I intend to do is to rent it out and I'm offering you first refusal.'

Ginny sat down with a thump, Ruth went over to the sink and washed her hands and dried them. Very thoroughly. Neither of them spoke for several minutes, then Ruth said icily, 'And where, might I ask, would you get the money from to buy this property?'

'Mother!' Ginny said, aghast. 'That's none of our business.'

'It is if it's his wife's money. Have you thought of that?' Ruth asked. 'I for one would want nothing to do with property bought with *her* money, and if you've got any pride, neither would you, girl.'

'It isn't my wife's money,' Nathan said, keeping his voice level with difficulty. He paused, then went on, 'For your information,

Mrs Appleyard, although it has nothing whatever to do with the matter in question, I no longer have a wife. Isobel divorced me earlier in the year, much to my relief. I have nothing to do with her, nor her father, who, I discovered recently, has made his fortune through arms dealing, which I find despicable. But that's by the way.'

Bobby had come up to him and was tugging at his arm. With a smile, he lifted her on to his knee and gave her kiss, then he produced a bunch of keys from his pocket for her to play with. 'To set your mind at rest still further, Mrs Appleyard,' he went on, 'although this is not a confidence I share with many people, I have made quite a lot of money from my paintings. They seem to be very popular in some quarters and sell very well. That's one reason why I didn't bother to sign up with another yacht this summer. I'm far too busy with the paintings I've been commissioned to do. But be that as it may, and to get back to the reason I've come here today. The property is mine if I want it and I'm offering to rent it out to you if you would like it.' He lifted Bobby gently down to the floor and got to his feet.

'I'll leave you to think about it and to talk it over with Will. There's no immediate hurry . . . '

'Yes. Yes, please, Nathan,' Ginny said, her eyes shining. 'We'd like it.'

'Wait a minute,' Ruth said cautiously. 'We don't know what the rent will be.'

'Not more than you can afford, Mrs Appleyard, I can assure you,' Nathan said with a smile. He turned to Ginny. 'I've been all over it. It's in quite good condition. Needs a lick of paint, of course, but I'll get that done. And there's plenty of room. Four bedrooms, one of them very small, and three rooms behind the shop, one of which could be converted into a bedroom for Will if that would make life easier.'

'No.' Ginny shook her head. 'He wouldn't like that. He manages the stairs perfectly well. He goes up and down on his bottom.'

'How big is the kitchen?' Ruth asked, interested in spite of herself.

'Oh, it's a nice big kitchen.'

'Room for a gas cooker?'

'Two if you wanted them,' he said, 'and there's already a kitchen range with a boiler beside it so you'd have constant hot water.'

Ruth's eyes widened in spite of herself. 'And an inside tap?' Ruth was proud of her inside tap.

He nodded, trying not to smile. 'Yes, and a nice deep sink.'

'We'll think about it,' Ruth said as if it was

she who was bestowing the favour.

'We don't need to think about it, Mother,' Ginny said impatiently. 'It's exactly what we want.' She beamed at Nathan and would have thrown her arms round his neck if Ruth hadn't been there.

'You'd better have a word with Will before you finally make up your mind,' Ruth warned. 'In his present frame of mind the last thing you want is for him to think you're making decisions behind his back.'

'Yes, you're right.' Ginny pinched her lip, frowning. Then her face cleared as an idea dawned and she turned to Nathan. 'You said you were going to see him this morning, Nathan, so why don't *you* tell him?' She smiled at him. 'Ask him what he thinks of the idea? Talk it over with him, man to man?'

'What if he doesn't like the idea?' Nathan asked.

Ginny picked up his hat and gave it to him. 'We'll cross that bridge when we come to it. In the meantime, we'll keep our fingers crossed.'

★　★　★

It was late in the afternoon before Ginny arrived home because she had taken a wide detour in order to deliver boxes of cakes and pies to some half dozen or so addresses on her way.

She pushed open the door, apprehensive as to what Will's reaction might be to Nathan's suggestion.

But Will wasn't there.

She hurried down the yard to see if he was on the quay but there was no sign of him. Puzzled, she went back to the house.

As she passed Granny Crabtree's cottage the old lady poked her head round the door. 'If you're looking for Will, he's out,' she said.

'I can see that,' Ginny said, tiredness and anxiety making her short-tempered. 'Do you know where he's gone?'

'No. He went off with that young Mr Bellamy about an hour and a half ago.'

Ginny frowned. 'On his crutches?'

Granny Crabtree nodded. 'Seemed to be getting along on 'em like a house on fire.'

Still puzzled, Ginny peeled potatoes and carrots to have with the freshly baked meat pasties she had brought home with her. While the vegetables were cooking she undressed the children and put them into their pyjamas ready for bed. They were already tucking into their meal by the time Will returned with Nathan.

'You'll stop and hev a bite with us, boy, won't ye?' Will asked, sinking gratefully into his chair. 'Ah, thass better. Them crutches are hard on th'old armpits. There's enough for Nathan to share, ain't there, Ginny?'

'Yes, I brought extra pasties home and there are plenty of vegetables.' She smiled at Will. 'I wondered where on earth you'd got to. I've been down on the quay to look for you . . . '

'Ah, you'll never guess,' he said, mysteriously. Then his face broadened into a smile. 'I've bin with Nathan to hev a look at this place he's thinkin' of buyin'.'

'How did you manage that?' Ginny asked in amazement. 'You had trouble getting as far as the end of the yard only yesterday.'

'Ah, I hadn't got the hang of usin' the crutches right, had I, Nathan.'

'We experimented a bit round the kitchen table,' Nathan said. 'It was a case of getting the balance and the swing right.'

'Yes. Nathan tried different ways with the crutches till he found what he thought 'ud do, then I had a go. We worked it between us. I can manage fine, now.'

'That's really good. And you say you managed to get as far as this place Nathan's buying?' she asked warily, noticing the lines of tiredness etched on his face from the effort of the walk he'd taken.

He nodded. 'Thass a nice place. Little bit

o' garden at the back for the kiddies to play in, good-sized shop at the front an' the livin' rooms are bigger'n we've got here.'

'And there's a shed in the garden where Will can work,' Nathan added.

Ginny raised her eyebrows.

Will went on, 'Might take up paintin'. Nathan says he'll learn me a few wrinkles. Or I might take up woodwork. I've always thought I'd like to make musical boxes. You can buy the movements — the bits that make the tunes — so all I'd hev to do is make the boxes to put 'em in.'

Ginny heaved a sigh of relief. She didn't know what Nathan had said to Will but it had obviously cheered him up. 'So you think it might be a good idea for us to rent this place, if Nathan decides to buy it, of course.' She shot Nathan a glance.

'Oh, he's decided. He's goin' into Colchester to sign on the dotted line termorrer, ain't ye, boy?'

Nathan nodded. 'If that's what you'd both like,' he said with a smile.

'Thank you, Nathan,' Ginny said, her eyes brimming with grateful tears.

Later that night, when they were in bed, Will said, 'I wasn't very keen to take that shop, at first. I thought it smacked o' charity. But Nathan put it to me that I'd had a rough deal over me legs, which is true. He said he felt bad about that accident, blamed hisself because he didn't get to me sooner, although I can't see he could hev done any more for me than he did. Anyway, he reckons that if he rents that shop to us that'll make amends a bit and he won't feel so bad about me bein' crippled.' He chuckled. 'You'd almost think we'd be doin' him a favour by takin' the place, to hear him talk.'

Ginny was silent.

'He's a good friend to me,' he added.

'Yes.' Ginny closed her eyes and prayed that Will would never discover just how much of a friend Nathan was to her.

★ ★ ★

Never enthusiastic over Ginny taking the shop, Ruth's reaction when she was told that it was going forward and that they would be moving within a month was lukewarm. She had been so sure that Will would never agree to it that it was almost as if she felt that he — her last line of defence — had let her down.

'I think you'll be very foolish if you take that shop on,' she told Ginny when she called in at Quay Yard after leaving her grocery list at Stacey's. She sat herself down, her shopping basket on her lap, preparing for an argument. 'For a start you'll have rent to pay . . .'

Ginny looked up from her ironing. 'We pay rent here, Mother,' she pointed out.

'Yes, but it'll be more. And how do you think you're going to keep that shop stocked with cakes, I should like to know. It'll take more than two days baking a week, I can tell you.'

'I realise that and I'm hoping you'll work with me.' Ginny folded Will's shirt and began on Bobby's liberty bodice. 'The kitchen is big enough for us both to work in without getting under one another's feet.'

Ruth straightened her back. 'Are you suggesting my kitchen is cramped?'

Ginny sighed. 'Of course not. But there's no denying the one behind the shop is bigger. And there'll be hot water on tap.'

Ruth was silent for several minutes, watching Ginny's iron move back and forth.

'I wouldn't want to neglect our present customers,' she said at last, beginning to weaken.

'Of course not. They'll be our first priority.' Ginny started on a pillow case.

Ruth frowned. 'It's just that, well, I'm not sure this is a very good time to set up a shop.'

Ginny looked up. 'What do you mean?'

'Well, I listen to the wireless a lot and this Herr Hitler man, it seems to me he's getting too big for his boots. There'll be trouble before long, if I'm not mistaken.'

'What *are* you talking about, Mother?' Ginny said with an impatient laugh.

'Well, he's taking over all these foreign countries. He's already walked into Austria and now he's got his sights on Czechoslovakia. I mean, where will it all end?'

'I know what you're saying, Mother. I listen to the wireless, too. But whatever Herr Hitler does I can't see it's going to make any difference to whether or not we open a cake shop.'

'But what if there's a war?'

'Oh, Mother, don't be so pessimistic. There's not going to be a war. And even if there was, people would still have to eat, wouldn't they.'

'Yes, I suppose you're right.' Ruth shifted her basket. 'There's certainly more employment about now that the shipyard has opened again. And I hear Paxman's are looking for more men, so perhaps a shop might not be such a bad thing,' she mused.

'We'll be partners,' Ginny said eagerly. 'Just like we are now. Profits split down the middle. Only instead of me coming to you, you'll come and cook with me, because we'll have the shop to look after.'

'We'll have to bake every day,' Ruth pointed out.

'Of course. And we can sell the stale ones off cheap.'

'Will could serve in the shop . . . '

'No, Mother. He flatly refuses to do that so don't you suggest it to him. He'll have his own workshop out in the garden.'

'What's he going to make?'

'I don't know. He hasn't decided yet. He thinks he might like to make musical boxes.'

'What? With those great ham fists of his? Never.'

'Don't you dare let him hear you say that, Mother,' Ginny said furiously. 'Whatever he decides to do it's up to us to encourage him. Poor devil, he must try his hand at something or he'll go mad. Ssh, here he comes now.' She nodded towards the window as Will came swinging up the yard on his crutches.

He came in at the open door. 'I bin talkin' to Nathan,' he announced. 'He says the workmen will hev finished by the end of the week so we can move in as soon as we like.' He rubbed his hands together and grinned at Ruth. 'What d'ye think o' that, Ruthy? We'll be outa here in a fortnight.'

Ruth gave him a wintry smile. 'I just hope you know what you're doing,' she said frostily.

'And don't call me Ruthy.'

Ginny looked from Will to her mother and back again. She hoped their old animosity wasn't going to surface again.

28

During the evening, after the children were in bed and Will was sitting smoking his pipe while Ginny sat at the table with her mending basket he remarked, 'I never said anything while your mother was here because I didn't want her interferin', but Nathan want you to go an' hev a look at the house. See if there's anything else you want doin', sort out where you want the counter in the shop, things like that.' He puffed on his pipe for several minutes, then he remarked, 'Nathan's good to us, Ginny, ain't he.'

'Yes, Will, he is.' She continued with her mending. 'When does he want us to go to the house?' she asked after a bit.

'Oh, there ain't no need for me to drag all the way up there,' he said complacently. 'You an' him can sort it out between ye. He said he'll be there in the mornin', if you could call in.'

She gazed at him, sitting contentedly with his pipe. His trust in her was absolute. He had no idea of the turmoil she went through whenever she was in Nathan's presence, how she longed for his arms round her and his lips on hers. In a way she was glad that Will's lovemaking — if such it could be called — was, and always had been, perfunctory to say the least, so there was no danger of her being carried away and whispering Nathan's name instead of Will's.

She closed her eyes, praying that she would have the strength never to betray the trust Will had in her.

The next morning she got up determined not to make any extra effort with her dress simply because she would be seeing Nathan. But she had a pretty scarf with colours in it that exactly matched the blouse she was wearing so it seemed a pity not to wear it, and her hair was very flyaway because she had washed it the previous evening so it was common sense to pin it back with a tortoiseshell slide.

'Pretty, Mummy,' Bobby said, fingering the scarf as Ginny brushed her hair for her and fastened it with a floppy pink bow.

'An' you're a pretty little gel, too,' Will said affectionately.

Ginny's heart rose in her throat. She lived in constant fear that he would see the resemblance to Nathan in Bobby's face.

He chucked the little girl under the chin. 'You get more like your mother every day,' he said, giving her a kiss.

Ginny relaxed. 'We shan't be long, Will,' she said, tucking George into his pram and manoeuvring it down the step into the yard.

'Take yer time. I shall go for a little walk on the quay presently,' he replied. 'There's bound to be somebody there I can talk to for five minutes.'

She walked along to the shop offering up a silent prayer of thankfulness that Will appeared to have accepted his disability with such stoicism.

Nathan was there when they arrived. He was wearing dungarees covered in paint and suddenly Ginny felt stupid and overdressed in her silk scarf and tortoiseshell slide.

'I was just giving the kitchen a lick of paint. It makes quite a change from painting pictures,' he said with a laugh. Then he became serious. 'I do hope you'll like the colour, Ginny. Come and see. It's not a very sunny room so I thought to keep it bright with creamy yellow walls and white paint. But I can change it if you don't like it.' He followed her into the kitchen, looking a trifle anxious. 'I got it from Mr Chaney on the corner and he said . . . '

'Oh, no, I do like it. It's a nice bright colour, Nathan,' she said, looking round. She turned to him with an anxious frown. 'But you shouldn't do all this for us. I could easily do it myself, after we've moved.'

'I know. But I wanted to do it for you, Ginny,' he said quietly. He turned to Bobby, who was amusing herself by playing imaginary hopscotch on the red quarry tiles. 'There's something for you in the garden, Bobby,' he said, putting his hand on her head. 'Go and look.'

'A swing! Oh, look, Mummy, it's a swing!' Bobby ran out of the back door on to the tiny patch of lawn and hitched herself on to the swing. 'Come and push me, Uncle Nathan.'

Nathan went out and gave her several pushes while she squealed with delight, then he came back inside to where Ginny stood, watching from the window.

'This has got to stop, Nathan,' she said in a low voice. 'You mustn't do so much for us. You know we can never repay you.'

He came and stood just behind her, resting his hand on her shoulder. 'Ginny, whatever I can do for you will never be enough,' he said quietly. 'I'd pluck the moon and the stars out of heaven if I thought it would make you happy. God knows, I've caused you enough unhappiness in your life, never mind the misery I've suffered myself. If it hadn't been for my crass stupidity we'd have been married by now and you wouldn't be tied to a man you don't love. And to think I saved his life only to saddle you with more trouble.' His hand tightened on her shoulder. 'Oh, Ginny, my love, my dear love, if only . . . '

She twisted away from him. 'Don't, Nathan. Don't make it even more difficult than it is already.'

'I just want to take you in my arms . . . '

'I know. And that's where I want to be, but it's impossible. Do you think Will would have agreed to me coming to see you here today if he hadn't trusted me — and you — completely?'

'I know. But it's hard, Ginny. And you're so lovely.' He turned away and his voice was not quite steady. 'I just want to make up for all the hurt I've caused you over the years.'

There was a cry from outside and Bobby came running in. 'I fell off. Hurt my knee,' she cried.

'Never mind, sweetheart, I'll kiss it better. Look, there's no blood.' Ginny kissed the knee and Bobby's forehead. 'There. All better.' She smiled and gave her a hug.

Bobby smiled up at Nathan. 'Mummy kissed it better,' she said happily and ran outside again.

'Can you kiss a broken heart and make it better, Ginny?' Nathan asked with a wry smile.

She stared out of the window to where

Bobby was struggling back on to her swing. 'Sometimes I wonder which is worse,' she said, speaking as much to herself as to him. 'When you go away and I don't see you at all or when you are near and I see you but daren't touch you, daren't let it show how much you mean to me, when I have to pretend you are just Will's good friend. And you *are*. You're Will's very good friend. He would miss you dreadfully if you weren't around. But if he knew about — us, he would never speak to you again and that would mean I should never see you again. I can't risk that.'

He picked up her hand and kissed it. 'You're right, of course, Ginny.' His mouth twisted. 'Women are supposed to be the weaker sex but you're far stronger than me in this. All I want to do is carry you off somewhere . . . '

'Not in those dirty old dungarees.' She laughed. It was a shaky little laugh but it broke the spell. She went on, trying to make her voice businesslike, 'Now, what else is there you wanted me to look at? I have to get back, you know, I've got to pack boxes ready for the move.'

'Yes, of course.' He cleared his throat in an effort to become businesslike too. 'Well, I'd like you to take a look at all the rooms. I don't think anywhere else needs painting, but see what you think about the wallpaper in the bedrooms.'

He followed her up the stairs and from room to room. When she had finished her inspection she turned to him. 'It's wonderful, Nathan, absolutely wonderful.' She shook her head, her eyes brimming with tears. 'I can't thank you enough.' Impulsively, she leaned forward and lightly kissed his cheek.

He caught her by the wrist and held her, his face inches from hers. 'You can't expect me to play by the rules if you go breaking them like that,' he said quietly as, looking deep into her eyes he drew her into his arms and began to kiss her, gently at first, but with mounting passion as he felt her respond and her lips parted under his.

At last he lifted his head. 'I'm sorry, Ginny,' he said unsteadily. 'I promise it won't happen again.'

She laid her head briefly on his shoulder. 'No, it mustn't happen again, my love.'

They clung together for a brief moment, then with a great effort he put her from him. 'We'd better go downstairs before it does.'

Despite the turmoil inside her Ginny somehow managed to fix her attention on the matter of counters, glass showcases, cash registers and the like.

'You haven't yet said what the rent will be,' she reminded him as he made notes on a scrap of paper.

He looked up and gave a shrug. 'I should think the same as you are paying at Quay Yard, if you can manage it.'

'But the house at Quay Yard is only half the size of this one,' Ginny protested. 'And there's the shop as well. I'm sure it ought to be at least double what we're paying now.'

'Let's say we'll review it when you begin to make a profit.' He put the paper into his pocket. 'You know very well you could live here rent free for all I'd care, Ginny,' he said with a sigh, 'But I know that wouldn't do, so we'll leave it as I suggested. The same as you're paying now.'

'Thank you, Nathan,' she said, but the look in her eyes was all the thanks he needed.

Ginny and her family moved into the house behind the shop at the beginning of August and the shop opened a week later. Both Ginny and her mother had been baking until gone ten o'clock the previous night and then Ruth was back again at five the next morning to begin again. They baked pies of all kinds, beef, steak and kidney, chicken and ham, cheese and onion, and more than a dozen different kinds of mouth-watering cakes and pastries, from custard tarts to iced fancies, from gingerbread men to cream slices.

When a selection of everything they had baked was carefully displayed on neat paper doilys on the shelves Ruth looked at Ginny.

'Do you think we've done too much?' she said doubtfully.

'No,' Ginny said. 'We need to show what we can do. We'll soon find out what sells best.' She pushed her hair wearily back from her forehead. 'We can sell off what's left at half price tomorrow. Nothing will be wasted, I'm sure.'

She was right. The succulent smell from the open door of the shop brought the customers in and by three o'clock in the afternoon there were only three jam tarts and a currant cake left.

When these too had gone Ginny turned to her mother. 'See? I told you we hadn't baked too much.'

'Yes, but it's probably only a flash in the pan,' Ruth replied pessimistically.

She was wrong. Although sales didn't go on at quite such a hectic level, nevertheless business continued to be good and Ginny and her mother were kept busy, Ruth baking almost continuously either at her own home or in Ginny's kitchen, Ginny confining her share of the baking to early mornings or late in the evenings because the rest of her day was taken up with looking after the shop and the children. But even though she had to work hard she was happy because the cake shop was soon making enough to live on and to pay the rent and sometimes there was even a little bit over, which she put away in a tin on the dresser in the kitchen towards a rainy day.

She was so taken up with her new venture that at first she didn't notice that Will was becoming increasingly restless and irritable. Although he rarely complained, she knew that the state of his legs irked him and he was often in pain from them, particularly as the weather got colder, but there was little she could do about that except to give him aspirin and encourage him to rest. She was constantly amazed at his fortitude in accepting the fact that he would always have to drag himself round and he was becoming quite nimble on his crutches.

Much of his time was spent in his little workshop in the garden where he was teaching himself to carve little wooden figures. He had a bench there and a stool so that he could sit to do the work. Ginny had suggested that when he became proficient the figures might sell in the shop, which would earn him a little money as Christmas approached.

The trouble was, he was no good at it and

he knew it. He was a mariner. He had spent his life at sea, heaving on ropes and hauling in nets full of fish and however hard he tried and however much he practised his great ham fists couldn't control the delicate carving chisels that Ginny had bought him with the first profits from the shop. He tried carving ships but could never get one side to match the other; he carved houses with walls that were nowhere near parallel and had crooked windows; he carved unrecognisable figures, then the chisel would slip and he would slice off an arm or a leg.

Things came to a head one evening after a particularly busy day in the shop.

'Maybe you should try something a little less complicated, dear,' Ginny suggested when he threw a toy soldier he had accidentally decapitated on to the table. Not that it mattered, since one leg was a good deal shorter and thicker than the other. She picked up the soldier and turned it over in her hands, trying to think of a way to console him when all she really wanted to do was lay her weary bones down and sleep.

'Like what?'

'Oh, I don't know.' She leaned her head on her hand and briefly closed her eyes. 'Farmyard animals?'

'With no legs, or crooked ears?' He looked

down at his hands. 'Thass no good, Ginny, these hands weren't made for this kind of work. I'm a fisherman. A good fisherman. Thass what I know. Thass what I can do. Only I ain't got the bloody legs for it.' He struggled to his feet. He was quite adept at positioning his crutches and swinging himself out of the chair. 'I'm orf to bed.'

'And I'm right behind you. I'm nearly dead on my feet,' she said with a sigh.

'So don't try anything on, Will,' he said sarcastically over his shoulder. 'I git the message, don't worry. I'll leave ye alone.'

She didn't reply to this barb but waited until he had gone upstairs, heaving himself from one stair tread to the next on his backside, then followed him up to bed.

The next morning when Ruth bustled in with a basketful of cheese and ham pies on one arm and a bag of rock cakes in her other hand he was sitting and staring into the fire while Ginny drizzled icing on to fancy cakes she had baked that morning.

'What's the matter with you?' Ruth asked, directing the question at him.

He looked up at her but before he could answer the shop bell rang.

'I'll go,' Ruth said. A minute later she was back. 'Are there any sausage rolls?'

'They'll be ready in half an hour. They're

still in the oven,' Ginny said. She frowned. 'If they say how many they want we'll put them aside.'

When Ruth came in from the shop again Will said, 'If you wanta know wass the matter with me I'm waitin' for somebody to make me some breakfast.'

'Oh, I'll do it in a minute. When I've finished this,' Ginny said impatiently.

'Can't you make your own breakfast?' Ruth demanded. 'You're big enough to make yourself a cup of tea and a slice of toast, I'd have thought.'

'Thass women's work,' he said, reaching for a cake and putting it into his mouth whole.

'Don't eat the cakes, Will, they're for the shop,' Ginny said sharply. 'I'll make a cup of tea as soon as I've done this. I could do with a cup and I expect Mum could, too.'

'Have the children had their breakfast?' Ruth said, picking up George, who had been playing under the table with one of his father's 'gone wrong' models, while Bobby played with her doll in the corner.

'Yes, ages ago,' Ginny said, wiping her arm across her forehead. She straightened up from the table. 'Right. That's that. I'll just take them through to the shop ... Oh, drat. There's the shop door again. Can you take the sausage rolls out of the oven, Mum?' She hurried through to the shop.

Ruth put George gently on the floor and went to the oven. 'It wouldn't hurt you to look after the shop sometimes, Will,' she said over her shoulder. 'It would help Ginny.'

'Thass women's work,' Will repeated what he had said earlier. 'And you needn't come here tellin' me what I should an' shouldn't do, Missus. This ain't your house, remember.'

'No. You're quite right, Will.' Ruth made a supreme effort not to antagonise him as she expertly slid the sausage rolls on to the cooling racks. 'How are the models going?' she asked brightly. 'Have you got any ready to go in the shop, yet?'

'No, I bloody ain't,' he said rudely.

'Well, if you want to have them in the shop for Christmas . . . ' Ruth smiled at him, her eyebrows raised questioningly.

'I don't. An' you can mind your own business.' He glowered at her then turned and stared into the fire.

'I'll make some toast.' Ruth turned away, her efforts at being sociable getting nowhere.

Will ate six slices of toast and drank three cups of tea without saying a word to either his wife or his mother-in-law, then he heaved himself to his feet. 'Help me on with me coat,' he commanded Ginny. 'I'm goin' out.' He waited while she buttoned him into his reefer jacket then announced. 'Dunno when I'll be back.'

'What's got into him today?' Ruth asked when he had gone.

Ginny poured herself another cup of tea and bit into a second slice of toast. 'I think he's feeling a bit under the weather,' she said vaguely.

But it was more than that and she knew it. The trouble was, it was a problem that she had no idea how to resolve.

29

Will was gone all day. Several times Ginny had been on the point of taking off her overall and going to look for him, then something had happened — her mother had gone home to fetch more sausage rolls so she couldn't leave the shop, Bobby had fallen off her swing and cut her knee — so she hadn't gone. But she kept expecting him to return any minute, especially when it began to get dark.

'I expect he's gone to see his mother,' Ruth said when she voiced her anxiety as she bathed the children in the tin bath in front of the fire.

'Yes, you're probably right.' She cuddled them dry in the big towel and put them in their nightclothes and gave them a mug of milk each. Then she took them upstairs and tucked them into bed, Bobby's fair curls on one pillow and George's dark head on the other. She dropped a kiss on each rosy cheek, thanking God for two healthy and happy children and went downstairs.

An hour later Will came home — or rather was brought home. He was blind drunk. Ginny looked at him in disgust, relieved that the children were both in bed so they didn't see the state their father was in.

But Ruth was still there, helping Ginny to clear up and prepare for the following day.

'You still here, you miserable owd bitch?' he shouted as two of his old cronies eased him into his chair. 'Ain't you got a 'ome of your own?'

'Be quiet, Will,' Ginny said crisply. Then to the two men, 'Don't leave him there. I don't want him cluttering up my kitchen. Put him on the sofa in the other room and let him sleep it off. He'll never get up the stairs, the state he's in.'

'We could carry 'im up, Missus,' one of them said and Ginny noticed that he was none too steady on his feet.

'No, thank you. I don't want him in my bed and I don't want to risk him waking the children.' She nodded in the direction of the sitting room that was rarely used. 'Put him in there and I'll throw a blanket over him.'

When the two men came out again she rounded on them. 'What possessed you to let him get into such a state?' she demanded. 'And anyway, where did he get the money from?'

They stared at her in owlish surprise. They had expected gratitude, not this tirade. 'Well, Missus, 'e'd bin sittin' in the hut on the quay all day talkin' to one an' another an' 'e seemed prop'ly down in the dumps, poor beggar,' the shorter of the two men explained in a rather rambling way. 'That was cold, too, so when the Rose and Crown opened we all got together and took him in, thinkin' we'd warm 'im up a bit.' He twisted his cap in his hands. 'Everybody there was pleased to see 'im, even 'is owd mum — she's got 'er own chair up the corner now, she spend so much time there — 'cause 'e 'adn't bin in the Rose for near on a year. Well, o' course, everybody there said how sorry they was about his legs an' how nice it was to see him in the Rose again an' one an' another bought him a pint or a tot o' rum. He enjoyed hisself so much that afore we knew where we were that was gone eight o'clock an' 'e'd 'ad a drop too much. So we thought we'd better fetch 'im 'ome.'

'We coulda kep' 'im there till closin' time, but we didn't, we brung 'im 'ome,' the other one said, swaying gently on his feet and looking for approval.

Ginny looked at them both disdainfully. 'If you'd kept him there till closing time you wouldn't have been in a fit state to find your own homes, let alone his,' she said scathingly.

The two men looked crestfallen. They had expected her to be grateful to them. 'Hev you got a few stale cakes we could take home for the littl'uns?' one asked hopefully.

She pursed her lips, angry that they should have had the temerity to ask. 'No, I haven't. We'd sold out of everything before four o'clock today.' She began to propel them towards the door. 'But if you'd given your wives the money instead of tipping it all down your necks they'd have been able to come and buy some fresh ones.' She closed the door firmly behind them.

She fetched a blanket from upstairs and covered her snoring husband, then went back to the kitchen and flopped down into the Windsor chair by the fire and rested her head on her hand.

'I was afraid that might happen,' she said with a sigh.

'Why? What do you mean?' Ruth asked.

She looked up, her face bleak. 'Will's realised he's no good at working with wood, he's too ham-fisted. All those little wooden figures . . . ' she spread her hands and sighed. 'I've tried to encourage him. I thought he might get better with practice but it's no use, he just can't do it. And he can't go out fishing because of his legs, so he feels completely useless.' She shook her head. 'I don't know what to suggest he might do.'

Ruth sat down at the table. 'It's a terrible

hard row you have to hoe, my girl,' she said sadly. 'And it's all my fault.'

Ginny's head jerked up. 'What do you mean? It wasn't your fault the smack sank.'

Ruth's shoulders sagged. 'No, that wasn't anybody's fault. But it was my fault you married him in there.' She nodded towards the closed door, behind which Will's snores could be heard. 'I should never have forced you to marry him,' she continued, her voice quiet and despairing. 'We'd have managed. We'd have ridden out the shame. A bastard child isn't the end of the world. We'd have been all right, the three of us. Goodness knows, Bobby wouldn't have been the first child to be brought up without a father.' She gave a deep sigh.

'What's done is done. You did what you thought was best,' Ginny said resignedly.

'That's just the trouble. I didn't force you to marry him because I thought it was best,' Ruth admitted wretchedly. 'I did it because I had to get married when the same thing happened to me so I didn't see why you shouldn't do the same. I suppose you could almost call it spite.'

Ginny sat up straight in her chair. 'You mean Dad wasn't my father?' she asked, horrified.

'Oh, no, nothing like that,' Ruth said

quickly. 'Robert's your father, there's no doubt about that. And he was keen enough to marry me when he knew you were on the way. It was me that didn't want to.'

Ginny relaxed. 'That's all right, then.' After a minute she asked, 'But why didn't you want to marry Dad?'

'It wasn't just that I didn't want to marry Robert, I didn't want to get married at all,' Ruth explained. 'You see, I was under-cook at Wyford Park at the time. I'd been there ever since I left school and as Cook was getting near to retirement I was all set to step into her shoes. That was what I had always wanted to do, to be Cook in a big house. I never had any wish to marry and raise a family.'

She paused and stared into the fire, her thoughts elsewhere. Then she pulled herself together and went on, 'But then I met your father at the fair. He was tall and handsome and it was quite nice to have a young man paying me attention. It had never happened to me before. Well, I met him several times after that, he'd come up to the Park whenever his boat was in and we'd go for a walk by the river. I never intended anything serious, but I was young and I suppose I got a bit carried away by his attentions. The next thing I knew was I was pregnant — oh, I'd known I was taking a risk, I wasn't entirely ignorant about such things, but I suppose I thought it couldn't happen to me, silly little fool that I was.'

She gave a mirthless little laugh and continued, 'I didn't say anything to anyone. I kept hoping I'd made a mistake, got my dates wrong, or that I'd miscarry and nobody need be any the wiser. I'd no family to help me, I'd been brought up by a maiden aunt after my mother died and she'd been only too glad to get rid of me. But as the weeks went on and my clothes got tighter Cook became suspicious and in the end I had to leave.'

Ginny licked her lips. She was seeing a side of her mother she hadn't known existed. 'What did you do?' she asked.

Ruth gave a shrug. 'The only thing I could do. I had to tell Robert.'

'What did he say?'

'Oh, he was very kind. In fact, he insisted on us being married right away.' She gave a slight smile. 'I think he was very happy about the prospect of being a father. But I wasn't. I never felt I was cut out to be a mother, it wasn't what I wanted, at all. I felt trapped in that poky little house in Quay Yard after being in service for over eight years in a big house with rolling grounds and I resented having to give up my lovely life there. Looking back, I can see I was lucky Robert was so keen for us to be married, but I didn't think so at the time, nor for years afterwards.' She paused, then went on more slowly, 'I don't think I stopped to think what my real motive was in forcing you into marriage, Ginny. I told myself it was the shame of it all that I couldn't face. I'd always held myself to be a cut above the people we lived amongst and I couldn't bear the thought of them gloating over our downfall. But I realise now that it went deeper than that. The real reason was that I'd had to pay for my mistake with a marriage I didn't want, so why shouldn't I make you do the same.' She looked up at Ginny and her eyes were full of pain. 'There, I've admitted it. It was a shameful thing to do and I've suffered for it every day of my life since, as I've watched you struggling with the life I condemned you to by my vindictiveness.' She turned away. 'I won't blame you if you turn me out and tell me you never want to see me again, Ginny.'

Ginny shook her head. 'There's no point in that. We have a business to run.' She looked thoughtfully at her mother. 'And strange as it may seem, I bear you no malice. Perhaps I understand you better than you realise.' She was silent for a long time. Then she said, 'I'm just so thankful you didn't say Dad wasn't my real father. I don't think I could have borne that. I loved him so much.'

'Oh, there's no doubt about that. Robert was the only man I ever went with and I was lucky, he was a good, honest and upright man,' Ruth said, her voice heavy with relief. 'He treated me well and he thought the world of you.' She looked hard at Ginny, whose eyes had filled with tears at the mention of her beloved father. 'I can't expect you to forgive me for what I've done to you, my girl. All I can say is that I regret it from the bottom of my heart.' She reached over and took Ginny's hand. 'If only you could have married Nathan, Ginny . . . '

Gently, Ginny removed her hand and got to her feet. 'That was not an option, at the time, Mother. And now it's too late. Things are as they are, so I have to make the best of them. Will took me on when I was pregnant with another man's child and now I've got two lovely children, so I've got a lot to be thankful for.' She gave a funny, quirky smile. 'We've managed to get along together reasonably well for the past three or four years. It's all right as long as I take life one day at a time and try not to look ahead to the future.' She blew her nose and said briskly, looking round the kitchen, 'Now, I think we've finished here for tonight. You're welcome to stay the night as it's getting late, or would you rather go home?'

Ruth took the hint and stood up. 'I'll go home. I must be up early in the morning to make mince pies. People are already asking for them even though it isn't Christmas yet.'

After Ruth had gone home Ginny went to bed and lay thinking over what her mother had said. She could begin to understand now why she had always been so cold and aloof towards everybody. It must have been very difficult to adjust to a tiny cottage with no more than a cobbled yard after living in a big house with green rolling grounds, even as a servant. Ginny could even believe that deep down and probably unknowingly, her mother might have blamed her, Ginny, for her own downfall, and had forced her into a loveless marriage as some kind of punishment. It was a sobering thought.

The next day Will woke with a bad head and an even worse temper. When Nathan called, as he often did, for a meat pie, Ginny sent him through to talk to Will.

'He's like a bear with a sore head,' she warned. 'And it's not altogether because he got drunk last night.' She told him about his failure with the little wooden figures.

'I'll go and see him in a minute,' Nathan said. 'But I want a word with you, too, Ginny, since there's nobody in the shop. No, it's all right, it's nothing personal,' he said, as a wary look crossed her face. 'Although I wish it could be,' he added softly.

'What is it, then?' she asked, furious with herself for blushing like a schoolgirl at his words.

'I want to know how things are going with the shop,' he said. 'I want to know if it's a success. I want to make sure you can afford the rent you're paying.' He paused and studied her. 'And I want the truth, Ginny.'

She straightened two doughnuts on their doily and looked round the shop.

'We did very well when we started,' she said. 'Like all new shops, people came to sample our wares. And we still have regular customers, like you, and your mother and the other yacht captains' wives. But we had heard that the shipyard was going to open again, which gave us courage to go ahead because we thought it would bring in quite a bit of trade. But up to now nothing's happened in that direction so there's still quite a lot of unemployment in the village, which means there's not very much money about.' She gave a little laugh. 'Most of our cakes now are sold half price. People wait till the second day before they buy them so they don't have to pay full price.' She shrugged. 'I don't blame them, it's not as if they're stale after one day.

But it cuts the profits.'

'You don't have to pay the rent, Ginny. You know that,' Nathan said.

'Oh, we can manage. The insurance from the smack has come through so we've got money to tide us over till things pick up — if they ever do.'

'Have you ever thought of displaying your pencil drawings?' he asked thoughtfully. 'You've got quite a bit of wall space and they'd look good. After all, they'll never sell if nobody can see them.'

'Oh, I don't think they're good enough for anybody to buy,' Ginny said hurriedly.

'That you'll never know unless you display them,' he said with a smile. 'And if they don't sell you won't have lost anything because they'll still look good on the walls. Think about it.' He lifted up the counter flap. 'Now, I'll go through and beard the lion. See if I can put him in a better mood.' His smile widened. 'Is my favourite god-daughter in?'

'No, I'm afraid not. She's gone home with her granny to make custard tarts.'

'Oh, that's a pity,' he said, his mouth turning down at the corners. 'She always brightens my day. Just like her mother.' He whispered the last words in Ginny's ear as he passed, making her blush yet again.

$\star$ $\star$ $\star$

'Nathan's gettin' a bit above himself, ain't he?' Will asked, that night, as Ginny turned out the light and got into bed bedside him.

'What do you mean?' she asked, a little finger of fear clutching her heart as her mind spun rapidly through any possible reasons for suspicion Will might have discovered.

'Comin' here an lecturin' me on what I oughta be doin',' he said grumpily. 'Thass all very well for him. He ain't the one with smashed legs, is 'e! He ain't the one who can't git 'is fingers to work a chisel. He can sit an' paint them pictures of his to his heart's content an' know some damn fool'll buy 'em.'

'Have you ever tried to paint, Will?' she asked, trying to suppress a yawn.

'No, thass sissy's work,' he said scornfully.

'Not if you can earn twenty or thirty pounds doing it,' she reminded him.

'Well, I ain't gonna try.' He was silent, but she knew there was more to come from the tense way he was holding himself. After some time he said, 'Nathan reckons I oughta go an' see Billy Barr. See if he'll give me a job in the sail loft.'

'Oh.' She was careful to say nothing more.

'I said I couldn't work a sewin' machine to make sails but Nathan reckons I could put the cringles in. There's splicin' to be done there, too. I can splice a rope as good as the next man.'

'Do you think you might go and see him, then?'

'Who?'

'Billy Barr. Do you think you might ask him for a job?'

'I'll think about it. But not because Nathan said so. I ain't takin' orders from him. I ain't hevin' him order my life about.'

'I thought you liked Nathan. I thought he was your friend,' she said.

'Not when he come here tellin' me what I oughta do. I don't take orders from nobody.' He was quiet for some time and she was just dropping off to sleep when he turned suddenly and pulling up her nightdress rolled on top of her.

'Oh! For goodness sake . . . What are you doing?' She was still half asleep.

'What d'you think I'm doin',' he growled. 'I'm doin' what *I* wanta do, not what Nathan Bellamy say I oughta do. Now shut up an' keep still.'

30

Christmas came and went. The shop was busy right up to Christmas Eve and on Christmas Day both Ginny and Ruth were almost too tired to cook the large chicken Ruth had provided. But the children squealed with delight at the presents Father Christmas had left them and even Will made himself sociable, especially as Ruth had put a bottle of rum in his stocking.

The New Year came in on a sombre note. In spite of Mr Chamberlain's earnest assurance that there would be 'peace in our time' the clouds of war seemed to be rumbling ominously. Schoolchildren were given gas masks and there were rumours of the possibility of air-raid shelters being distributed to those London homes that were 'most likely to be bombed'. People were edgy and nervous and lurid tales of 'what happened in the last war' abounded. Another ominous sign was that most of the big yachts that usually wintered in the river had disappeared, requisitioned by the government for naval purposes. *Aurora* was not among these; she had already been sold by Sir Titus for an inflated price.

The months wore on and Ginny became increasingly worried about the cake shop because now that the yachts had gone there was no trade at all from the yacht owners and their visitors. However, the yacht captains' wives were still faithful. Although their husbands had for the most part been forced to retire from yachting, it had provided a very good living while it lasted and the more prudent among the captains had invested carefully and were now more than comfortably off. Their wives were only too happy to take advantage of this fact. But as Ruth pointed out, whilst baking for half a dozen yacht captains' wives in her kitchen had been quite profitable, it was hardly sufficient to maintain a shop. Nevertheless, there was no shortage of customers for yesterday's cakes, if they were sold cheaply enough. Ginny sometimes felt she was walking a tightrope.

And Will did nothing to help.

Since Nathan had suggested that he might ask for work at the sailmakers he had spent hours in his workshop splicing bits of rope.

When Ginny questioned him he barked, 'I gotta see if I can do it, ain't I? No good me goin' for a job I can't do.'

'I'm sure Mr Barr would be happy to teach you,' Ginny said. 'He wouldn't expect you to know what to do without being told. He knows you're a fisherman.'

'Was!' he corrected irritably.

She ignored that. 'I think you should go and see him,' she said.

The next day he went out. She watched him down the road and marvelled at how agile he had become on his crutches, swinging his body from side to side as he went. As a result, the muscles in his arms and shoulders had become very strong and powerful and she reasoned that there must be some kind of work he could do, as long as he could sit down to it.

He was gone most of the day, which pleased her and she went about her work humming.

'You sound happy,' Ruth remarked when she came into the kitchen for more Chelsea buns.

'Yes. Will's gone to see Mr Barr at the sail loft, and he's been gone such a long time that I reckon he's been taken on right away.'

'Either that or he's fetched up at the Rose and Crown,' Ruth said pithily.

'He can't go there, he hasn't got any money.'

'No, but he's got so-called friends.'

'Oh, give him credit for a bit of decency, Mother,' Ginny said impatiently. 'He wouldn't sponge off his friends.' She arranged the Chelsea buns on a plate and handed it to Ruth. 'There, that's the last of them. They've gone well today.'

'Yes, so have the iced fancies. Maybe things are picking up.' Ruth went back into the shop.

Will came home in the middle of the afternoon. He didn't seem quite so agile on his crutches and Ginny could smell the beer on his breath.

'Did you go and see Mr Barr?' she asked.

'Yes, I did.' He flopped down in his chair looking very pleased with himself.

'Well?' She put her hands on her hips. 'I suppose he said there's not a lot of call for sails to be made now the yachts have gone.'

'No, he didn't, then,' Will said triumphantly. 'He's happy to put me on an' he says I can start termorrer. Seems he's rushed off his feet because he's got a big order from the Admiralty . . . '

'Is it something to do with war?'

'Yes. Well, gettin' ready for it. Jest in case.'

'Oh, dear,' Ginny said, looking alarmed. 'I don't like the sound of that.'

'No, but I reckon thass what's comin'. Well, anyway, Billy Barr's got a big order for canvas covers for guns an' suchlike an' one of his men has left to join the army so he'll be glad to take me on if I can manage the foot pedal on the stitchin' machines.' He looked down at his feet. 'I reckon I can manage all right. Thass not as if it'll need too much pressure, not like hevin' to bear the weight of me whole body. Anyway, I shall give it a try.' He leaned back in his chair, looking very pleased with himself.

She rescued George from the coal scuttle and placed him on his father's lap. 'So you just popped in to the Rose and Crown to celebrate,' she said mildly.

'Coupla pints, thass all.' He bounced George up and down on his knee, making the little boy squeal with delight.

Ginny said no more. It was a relief to see Will happy; for the moment she was content.

He went off happily the next morning, a bag with sandwiches and a flask of tea slung round his neck because although it was not far to the sail loft he agreed with Ginny that he would have difficulty in managing the journey there and back twice as well as doing a day's work. She watched him go, breathing a silent prayer that all would go well for him.

Her prayer was answered. He came home in high spirits.

'I wasn't the only one Billy Barr set on today,' he said gleefully as he tucked into the plate of stew she had saved for him. 'He set another chap on too, a Brightlingsea bloke, but he was as ham-fisted as they come. Couldn't manage the machine nohow. He got himself in a terrible muddle. I couldn't see the problem, meself. I never had any trouble at all.' He leaned back and flexed his shoulders. 'Thass tirin', though, hunched over them great stitchin' machines all day and heavin' lumps o' canvas around. They ain't like that sewin' machine o' yours, girl.'

'My sewing machine wasn't designed to stitch canvas,' she reminded him with a smile.

When Friday came Will waited until he had finished his meal, then opened his pay packet. Ginny, busily bathing the children in the tin bath in front of the fire, watched him out of the corner of her eye. He laid two pennies side by side on the table.

'Thass a Friday night penny for the kiddies,' he said proudly. 'They'll get one every week from their owd dad.'

'And what about me?' Ginny asked with a smile, towelling George dry. 'Don't I get a Friday night penny or two?'

He looked at her in some surprise. 'Why should I give you money? You've got the shop.'

'The shop isn't doing all that well, you know that,' she said, buttoning the little boy into his pyjamas. 'In fact, if you hadn't found work I don't quite know what we'd have done. We already owe Nathan a fortnight's rent.'

Will poked about in his pay packet and grudgingly fished out two half-crowns. 'There y'are. Thass all you're gonna get. The rest is mine. I've worked for it an' I'm keepin' it.'

'But Bobby's shoes need mending and George's are too small for him. I was hoping your money would pay for that,' she said, disappointed.

'Ah, I thought as much.' Will banged his fist down on the table, his mood suddenly changing. 'No sooner do I earn a copper than you're after it. Well, the kids've waited this long for shoes so that won't hurt 'em to wait a bit longer.' He picked up his crutches and heaved himself to his feet.

'I'm orf out. I allus used to hev a drink of a Friday night so I don't see why I shouldn't go to the Rose an' Crown for an hour. Thass long enough since I've had two farthin's to rub together in me pocket, thanks to your tight fist, Missus.'

Ginny sighed. She knew it was no use arguing with him so she contented herself with saying, 'I hope you won't be too late back. Saturday can be quite a busy day in the shop.'

'Thass your concern, not mine,' he said unsympathetically.

When Will came back she had just finished clearing up the kitchen and the last batch of cakes was out of the oven and on the cooling tray.

He stood in the doorway, blinking in the light, then moved forward to help himself to a jam tart.

'Leave them! They're not for you,' she said, her voice sharp with tiredness as she stepped in his way.

He gave her a push that sent her reeling against the dresser. Then he deliberately picked up two jam tarts and rammed them both into his mouth. 'They're better warm,' he grinned, spraying pastry as he spoke. 'I allus like a warm tart. Better a warm tart than a cold wife, thass what I say.' He went to pick up a third tart but Ginny caught his arm.

'You're not having any more,' she hissed.

'Who says so?' He shook her off roughly, catching her off balance so that she fell again, hitting her cheek on the edge of the table.

She sat on the floor, nursing her cheek and heard him go to the stairs. After a minute, he called, 'You'll hev to give me a hand. I can't git up the stairs. These bloody crutches . . . keep gettin' in the way . . . '

She got to her feet and went to him. 'I'm not helping you. If you're too drunk to get up the stairs you'll have to stay down here and sleep on the settee,' she said coldly. 'I'll bring you a blanket.'

He looked up at her. 'What've you done to your face?' he asked, trying to focus his eyes.

'I hit it on the table when you pushed me over. Now, get out of my way so that I can fetch you a blanket. I'm very tired. I want to go to bed.'

Predictably, the next morning he had a hangover, but Ginny made him get up and go to work.

'It's only for the morning. You don't have to work Saturday afternoon,' she said, hanging a bag containing a flask of coffee round his neck. 'But you don't want to risk getting the sack for not turning up on your first week, do you.'

'You'll be sorry if I put the needle through me finger 'cause I can't see straight,' he warned.

'Not half as sorry as you will,' she replied, half pushing him out of the door.

He was in a much better mood by the time he came home. Nathan was with him and he was busy telling him what he'd been doing all the week.

'We're makin' canvas covers. Thass all a bit hush-hush, but there ain't much doubt what thass all for. I reckon they're for guns and ammunition boxes, things like that.'

'And you're managing all right?' Nathan asked.

'Yes. As long as I can sit on me arse I'm as good as the next man,' Will said expansively. He pushed open the shop door and ignoring Ruth, who was standing behind the counter, said 'Come through to the kitchen. I'll get Ginny to make us a cuppa tea.'

With a nod towards Ruth, Nathan followed him.

'Sit down, bor,' Will said. He turned to Ginny, who was busy washing tins at the sink. 'Come on, girl, look lively. I've brought Nathan home for a cuppa tea.'

'You'll have to wait a minute, till I've finished this,' she said, without turning round.

'It's all right, there's no hurry, Ginny,' Nathan said, squatting down on the floor to help George build a castle with his bricks.

She finished what she was doing and went straight to the stove. But eventually, when the tea was made and poured she was forced to look at him.

'Ginny!' He got to his feet, full of concern. 'What have you done to your face? How did you get that bruise on your cheek?' With difficulty he prevented himself from putting a hand out to touch it.

'She tripped over, didn't you, girl?' Will said casually. 'Fell over her big feet and hit her head on the table, daft besom.'

'Is that right?' Nathan said, looking at her suspicious.

She nodded, putting her hand briefly up to her cheek. 'Something like that. It probably looks worse than it is.'

'You're working much too hard, Ginny,' Nathan said. She could hear the concern in his voice and she was worried in case Will heard it, too.

'Nonsense,' she said cheerfully. 'In any case, it's work I love doing.' She changed the subject. 'If you've called for your meat pies, Nathan, they're all ready and waiting for you in the shop.'

'Yes. I'll take them when I go. But I've really come because there's something I want to tell you . . . both.' He added the last word just in time.

'What's that? You got some exhibition on?' Will asked, slurping his tea.

'No, nothing like that.' Nathan sat down opposite Will. 'I've come to tell you I shall be going away before long,' he said, looking at him and not Ginny as he spoke.

'Going away? Where to, for goodness sake?' Ginny asked, keeping her voice light with difficulty. Now she knew what it meant to

470

have a sinking heart. She really felt as if her heart had plummeted, right down through her body and into her shoes.

'Had enough o' Wyford, hev ye?' Will chuckled. 'Goin' back to Lunnon town?'

'Good heavens, no!' Nathan said, shocked. 'That's the last thing I'd think of doing. No, I've thought about it a lot and I've decided to join the Royal Navy. With my experience on the yachts and fishing boats I shouldn't have any trouble getting in, especially with my father's connections.'

Suddenly, Bobby, who had been playing with her dolls in the corner, ran across the room and climbed on to his lap and threw her arms round him. 'No, Uncle Nathan. You can't go away. I won't let you. You've got to stay here with me.'

Ginny smiled at the child on Nathan's lap, then the smile froze on her face as she saw with total clarity the likeness between the two of them. Swiftly, she took Bobby from him and set her on her feet.

'Little pitchers should be seen and not heard,' she said, kissing the top of her head and giving her a pat on the bottom at the same time. 'Why don't you go out and have a swing?'

'But I don't want Uncle Nathan to go away,' Bobby protested.

'Neither do we, dear. But I don't suppose it will be for long,' her mother said reassuringly.

'Oh, that's all right, then.' Obediently, she ran out through the open door to her swing.

'You're a lucky bugger,' Will said gloomily, pouring his tea into his saucer and drinking it noisily. 'Wish I could come with you.'

'When do you expect to go, Nathan?' Ginny asked, amazed that her voice wasn't betraying the turmoil inside her.

'In about a fortnight, I think,' he replied. He paused and drank some of his tea, then went on, 'To my mind, whatever Mr Chamberlain tries to tell us, there'll be war before many more months. It's unavoidable, all the signs are there. In which case it'll only be a matter of time before all able-bodied men get their call-up papers. Well, that's all right by me, I'm quite prepared to fight for King and country. But if I'm going to fight I'd prefer to fight at sea rather than on dry land, so I thought I'd volunteer, then I'd have the choice.'

Ginny drank her tea, holding her cup with hands that were shaking. She couldn't begin to imagine life without Nathan. Even though he was forced to remain in the background of her life, the knowledge that he was there, knowing that she would often see him, however briefly, gave her the strength to keep going from day to day. Without that knowledge she wondered how she would find the strength to carry on, or whether she might disintegrate, fall into little pieces that only Nathan could put back together again.

Realising that she must say something, she forced her lips into a smile and said, 'I'm sure you'll look very dashing in your uniform.'

'I'll come and see you when I get it, then you can judge for yourself,' he said, smiling back at her with a smile that didn't reach his eyes.

Will was frowning. 'I reckon you're right about a war, Nathan. I reckon if Hitler once sets his foot into Poland that'll be it. We shall be in it up to our necks. But do you reckon he will?'

'I'm certain of it. The man's power crazy. He's already gone into Austria and Czechoslovakia without being hindered so he won't stop now. And have you seen in the paper what's happening to the Jews?'

'Aye. An' I listen to the news on the wireless, too . . . '

Ginny got up from her seat and went into the garden, leaving the two men talking about the impending war. It was a gloriously sunny July day, without a cloud in the sky. The birds were singing, the garden was a riot of summer flowers and Bobby was happily playing on her swing. It was all so peaceful, so normal, so beautiful, that she simply couldn't believe that all the talk of war could ever be more than talk. It was unthinkable. Almost as unthinkable as Nathan leaving Wyford and going away.

31

Nathan left Wyford two weeks later. Glancing out through the shop window, Ruth saw him on the other side of the road, walking to the station, his suitcase in his hand. She also saw him hesitate, look at his watch, then cross the road and push open the shop door. She smiled and nodded in the direction of the kitchen.

'Ginny's in there,' she said.

'Thanks.' He put down his suitcase and went through, ducking his head as he went.

He stood for a moment, just looking at her as she stood at the table, ironing. Then he said, 'I'm sorry. I found I couldn't walk past without coming and saying goodbye, Ginny,' he said apologetically.

Ginny put down her iron. 'I don't think I could have borne it if you had,' she said. She bent her head. 'Not that I can bear it, anyway.' She looked up at him, her eyes bleak. 'Oh, Nathan, what am I going to do? How am I going to . . . ?' She bit her lip and looked out at the garden, where the two children were playing happily. 'It's only the thought that I shall see you sometimes

. . . hear your voice . . . know that you're not far away . . . ' She shook her head. 'I can't explain, but somehow it gives me strength, just to know . . . '

He moved forward and put his arm round her. It was the first physical contact they had had for a long time and she leaned against him, savouring the feel of his tweed jacket under her cheek. 'I understand, sweetheart,' he whispered. 'And I feel the same. But it's not enough, is it? All this time and never being able to show you how much I love you. Never being able to kiss you, to hold you in my arms like this.' His other arm went round her and he held her close.

'Oh, if only I could stay here for ever,' she sighed.

His arms tightened. 'If only you could, my dearest love,' he whispered back, leaning his cheek on her hair. 'But it's not possible, is it. Will is your husband, he trusts you and you won't betray his trust.'

'No,' she said, her voice muffled. 'I couldn't live with myself if I did.'

'I know,' he said gently, 'And I respect you for it. In any case I wouldn't want to cheapen our love with some sordid affair, it's much too precious to me for that.' He loosened his hold slightly. 'But it's no use, I can't go on wanting you the way I do, knowing you can never be mine. Sometimes I have difficulty even being civil to Will because I'm so jealous. Especially as I know he doesn't have half the feeling for you that I do. At night sometimes I imagine what our lives together would be like, the things I could do for you, the places we could go. I torture myself with all kinds of wonderful plans. Then I come back to earth and realise that it can never be. So that's why I've decided that the best thing will be for me to go away, to join the navy.' His voice roughened. 'It'll be a new life, new start . . . '

She twisted up to look at him. 'But you'll come back?' she asked, alarmed. 'You're not saying you'll never come back to Wyford?' She didn't wait for him to answer but went on, 'I'll pray every night of my life that you'll come back safe. If . . . if anything happened to you I think it would kill me, too.'

He gave her a little shake. 'Nothing's going to happen to me, darling,' he said with a smile. 'I'm only joining the Royal Navy, not the Foreign Legion.'

'But if there's a war . . . '

He bent and kissed her, very gently. 'We'll cross that bridge when we come to it.' He kissed her again, urgently, desperately. Then he held her close, stroking her hair. 'But whatever happens, my darling, never forget that I love you more than words can ever tell.'

Before she could reply he had released her and gone.

She stood for a moment, her eyes closed, touching her lips where he had kissed her. Then, because there was no other alternative she resumed her ironing, her tears sizzling on the hot iron as she worked. With Nathan's departure a light had gone out of her life.

She told Will of Nathan's visit when he got home that night.

'He's gone to join the navy,' she said, amazed at how matter-of-fact her voice sounded.

'Lucky bugger. Wish it was me,' he said bitterly.

So do I, she thought with equal bitterness.

★   ★   ★

Not many days after Nathan had left Mabel Bellamy, his mother, came into the shop. She was looking quite distraught. 'No doubt you've heard that my Nathan's gone away, joined the navy,' she said, as Ginny put her cakes into a bag.

'Yes, he came and told us,' Ginny said, keeping her voice level with some difficulty.

'Well, would you believe it? Now his father's decided to do the same.' Mabel rammed the cakes savagely into her shopping basket. 'I told Hector he was being ridiculous to even consider such a thing. After all, he's forty-seven; he has no need to do another day's work as long as he lives if he doesn't want to because he made a very good living from yachting and he's invested wisely. But he's quite determined. He says if there's going to be a war he wants to do his bit, the stupid man.'

'That's very patriotic of him, Mrs Bellamy,' Ginny said, trying to say the right thing.

'Patriotic, my foot. He just doesn't want to be left out, that's all it is,' Mabel snapped.

Ginny frowned. 'Does Captain Bellamy really think there's going to be a war, then?'

Mabel sat down heavily on the chair provided on her side of the counter. 'Yes, he's convinced of it,' she said, her voice taut with anxiety. 'He says all the signs are there, the only question is, when will it start.' She sighed. 'He's right, of course. I keep trying to tell myself that it'll all blow over and nothing will come of it but whenever you pick up a newspaper or listen to the wireless all you read about is air-raid shelters and gas masks and evacuating children from big cities in case of bombing.' She pulled out her handkerchief and dabbed her eyes. 'It's dreadful.' She looked up at Ginny. 'I think it's very selfish of Hector to go off and leave me with all this uncertainty hanging over us all. What am I going to do? Who can I turn to with both my husband and my son gone? Who can I share all my worries with?'

'You can always come and talk to me if it will help, Mrs Bellamy,' Ginny told her. 'And I know my mother would say the same.'

Mabel nodded and gave her a watery smile. 'Thank you, Ginny. That's very kind.' She got to her feet. 'You're a good girl. Nathan should have married you when he had the chance. He was a fool.' She went to the door. 'But maybe he'll find some nice Scottish lassie and marry her. You've heard he's being sent to Scotland?'

Ginny shook her head. 'No, I didn't know that,' she said bleakly.

★ ★ ★

Will was happier than at any time since his accident. He had regained his self-respect because he had found that he could work for a living in spite of his crippled legs. More to the point he enjoyed the work he did on what he called 'them owd stitchin' machines'. Every morning he would cheerfully heave himself off to work, with his lunch bag slung round his neck or on his back, returning at night, tired but contented with his lot.

'Can't tell you what we're makin' 'cause thass all hush-hush,' he told Ginny importantly. 'Thass all to do with the war.'

Ginny smiled a little at this, remembering he had already told her he was making canvas covers for guns and ammunition cases, but it occurred to her that perhaps now there were other, more sinister items being stitched in Billy Barr's sail loft. Her imagination baulked at what they might be.

'But there isn't a war and please God there won't be one,' she insisted. 'War. That's a horrible word.'

'I know. But I reckon thass a word you'll hev to get used to, girl. I'll give it till the end o' the year before war's declared. No longer.'

'Oh, Will, I hope you're wrong,' she said.

'So do I, girl. But I don't think I am.'

Every Friday night when he came home with his wages he carefully doled out a quarter share for Ginny to keep house on. This he considered fair, since she also had the money she earned from the cake shop, which she had never seen fit to share with him — the fact that the cake shop rarely made enough to do much more than pay its way didn't concern him. The rest of his wages he considered were his own, to spend as he chose. And he chose to spend a good deal of it on Friday nights at the Rose and Crown. It was the only night of the week he got drunk so Ginny tried not to complain, but she always made sure the children were tucked up in bed out of the way when he arrived home and did her best to keep him quiet so that he didn't wake them up. Occasionally, they would spend Friday night with Granny Ruth, which both they and she enjoyed, leaving Ginny to wait alone for her husband to be brought home, either singing at the top of his voice or morose and bad-tempered. Either way, she would leave him to sleep it off on the settee in the room next to the kitchen and was ready with aspirin and black coffee the next morning as he vowed blearily never to touch another drop of alcohol as long as he lived.

But one Friday evening, when she was still busy making the pastry that would be made into jam tarts early the next day he arrived home unexpectedly early. It was only nine o'clock and he was stone-cold sober.

'You're back early, dear,' she said, trying not to sound surprised. 'Aren't you well?'

'Never better,' he replied grimly, swinging himself over to his chair and lowering himself into it.

She began to dust the flour off her hands. 'Shall I make you a cup of tea?'

'No.'

'Oh, very well. I'll just finish making this pastry and put it to cool . . . '

'Sit down,' he barked.

She was too surprised to do anything but obey. 'What is it, Will?' she asked, frowning. 'What's wrong?'

'You've made me look a bloody fool, thass wass wrong,' he said savagely.

Her jaw dropped. 'Me? How? Why? What have I done?'

He didn't answer her question. Instead he said, 'I saw a friend o' yours in the pub tonight.'

'Oh, yes? And who was that?' she asked, her mind busily going through all the people she was even vaguely friendly with. Few of them, apart from Annie Kesgrave, regularly frequented the Rose and Crown, and he was hardly likely to refer to his own mother merely as Ginny's friend. She pulled her mind back to what he was saying.

' . . . this chap. Used to live in Wyford till a few years ago, then he went out to Australia. Sheep farmin'. Know who I'm talkin' about? The name Roger Mayhew ring a bell?' He didn't take his eyes off her face as he spoke.

'Roger? He's come back to Wyford? Well, I never,' she said, managing to make her tone sound normal, although her mouth had suddenly gone dry.

'He was askin' after you.'

She gave a little laugh that sounded nervous even to her own ears. 'He asked the right person, then, if he asked you.'

'Oh, yes. I told him we was married.' He was still watching her and she felt like a mouse being watched by a cat. His voice rose ominously. 'I also told him — on the quiet, so nobody else could hear — that I didn't think much o' the way he'd gone off an' left you with a bun in the oven. But that I'd taken on his leavin's an' was bringin' up his little gal as if she was mine.' He paused. 'An' do you know what he said?'

She could well imagine. She shifted guiltily in her chair.

He slapped his fist down on the table. 'I'll tell you what he said. He said he didn't know what I was talkin' about. An' when I reminded him that he'd been engaged to you, if I wasn't very much mistaken, he said, yes, he had, but for my information, if you was in the fam'ly way when the engagement was broke off it couldn't hev bin him to blame because you hadn't never let him get into your knickers, much as he'd hev liked to. So if I was bringin' up somebody else's brat I'd better start lookin' for somebody who'd had better luck than him.' He leaned back in his chair and stared at her. 'So who's bin tellin' me lies, him or you?'

'Nobody's told you lies, Will,' she said quietly. 'If you think about it, I never, ever told you that Roger was the father of my child, you just assumed he was. You assumed he got me pregnant and when he found out escaped to Australia because he didn't want the responsibility.' She shrugged. 'It wasn't true, Roger wasn't that kind of man, but I didn't see any harm in letting you put two and two together to make five because I never expected Roger would ever come back to England.' She lifted her chin. 'I never lied to you, Will. I just never told you the truth.'

'So what is the truth?'

She shrugged again. 'Does it matter? Bobby's your daughter, that's what she thinks, that's what the world thinks. Why dredge up the past?'

He ground his teeth. 'Because I've got the right to know.'

'Then take yourself upstairs and look at her.' She passed her hand over her face. 'That's all you'll need to do. Just look at her. You'll see who her father is. And you'll wonder how it is you've never seen it before.'

His mouth clamped in a thin, straight line, he picked up his crutches and hauled himself to his feet. Then he went upstairs, bumping noisily from one stair to the next. After what seemed an age he came down by the same method.

He sat down in his chair again, staring at the floor. At last he looked up. 'Nathan?'

She nodded.

His eyes narrowed. 'Hev you bin carryin' on with him behind my back all these years? All this time when I've bin callin' him my friend?'

'No, Will, I haven't. I swear to God I haven't,' she said.

'How can I tell whether to believe you? You lied to me once . . .'

'I *didn't* lie to you, Will. I've *never* lied to you and I'm not lying to you now.' Her voice rose. 'As God's my witness, Nathan has never been anything more than a friend to me since I married you.'

'And before? He musta meant suthin' to you or he couldn't hev got you in the fam'ly way.'

She nodded. 'He did. He meant everything in the world to me. We were in love and we were going to be married.' Her mouth twisted. 'But that woman in London, Isobel Armitage, tricked him into marrying her instead. It was all a dreadful, horrible mess.' She gave a great sigh.

'Do you still love him?'

She looked up. 'That's hardly a fair question, Will. You can't turn love on and off like a tap. But it's over between us, because it has to be. We're friends. Nothing more. That I swear.'

He thumped his crutch on the floor. 'All I can say is, he'd better not come near this house again, the slimey bugger. I'll kill 'im with me bare hands!'

'You don't mean that, Will,' she said, shaking her head. 'Have you forgotten he saved your life? And not once, but twice,' she reminded him. 'Don't you reckon that if we'd been carrying on behind your back he'd have let you drown? From what you've told me about it he could easily have done that. But he didn't, he risked his own life to save you.'

He chewed his moustache. 'All the same . . .'

She waved her hand. 'It doesn't really matter what you think,' she said wearily, 'because Nathan's gone now and he's not likely to come back. Not for a long time, anyway.'

'Do you care?' he asked, glaring at her.

'I care that you shouldn't turn against Bobby,' she said, not answering his question. 'You've always been good to her and treated her exactly the same way as you treat George. I wouldn't want that to change, just because you now know she belongs to Nathan and not Roger Mayhew.'

'Thass not the little maid's fault,' he said grudgingly. 'She didn't choose her father.'

Ginny relaxed a little, grateful for this concession. 'Then can we forget this conversation and carry on like we've always done, Will?' she said. 'Considering how it began, with little enough feeling on either side, we've not had a bad marriage. No worse than a lot of people, at any rate.'

'How do you feel about me now?' The question was totally unexpected, coming from Will.

She was silent for some time, then she put her head on one side and looked at him. 'Put it this way, Will,' she said slowly. 'I shall always be grateful to you for taking me on when you knew I was pregnant and never holding it against me or taunting me with it. And the way you accepted Bobby as if she was your own, from the moment she was born.' She paused, then went on, 'I admire the way you cope with your legs. You don't often complain, although I know they're painful at times and I know you get frustrated because you can't walk about like other men. I know you miss the sea, too.' She hunched her shoulders. 'I've got used to having you around, to seeing you smile and chuckle at the antics of the children.' She smiled. 'I reckon I'd miss you if you weren't here, Will, if only because of the smell of that filthy old pipe.'

He nodded. 'Thass good. Because I dunno how I'd get on without you, girl, straight up, I don't,' he said gruffly. He struggled to his feet. 'I'm orf to bed.'

After he'd gone Ginny sat for a long time, simply staring into space. She recognised his last statement for what it was, the nearest he could ever get to saying 'I love you.'

And in a way she supposed she loved him, too, but it was a quiet, companionable love, not the searing passion she felt for Nathan. She had told Will she would miss him if he wasn't there, and so she would, for a time, but she wouldn't have the enormous hole in her life, a hole that she could only plug by being permanently busy and not looking any further forward than the next day, that Nathan had left. She recognised that there were many different kinds of love and the love she felt for Will was dross against the pure gold of her love for Nathan.

She got to her feet and went up the stairs and got into bed beside her husband.

32

Will's prediction came true and sooner than he had forecast. Hitler carried out his threat and invaded Poland with the result that at eleven o'clock on Sunday, 3 September 1939 Mr Chamberlain made his portentous announcement that the country was at war. As Ginny sat with Will, listening to the awful news on the wireless, she felt in a funny kind of way as if time had suddenly come to a standstill. Nothing had changed. The sun was still shining in through the open door, the birds continued to sing in the old apple tree where Bobby's swing hung, the children still played happily on the step.

'Ah, that won't last long,' Will said, shifting uneasily in his chair. As he spoke, Ginny realised with a start that she had been holding her breath, waiting for something — she didn't know what, to happen.

He nodded his head. 'You mark my words. That'll all be over by Christmas.'

She got up and turned the wireless off. 'Please God, you're right,' she said fervently as she sat down again and lifted George on to her lap, rocking him absent-mindedly. 'What happens now, Will? Will we be invaded by the Germans? What do you reckon's going to happen next?'

'Dunno. We shall hetta wait an' see, shan't we.' Will stoked his pipe as he spoke.

Ginny watched him. After a bit, she said, 'I'm a bit worried about Mum living on her own, Will. After all, we don't know what's going to happen. We could all be killed in our beds, Or worse.'

'Don't be daft, woman,' he said sharply.

'Well, you just said yourself we don't know what's going to happen.'

'I know. But thass daft talk. I'll see you don't come to no harm.'

'I know you will. But that's what I mean about Mum being on her own, Will, she hasn't got Dad to look after her. Do you think we might ask her to come and live with us? Just for the duration of the war? I know you don't get on all that well with her, but she'd be a good help to me . . . '

He shrugged. 'Don't see that'll make that much difference, seein' as she spend most of her time here anyway.'

'That's not true, Will. She's never here on Sundays,' Ginny said defensively. 'She's not here today.'

Will nodded towards the back garden. Ruth was just coming up the path. 'Speak of the devil . . . ' he said laconically.

Ruth came in, her face ashen. 'It's happened,' she said, wringing her hands. 'I never thought it would but it has. Now we shall have Hitler's men overrunning the place and we shall all be killed in our beds.' She sat down, bolt upright on a chair by the table and looked from Ginny to Will and back again. 'I shall buy a gun, that's what I shall do,' she said, nodding her head with every word. 'They won't take me alive, I'll see to that.' She stood up again and began to walk about the room.

Ginny put George down and went over and put her arm round her mother. 'Calm down, Mother, for goodness sake. It's not like you to be so melodramatic. Sit down and I'll make a cup of tea.'

'Tea! How can you think of tea at a time like this?' Ruth sat down and then got up again. 'I don't know what we're going to do.'

'We're not going to do anything at the moment. Now, sit down and pull yourself together. This is not like you at all.'

'It's all very well for you, but I can remember the last war. We don't want to go through all that again, I can tell you.' Suddenly, she cocked an ear. 'Listen, is that an aeroplane? Oh, my Lord, they're coming after us already.'

'They won't come after you, Ruthy, don't you worry,' Will chuckled. 'One look from you and they'll turn and scarper. Britain's secret weapon, Ruthy Appleyard's witherin' look.'

'Don't joke. It's not funny,' she said, too agitated to rise to his bait.

'You're right there. Your witherin' look 'ud frighten the devil back to hell.'

'Oh, stop it, you two,' Ginny said crossly, handing the tea round. 'Now listen, Mother. Will and I have been talking. We want you to come and live here with us while this war is on. It probably won't be for long, but I daresay you'd feel safer here with us while it lasts, wouldn't you?'

Ruth nodded eagerly. 'Reckon I would.' Her face clouded. 'But I don't know . . . it didn't work out very well before when we lived together, did it?'

'No, but this house is a lot bigger than the one in Quay Yard, remember. There's plenty of room here. We could clear the boxes out of the room at the back and you could have that for a sitting room if you want it. And there's a spare bedroom upstairs.'

'What do you think, Will?' Ruth asked, turning to him.

He shrugged. 'Don't make no difference to me. You're here most of the time, anyway.'

'No, I'm not.'

'Well, you ollus seem to be here when I'm home.'

'That's not true. I don't get here till . . . '

'Now then, don't start arguing, Mother.' She drained her tea. 'Think about it and let us know.'

'I don't need to think about it. I'll come, if you'll have me,' Ruth said quickly. 'Mrs Robinson, next door to me, was saying there'll be evacuees coming here from the East End of London in the next day or two. I don't like the idea of that. I don't want somebody else's snotty-nosed children foisted on me. I'd rather come here and look after yours.'

'Our children ain't snotty-nosed,' Will said mildly.

'No, I know they're not.' She gave him an impatient glance. She pinched her lip. 'Perhaps I could offer my house to a family. Some poor heart might be glad of it to get away from the bombs.'

'What bombs?' Will asked, raising his eyebrows.

'The bombs they're expecting to fall on London.' Ruth glared at him. 'Don't you read the papers? Why do you think they've been handing out those Anderson shelter things?'

Ginny ignored that. 'You'd have to make it

494

right with your landlord,' she reminded her.

'Yes. But I don't think it'll bother him.' She got to her feet. 'Well, if you're sure you don't mind I'll go and fetch my things right away.' She didn't wait for an answer. 'Do you want to come and help Granny pack, Bobby? I'm coming to live with you for a few weeks.'

'Oh, goody, goody,' Bobby said, slipping her hand into Ruth's.

'Will you wanta borry a handcart?' Will said, puffing his pipe and gazing up at the ceiling. 'Jest remember we ain't got room for a pianner.'

'I haven't got a piano, as you very well know,' Ruth said, once again rising to his bait. She looked at Ginny. 'But I might get the carrier to bring my new sideboard, if you wouldn't mind.'

'Yes, don't leave that behind, whatever you do,' Will said from behind a cloud of tobacco smoke. 'Once the Germans get hold of your new sideboard that'll be Britain done for.'

'Don't take any notice of him, there'll be plenty of room for it,' Ginny said quickly, shooting Will a warning glance. 'Of course you don't want to leave it behind if the house is going to be let to somebody else.'

★　★　★

In fact, Ginny found it useful having her mother living in the house. Together they stitched blackout curtains for every room, and Ginny made a blind for the big shop window. They also bought reels of sticky tape and made criss-cross patterns over all the windows to prevent them shattering in bomb blast.

When it was all done an ARP warden came and officiously checked everything and left them with a stirrup pump and a bucket of sand together with instructions on what to do if incendiary bombs dropped on the house. This set Ginny worrying because they had no air-raid shelter.

'No need to worry about that. You can put the children in the cupboard under the stairs if there's an air raid,' Will told her. 'They'll be as safe as houses there. And if you're frit you and your mother can get in with 'em.'

'What about you?' Ginny asked, only slightly less worried.

'Don't you worry about me. I can look after meself. I shall be out and about seein' wass goin' on.' He didn't add that he would be far happier taking his chance in the open air than cooped up in a cupboard.

It seemed as if the whole country was holding its breath, waiting for something to happen now that war had been declared. The windows and doors of public buildings disappeared under thick blast walls of sandbags, and public air-raid shelters were hastily dug wherever there was a patch of green big enough. Late summer turned to autumn and darkness came earlier and earlier and was total. Not a chink of light from any window, not a single street lamp. Even car and bicycle headlamps were allowed to be no more than shaded slits. But before long the authorities were forced to order white stripes to be painted on any obstructions and on the edges of steps and pavements because there had been so many accidents caused by people walking into things or tripping up in what became known as the blackout.

Preparations all made, they waited for the invasion by the enemy. But nothing happened. In fact, the only thing the village was invaded by was a train-load of sorry-looking children, evacuated from the East End of London, who stayed for a few months and then were either sent somewhere else because the authorities realised that Wyford was well in the path of hit-and-run raiders, or went home because their parents resented paying the six shillings a week towards their keep and there didn't seem to be anything dangerous happening anyway.

Ginny and her mother had never been so

busy. With the reopening of the shipyards there was more money about and everybody seemed to have a craving for sweet things, as if they had a premonition that soon such commodities would be in short supply so they must make the most of them while they were available.

Mabel Bellamy often came into the shop, as much for somebody to talk to as because she needed anything. Ginny was always glad to see her, hoping to glean news of Nathan.

'Did you know I've got your husband's sister, Gladys, working for me now, Ginny?' she asked one day. 'She came to me after she left the Sheldrakes' in Belle Vue Road.' She put her hand up to her mouth and added secretively, 'Between you and me and the door post I don't think she was treated very well there.' Then, in a louder voice, 'Hector said I ought to have somebody living in the house with me while he was away and he was quite happy to pay for me to have a maid. Gladys is very willing, I must say, although she's no cook, I'm afraid.' She lowered her voice again. 'Of course, with a mother like hers you can't wonder.'

'Have you heard from the captain? Or Nathan?' Ginny asked, trying to sound casual.

'Yes. I had a letter from my husband a

couple of days ago. He's on a destroyer, that's all I know. And Nathan's been moved. He's on a minesweeper. I had a letter from him last week, but of course neither of them can say much. If they mention what they're doing the censor blue-pencils it out so you can't read it. It's horrible, knowing your letters have been read by some stranger before you receive them, but at least I get letters so I know they're both all right.' She left the shop, a small, anxious-looking figure, a far cry from the haughty yacht captain's wife of only a few months ago.

* * *

The New Year brought food rationing although Ginny was allowed extra sugar and fat because of the shop. In anticipation that this would happen Ruth had made a small mountain of jam with blackberries she and the children had picked in the nearby fields and woods in the autumn and with apples and plums from neighbouring trees so she was able to continue to make her delicious fruit pies. She enjoyed experimenting too, managing to concoct appetising cakes and pies using bilious-looking dried egg and what seemed to Ginny to be the minimum ingredients. Rabbit pies, made with wild rabbits caught in the fields by the local lads and bought from them for sixpence, became very popular, too, as did the vegetable pasties made with vegetables that Ginny, obeying the Government's order to 'Dig for Victory', grew by digging up the flower beds and grass in her garden. Thanks to these efforts, the shop continued to pay its way.

Ruth and Will seemed to be on reasonably good terms, much to Ginny's relief. At first Ruth made a point of spending her evenings in her own sitting room, listening to her wireless and knitting. But coal became in short supply during the winter, which was exceptionally harsh, with deep snow and temperatures well below freezing, so it seemed more sensible for her to stay and share the warm kitchen with Will and Ginny.

It was unfortunate that Ruth and Will didn't like the same radio programmes. Ruth enjoyed Sandy Macpherson, who played popular tunes on the theatre organ but Will was tone-deaf and hated it. On the other hand, Will loved Tommy Handley in ITMA, a fast-talking comedy, which Ruth couldn't bear because she couldn't understand what the people were saying, so she ignored it and talked all the way through it. But apart from these little irritations life was harmonious enough and the time came when Ruth and

Will could even discuss the way the war was going without starting up a small battle of their own.

As Ginny dealt with rationing and shortages, the blackout, customers complaining about the lack of the more extravagant cream cakes, and Will coming home very late, tired and tetchy because a consignment of goods had to be finished and despatched, always at the back of her mind was the nagging worry about Nathan. It was something she was learning to live with, always there, her first thought in the morning and her last thought at night as she offered up a fervent prayer for his continued safety.

Now and again, when Mabel came into the shop she would talk about him.

'My Nathan's been made up to lieutenant now,' she said proudly, one day. 'He says it's because he's familiar with the area he'll be working in. Apparently, he's been given command of his own minesweeper. But he doesn't say where it is.' She frowned. 'It's most annoying. They should let relatives know where their loved ones are. It would help to set their minds at rest.' She picked up her bag and left the shop and Ginny noticed that her coat was beginning to hang more loosely on her shoulders.

'What do minesweepers do, Will?' Ginny

asked innocently as he was eating a late meal, not having arrived home until gone eight o'clock.

'They go along and clear away enemy mines, so the supply ships an' suchlike can get through. Why?'

'No reason. I just wondered.' She carried on with her knitting. 'Is it dangerous?'

'Reckon so. 'Tis if they make a mistake an' hit one. Is there any more o' that pie?'

'If you eat it tonight there won't be any tomorrow,' Ruth said from her armchair.

'Then I shall hev to hev suthin' else, shan't I?' he replied.

'There might not be anything else,' she said.

'Ther'd better be. I'm a workin' man. I need my grub.'

'That's all very well . . . '

'No doubt we'll find something,' Ginny interrupted, putting an end to the argument. Sometimes she felt as if she was treading on egg shells, keeping the peace between the two of them.

But the arguments between Ruth and Will lost their importance the blustery day in late March when Mabel rushed into the shop waving a yellow envelope and looking very unlike her usual self. Her hair was untidy and she had forgotten to put on her lipstick and powder.

'It's Nathan,' she said, waving a telegram in front of Ginny. 'His boat's been sunk.' She sat down on the chair beside the counter and rocked back and forth. 'My boy, my only boy, drowned.'

'Is that what the telegram says?' Ginny asked, white to the lips.

Mabel waved the telegram in front of her. 'Missing, it says. He's missing, believed drowned.'

Ginny read the telegram, trying to make the words say something less final, trying to find some vestige of hope. 'It says he's missing, *believed* drowned. It doesn't say he's definitely drowned,' she said. She felt odd, as if she was floating in space, yet at the same time her insides felt dead, as heavy as lead. She felt numb, too numb to cry.

Mabel shook her head. 'That's what they say when they don't recover the body. Hector told me that, once,' she said wiping her eyes.

'Come through to the kitchen and I'll make you a cup of tea, Mrs Bellamy.' She led the way, amazed that her voice sounded so normal.

Ruth was there, taking the last batch of rather yellow-looking fairy cakes out of the oven. 'That's what dried egg does,' she said, straightening up, 'turns things yellow. But they taste all right, that's the main thing.' She looked at Ginny, then at Mabel. 'What's wrong?'

'It's Nathan,' Ginny said, her voice flat. 'His ship has hit a mine and Nathan's missing, believed drowned.'

Mabel held out the telegram for Ruth to read. She was crying unrestrainedly now.

Ginny made the tea while Ruth comforted Mabel. She was amazed that she could carry on doing these ordinary things when her world had collapsed under her. Nathan was dead. She would never see him again. The words hammered on and on in her brain as she poured tea and pushed it across to her mother and Mabel. She sat down and picked up her cup, her elbows on the table. The tea scalded her mouth but she didn't notice.

'Wait a minute. I'll get a tot of whisky to put in that tea. You both look as if you could do with it,' Ruth said.

The tea didn't taste any different when it had the whisky in it and Ginny still felt dead inside when she had finished it.

'I'll come and see you tomorrow, Mrs Bellamy,' she said as she let Mabel out through the shop.

Mabel gave her a watery smile. 'Yes, do, Ginny. There's something . . . something Nathan wanted you to have if . . . well, come and see me and I'll tell you . . . ' she hurried off into the gloom, a lonely, bereft little figure.

Ginny went back inside.

'Are you all right?' Ruth asked as she walked into the kitchen.

Ginny nodded and began the washing-up. 'Yes, I'll be all right.' She bit her lip. 'It's just that . . . it's so final. The future . . . there's nothing . . . '

Her mother came over and laid a hand on her shoulder. 'There never was a future for you and Nathan, Ginny. You knew that. You were only eating your heart out if you thought it could ever be any different. Your future is with Will and the children.'

Ginny nodded. 'Yes. My future is with Will and the children. I'll always have the children.' Always a reminder of Nathan in Roberta.

33

It was Ruth who told Will of Nathan's death. She told him as Ginny was kneeling over a bowl of water, bathing his twisted legs and feet. She had recently begun to do this every night now to try and ease the arthritic pain he suffered and which made him increasingly bad-tempered and tetchy.

'Mabel Bellamy came into the shop today and told us Nathan's boat's hit a mine and been blown up and Nathan's missing, believed drowned,' she said without looking up from her knitting.

Will's head jerked up. 'Is that right?' he asked disbelievingly. He was quiet for several minutes, shaking his head. 'Oh, the poor bugger,' he whispered at last. He stared into the fire. 'Well, if he wasn't blown to bits he'll be drowned, all right. Nobody 'ud last long if they was tipped out into the sea, not at this time o' year, thass for sure,' he murmured, speaking more to himself than to the women in the room. 'Ten minutes at the most, I reckon. Thass why a lot o' the old fishermen wouldn't learn to swim, y'know. They reckoned if they was goin' overboard that was better to drown an' get it over with than swim about tryin' to stay alive an' freeze to death. An' thass why I never learned.'

'Nathan could swim,' Ginny said quietly, lifting his foot out of the water and drying it. 'We used to go in off the quay when we were children. He often used to swim across to the other side and back. He was a strong swimmer.'

'Ah, yes, but that was summer time, when it was hot an' he hadn't got much on. Thass a different thing altogether in the winter, in freezin' temperatures and a heavin' sea, an' weighed down with all his gear, includin' boots.' He shook his head. 'Nah. I wouldn't give much for his chances, poor sod.'

'Well, don't go on about it,' Ginny said, more sharply than she had intended. She finished drying his feet and emptied the water down the sink.

'Ah, thass better,' he said, bending down and moving his legs towards the fire. He glanced up at Ginny. 'Well, all I can say is, I'm sorry for the poor bugger, but he's gone an' thass the end of it.' He reached for his pipe and lit it. 'So you might as well stop hankerin' after him now he's dead an' start bein' a better wife to me.'

'I've always been a good wife to you, Will,' she said, her voice low with fury.

'Yes, she has, I'll vouch for that,' Ruth said, jabbing a knitting needle in his direction before starting another row of knitting. 'You've never gone short of anything.'

'You mind your own business, you interferin' old besom,' Will said, rounding on her. 'How would you know what I hev or hevn't gone short of? Unless you listened at the bedroom door. An' I wouldn't put that past you, you nosy old bitch.'

'Oh, stop it, you two,' Ginny said wearily. 'I'm going to make the cocoa and then I'm going to bed. Do you want some, Will?'

'No. I think I'll go down to the Rose and Crown for a pint. Hear what they've got to say about Nathan in the bar.'

'Your legs and feet can't be that bad, then, if you can fetch yourself back there after your day's work,' Ruth said sarcastically.

'I'd walk to Timbuktu to get outa your sight, make no mistake,' he sniped back.

'It might be cheaper than tipping all your money down your throat at the pub,' she shot at him.

'Oh, leave it, Mum,' Ginny said with a sigh, giving her a warning look. 'If he wants to go, let him. It's up to him.' She helped him on with this coat and handed him his cap. 'Will you be late back, Will?'

'Might be. Might not,' he replied, fitting his

crutches under his arms and going to the door.

'There's no need to take it out on Ginny, just because you're mad at me,' Ruth said sharply.

'Oh, shut up, woman, an' go to bed.' He swung himself out of the house.

Ginny made cocoa for herself and her mother and sat down at the table. 'I do wish you and Will wouldn't goad each other so much,' she said, pushing her hand through her hair. 'I thought you were getting on better together but lately you've done nothing but snipe and carp at one another. I'm getting thoroughly sick and tired of it.'

'Well, he makes me mad, the way he seems to think he's the only one who does any work,' Ruth said, taking a gulp of her drink and burning her mouth. 'After all, he only has to walk down to the sail loft and back each day. The rest of the time he's sitting on his backside to do his work, while you've been run off your feet cooking, cleaning and looking after the shop, never mind seeing to the children. Yet when he gets home he doesn't lift a finger, but expects you to run about after him, bathing his feet and legs and waiting on him hand and foot all the time.' She took another, more careful, sip of her cocoa.

'Well, don't go on about it, Mum.' Ginny got to her feet and tipped the remains of her cocoa down the sink. 'I'm tired. I'm going to bed.'

Her mother looked up. 'Yes, you're as white as a sheet. Are you all right?'

'As all right as I'll ever be,' Ginny said with a weary little smile.

'What do you mean by that?'

'Nothing. Goodnight, Mother.'

She went up the stairs, checked that the children were sleeping peacefully, undressed and climbed into bed. Yes, she was as all right as she would ever be now that there was no possibility of ever seeing Nathan again or hearing his voice. No chance that he would ever come into the shop for his favourite meat pie, no chance of him ever taking Bobby on his knee and talking to her, no chance of seeing his smile. She hadn't realised quite how much she had depended on just knowing he was somewhere in the world, loving her as she loved him. This knowledge had given her the strength to carry on — to dream that one day, she had no idea how, they would be together.

She stared up into the darkness, dry-eyed; her grief, like her love for Nathan, locked so deeply inside her that she could find no relief, only a cold deadness, as if a part of her died with him.

When Will came home she feigned sleep and for once he didn't disturb her.

★ ★ ★

The next day was Saturday and a busy day in the shop. Will was at work; he worked until seven o'clock all the week and till four on Saturdays and Sundays like the rest of the men in the village who were on war work.

'I promised to go and see Mrs Bellamy today,' Ginny said when she came downstairs after putting the children to bed, 'but I haven't had a chance all day.'

'You can go now,' Ruth said. 'I'll wash up the supper things.'

'What d'you wanta go an' see her for?' Will demanded.

'Because I promised I would. And because she's just lost her son. That's why,' Ginny said shortly.

'What about my feet?' Will demanded. 'Ain't you gonna bathe them afore you go?'

'No. I'll do them when I get back.' Ginny took her coat from the hook behind the door and rammed her hat on.

'Oh, never mind about me. I don't count in this house. I might as well go down the pub.'

'You do that,' Ruth said, beginning to clear the table.

Will rounded on her. 'I shall please meself. You needn't think you can turn me outa me own house, you interferin' old biddy.'

'Oh, for goodness sake, stop squabbling, you two,' Ginny said with a sigh.

Ruth looked offended. 'I only said . . . '

Ginny slammed the door, leaving them to argue and went out into the pitch-black street, with a tiny torch showing only a pinpoint of light to help her on her way. There was no moon but millions of stars twinkled overhead, shining brightly in the velvet blackness that surrounded her. She had often drawn comfort from the fact that Nathan might be looking up at those same stars. But not any more. She sniffed, but no tears came because she was dead inside.

Mabel Bellamy was pathetically pleased to see her and brushed aside her apologies for not coming earlier. 'It's all right, my dear, I know how busy you are. I'm just grateful you've found the time to come at all,' she said, taking her coat and drawing her towards the fire. 'Sit down and I'll get Gladys to make some tea.'

'Thank you, Mrs Bellamy.' Ginny sank down into the comfortable armchair and by the time Mabel came back she was asleep.

She woke with a start when she heard the rattle of the cups. 'Oh, I'm so sorry . . . '

'That's all right. I was longer than I expected. I made the tea myself because Gladys was busy with the ironing.'

'All the same, it was rude of me to fall asleep like that.'

'You're tired, Ginny. We're all tired. This war is wearing everybody out, isn't it. Long working hours. Worry. Uncertainty.' She handed Ginny her tea and Ginny noticed that although her eyes were red and swollen with crying and her face looked ravaged her expression was now calm. 'My husband has got a few days' compassionate leave. He should be home tomorrow,' she said.

'Oh, I'm so glad. I'm sure he'll help you to . . . ' she didn't know how to finish the sentence but Mabel didn't seem to notice.

'Yes. I've spoken to him on the telephone, of course. Naturally, he's very upset. Nathan was all we had. We couldn't have any more children . . . ' her voice trailed off and she stared into the fire. 'Now we haven't even got him. We've nothing. Nobody.'

Ginny was silent for several minutes, then she put her cup down carefully on the tray. 'That's not quite true, Mrs Bellamy,' she said slowly.

'What do you mean?' Mabel said with a frown.

'It's not quite true that you have nobody. You see, you have a granddaughter.' She hadn't meant to say it but she suddenly realised it was the one thing that might give Mabel some crumb of comfort.

'How do you know that?' Mabel asked suspiciously. 'I thought that wife of his couldn't have children. Anyway, we would have known.'

'She doesn't belong to Isobel Armitage,' Ginny said quietly. 'She belongs to me. My little Roberta is Nathan's daughter. Your granddaughter, Mrs Bellamy.'

Mabel covered her mouth with her hand, and her eyes, wide with surprise, filled with tears. 'Your Roberta!'

Ginny nodded.

'But how . . . ?' Mystified, Mabel sniffed and blew her nose. 'I don't see . . . '

Ginny held her cup out. 'May I have some more tea? Then I'll tell you. It's quite a complicated story.'

Between sips of tea Ginny told Mabel her story, how she and Nathan had discovered their love for each other on the night of her father's funeral, how they had intended to be married and would have been had not Isobel tricked him into marrying her. How, as a result Ginny, finding herself pregnant, had been forced by her mother to marry Will Kesgrave.

'Oh, what a terrible mess,' Mabel said when she had finished. She poured herself more tea. 'You know, I thought at first Nathan was doing all right for himself, with that Armitage woman, but I soon realised she was a bad lot. He ought to have married you, my dear, I can see that now. At least you would have had a few years together . . . Whereas neither of you has been happy, have you.'

Ginny put her cup down carefully. 'It's quite true, I didn't want to marry Will Kesgrave in the first place and I knew from the start I could never love him, not the way I love . . . loved . . . Nathan.' She paused and took a deep breath. 'But although Will is a bit rough and ready his heart's in the right place. He knew I was pregnant when he married me, although he didn't know it was Nathan's child I was carrying. And he's never shown the slightest difference between Bobby and his own son. He's always treated Bobby and George exactly the same. Mind you, that's not to say he hasn't given both of them a smack from time to time. But that's understandable. He's had a lot to put up with since the accident to his legs. He's always in pain from them and it seems to be getting worse.'

'You're very loyal, Ginny. Are you happy with him?'

Ginny frowned. 'Happy? He's my husband. Happiness doesn't really come into it.' She shrugged. 'We get along all right.'

'But you can't say you love him.'

'There are so many different kinds of love, aren't there. I'm fond enough of him, I suppose and I think he's quite fond of me, in his way. It's not something we ever talk about, to tell you the truth. Things are as they are and we have to make the best of it.'

Mabel was quiet for a long time, then she said, 'Thank you for telling me all this, Ginny. I'm sorry things have turned out for you the way they have but I can't tell you what a comfort it is to me to know that Bobby is Nathan's daughter. It's almost like being given a little piece of him back.' She paused and then asked, almost shyly, 'Perhaps you'll allow me to get to know her a little better, maybe I could have her to tea now and again?'

'Of course,' Ginny said warmly. 'But we must be careful. I wouldn't want Will to find out I'd told you that Bobby is Nathan's child.'

'He knows, then. I thought you said . . .'

'Oh, yes, he found out, eventually. Said he'd never have Nathan in the house again, once he discovered the truth. They'd been good friends before that.' She gave a sniff. 'Well, he won't have to, now, will he.'

'It was understandable, I suppose.' Again Mabel was quiet. After a while she got to her feet. 'I told you I had something to show you. Come with me. It's upstairs in my sewing room.'

Puzzled, Ginny followed her out of the room and up the stairs to Mabel's sewing room. It had a neat, unused look about it, the sewing machine was covered, her sewing box beside it. Everything was in its place except that against one wall, at the end of the chenille-covered single bed, stood a large flat package wrapped in brown paper. Mabel went to it and began to untie the string. 'I don't know what he did with the rest of his paintings but he asked me to look after this one and to give it to you if he didn't come back.'

'I've always thought I'd like to have one of Nathan's paintings but not under these circumstances,' Ginny said. Suddenly, it was almost more than she could bear, even to look at it. 'Have you seen it?' she asked, staring out of the window. 'Do you know which one it is?'

'Oh, yes. I've seen it. It's very good. Look.' Mabel finished untying the string and took off the wrapping.

Slowly, Ginny turned her head and looked. She caught her breath, because it was almost like looking into a mirror, except that the Ginny in the picture had a half smile on her face and her hair was loose, lying across one shoulder, just as it used to be when she was nineteen.

'He told me he painted it during the time he was in London. From memory.' Mabel put her hand on Ginny's arm. 'I think he may have been trying to paint you out of his mind but he never could. That's how much he loved you, my dear.'

Now the tears began to flow. Tears that Ginny had thought she would never shed because her grief was locked so deeply inside her. She sat down on the little bed and wept tears of utter despair, melting the cold block of ice that had lain inside her ever since she heard of Nathan's death. Mabel held her close and stroked her hair, crying with her for the man they both loved so much and wishing that things could have been different, that she could at least have been comforting Ginny as Nathan's wife. But it was too late. Too late.

Mabel let Ginny cry until she had no tears

left, then she led her to the bathroom so that she could wash her face.

'Better now?' she asked sympathetically. 'I could see that was what you needed, dear. I could see you were holding your feelings so tightly in check that it was bound to come out. I'm just glad I was here to hold you when it did, for Nathan's sake.' She blew her nose and continued, 'There's something else. Downstairs. Can you bear it?'

Ginny nodded.

'Good. I must say it didn't make any sense to me at first but it does now.'

They went downstairs together and Mabel went to a small safe in the wall. 'Nathan left these here for me to look after,' she said. 'They are the deeds to your shop, Ginny.' She handed the package to her. 'You'll find the shop is in your name. He told me he put it in your name when he bought it although he didn't want you to know. Another thing, all the rent you've paid has been put in a separate bank account, also in your name.'

Ginny sat down with a bump. She already felt emotionally drained from all her weeping and she simply couldn't take in what Mabel was telling her. She looked from the package to Mabel and back, frowning. 'I don't understand,' she said. 'Why would he do this?'

'Because he loved you,' Mabel said simply. She sat down and took Ginny's free hand in hers. 'Heaven forbid that I should cause any kind of rift between you and your husband, dear, but I wonder if it might be wiser not to say anything to him about this? Just for a while, at any rate.'

Ginny nodded and passed a hand over her forehead. 'I think you're probably right. Will can be a bit . . . jealous, at times.' She was silent for a bit, then she said, 'I think probably the best thing will be for me to go on paying rent like I've always done. It can go in the bank to provide a little nest egg for Roberta when she grows up.'

Mabel smiled approvingly. 'I'm sure Nathan would have liked that, dear.'

Ginny handed back the deeds. 'I mustn't take these home. Do you mind putting them back in your safe?'

'Of course not, my dear.'

Ginny got up to go and Mabel kissed her as she reached the door. 'Thank you so much for coming to see me, Ginny,' she said. 'You've been a great help and comfort to me. Please come again, and remember, if there is ever anything I can do for you, you've only got to ask. You and Nathan may never have been married but I feel you're as much my daughter-in-law as if you had been.'

'Thank you, Mrs Bellamy.'

'Mabel. Please call me Mabel.'

'Thank you, Mabel.'

Ginny walked home in the thick darkness. Her grief was just as deep but the icy deadness that had cloaked it was gone, replaced by the warm certainty of Nathan's love.

Added to that she knew she had found a real friend in Mabel Bellamy.

34

Ginny made her way home feeling much calmer and more at peace. Nothing had changed, Nathan was dead, she would never see him again or hear his voice, but she had found an outlet for the grief that had been locked inside her, she had wept away that terrible icy emptiness and she felt better for it. And now she had tangible proof, if she had needed it, of his unwavering love for her. It was there in the portrait of her he had painted whilst he was in London. He had caught her expression exactly, even though he hadn't had so much as a snapshot to remind him. Looking at it she could almost see his love in the brushstrokes. It was quite uncanny, but not spookily so, rather it had given her a warm glow as she gazed at it. Her only regret was that she would never be able to hang the portrait at home, because it would never do to show it to Will. It was just the kind of thing that would drive him into a jealous rage and then there was no telling what he might do to it; he was quite likely to smash it up or deface it. Ginny knew her husband too well to risk even letting him see it.

There was the house and shop, too. She smiled to herself in the darkness. She was a woman of property, although she hadn't known it until tonight. But she didn't regard it as belonging to her; from the moment Mabel had shown her the deeds she had known that it should rightly belong to Roberta. She would simply hold it in trust for Nathan's daughter until she came of age. Then she would hand it over to her. Nathan would like that, she was sure. But for the time being everything would continue as it had been; she knew the secret would be safe with Mrs Bellamy and the captain.

When she arrived home all was quiet. Ruth was sitting by the fire, dozing, her knitting on her lap.

'Where's Will?' Ginny asked.

Ruth picked up her knitting, trying to look as if she hadn't been asleep. 'He took himself off to the pub soon after you left.'

'Did you bathe his legs for him?'

'I did not! You won't catch me washing his feet! Anyway, I can't see why he can't do it for himself, instead of always expecting you to get down on your knees and do it for him.' She wound the wool round the ball and jabbed her needles into it and put her knitting away in her knitting bag. 'I'm going to bed now you're home.' She got up and went to the stairfoot door. 'How was Mrs Bellamy?' she asked as an afterthought.

'We talked for a long time. It helped us both,' Ginny replied enigmatically. 'The captain's coming home. He's got few days' compassionate leave.'

'Ah, it's a sad business. Nathan was a nice young man. One of the best.' She eyed Ginny. 'Are you all right?'

Ginny nodded briefly. 'I'll manage.'

And that was how it was, Ginny decided as day followed miserable day. She managed. Yet in spite of her misery she knew that nothing in her life had really changed with Nathan's death. He could never have been part of her future. Her future lay with Will, her husband. She told herself this over and over again as she cooked and cleaned, looked after the children and played with them when she had the time. She paid extra attention to Will in an effort to keep some spark alive in their marriage, attending to his every need, bathing his crippled legs and feet for him every night and never turning away from his increasingly rare attentions in bed.

But she had no heart for anything that she did, although she smiled and joked with her customers, trying with them to make light of rationing and shortages and the crippling restrictions they were all suffering.

It didn't help that the air-raid siren went, night after night, disturbing everyone's sleep. The people that had dug Anderson shelters into their gardens sometimes slept in them all night so that they wouldn't have the disturbance of moving out of their warm beds when the siren went. But the shelters were cold and damp and not very comfortable so they still got up the next morning feeling jaded and tired, to begin another long day's work in the shipyard or factory.

For Ginny, it was a case of taking the children, rosy with sleep, from their beds and carrying them down, wrapped in blankets, to the mattress kept in the cupboard under the stairs. Sometimes she crawled in with them, but more often she would sit in the chair by the dead embers of the fire, wrapped in her dressing gown, dozing in the lulls between the sound of gunfire or distant bombs falling. Ruth flatly refused to move, saying she preferred to die in the comfort of her own bed and Will often didn't wake at all and if he did would prowl around outside, watching the searchlights rake the sky, and the red tracer bullets from the ack-ack guns arc away into the blackness, the white lines he had painted on his crutches and the smell of his tobacco smoke warning of his presence in the blackout.

A combination of anxiety over the progress of the war, shortages, lack of sleep and long working hours began to take their toll on everyone. Both Ginny and Ruth joined the Women's Voluntary Service; Ruth was rarely without a piece of khaki or airforce blue knitting in her hands as she knitted comforts for the troops and Ginny helped to organise the selling of national savings stamps in the village. Will began taking refuge at the Rose and Crown more and more often, till some evenings he didn't bother to come home for his evening meal but went straight there, arriving back late and drunk, demanding both his dinner and that Ginny bathe his legs and feet. She learned better than to go to bed before this ritual had taken place or he would wake her and drag her out of bed to do it.

Ruth sometimes retired early so she didn't often see what was going on but if she was late to bed she made no bones about her disapproval.

'Why can't you leave the girl to sleep. She's been run off her feet all day,' she said when Will reeled in shouting for Ginny.

'She's no business to go to bed when she knows very well I shall want my legs done,' he said over his shoulder as he lurched to the stairfoot door. 'GINNEEee!'

'Be quiet, you'll wake the children,' Ruth hissed.

'Then she'd better come down, hadn't she.' He slammed the door shut. 'I'm hungry. I ain't had me dinner yet.'

'Then you should have been home at the proper time. But if you want it now it's on the gas, keeping hot over a saucepan.'

He sat down at the table, knife and fork in hand. 'All right, you can get it for me.'

'Get it yourself. I'm not waiting on you hand and foot.'

Before he could reply Ginny appeared, yawning, her hair tousled, knotting her dressing-gown cord as she came. 'Oh, for goodness sake, Will, can't you make a bit less noise when you come home,' she said irritably.

'Well, I want me dinner and I want me legs done.'

'Your dinner's on the stove. I told you that,' Ruth said.

'I ain't talkin' to you. Git me dinner, Ginny. You can do me legs while I eat it.'

Ginny fetched his plate and put it in front of him. Then she took a bowl of water and began to bathe his swollen legs and feet. 'They look sore, Will,' she said sympathetically, drying them carefully.

'They are sore. Bloody sore,' he said, speaking with his mouth full. 'Thass why I hev to go to the pub before I come home at night sometimes. I couldn't manage that walk twice in a day.'

'You don't have to go to the pub,' Ruth said caustically. 'Nobody's forcing you.'

'Nobody's forcing you to get on my tits, but you do,' he answered, shooting her a venomous look.

'Oh, don't start, you two,' Ginny said, sighing wearily. She rubbed salve into his legs and feet, by which time he had finished his meal. 'There you are,' she said, taking his empty plate and putting it on the draining board. 'You've had your dinner and I've done your feet. Is there anything else you want before I go back to bed?'

'Do what you like.' He slid across to his chair by the fire and lit his pipe.

She began to climb the stairs. She often felt that if Will was to put as much energy into the marriage as she was doing they might have a better chance of happiness together. As it was his only thought these days was for his own comfort.

She was barely halfway up the stairs when the siren went. 'Oh, damn,' she said under her breath and hurried on up to fetch the children and bring them down to their little shelter under the stairs.

It was a full two hours before the all-clear sounded and they could all go back to bed and get some much-needed sleep.

★ ★ ★

March gave way to April and Ginny was vaguely surprised to see the trees blossoming and daffodils blooming just as they had always done before the terrible shadow had fallen over the world. But nature had no interest in man's folly and continued to bring sanity and colour into a world that had gone temporarily insane.

Ginny picked a bunch of daffodils from the one corner of the garden not given over to growing vegetables and put them on the counter in the shop. She was amazed at the effect they had. Customers seemed to smile more, and several people remarked how much they brightened up the shop — and their day. Ginny resolved to keep a vase of flowers in the shop whenever she could. She was sure Mabel would often provide her with a bunch, since her garden — a riot of colour in the summer — had not yet been given over to growing potatoes.

As the weeks went by Ginny was never quite sure whether the pain of Nathan's death grew less or whether she simply became used to carrying it around with her. She rather suspected it was the latter. She had lost a very dear friend — she tried hard to convince herself that he was nothing more than that — but the terrible sense of loss remained and she coped with it by always being busy, never giving herself time to stop and think. Inevitably, she grew thinner, but she brushed aside her mother's concern.

'Everybody's getting thinner. How can anybody expect to get fat on four ounces of butter and four ounces of bacon a week? And you could get the meat ration in your eye.'

'And most of your meat ration goes to Will. And don't tell me it doesn't because I've seen it.'

'Well,' Ginny gave a shrug. 'He's a working man. He needs it.'

'And so do you.'

Ginny looked at the clock. 'It's nearly closing time,' she said, putting an end to the conversation. 'I'll go and take the cake plates out of the shop window and wash them up. I only leave them on the shelves for decoration because they're always empty by eleven in the morning.'

She went through to the shop, fastening a wisp of hair back under her hair slide as she went. It was as she was leaning over to take out the last plate that she saw a figure crossing the road. For a moment, her heart leapt up into her mouth because the figure was so like Nathan it was uncanny. It had happened before: something in the walk of a complete stranger, or the set of his head perhaps, had reminded her of Nathan and set her heart pounding.

Then the shop door opened and there he stood, a tall figure in his naval sweater, his cap perched at a rather rakish angle because of the plaster on his temple.

The plate she was holding slipped out of her hand and fell to the floor with a crash. 'Nathan?' she said uncertainly, not trusting her own eyes because she knew it couldn't really be him.

He nodded and a smile lit up his face. 'Yes, Ginny, it's really me,' he said.

Ginny never knew who took the first step but before she realised it she was in his arms and he was holding her, rocking back and forth with her as if he would never let her go.

'Good grief!' It was Ruth. She had come to investigate the sound of breaking china and found them locked together, oblivious of the world. 'Nathan! Is it really you?' She gaped at him for a few seconds, then said briskly, 'Well, don't stand there like that right in front of the shop window where everyone can see, you'll get yourselves talked about. Come through to the back room.'

She bustled about making tea while Nathan and Ginny sat at the table, feasting their eyes on each other. Nathan had taken Bobby on to his lap and was cuddling her and stroking her hair, while George, not to be outdone, had climbed on to Ginny's lap, a little shy of this man who he couldn't be quite sure was Uncle Nathan because he looked different, somehow.

'We were told you were missing, believed drowned,' Ginny said. She leaned over and touched his arm. 'You *are* real, aren't you? Only sometimes . . . '

He put his hand over hers. 'I know, Ginny. And yes, I'm real.'

'What happened?'

'I'm not too sure, really, it all happened so quickly. I think a mine must have blown up under us. I remember being in the water and thinking I'd had it. It was so cold I knew I couldn't last long. I was hanging on to something, I don't know what it was, might have been a life raft, but I was too weak to get onto it and I could feel my hands getting colder and I knew I couldn't hold on much longer. The next thing I knew a fishing boat had picked me up; I must have been half dead by this time, and they were pouring brandy into me and trying to patch up my head. I must have banged it or been hit on the head by something or other. I flaked out then and apparently didn't come to for nearly a week. They took me back to some little village or other in the north of Scotland, I'm not sure even now where it was, and looked after me. Nobody knew who I was and I of course, being unconscious, couldn't tell them. I think they thought I was a German spy at first.' He gave a crooked little smile. 'When I finally came round they kept asking me who Ginny was. Apparently, I'd been shouting for Ginny and using the most obscene language because she didn't come.' He rubbed his chin and looked a bit sheepish. 'I can't understand it, I'm not given to using more than the odd swear word as a rule.'

Ginny flushed. 'You're safe. Nothing else matters,' she said softly, looking at him with eyes full of love.

Ruth was watching, her heart full of foreboding. In some ways she was almost sorry Nathan had come back, fearful that his return from the dead would rekindle the old longing in Ginny's heart. 'Does your mother know you're alive?' she asked, ever practical.

'No. I thought the people at the hospital they took me to had informed her I was safe but apparently they hadn't. But when they said they were going to let me out this morning I thought I'd surprise her. To tell you the truth I didn't want to risk the kind of welcoming committee that seems to be the fashion these days.' He dropped a kiss on Bobby's curly head, put her down and got to his feet. 'I'd better go now. I wasn't going to call here but I saw Ginny and . . . ' he sighed, 'I couldn't help myself.'

'We'll see you again before you go back?' Ginny asked, accompanying him to the door, reluctant to let him go.

'I hope so. If Will . . . '

'Oh, I'm sure Will will want to see you,' she said with more confidence than she felt.

'Ginny?' He looked at her, his eyes warm. 'How are things between you and Will? Are you happy?'

She shrugged. 'Happy?' She shrugged again. 'I guess I'd be lost without him after five years of being married to him.'

'So nothing's changed?' he asked softly.

She shook her head, her eyes shining with tears. 'No, Nathan. Nothing's changed.'

Will was home early for once. As he waited for Ginny to pull off his boots and bathe his legs Bobby climbed on his knee.

'Uncle Nathan came to see us this afternoon, Daddy,' she said excitedly. 'I sat on his knee.'

534

Will frowned. 'Is she hevin' me on?' he asked Ginny.

'No.' Ginny couldn't help smiling. 'He called when he came off the train, on his way home.'

Will chewed his moustache. 'So he weren't blowed up, then.'

'Yes, his ship was blown up but he was picked up by a fishing boat and taken to a village in the north of Scotland.' Ginny giggled, feeling irrepressibly happy. 'They looked after him but they thought at first he was a German spy.' She unlaced his boot and eased it off. 'Isn't it wonderful, Will, to think he's alive and well?' She looked up at him, her face more animated than he'd seen it for weeks.

'I'm glad he's all right,' he said grudgingly, 'but he'd better not come sniffin' round here. I don't want him upsettin' our applecart.'

'I thought you'd be pleased to see him,' Ginny said, disappointed. 'I told him you would.'

'Why should I be pleased to see the man who's been all over my wife an' still can't leave her alone, by all accounts,' he said angrily.

She sat back on her heels. 'Will, be reasonable. Nathan is our friend, yours as well as mine. He's the man who saved your life, remember. Twice. Each time he could have left you to drown, but he didn't. Would he have done that if he'd had designs on me?'

Will sniffed and looked pointedly down at the little girl on his knee.

Ginny saw his look and gave a vicious pull at his boot, making him yelp with pain. 'What happened between him and me happened before you and I were married,' she said between clenched teeth. 'There's been nothing since. I've told you that, many times. He's just a very good friend. *Our* very good friend.'

'Well, I don't want him in my house.'

Ginny clamped her lips shut on the retort that it wasn't his house, it was Nathan's, knowing it would be like showing a red rag to a bull. Then she realised that the house didn't belong to Nathan at all, it belonged to her.

If Will were to find that out, in his present frame of mind he would be ready to commit murder.

35

Ginny didn't see Nathan again before he went back. It was better that way since there could be no future for them together. Ever. She even tried to keep her eyes averted from the shop window when she was serving so there was no danger of seeing him walk past, because the pain of wanting him was too unbearable.

Ruth sent a message via Mabel, who was understandably ecstatic at having her son back alive, that Will would prefer Nathan not to visit.

Mabel shook her head, her eyes full of sympathy as Ruth explained the situation. 'It's a shame,' she said, 'They used to be such good friends. And Nathan is Roberta's godfather, too.' The two women exchanged glances, each busy with her own thoughts on Roberta's parentage but neither speaking of it.

'Will's still jealous, that's the trouble,' Ruth said sadly. 'And I'm not saying he hasn't every right to be. Not that there's ever been any hanky-panky between Ginny and Nathan, not since Will and Ginny married, I'm quite sure of that. But her heart's with Nathan, you can see that at a glance.'

Mabel nodded. 'Nathan's the same.' She sighed. 'I just wish things could have worked out differently for them,' she said quietly.

'Amen to that,' Ruth replied. 'But I'm afraid it's too late now.'

Ginny bit her lip against threatening tears when Ruth told her Nathan wouldn't be visiting again. Then she tossed her head in an attempt at nonchalance. 'It's probably just as well, Mum,' she said. 'I don't want to upset Will. He works so hard and his feet and legs pain him so much these days that it's no wonder he gets short-tempered at times.' She gave an apology for a laugh. 'I wouldn't want Will getting mad at Nathan and trying to throw him out. I wouldn't know whose side to take, Will's because he's my husband or Nathan's because he's a wounded sailor!'

After Nathan had gone back Mabel kept Ruth and Ginny up-to-date with news of him.

'He's got a shore-based job, because he's still getting headaches from the blow on his head when his ship sank,' she told them happily. 'I'm glad about that; at least I know he's safe.'

But the war wasn't going well. The British army was being pushed back towards the French coast and by the beginning of June

Nathan was back at sea and involved with the great evacuation of troops from Dunkirk.

Everybody was worried and depressed, although an ignominious defeat was turned into a heroic victory by all the little ships that crossed the Channel again and again to rescue the troops from the French beaches. All the fishing boats from Wyford joined in the rescue and the *Nancy Margaret* never returned, bringing home to the village yet again the full horror of war.

And now, with German troops only a few miles away on the other side of the Channel the fear of invasion was very real. Beaches where children had played and splashed at the water's edge in happier times were barricaded; barbed-wire defences and concrete pill boxes appeared everywhere.

Ginny and Ruth struggled to keep the cake shop going. They were allowed a few extra rations because of the business and both Ginny's and Ruth's creativity was tested to the limit in an effort to make them stretch as far as possible. Ruth's potato and onion pies became a particular favourite and Ginny made slab cake — she called it fruit cake because it had a scattering of currants in it — partly sweetened with grated carrot and parsnip.

Will worked longer and longer hours. His

shoulders became rounded from crouching over the big sewing machine all day and his hands became calloused from the thick canvas he stitched. As well as working on naval requirements he was also involved in making khaki gas mask bags for servicemen and gaiters for the army. Some of the things he made were so peculiar that he had no idea what they would ever be used for.

Inevitably, with the combination of over-work and anxiety tempers became frayed. Ginny found herself being unnecessarily sharp with the children and then defending them when Ruth admonished them for being too noisy. When Will was at home he and Ruth bickered.

'You've been at the margarine again, haven't you?' she asked accusingly one morning when she had cleared away the breakfast things and was about to start cooking. 'There was a good half pound here, now there's only six ounces.'

'Well, I gotta put suthin' on me bread an' jam,' he said, defending himself.

'Oh, Will,' Ginny said, looking up from buttoning George into his trousers. 'You know the rule is bread and jam or bread and butter. You can't have both, the rations won't stretch to it.'

'Butter!' he roared. 'I'd like to know the

last time I tasted butter!'

'I mix the butter and marg ration together, it makes the butter go further,' she told him. 'But that's no excuse. You've been using the shop rations and you mustn't do that. We shall have the people from the ministry after us.'

He shrugged. 'I never took much.'

'You leave the shop rations alone in future,' Ruth said, squeezing out some stale bread that had been soaking in water to soften it, ready to make bread puddings. 'We shall have to keep them under lock and key, Ginny, then he won't be able to get at them.'

'Oh, you shut up and get on with yer stirrin', you miserable old biddy, you're good at that.' He looked at the clock and reached for his crutches. 'Time I wasn't here. Is me dinner packed, Ginny?'

'Yes. It's there. On the table, right in front of your nose.' She gave George a gentle pat on the bottom and got to her feet to help Will on with his coat, which he couldn't manage on his own. Then she hung his gas mask and the bag with his dinner in it round his neck and gave him a peck on the cheek as she always did. 'Have a good day. See you tonight.'

'Don't work too hard.' It was his usual rejoinder.

After Will had gone and the children were sent to play out in the patch of garden that wasn't given over to growing vegetables, the two women worked quietly for a while, Ruth making bread puddings, Ginny making pastry with rather grey-looking wartime flour.

'I've been thinking, Ginny,' Ruth said, after a bit. 'The people that were living in my house have moved and gone back to wherever they came from. Perhaps I should go back home to live.'

Ginny looked up with a frown. 'Oh, Mum, I don't know about that. Suppose the Germans come and you're there on your own . . . '

Ruth shrugged. 'I'll have to take my chance. Same as everybody else.'

'Why do you suddenly want to go back there?'

'I miss my little house. And it'd be more peaceful here for you. Will and I don't get on and there's no use pretending that we do.'

'Perhaps if you made a bit more effort you'd manage to tolerate each other better?'

'A bit more effort?' Ruth's eyebrows shot up nearly to her hairline. 'I fall over backwards to be pleasant to that man and all he does is snap and snarl at me. He's the rudest man I ever met, and that's saying something.'

'I'll have a word with him,' Ginny promised.

'It won't do any good, my girl.' Ruth put the bread puddings in the oven and sat down, pushing her hair back with the back of her wrist. 'We're all tired, Ginny. Not just us, it's everyone you speak to. We hardly get a night's sleep because of the air raids, we're all working all the hours God created and at the same time worried sick over what's going to happen next. Can you wonder we all live on our nerves?'

Ginny lifted the pastry on to the pastry board and began to roll it out. 'I don't think I could manage the shop without you,' she said, frowning anxiously.

'Don't be silly. You won't have to. I'll be here during the day. I'd come after Will's gone to work and leave before he gets home.' She stared into the fire. 'And there's another thing. I don't like to see the way Will orders you about and expects you to wait on him hand, foot and finger. You're not his slave but he treats you as if you were. It might be a cowardly thing for me to say, but the truth is, if I wasn't living here I wouldn't see it, then I wouldn't get so upset about it.'

'Well, you can't really blame him. He works very hard, Mum.'

'So do you, my girl. That's no excuse for

the way he treats you.' Ruth got to her feet. 'No. It's no use arguing with me, I've been thinking about it ever since those people left my house. I'm going back there. Mind you,' she said as an afterthought, 'I reckon they've left a rare old mess for me to clean up. I don't know that I'll fancy living there again.'

'You don't need to see it. I'll go and clean it up for you. If you're quite determined to go back there I'll go round after we've had our supper and have a look. See what needs to be done. You can put the children to bed and read them a story. How about that?'

'It'll take you more than one evening, I reckon.'

'I'll see, won't I. Anyway, it won't matter, you're not in that much of a hurry, are you?'

'No, I suppose not.'

Ginny went round to the house in Denton Terrace that evening. It had a rather rank smell as she opened the door and she realised that the kitchen would need a good deal of work, especially the gas cooker, which was thick with grease. But the rest of the house was reasonably clean, although covered in dust. Four or five evenings would set it straight. But knowing her mother's fetish for cleanliness Ginny thought it best not to let her see the place until it was all pristine again or she would never stop complaining about the way other people had treated her furniture.

She started the next evening with the bedrooms, clearing cobwebs, washing paint, beating rugs and scrubbing floors. It took a little longer than she had anticipated because she was very thorough, even lining the drawers with fresh newspaper, knowing that her mother would poke and pry into every last corner. Allowing one evening for each room and two for the kitchen she estimated she should be finished in a week.

Ruth was in bed by the time she arrived home. Will was sitting in his chair waiting for her to attend to his feet and legs.

'What time do you think this is?' he asked, pointing to the clock, for all the world like some Victorian father.

'Goodness, it's after ten o'clock. I didn't realise it was that late.' She hurried to fetch water and a towel.

'She's goin' back to her kennel, then,' he said, puffing on his pipe, more good-humoured now that she was kneeling at his feet.

'Yes, Mum's going home, if that's what you mean. I'm getting the place ready for her. She should be gone by the end of next week.'

'Good riddance to bad rubbish. Thass all I can say,' he remarked.

'Oh, don't be like that, Will. Remember it's my mother you're talking about.'

'I don't remember you was ever very complimentary about my poor old mum, God rest her soul.' Will's mother had died just after the outbreak of war.

'I was never as disrespectful about her as you are about my mother.'

'You didn't hev to be. You didn't hev to live with her.'

Ginny enjoyed her evenings working at the cottage in Denton Terrace. She even sang as she worked to the music on the wireless. Henry Hall, with his signature tune, 'Here's to the Next Time', was one of her favourites and she liked to hear the records on *Forces' Favourites* — she knew all the words to 'Who's Been Polishing the Sun' and several of the songs the Inkspots sang, in particular, 'Why Do You Whisper Green Grass?' She would sing them all at the top of her voice as she worked, until someone in the house next door banged on the wall and told her in no uncertain terms to 'put a sock in it'.

She even wondered, as she listened, whether she dare put in a request for a record to be played for Nathan, but decided against it. Will didn't often listen to those sorts of programmes on the wireless but there was always the chance that he might.

Ginny left the kitchen in her mother's house till last. The night she intended to tackle it Will was home from work early. 'No pub tonight?' she asked, dishing up his supper.

'I might go later. Me legs are playin' me up suthin' cruel.'

'I'll bathe them before I go out.'

He didn't even say thank you, Ruth noticed, pursing her lips. But she wisely said nothing.

After Ginny had gone Ruth put the children to bed and began washing up the supper things, making no attempt to be quiet even though Will had gone to sleep in his chair, his pipe fallen out of his hand on to the hearth. From time to time she shot him a glance of pure loathing.

She regretted from the bottom of her heart that she had forced Ginny into this marriage. It had been pure vindictiveness on her part, she admitted it now, and she was ashamed. They would have managed, the three of them, she Ginny and Bobby. They wouldn't have been the first family to bring up an illegitimate child. She had had no right to ruin her daughter's life just because her own hadn't turned out the way she would have chosen. But she had suffered for it, God knew she had suffered, watching Ginny trying to make the best of her life with this uncouth, boorish man. She shot him a venomous look and slammed a saucepan down on the draining board, dislodging several enamel lids so that they clattered to the floor.

'Wassat!' Will woke with a start and looked round to see where the noise had come from. 'You knocked them lids on the floor on purpose to wake me up, you old bitch,' he shouted at her, pointing to them.

'No, I didn't. They fell off because the draining board was too full. If you'd had anything about you you'd have lent a hand and dried the supper things for me instead of going to sleep, you lazy lout. You're not the only one who's done a full day's work, you know. And some of us haven't finished yet.' She began to dry the heap of saucepans and dishes on the draining board. 'Anyway, I thought you were going down to the pub.'

'I'll go when I'm good and ready and not before.' He rammed more tobacco into his pipe and lit it. 'If you don't like my company you know where to go. And the sooner you go there the better. Ain't Ginny nearly finished cleanin' the place up?'

'I think she said she'll finish it tomorrow.'

'Can't see why you couldn't do it yerself.'

'She wouldn't let me. That's why. But don't worry. I'll be packing my bag when I get back from church on Sunday.' She gave a mirthless laugh. 'Sunday! Supposed to be a day of rest. Not that there's ever much of that in this house.'

'Pious old bitch,' he muttered. 'What about the rest of us? I shall be at work all day too, y'know. Seven days a week, I hev to keep goin'. I couldn't go to church if I wanted to.'

'Ha! The day you set foot inside the church the roof'll fall in.' She finished putting the plates on the dresser shelf, sat down and picked up her knitting.

'Oh, I'm goin' down the pub. I can't sit an' look at you all night. I've had enough,' he said, struggling to his feet and fitting his crutches under his arms. He took his donkey jacket, on which Ginny had sewn leather patches where the crutches had worn it under the arms, off its hook behind the door. 'You'll hev to help me on with this,' he said, hating her and himself that he had to ask.

She looked up briefly. 'You'll have to wait a minute till I've finished this row. I think I've dropped a stitch.'

'Oh, bugger it, I'll do it meself.'

'Yes, it's time you made an effort,' said Ruth, concentrating on what she was doing. 'You expect Ginny to wait on you far too much to my way of thinking.'

She didn't look up as he tried to juggle his

coat with his crutches, trying to balance on one crutch while he pulled the coat up over one arm, then balancing on the other to finish shrugging it on, so she didn't see what happened next. She just heard the crash as he fell to the floor, crutches and coat flying, cursing her with words she had never heard before and prayed to God she would never hear again.

She stared at him lying there for a minute, her face a mask of distaste. Then, taking her time, she put down her knitting and got to her feet, standing by as he tried to struggle to his knees, unable to pull himself up any further without help.

'If it wasn't for you I wouldn't be strugglin' here crippled like this,' he grunted, breathless with effort.

'What do you mean?'

'It was the mast off *your* bloody smack that smashed my legs.'

'If you'd been a better seaman you wouldn't have lost *my* smack. Or rather, my husband's smack. I should never have trusted you with it. Nor my daughter.'

'No, it was only because she was in the fam'ly way and you wanted a husband for her that you let me hev it. And I was fool enough to think I was on to a good thing. Little did I know! I wish to God I'd never had anything to do with you, you schemin' old bitch.'

'You don't wish it any more than I do.' She stared at him a moment more, then picked up one of his crutches, both of which had shot out of his reach as he fell, and handed it to him without a word.

He snatched it from her and as she bent to pick up the other one he swung it and caught her with a sudden blow to the side of the head that knocked her to the floor. Then he hit her again.

36

It was after ten o'clock by the time Ginny arrived home. She'd had a good evening, she'd worked hard and the results were gratifying. The gas cooker sparkled and the whole kitchen shone. She'd done a lot of thinking, too, during these evenings she had spent working alone and she was determined that once her mother had gone back to her own home that she would make something of her life with Will. As she had said to herself over and over again during the five years of being married to him, he was not a bad man. Weak, perhaps, but not bad. And it was no wonder he was sometimes bad-tempered; his crippled legs and feet pained him a good deal. If only she could persuade him that she had put Nathan out of her mind once and for all things would improve, she was sure of it. Humming under her breath she let herself in through the shop door and went through to the kitchen. Something seemed to be obstructing the door, so she gave it an extra push and sidled round it into the room, nearly falling over Will, who was half lying, half leaning against it.

'Will! Whatever's the matter? Are you hurt? Here, let me help you up.' Ginny bent over him and it was then she saw her mother, lying near the hearth. She stood up, her mouth dropping open. 'What . . . ?'

'The old bitch wouldn't help me on with me coat. You know I can't manage, not with me crutches an' I fell over. That was her fault. She'd made me look a fool and I was that mad, as soon as she got near I hit her,' he said impatiently, holding out his hand for his crutch. 'She'll be all right when she comes round. Here, give me a hand.'

Automatically, Ginny handed him his crutches and helped him to his feet, then she left him and went over to where her mother was lying. 'How long ago was this?' she asked over her shoulder.

'Dunno.' He looked at the clock. 'Must be a coupla hours, I reckon. I couldn't get up so I musta fell asleep. I never woke till you came in.'

She straightened up, her face very white. 'How many times did you hit her, Will?' she asked, her voice quiet.

'Dunno. Two or three times. I didn't hit her *hard*. Jes' rapped her round the skull once or twice with me crutch to let her know I was good an' mad.' He came over to Ginny, and stood watching as she knelt beside her mother, smoothing away her hair where a trickle of blood oozed from an ugly bruise.

After a few minutes Ginny got to her feet. 'I think I'd better call the doctor. I don't think we should move her. Not till he's seen her. I'll go and fetch him. I shan't be long.'

'Ain't no need for that. She'll be all right.' His voice followed her, rising in sudden anxiety.

She was back in less than five minutes with the same doctor, slightly more experienced now, who had pronounced her father dead only five years ago.

After a brief examination he sat back on his heels. 'I understand you hit her with your crutch, Mr Kesgrave,' he said, his eyes still on Ruth's still form.

'Thass right. Well, th'old bitch wouldn't help me. You can see I'm crippled. I need helpin'.'

'How many times did you hit her?'

He shrugged. 'Dunno. Once. Twice. I can't remember. I was mad at her an' thass the truth. I'm sorry if I've knocked her unconscious but she was askin' for it.'

The doctor turned slowly to face him. 'I think you hit her more than once or twice, Mr Kesgrave.'

He shook his head. 'No. No. I never hit her more'n about twice. I know I never did.'

'But you hit her hard.'

'I'm a cripple, Doctor. I ain't strong. I couldn't hev hit her hard, now, could I?' There was a hint of a whine in Will's voice.

'That's a debatable point. Dragging yourself about on crutches will have strengthened your arms and shoulders very much, I would say. More so than most men.'

'I dunno what you mean.'

The doctor turned back to the figure on the floor. 'I mean has it occurred to you that you might have killed her?'

The colour drained from his face. 'Killed her! I never killed her! I only hit her with me crutch. I couldn't hev killed her. I never hit her hard enough.'

The doctor got to his feet without speaking.

'No. No. You're wrong, doctor. She can't be dead.' Ginny dropped to her knees beside her mother and went to lift her head on to her lap.

The doctor put his hand out and restrained her. 'I'm afraid you mustn't touch her. Everything must be left as it is till the police get here.'

'Police? Oh, God, I must be dreaming. I can't believe . . . this can't be happening.' She got up and slumped down at the table and put her head in her hands. After a minute she looked up. 'It's not true, is it? There's some mistake. Will wouldn't . . . she can't be dead.'

A man on his way home from the pub was sent to fetch the local policeman, who took one look and decided it was too much for him and sent for detectives from Colchester. Ginny was led into the next room and before long Mabel Bellamy and Gladys, Will's sister, were there — Ginny never knew who fetched them but she was grateful for their presence because for some strange reason she couldn't stop shivering. Mabel held her while Gladys — a little nervous in the presence of all these strange policemen — found a blanket and wrapped her in it, then made some tea which she drank gratefully.

After what seemed a long time they were all allowed back into the kitchen, where Ruth's body had been covered by a sheet. Between gulps of her third cup of tea Ginny managed to tell them what she had found when she arrived home.

'And you didn't touch anything?'

She looked surprised. 'I helped Will up but I didn't touch Mum because I didn't want to risk doing more damage.'

'And where exactly did you find your husband?'

The questions went on and on while the sergeant made notes at his boss's dictation, then they took Will away to make a statement.

'Will he be back tonight?' Ginny asked as they helped him through the door.

The detective looked at her. She looked lost and bewildered, poor girl. She couldn't have been more than about twenty-five or so he didn't reckon, too young to be mixed up in a nasty business like this. 'I'm afraid your husband may not be home for quite a long time, Mrs Kesgrave,' he said sadly.

The days passed. Ginny didn't open the shop because she hadn't got anything to put in it and she had no heart for baking. Her time was fully occupied with looking after the children because everything she did was such an effort that she felt as if she was ploughing through treacle. After they had gone to bed she got out her sketch pad and sketched odd little scenes that didn't make sense.

Mabel was a tower of strength and wanted her to go and stay with her, but Ginny was determined to keep the children's lives as normal as possible so she remained at home. Normal! As far as she was concerned nothing would ever be normal again.

The inquest on Ruth showed that she had died from blows to the head consistent with being hit with a wooden object. Will's crutch was found to have traces of blood and grey hair on it.

Ruth was laid to rest beside her husband. It was intended to be a quiet funeral but so many of their customers from the cake shop wanted to show their sympathy and support for Ginny that the church was full and a large crowd even followed the cortège up the hill to the cemetery for the burial.

Ginny went through the whole thing dry-eyed. Ruth had dominated her life, guiding it in a direction that had caused nothing but unhappiness and heartache. There was even some kind of cruel justice in the fact that she had died at the hand of the man she had manipulated into serving her purpose. Ginny felt sorry for her but that was as far as it went. She knew that her mother had never really loved her, blaming her for spoiling her life, and she realised with something of a shock that she didn't love — and probably never had — loved her mother, partly for the same reason.

Some time later Will was sent for trial at Chelmsford Crown Court.

'Do you want to go to the trial?' Mabel asked Ginny. She called every day and would have taken the children to live with her but Ginny couldn't bear them out of her sight. 'Hector is coming home on leave and he says he'll be happy to come with you if you want to go. I'll look after the children for you.'

Ginny looked at her, frowning. 'I don't have to go, do I? They won't want me to testify, will they?'

'No. A wife doesn't have to testify against her husband.' Mabel poured the tea that Ginny had made and forgotten to pour. The poor girl looked lost, worn out with grief and worry.

'I went to see him in prison,' Ginny said, sipping her tea with small bird-like pecks. 'It was awful. He said he was glad he'd killed my mother. He said she deserved to die because if it hadn't been for her he would never have got married to me and would still have the use of his legs.' Tears were running unchecked down her cheeks.

Mabel frowned. 'What did he mean by that?'

'Well, it was Mum's idea that he should skipper the smack in return for marrying me. If he hadn't been on the smack the mast wouldn't have fallen on him . . . ' she waved her hand wearily. 'Oh, he'd got it all worked out. I think he's losing his mind, to tell you the truth.' She shook her head. 'I couldn't go through listening to him ranting on like that again. I'd rather not see him at all.'

'Somebody should go. I'll ask Hector.'

Hector listened to what Mabel had to say and agreed to go to the trial.

'Have you let Nathan know what's going on?' he asked.

'I've written to him, but you know how long it takes for letters to reach him when he's on the high seas. I've no idea where his ship is at the moment, have you, Hector?'

Hector shook his head. 'Classified secret.' He scratched his chin. 'Has Ginny asked about him?'

'No. It's very strange. She's never even mentioned his name.'

'Got too much else to think about, poor girl.'

'I do what I can for her, Hector,' Mabel said, slightly offended.

He leaned over and kissed her briefly. 'I know you do, my dear. And I'm sure she's grateful for it.'

He was right; Ginny was grateful to Mabel and she looked forward to her daily visit, someone to talk to, to go over the horrible events with, time after time, to talk them out of her system. And Mabel, understanding Ginny's need to relive the horror, let her talk and weep and talk again.

It was Mabel who explained to Bobby that neither her daddy nor her granny would be coming back again.

'Have they gone away together?' she asked. Then, not waiting for Mabel to reply, 'That's nice. They'll be company for each other, won't they? Will I be able to go and stay with them?'

'No, sweetheart, I don't think so. You'll say with Mummy.'

Bobby stuck her thumb in her mouth, as she did when she was thinking very hard. 'I'd rather be with Mummy. She doesn't get cross with us like Granny and Daddy.' She slid off Mabel's lap and went off to her swing.

'Thank God she doesn't understand,' Ginny said wearily.

Mabel was with Ginny when Hector returned from the trial. He was in a sombre mood and shook his head almost imperceptibly at Mabel's questioning eyebrows.

Ginny looked at Hector, then took a drag on her cigarette, a habit she had only recently taken up. 'He'll hang, won't he.' It was a statement rather than a question.

Hector nodded. 'The defence tried to make a case for manslaughter but Will did nothing to help himself.' He thought it wise not to tell Ginny how Will had shouted that he'd killed the old bitch and was glad he'd done it and he'd do the same thing again if he had the chance. 'He murdered her. He admitted it so they had no option but to bring in a verdict of guilty.'

Ginny stubbed out her cigarette. 'I'll make some tea.'

Much later, Mabel put her hand on Ginny's arm. 'If there's anything you'd like us to do, my dear . . . If you want to go and see him . . . '

Ginny shook her head. 'I don't want to see him and I doubt if he'd want to see me.' She took a deep breath. 'When is he . . . ?' She stopped and tried again. 'When is it . . . ?

Hector understood what she was trying to say. 'It's to take place at nine o'clock on the eighteenth.'

'There's no chance of a reprieve?' Mabel asked anxiously.

'None whatever.'

Ginny licked her lips. 'Could you look after the children for me? I'd like to be in church when . . . when it happens.'

'Of course, my dear.'

★ ★ ★

Ginny dressed very carefully on the morning of the eighteenth. Not in black, there were no clothing coupons to spare for black mourning, so the black armband she was wearing for her mother had to suffice. At half past eight she left the children with Mabel and walked along to the church.

It was cool and dim inside, and the morning sunlight was shafting through the stained-glass window over the altar, throwing a mosaic of colour on to the floor of the chancel. She slid into a pew halfway along the nave and sat with her hands in her lap, savouring the musty smell of old hassocks and hymn books, wax polish and candle grease, waiting, her mind such a jumble of thoughts that nothing made sense.

As the church clock began to strike the hour she slid to her knees and prayed, 'Oh, God have mercy on his soul.'

She didn't know how long she stayed there but at last she got up from her knees and went slowly out of the church, blinking at the sudden brightness of the day. High above in the blue sky a skylark was singing and she looked up and saw the tiny bird, hovering, free as the air. The thought struck her that perhaps now Will too was free; free from the life that had been such a burden to him for the past few years.

With a sudden lift of her shoulders she realised that she too was free. No longer would she have to bend to the will of either her husband or her mother. No longer would she have to act as a buffer between them, keeping them apart, keeping the peace between them. Surprisingly, the thought left her feeling strangely empty.

Her thoughts turned to Nathan. It was a luxury she had rarely allowed herself over the past months although she had written to him once. It had been during one of the many dark, lonely nights when sleep had eluded her, as it so often did. She had tried to write unemotionally, simply telling him what had happened, but it had been impossible to write of such horrific events dispassionately. Afterwards she had worried, fearful that it had been wrong to burden him with her troubles when he was in the midst of fighting a war. She consoled herself that the letter had probably not caught up with him yet if he was on the high seas.

She reached the house and let herself in through the empty, spotlessly clean shop. She was not sure she could stay here now, it would always hold too many horrific memories. She went through to the kitchen to make herself a cup of tea before going to fetch the children from Mabel.

As she stood at the sink filling the kettle she looked out at the garden. In her mind's eye she saw Nathan, sitting on the swing, with George on his lap, his arm round Bobby, who was leaning against him. It was such a wonderful picture to have conjured up that it brought tears to her eyes.

She turned away from the sink, but at that moment she saw a movement and heard a cry, 'Mummy!'

She spun round. Bobby was running up the path, Nathan, carrying George, right behind her.

She opened the door. 'You're real!' she whispered, staring at him, bemused.

He put George down gently and took her hands. 'Yes, I'm real, Ginny,' he said quietly. 'I got your letter. It earned me ten days' compassionate leave and a flight home. I came as quickly as I could. I wanted to be with you when . . . ' he hesitated. 'I'm sorry. I was just too late . . . '

She shook her head. 'No. No. It was better that way,' she said wearily. 'I went to church. I needed to be on my own . . . ' Her voice tailed off.

'But not any more?' He looked at her anxiously.

She shook her head and sighed a little as she walked into the circle of his arms. 'No, Nathan. I don't want to be on my own ever again,' she said, resting her head on his shoulder. 'I want to be with you. And the children.'

'Good. Because that's what I want, too, my love,' he said, holding her close.

Ginny felt a tug at her skirt. Bobby was

looking anxiously up at her.

'George is hungry,' she said. 'He would like a biscuit. And so would I.'

Ginny picked up George as Nathan squatted on his haunches so that his face was on a level with Bobby's. 'As it's nearly dinner time, I think a much better idea would be for us all to go back to Granny Mabel's, don't you, Bobby? She told me when I fetched you that she'd be making a nice shepherd's pie for us.'

'What for, all of us? The whole family?' Bobby asked, her eyes widening.

Nathan put his arm round her. 'Yes, Bobby. The whole family,' he said, looking up at Ginny and smiling. For the first time Ginny smiled, too.

THE END

We do hope that you have enjoyed reading this large print book.

Did you know that all of our titles are available for purchase?

We publish a wide range of high quality large print books including:
Romances, Mysteries, Classics
General Fiction
Non Fiction and Westerns

Special interest titles available in large print are:
The Little Oxford Dictionary
Music Book
Song Book
Hymn Book
Service Book

Also available from us courtesy of Oxford University Press:
Young Readers' Dictionary
(large print edition)
Young Readers' Thesaurus
(large print edition)

For further information or a free brochure, please contact us at:
Ulverscroft Large Print Books Ltd.,
The Green, Bradgate Road, Anstey,
Leicester, LE7 7FU, England.
Tel: (00 44) 0116 236 4325
Fax: (00 44) 0116 234 0205

Other titles published by
The House of Ulverscroft:

TO BE A FINE LADY

Elizabeth Jeffrey

Found as a baby wrapped in a luxurious blue velvet cloak, Joanna was brought up by the cruel farmer who found her, and put to work on his land just as soon as she could walk. Despite such hardship, Jo dreams of a reunion with her true mother, convinced that she must be a fine lady. When local factory owner Abraham Silkin decides that she has the potential to make him a good wife, Jo believes her dreams are finally coming true, but she hasn't bargained on her forbidden attraction to Abraham's godson!